UNFINISHED TALES OF THE

AMULET

And Other Dark Stories

THE AMULET

For millennia it has existed, its power overwhelming and its effects horrifying. The Amulet destroys all who find it and lays to ruin all lives in its wake. It is everywhere and it is evil, it is The Amulet. These stories are mere drops in the bucket of its terror.

Stew Miller
Author

HOPKINS' HOUSE
PUBLISHING

The Thank Yous

Firstly, I want to thank my family. My wife, Amy, and my kids, Charlie, Simon, and Addison, thank you so much, mainly for always being there to read or look over my work and always offering an honest opinion, even if I beg you. I love you all endlessly.

A big thanks to my Publishers at Hopkins' House Publishing. Never in my 48 years on Earth did I imagine I'd have a publisher (I always thought it an unattainable dream), let alone two books I am extremely proud of. (And yes, there are more to come) So thank you again.

And, of course, to all of my readers over the years, thank you. Some of you have known my work from decades ago and continue to follow my writing and artwork, and some of you I have met along the way. Thank you all to my friends and fellow writers who have taken the time to give me a lovely bit of positivity for the back cover; I appreciate every word. Thanks to anyone who is holding a finished copy of this book in their hands right now. It's because of you that I keep doing all of this.

September 23, 2022

UNFINISHED TALES OF THE AMULET
And Other Dark Stories

By Stew Miller

What is Flash Fiction? Well, it's pretty much what it sounds like. It's little bits of stories, all fictional, with a quick-hitting plot point, rapidly identifiable characters, and a satisfying jolt somewhere within. Typically, they're short, less in length than a traditional 'Short Story,' making them a little more difficult to write. Is there an ending? There should be; that's true. But some of these, some of my pieces of Flash Fiction, do not have an ending. Maybe I never got around to finishing them, or maybe I couldn't think of anything, or, most likely, I said all I had to say in the little bit you've read, and that's... well, *it*. But rest assured, these all pack a punch, a jab, a hook, or, in a few of the stronger cases, and nice and tidy Knock Out. These were all once tales I wrote years ago (the most recent being around 10 years) for a blog post that stagnated and withered on the Web (as it were) like many so often do. So, I decided the best way to go, before these are completely lost to degradation and outright forgetfulness, was to put them to paper and make this book you hold in your hands now.

Each of these stories didn't originally start out as having a common theme. In fact, if memory serves, they were never meant to be connected in any way at all. But, as I started adding more and more, it made sense to me then to begin using an AMULET as a common thread interconnecting every tale herein.

Though I am an artist (the Amulet design is all mine, and you might know of my other book mentioned somewhere in these pages), it seemed better to not make the pictures too much like illustrations. I'll leave those for a third book. Oh, and there are a few extra treats at the end of The Amulet Anthology. They are stories I worked on for someone else and another publication I am frequently a part of. Still, they never reached completion (save for one, but I was so happy with it that I wanted to include it here as well), and the project kind of died. So, rather than let them rot on the vine, I've included them as well. Though they aren't, strictly speaking, part of the AMULET lore, they'd likely fit right in with a few tweaks. Here you'll read them in their original forms.

Well, that's about it. That's all you need to know to prepare yourself for a journey through these many pages. I truly hope you enjoy some (or all) of my terrifying tales… of The AMULET.

Tales of the Amulet
Part 1: The Beast Within

Sam didn't have a choice. He was cuffed in irons to a couple of solid slabs of cement. He knew he was a werewolf; the town knew he was a werewolf... hell, the next town over knew he was a werewolf. Of this fact, there was no denying. The problem was that Sam LeFleur happened to be the mayor of Tumbleweed Gulch, and the town as a whole -though completely in the know of Sam's permanent lycanthropy- loved him. He was fair, mildly stern (mayhap an oxymoron, but the truth none the less), friendly, courteous almost to a fault, and never underhanded or dirty. Be that as it may, Sam was a ravaging, murderous killer hiding beneath human flesh, and it took naught but a full moon to unleash the fury within him. Sam prided himself on maintaining peace and a modicum of justice -more so than could be said for most other Western towns- and upheld high standards for his citizens that would best even those in Dodge City or, God forbid, Tombstone. So, as he hung his head and waited for the inevitable, he spoke silently a prayer that just once, the coming complete lunar face wouldn't turn him into the rampaging monster he'd come to reluctantly live with. Yet, as the clouds cleared and Sam glanced heavenward, his loins sank, and the feeling of his bowels filling in an instant washed over him like Yellow Fever. His face shot taught, his eyes bulged, and his ribs and spine squeaked and groaned under the pressure of their transformation. His hands -aching under the curling as they arced themselves into entirely new shapes- forced a yelp of agony from Sam's rearranging throat, and it exited his mouth more akin to a yowl. His knees buckled, the bones and tendons in his legs loosed and rewound, and a short tail burst with a crack- above his buttocks. The chains were strong. They were made with the finest metals from the most experienced blacksmiths in town. Yet, with the expanse of Sam's- newly located muscles, they bent and splintered and burst apart, showering the area with shards of the chain. Sam shook his furred hide, licked his chops, and announced his evil presence to the pale moon with a defiant howl. And then he was off.

Morning came. Sam woke in the meadow fifteen miles outside of town on Farmer Gillin's property. The carcasses of no less than six sheep lay strewn about the area. Sam sighed, stood, and made his way to the house. He knocked, looked about as sheepish as his fresh kills, nodded an apology to the sad nod of Gillin's, and signed an IOU voucher for the cost of the sheep. He was good for it. Then, under a shroud of shame, Sam trudged back to town to begin his day as Mayor. The moon wouldn't be completely full again for weeks. Just enough time to begin paying back his debts.

Tales of the Amulet
Part 2: It Had To Be Done

We'd been married for going on thirty years. Nothing unusual: standard fare, ups and downs, the ins and outs (*ha ha*), no kids, which was always an issue... but that's neither here nor there. But the day came in '87 when something not quite right happened. We had gone away on a jungle safari to Brazil. She'd always wanted to go; I was never a big fan of sweltering heat and huge bugs... but there ya go. Anyway, we went. It turned out to be a lot more fun than I'd imagined, despite the drenching mugginess and the mosquitoes the size of small birds... all in all, we had a lovely time. Well, after a week, we returned home none the worse for wear... until about three days later. My wife had come down with something. Something neither I nor any doctor we'd seen could rightly identify. She'd lost about fifty pounds, turned sallow and pallid, lost most of her hair, and developed pox-like warts all over her skin from head to toe. Her flesh would split and run, not so much blood but awful, horribly smelling rivulets of sour pus and thick, goopy liquid. She'd weep uncontrollably all the time, never with tears or emotion, just soulless sobbing full of agony and despair. Her friends would come, but they'd leave hurriedly disgusted, shaking their heads in awe. Eventually, life seemed to drain from her person, and all she could do was lie around, motionless and shallow. I had done everything I could do not to give up hope. I tried every medicine I could come upon from as many Internet stores as possible, selling remedies made from everything under the sun. But nothing ever worked... heck, nothing even made a small effect on her. Then, summer of '90, another drastic change took hold of her. Out of the blue, with no warning, she bolted from the bed she'd remained useless in for three years and began to attack me. Fortunately, I was a hair quicker and managed to get her into the basement, thanks to my old, empty shotgun mantle decoration. She toppled down the stairs, and there she stayed. Well, until yesterday. June 4th, '92, I burned our house to the ground with her trapped inside. I don't know what made her that way, but she was no longer my wife, my Muriel. Maybe now we can both be in the piece.

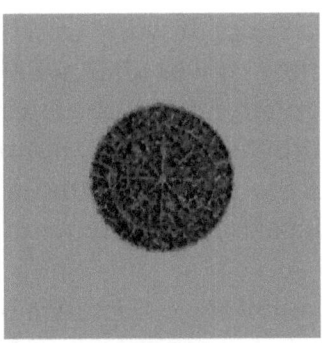

Tales Of The Amulet
Part 3: Something's In The Basement

Denny Harris had been chucking left-over carcass bits through his basement door for seemingly an eternity now. He didn't know what was scurrying around, living down there... what he did know was that it ate up every last bit of parts and leftovers he'd tossed down there. If Denny'd hunted and killed a deer, the legs, guts, nuts, and bits and pieces all got lobbed down the steps to the unnatural, guttural, hungry sounds of whatever was occupying the basement.

Denny's basement was what one could affectionately refer to as a "Michigan Basement," meaning it had massive rock walls -otherwise known as the home's foundation- and a full dirt floor. Most five-and-a-half foot tall folks were very uncomfortable standing upright down there, so Denny's six-six lanky-ass frame was almost at a full bend, hence his disdain and therefore un-desire to even go down there. In fact, it was all of fifteen years ago when Denny first heard the gravelly clawing coming up from the cavernous basement. At first, he just passed it off as the sump making its typical eerie and growly sounds, but when the thing lapsed into mewling and gargley whining, Denny was sure it wasn't the pump. At one point, he'd opened the door to make his way down fully armed with a metal claw rake and a Mag-style flashlight and was scared to the point of crying out to himself as he limped hurriedly back up the stairs. It wasn't anything he'd seen - he'd never *seen* anything- it was all in what he'd *heard*; he was almost certain the 'something' coughed out the word 'hungry.' No, he couldn't swear by it, but regardless, he began to feed it. Happily, if you please. Anything to keep from hearing that belched, pasty, phlegmy word again.

But lately, you see, something in Denny's basement was wanting *more*. It was no longer just satisfied with scraps and unwanted animal parts. No, recently, for some reason, it sounded hungrier and less satiated by what Denny was willing to offer it. So, Denny decided he'd have to move up the food chain just a bit; Denny would have to try something a little more human.

Every day Denny passed a man who did nothing for society but panhandle and survive off the crumbs of regular people. Denny was sure no one would particularly miss him. So, for the past week, Denny had taken to giving the hobo a bottle of juice every day; he'd gotten to know the bum's routine and kept up his regimen until Saturday. So, when Monday rolled around again, Denny had his juice in hand ready to make his new homeless friend happy, except this time it was laden with six thousand-milligram Vicodin, enough to nearly kill someone if not just drop them on their ass for a good long time. Denny went to work, left at three, and found the urchin barely breathing and semi-conscious behind the hedge where he slept. Denny, no slouch in the strength department thanks to his years on the college basketball team, snatched up the smelly, wet, and all-over sticky body and lugged him to his house, where he promptly set to work, hacking him to bits.

Denny served the thing in the basement with a pitchfork and a wheelbarrow. Nothing had ever made him grin more satisfyingly than the ecstatic moaning of his subterranean house guest. And even as he threw down arms, legs, and bits of broken human torso, Denny knew, somewhere inside, that he'd have to do this all over again. Soon. Too soon.

Tales of The Amulet
Part 4: Nightmare

Something was there. Right in the corner... I could almost feel it.

My breathing came in swift bursts. I consciously tried to regulate it; there wasn't much point in huffing and puffing myself into a heart attack. But the fear was in the driver's seat, and if it wanted to tighten my chest in crashing agony... well, it was going to whether I liked it or not.

I don't scare easily; I've been a rabid consumer of the horror genre (TV, movies, books... et al.) for nearly as long as I can recall. But damn it, when there's something in the room --right there in the corner-- the terror is as palpable as taste.

I think it moved. I start shuddering breaths again as I try --like a child in rapture at a TV show tries-- to tear my focus away from the... whatever it is... in the corner of my room, but I just cannot look away. It might leap if I'm not looking.

I feel and hear my throat catch and click as I try to swallow myself back into the fact that it's just a room, and whatever that shadow is not going-- shit, it moved again. Damn it. If I can move my legs a little, maybe the sound will make it twist a bit so I can... It moved again.

My legs don't want to work. It seems my unnatural fear has usurped my limbs and is insisting on holding me down like some flailing hospital patient. I don't like that at all. I need to move... I need to jostle myself back to my room and not this gaping, shadowed tomb I find myself stuck in. Movement is the key; it always seems to knock a little non-fiction back into one's head. I gotta try that again...

With a lot of conscious effort, I shifted my feet back and forth, making soft whisks under my sheet like a couple of anxious animals. And the corner shadow did more than move; it vibrated. -I swear, it looked like it was in two places at once, and it rotated between them: back and forth, back and forth like an other-worldly pendulum. It was in the shadows, and then it wasn't... and then it was. All I could do was stare. And I began to cry! Not in the saddened, heart-felt weeping of a sorrowful situation but out of absolute and all-encompassing fear. I was literally frightened to the point of tears.

But why? I knew it couldn't be real... right? It couldn't possibly be a thing and not just a something... a something right from my room like a shirt or... it moved again. This time I'm almost sure it --what? -- slithered? It is undulated and gesticulated like an eel! Oh shit, it really is a thing, isn't it? I'm questioning myself at this point... myself and what I know to be sanity and insanity...

And then I heard noises. I could hear what sounded like the television from the living room: monotonous, muted gabbing the way a blocking wall can make it sound. Somehow, I was only slightly more comforted...

Because I live alone...

The shadow coughed. A throaty, deep-crawled, guttural cough. And then it chuckled...

I can't lie here and write anymore... I need –

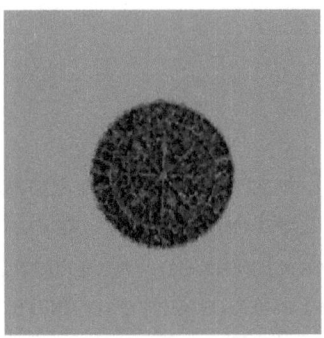

Tales of The Amulet

Part 5: Sometimes, When You Wish
You Were Anywhere Else

Taylor leaned languidly on his bent arm, resting his tired head on his hand. In his left, he twiddled and rolled his pencil across his fingers deftly like a magician.

Come one, come all! Marvel at the Terrific Taylor as he wondrously wobbles his precarious pencil twixt his dexterous digits!

Taylor was drifting again. His mind was swimming in and out of the moment as his eyes drooped ever more heavily. He blinked once, twice, attempting to struggle against the inevitable. He began to fall into a more purposeful breathing pattern. Soon, the hand that flitted the pencil began to drop, and the Ticonderoga hit the floor, eraser first, making a dull plip sound.

Taylor was in his own mind. The dull drone of the lecture on the Berlin Wall and its ultimate collapse continued unabated. Still, it sounded like it was being taught three classrooms away by a teacher created by Charles Schultz. Taylor's head slid down on his hand, and he subconsciously knew that in mere moments, it would make little difference how 'out of it' he was...

He was right.

The lights flicked off, and the steady rattle-hum of the movie projector whined to life behind him. As old and worthless as these archaic forms of classroom information were, they were darn good for at least a half-hour power nap. And that's just where Taylor was headed.

In the rapidly stretching distance, Taylor heard the warbling diatribe of the host of the film as it trailed off further and further away...

And sprang back into his mind like the return of a boomerang. Taylor was standing among his classroom cadets in the great meeting hall of the Second Infantry, Walking Dead Extermination Division. He loved how the circular patch over his right shoulder showed a skull emblazoned with the letters: WDED, with the DED written in dripping red letters. It was a cheesy acronym, but effective.

Taylor and his division had proven themselves worthy time and again by infiltrating the enemy lines and sending the zombies back to their former deaths. The commander stood tall among the ten- and eleven-year-old students, but he treated everyone equally. Each of the twenty-five children had a unique talent that was used with great skill in battle. Some created spit-wads embedded with push pins. Some made rubber band crossbows that launched flaming erasers. Others, like Taylor, used their mastery of deadly sharpened pencils to fight off the hordes. They were all trained to perfection, and the commander knew it and trusted them.

"Cadets!" The Commander continued, "Today is a big day for us! Today is the day we shatter the walls that separate us from the zombies, break into their stronghold, and acquire the thing that brought these monsters to life in the first place!"

Cheers rang up from the twenty-five little soldiers as they thrust their fists in the air triumphantly. Taylor was especially excited because he was the only one who had ever actually seen the instrument directly responsible for the zombie plague on earth: The dreaded Amulet.

Tales of The Amulet
Part 6: Trapped

One day, he was gliding high above the clouds: no worries, a happy family, and a comfortable lifestyle. Things looked good on the horizon, and the storm clouds built into towering, thundering maelstroms were safely in the distance. But then Hell came to William's life, and everything around him fell to pieces. William's life had become a ceaseless torrent of bad news.

William Michaels had a lovely wife, Elizabeth, and three amazing children: Marcus, Luke, and Olivia. They were never wealthy, but they were happy. The lived in a small house on the outskirts of town just across from a lovely, wooded area where they would always see deer, woodchucks, blue jays, and many other animals each season. It was beautiful, and they very much enjoyed their lives.

Elizabeth always had the better job -or at least the better-paying job- but this fact did little to take away from the love and complacency among them. They were happily married, despite Elizabeth's belief that William had often given up and only taken jobs that would just get them by rather than improve their situation. But the very much loved each other, and the kids also lived relatively stress-free lives. In fact, by all accounts, they were as typical an American family as you're likely to ever see.

But Elizabeth had a very dark and very sinister secret.

William arrived home one day, distraught and very upset. Elizabeth glanced up from the table, past the vegetables she was chopping, and noticed that her husband had a look of sorrow on his face. She had a cooler sensibility about her - which was quite typical, and though it looked snarky and uncaring, it was just her look- and arced an eyebrow with a modicum of concern. William pulled out a chair and sat heavily with a sigh. He looked at his wife past tear-blurred eyes and explained to her that the job he had grown to love was gone. She set down her knife, wiped her hands on her towel that dangled from the oven door, and walked to William with a mixed look of consternation and concern playing across her face. William sat slumped over in his chair, resting his head on unclenched fists, and breathed worried breaths. Elizabeth knew he needed comfort, but another side fought the urge to just melt into him and give him the satisfaction that everything would be okay. It wasn't, but she couldn't let him see that. She had to play it safer, so she tousled his hair, kissed his cheek gently, and told him she lived him. William nodded, replied to his love in kind, and shed a tear.

Elizabeth retired to the bedroom after dinner. She said she had a headache and needed to lie down. William was more than happy to assist the children with homework and bedtime stories. And soon, as the evening settled in, the house noise ebbed to a dull roar, and the only noise was the family room television. Elizabeth sat up from her bed and looked around at the looming shadows. The moonlight pierced through a thin slat of the window blinds and played a white stripe on Elizabeth's dresser. It was in that top drawer, under her underwear and bras, where she kept it. Secure -she always hoped- and nestled in an old brooch box. But tonight, the calling was as strong as it had ever been... and even stronger. She knew what was inside and what it could do, but tonight was not a night she wanted. But it wanted her.

It was 2002. William and Elizabeth had been married for three years, and things were getting better daily. In fact, just six months previous, they had welcomed little Marcus into the world. The pregnancy had been surprisingly issue-free, especially considering that Elizabeth was predisposed to potential problems. Strangely, it was almost as if that very predisposition was erased completely. Though they worried quite often, nothing ever came of it, and the nine-months sped by just as they do for thousands of others.
But Elizabeth knew something. She was told never to let on to her husband.
Four months into her pregnancy, she began experiencing terrible shooting pains up her legs, across her abdomen, and around her lower back. Something inside her told her that these were the precursors to premature and potentially stillbirth. She had to do something, but she couldn't tell William. He was far too busy attempting to secure a job, which, coupled with fearing for Elizabeth far too often, would only cause panic. She had to talk to someone.

-To Be Continued-

Tales of The Amulet
Part 7: Harvest of Sorrow

** Editor's Note**
-- What you're about to read is (aside from a few narrative elements to move the story along), word for word and scene for scene, an actual dream I had a few nights ago. After you read it, you'll likely be able to imagine the terror I woke from and the cold shivers that ran down my spine. Needless to say, I got up right after I woke up. Sleep wasn't going to come easily after that. --

It was a cold October morning. The rain drizzled in irritating sprinkles that wouldn't let up. The sky was a massive grey stone that masked any attempt of the sun to pierce its light through. It was dreary in every sense of the word. That dreariness carried over into the trip my wife and I had to make as we silently grabbed our jackets and headed for the car. Our journey was, to begin with, picking up a good friend of my wife's and bringing her to a new doctor in town. She had an inoperable brain tumor. This new practice was home to a brand-new medical procedure that worked like 'miracles.' Okay, not really miracles, but as close as humans are likely to get on their own, I guess. The doctors here were able to grow brand new pieces of you to replace the dying old ones. Pretty Science Fiction, right? Well, that's barely half of it.

I know, I know... but bear with me here. The gruesome and repugnant truth was that these doctors maintained a constant supply of un-living female torsos that actually 'gave birth' to whatever body part was needed. Each torso wasn't technically conscious or even really 'alive.' Because all they were were torsos: no heads, no limbs... just the torsos with the necessary nutrients fed into them and the required scientific adjustments to nurture the growing body part inside them. Yes, they had wombs out of which the parts would emerge. It isn't even correct since they came not from the traditional vaginal opening but a pre-created slit, almost like a Cesarean Section. It would open like a gaping mouth, and the new part would be excised. It's not a pretty visual, but it was an amazing procedure. Neither of us was too keen on witnessing this, but my wife's friend had learned all about it and was beyond excited to give it a go. And so, go, we did.

The building sat nestled in a wooded area just off the main road. Had we not caught a glimpse of the darkened brick facade, we might not have even seen it, as it was pretty concealed. Even the sign that proclaimed the name and address wasn't visible until we were practically on top of it. The drive was freshly paved, indicating that it had only been open for a short time. As we took the lazy 'S' to the doors where patients could be dropped off, we noticed a kindly nurse standing out front with a wheelchair already in tow. We had to wonder if she was just stationed there or because our friend's appointment was in about ten minutes. Either way, we slowed to a stop; my wife got out and led her friend to the nurse and to her medical chariot.

I parked and met them in the waiting room. From the second I walked in, I was uncomfortable. The ambiance was bland and uninviting: sharp angles, dark, muted colors, and a severity that made the whole room ache of a dank laboratory and less of a comforting anteroom. I sat next to my wife in one of the few chairs: bolt-straight and angry gray. Never before have I longed for tattered, year-old magazines. I stared at the reception area and the broken silhouette behind the mottled sliding glass. Etched on the front was a symbol I'd noticed with a cursory glance from the sign out front: it looked about the size of a tea saucer in this instance, and it was crisscrossed with odd glyphs and what looked like some kind of runes. It was the only thing in the room with a distinctive color: deep, blood-red that filled in the designs and ran the circumference of the bizarre amulet. It was stunning in its grotesqueness. Almost like a piece of frightening artwork that you fight between looking away in disgust and falling completely. I turned away and gave a wan smile to my wife. Her questioning brow led me to believe she'd noticed it, too.

A moment later a door on the opposite side silently swung open and the same nurse who'd met us at the outer doors poked her head through. She had a stolid look of consternation on her face until she noticed her patient sitting next to us in her wheelchair. I'm not sure what she was expecting, but her mood seemed to change, and a grin played across her mouth making her look almost sinister rather than the caring softness she was failing to pull off. I looked across my wife at her friend, and she sat up a little and let my wife pat her arm and give her a quick sense of security. The nurse nodded, walked behind the wheelchair, and wordlessly led our friend off into the innards of the office. The door swished behind them and the quite that followed was painful. I look at my wife; she at me, and we shared a sigh that was more worry than hope.

We sat. There wasn't too much to discuss, even if there was a rose-hued Mastodon in the room; we both wondered in our heads just what that bizarre sigil was and, come to think of it, why the crooked shadow behind the reception glass hadn't moved an inch. But we didn't talk. It was almost as if we were afraid to. It occurred to me that no sound at all had exited our mouths since we arrived. What were we scared of? Did we think we'd somehow sound differently? Were we expecting repercussions from the shadow behind the front desk? Neither of us knew, but neither of us shared. So, we sat.

Were it not for our watches, we'd never know the time, since - obviously- there were no clocks. Maybe obviously, but it's really unnerving when you can't just glance up at a clock and see the time. Even if you are wearing watches. There's just something oddly real about seeing a clock, especially in a place like a doctor's office. We noticed the time and several hours had passed without anyone relaying a progress report to us. This in and of itself was probably the weirdest part. There was always a doctor or a surgeon giving those waiting an update. But not this time. (*Time... hmm.*) The room itself became oppressive. The once annoying blandness of it became suddenly aggravating and all too small. I stood. My wife glanced at me side-long, but I waved her away with hand gesture meant to calm her, but it only served to make her stand, too. My ears pricked as I inched closer to the door through which our friend had been taken. I heard sounds like muffled beeping and an echoing chuffing. I pressed my hands to the door and then my ear. Behind me, my wife stood directly across from the reception glass watching for any movement. She shook her head, and I pushed my head to the door hard enough to hear a little better. Machines. Machines were chugging and chirping, the muted squeal of compressed air, and a low thrum from some other mechanism. It definitely sounded like an operating room, but somehow... foreboding. I pressed on the door and followed its trajectory as it opened into a poorly lit hallway.

I let the door whoosh closed. My wife likely stayed behind to ensure the shadow person didn't follow me. The hallway was about as well-lit as a backroom in an old museum. For a supposedly new building it felt ancient and creaky. Nothing about it screamed modern: the walls were dark and drab with no adornments whatsoever. As my eyes adjusted, it became clear that the hallway ended in another set of doors. From where I stood, about halfway down the ten-foot passage, I could easily hear the cacophonous electronics and apparatus working away beyond the end set of doors. Why was I scared? This was a doctor's office, not some abandoned prison morgue from one of those ghost hunting shows. Besides, I'm a grown man and this was getting ridiculous. I righted myself a little more professionally and headed for the doors and the sounds. Yet, tugging at the hairs on the back of my neck was just a little bit of fear that I couldn't shake.

I stood and faced the set of doors. The two square windows built into each door's top center were shaded and opaque. I glanced through one and saw only smokey halos and dulled glows. I turned and looked behind me. No one. The hallway was as barren as it was when I entered it. I wish I knew what was happening on the other side of the door through which I came, but I assumed that my wife was currently in the same spot I left her. At this point I really was at a zenith of decision: enter the doors and face whatever unknowns lay beyond, turn around, leave this house of oddities, and just hope for the best for our friend. Again, I had to question even why I was arguing with myself in the first place. This was silly. I leaned on the doors and shoved my way in.

Before me was a scene of such palpable horror that my breath was temporarily pressed from my body. The room looked like a movie set where Hellraiser and Aliens had somehow merged. Corroded hoses ran with filthy rivulets of indistinguishable fluid. Knots and bundles of dirty cordage hung like age-old cobwebs strewn from unseen connection to unseen connection. Haphazardly bundled wires like ancient holiday lights pulsated and glowed from one end of the blackened room to the other. Cables dripped, tubes shivered, black boxes with myriad switches and readouts hummed, and the wretched assembly line that housed the birthing torsos slowly moved in the distance. A click escaped my throat as I surveyed the ghastly images. I dared not move; the amalgam of electronics and whatnot seemed far too easily tripped over. As I returned my unblinking eyes to the moving terror that was the conveyor belt of un-living bodies, I saw their synchronized breaths as each chest ebbed and flowed in perfect unison. Each one sprouted a specific body part for any number of waiting patients, glistening with viscous liquid, and writhing in tandem with their unconscious host. And there, in the middle of the sickening mass, bulging from its own slit just above the torso's abdomen, was my wife's friend's new head staring blankly skyward. Her mouth yawned and a pink, bulbous tongue gibbered.

I held a scream as I burst back through the doors and sped down the hall. I encountered no one as I shot through the single door that led to the waiting room and nearly bowled over my wife. She let a squeal escape her mouth in utter surprise... it echoed thinly. I snatched her arm and we made for the exit. The fresh, cool air stung but it felt Heavenly compared to the stale, nauseating atmosphere of the office. As we sprinted the length of the parking lot to the car, I squeezed my wife's hand, letting her know there was far more to tell than she could imagine. I stole a glance behind me and noticed the same symbol from the glass partition. It seemed to be glowing an even brighter shade of red. I couldn't get the car door open fast enough.

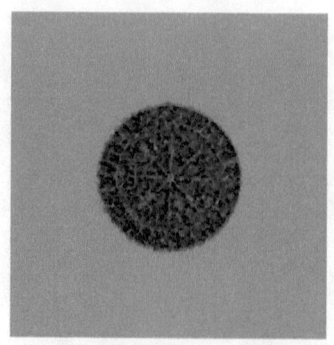

Tales of The Amulet
Part 8: Purple Prose

The ancient etchings ebbed and flowed
with crimson hue they ran
Archaic glyphs and sigils showed
Brought to his knees, all man

Its powers were imposing, true
its grasp on souls complete
To those who saw, it saw them, too
And to mortal lives: defeat

Known by names throughout its time
to its creators, they knew fear
And those who followed wrote in rhyme
of its legacy year to year

The Amulet; its modern name
grows stronger as it destroys
Its terror is a boundless game
With the tricks that it employs

The horror it contains; undeniable
it can drive mankind to madness
Attempts to ignore it; unreliable
In its path: death and sadness

With its pulsating face, it sees the 'you'
the beast within; it sets you free
No guard can shield; it sees right through
and creates a 'you' you can't unsee

The Amulet: Terror and evil made real
unluck and unrest be to those it finds
There is no cure; no way to heal
Its strength lies within man's own minds

So, pray, and hope, and pray again
that The Amulet stays far away
For its true cause is strife and sin
And it might find you some day.

Tales of The Amulet
Part 9: House

The planks they seethe with ancient ire
The boards and shingles creak
With age-old dust and breath respire
With soundless words they speak

Alone it stands in solitude
Beneath the crescent moon
A soul-less life it does exude
And shouts a song-less tune

Its glassy eyes and gabled face
Stare wanly, blankly, dead
The crooked hungry staircase
Beckons to be fed

Its body sheds, its columns peel
Its weathered woods corrode
It hungers for its latest meal
To enter this abode

But horrors live behind these walls
And long-dead spirits roam
For moans and echoes fill these halls
And ghosts still call it home

In days long gone, atrocious acts
Befell this once grand Inn
With blades that cut, and hatchet whacks
The house ran red with sin

T'was murder there, the locals said
And death to all who stayed
For checking in meant ending dead
T'was with their lives they paid

And so it went, for years and more
And soon t'was locked up tight
Just memories of the guests it bore
And their souls to walk at night

But now it sits, in disrepair
At the end of a lonesome drive
So do take heed, and do take care
If at its doors, you do arrive

For life still lives within its rooms
The ghastly wandering dead
And going in is certain doom
From evil, guilt, and dread

So, if you see, on lonely nights
The House that seems well met
Ignore those warm and welcome lights
For it's the House of the Amulet

Tales of The Amulet
Part 10: The Last Halloween

The full moon hovered like a dirty halo in the smoky night sky. Running footfalls and the distant whoops and catcalls of the last of the Trick-or-Treaters carried into the darkness like cacophonous notes borne on the breeze. Our pillowcases were loaded enough to be nearly heavy, and we'd each filled two apiece. I had mine slung over my shoulder; a nice accompaniment to my meticulously (and ironically) organized Hobo costume. My friend, Eric, was a racist ghost: eyeholes cut into a big, black sheet (a costume he now carried under his arm, claiming the damn thing was too hot). And Darren was a 70's Disco clubber complete with a giant, tacky (yet somehow horrifying) medallion-like amulet dangling from his neck. We looked ridiculous -all of us. But this was to be our last Halloween together... for various reasons. Eric was moving after the holidays out of state to live with his dad. Wyoming. Who lives in Wyoming? So, we sort of decided that since the three of us were being unceremoniously whittled down to a duo, we'd make this our last foray out into the Trick-or-Treating world. Besides, we were each pushing 15. It was time to pack it in, anyway. The wind had begun to pick up a bit. Unraked leaves took flight and spun in lazy circles as they chased each other in lopsided cyclones. The din of the last remaining kids faded into the night, and the three of us silently plodded up the side street to my house to conclude our evening. I was hungry, and not just for Snack Sized candy. My mom had actual food waiting for us...

"Hey, Stew... wait a sec." Eric said from a few paces behind me.

I stopped. Darren, too. He was even further in the lead than I was. His infamous perpetual hunger must have been dragging him by the stomach.

"Yeah. What's going on?" I asked as I turned toward Eric who had fallen back fifteen or twenty feet.

"Did you guys here that?"

Eric and I exchanged a quick glance and in eerie unison told Darren, "No."

"Guys I'm serious... it sounded... *deep*."

I chuckled, "Deep like introspective?"

Eric scowled. "No, shit head. Deep like *growly*... guttural."

Darren froze and cocked his ear. He cupped his hand to his temple as though he were really trying to listen.
"I hear... wind! Dumbass."

Darren and I burst into fits of mocking laughter. Eric blatantly ignored us and looked around.
"Shut the hell up! I heard it again!"

This time, so did I. And Eric was right: it was deep. Low, raspy... like a thrumming purr.
"Dude, chill. I heard it."

Darren's eyes opened wide. "Bullshit!"

"No. Eric's right. I think it's coming from over there. The Stillwell Lot... ya know, where that store was going to go a few years ago?"
I pointed off to the right of the sidewalk. The Stillwell Lot was a piece of property bought by local party store owner, Xavier Stillwell back in 2005. He owned six local liquor stores in the area, each with more escalated prices than the last. But as it turned out, the city didn't really want (or need) another Stillwell's, and the lot remained empty to this day. It was from there where the sound originated, as far as we could tell.

And then it came again. And it might have been closer.

II
The Chase

We stood absolutely still, and just listened. The crunchy chatter of dried leaves tumbling aimlessly in the wind seemed loud enough to be the hammered drumbeats of a marching band. And there, amid the crispy clatter of the long dead flora came that noise: hollow, gurgling, and churning. It sounded to us now not unlike the echoing whines of an empty stomach. This thought momentarily reminded me of my current state, but I snapped out of it as what could only be described as a lowing growl caught the wind and tore at our ears.

"Shhh... *there it is again!*" Eric said as looked at me, eyes round with fear.

"I definitely heard that. What the hell was that? It sounded like Darren's stomach through a megaphone!"

"Comedian." Darren scoffed as he, too, reluctantly nodded that he'd heard the noise. "But seriously, what could that have been? Is there a house with a giant-ass dog over there, or something?"

I shook my head, "I don't think so. As far as I know that whole lot all the way over to Park Street is just one, long, empty piece of overgrown land."

And I was pretty sure I was right. As we stood on Broad Street, Park ran parallel but about a full block-and-a-half away. It was a decent sized open area perfect for... well, another store that never happened. As it sat, the weeds had grown waist high, small saplings and shoots jutted out in small clumps, and grasses as thick as reeds sprouted like land-locked islands of bristling foliage. It was obviously late fall, so everything was dry and dead, and the stiffened bits of plant life whistled like an out-of-tune flute section. But the sounds we were hearing were nothing like the reedy shrills made by the blowing grasses.

"At the risk of sounding like a pansy, I vote we hike up our skirts and get the hell out of here." That was Eric, and those words will forever be etched into my memory because those would be the last words, I'd hear him say.

The thing that burst past me knocked me off my feet. I could smell its rank decay in its wake as it leaped at Eric and beat him to the ground. I heard him yelp as the breath was knocked from his lungs, and then the unmistakable deep, thrumming growl erupted from the thing that stood mere feet from me. I could hear Darren panic; strings of expletives flowing from his mouth in blaring screams as he tripped over his own feet attempting to get away. I scooted back, regained my own footing, and stared dumbfounded at the inky black mass that huffed its soured breath and bounced, spastically, on Eric's frame. Without a second thought, I gripped my weighty candy bag, and with a swing like a rail-spike driver, I brought it down on the beasts back like an unruly hammer.

What barked from its mouth was both the sound of agonizing surprise, and an almost human reaction: "OW!" The amalgam of beast and man suggested that this thing was directly from nightmares I'd long since grown unafraid of. Yet here it was. It turned its head as it purposefully lifted its frame from Eric. What I could see of its once-white teeth were stained pink and glistening rivulets ran down its damp chin. At some point over the last minute, it had bitten Eric. I didn't have time to figure out where. My body burned with fear; arcs of terror lanced up my spine and exploded into my skull. My eyes quivered and took in as much light as they could manage, giving everything a ghastly corona. My guts dropped a floor and piled up in a hot mass. I wanted -more than anything I'd ever wanted before- to run. But I was locked up. It took the gurgling cough of Eric to snap me out of it. The beast heard it too and turned its gaze back to its interrupted meal. Eric's eyes were huge as he silently pleaded with me. A large chunk of his cheek had been sheered from his face and I could see his back molars poking out of the muscle.

I shouted. It wasn't a word; it was just to release the pressure that had built into bursting in my head. It was loud enough to redirect the monster's attention. And then I felt the heat. Not coming from me but from behind me. I could see from my frozen peripheral vision a glowing light. To my left ran Darren, his candy sack emptied and now burning from the flames from his lighter. He swung it like a juggler's torch and screamed as he lunged it at the beast. At that, I could finally make out just what it was I was looking at: pitch-black fur covered a stocky, muscular frame, and fingered paws ended in scabrous claws. Its face was a mismatched and gnarled mess of fur and pustules, some of which had burst and run green into his nose and mouth. Its eyes glistened at the swirling flames and showed true signs of abject fear. It reared back in revulsion; its fangs sat deep in a mouth that was neither dog nor man but was the absolute worst of both.

It clamored from Eric's body, and I could see amid the dancing flames that it moved with human precision but looked uncomfortable doing so. It had a beast's musculature and obviously relied on that to move quickly when it wanted to. As it backed away from the fire, it lowered itself into a predatory pose, which was our cue to scramble. I reached for Eric (fortunately the smallest and lightest of the three of us) and heaved him over my shoulder, Fireman's style.

And then we ran.

III
Eric

We had an instant to make a choice, and it was a choice that none of us was going to be too fond of. If we continued to run down the street, we'd have to get to Main Street at the end and hang a right to get to my house. As it turned out, it was going to knock off about a third of our run if we just cut through the lot. Like I said: not the best option, but Darren knew it was true, too... we'd done it before on past Halloweens when we'd caused some form of mischief or another and wanted a quick escape before angry folks discovered us. It had been a year since any one of us had cut through the lot but now seemed like the best time and our only speedy option. The decision took less than ten seconds: Darren kept the monster outside of our space by waving the last of his rapidly burning pillowcase at it. It snarled and gurgled just beyond the light, ready to spring as soon as the fire burned out. We had no time. We nodded, we turned, Darren dropped the last of the smoldering cloth, and we took off at a sprint I'm sure I'd not performed in far too long.

Eric was much heavier than his bony frame would have ever led me to believe in any normal circumstance, but this wasn't that. He moaned and wept as he used his elbows to keep his head from banging into my back, which must have been incredibly uncomfortable since it was killing me. But I pushed it away; the distance to my house was only about a hundred yards, and the whipping limbs and stinging grass were already making the run as difficult as I could handle. Darren kept pace and frequently stole glances over his shoulder. It wasn't necessary. We could hear the monster breaking through the overgrown foliage like a loosed bull. We could hear its labored, wet rasps not too far beyond our own heels. It was gaining slowly, but it was gaining. Guttural yelps bellowed from its throat, and their sickening similarity to human cries were so unnerving that the sense of fear pushed me on a little faster.

Then Eric began to shift. His center of mass was now sliding down my back, and I was losing my grip. I tried to adjust without giving too much of my current speed, but in an instant, it was too late. Eric slid and fell, and I pitched forward, completely losing my balance. I skidded into the underbrush, tearing up my hands and face as I landed awkwardly. Darren stopped, too, reached down a hand and yanked me off the ground. We looked back, but we couldn't see Eric. But we could certainly hear the beast's footfalls and snarls pounding down on us, mere moments away.

"ERIC!" I shouted into the night.

A limp arm shot up out of the grass. He'd fallen a lot further back than I'd first realized. Darren and I made to return back to him, but our luck had completely run out. The moonlight caught the black form of the monster as it burst into circle in which we stood. It's wet, foaming breaths came rapidly and they caught in its throat as it struggled to breathe regularly. We backed up and ducked into some taller overgrowth. The beast lumbered closer to Eric's body, and it looked around, arrogantly triumphant. And that was it for my friend. The monster shot its muzzle into Eric's weakened body, and Darren and I heard the sloppy, chewing sounds as it fed.

As sick as it seems, we knew we had time now. It was over for Eric, and though I was horrified and scared beyond rational thought, we had to go. I tugged Darren's shirt, and we slowly moved out of the grass and took off at a run to cover the last thirty yards.

IV
Night

It only took a few seconds to fight the rest of the way through the weeds and saplings, and then we crashed the final few feet and out onto manicured lawn. We didn't stop running until we hit my yard which was two houses down from the backyard we'd broken through the field into. We dropped to the damp grass and breathed heavily in unison as we stared at the suddenly cloudless sky. I shivered uncontrollably thinking back a few moments ago as I watched one of my best friends being torn to fleshy threads before my eyes. It was almost too much... and then it was. I sprang to my knees and retched up the few pieces of candy I'd eaten along with most of that evening's dinner. Beside me, Darren began to weep. The weighty reality of what had just happened over the course of the last half hour hit us like a train wreck. How were we going to explain this? How were we going to tell our parents what had just happened? How were we going to tell Eric's parents? I had no idea. My mom and dad were literally four walls away, making snacks and waiting on our return. I sat in the grass next to Darren dumbfounded and overwhelmed with blanketing dread.

The night was uncomfortably quiet. It was one of those nights when the sounds from anything were amplified tenfold. And that was when we heard the howl. It wasn't quite animal, and it wasn't quite the distressing shout of a human... but we knew exactly what it was. And it sounded placated.

We had no choice. We had to go inside. Night was full-on, and ignoring our responsibility wasn't going to go away the later it got. We got up from the lawn and headed to my front door. We opened it; the warmth from the furnace swept us up and drew us in, as did the smells from the myriad snacks my mom had made. My dad sat in his recliner; 'An American Werewolf in London' was playing on AMC. Mom was fussing over a Sudoku at the kitchen table amid the plates of hot snacks. She looked up and smiled.

And there sat Eric, munching on a Pizza Roll. He turned to us and winked.

THE END

Tales of The Amulet
Part 11: Turkeys

Part 1-

Ed sighed and sat back on his porch rocker. It creaked under his ever-increasing girth; blame it on age, blame it on dessert-heck, blame it on complacency; it didn't need a name. He was getting heavier, and the arguing keen from the old chair only rubbed it in. He looked out over his yard. It appeared as vast as always: a tightly manicured lawn near his creaky deck and a flora-laden landscape across the back forty. He loved gazing out over his property and watching as the wildlife popped in and out of their hiding spots. It was six acres, all told, and he loved every square foot of it. It'd been him for going on thirty years now after he'd inherited it from his sickly mother. Her death was melancholy, but not unexpected. It was the cancer that did her in back in '82 when Ed was just forty-three. His life's aspirations never really bore fruit, so he packed up what meager collections he'd amassed and moved back to the house he'd grown up in. Lucky for him, the little town of Handlers Grove didn't have a decent hunting and fishing surplus shop, so Ed was kind enough to oblige and soon opened 'Ed's Outdoor'. And as he sat there on the cool November afternoon watching the hazed-over sun slowly march its way to its daily death, he knew Thanksgiving was coming. And so were the turkeys.

Part 2-

When Ed first took residence a few months after his mother's passing, nothing felt right. The house was still haunted by her; knick-knacks strewn about the walls, printed area rugs in mundane places, cabinets full of innocuous clutter, some bizarre disk-shaped trinket hanging from the mantle that immediately turned his stomach, and the stink. It positively reeked of his mom. It was her perfume and her smell that clouded her during her last days when Hospice had to take over. It was stale urine, dirty, fouled laundry, and the ever-cloying stench of a drawn-out death. As he stood there in the doorway facing the stairwell leading to his mother's old room, he clutched a box that contained nearly all the things he owned, and he wept. He stood there and cried like a baby boy who'd lost his favorite stuffed bear. Or his mother. The wave of emotion rolled over him like high tide. He didn't even cry at the funeral, for whatever reason. Call it masculinity. Call it potential embarrassment... whatever. But there he stood, and the floodgates opened wide. A few minutes passed and he regained control of himself after a few hitching breaths. Yes, he knew it was the scent that did it. His mother was still there, and he'd keep it that way. She was always good to him, despite her early divorce from his father, and the death of his stepfather a few years later. She was always there; she was always mom. He did, however, pack away her things. Too many reminders were just too painful. And then it was his home and his alone. And he was happy.

Part 3-

Being as far out into the country as he was, there was a never-ending parade of animals wandering his property. He'd begun setting salt licks out for deer, feeders for squirrels and birds, dishes of food for raccoon and coyote, and insect feeders as well when the season was right. It was like living in a preserve. But as the first year drew on toward late fall and into November, something strange occurred that Ed could never have been prepared for.

One day, late in the month, the turkeys came. At first it was a few and their guttural screams woke him from a dead sleep at first light around six thirty. He leaped from his bed clutching his chest trying desperately to calm his heart and his nerves. His eyes were wide and blurry as he flew to the window. He slid the curtains aside and there, strutting across his lawn laying waste to every piece of food he'd left out, were a dozen wild turkeys. They pecked at the seed, the salt, the treats for the coons... you name it, they were devouring it. And they were huge. Ed had seen wild turkeys before and they were typically scrawny and gaunt, not a lot of meat on them... but these bastards were massive! Bigger than farm-raised even, and by the looks of it, pushing thirty pounds each. But they weren't the sluggish, useless meaty birds you see on TV when Thanksgiving rolls around. Oh no, these birds were active and angry. But worst of all was their eyes. The turkeys looked at the house and Ed could see their eyes glowing bright red like taillights. And they didn't just glow, they throbbed.... pulsated. He watched, catching his breath in silence, as the turkeys decimated his wildlife spread. The birds wandered the yard, and Ed only hoped that they didn't catch wind of the deer he'd field dressed the night before. It was a surprisingly cold night, so he just left it hanging from the tree branch till he could deal with it the following day. Now, in fact. And it was becoming increasingly obvious that the turkeys smelled it. What followed was something out of a horror movie: beaks gnashing, meat stripped as though they were those piranha fish Ed had seen on those animal shows, and incessant cackling like a pack of angry wolves. They thrashed at each other, clawed faces, pecked, and pulled feathers. It was terrifying. Ed could only hold back his gorge as he watched the birds strip the carcass to bloody bone. Fortunately, he hadn't eaten yet.

Part 4-

That first year was a surprise, no doubt. But the year following Ed was a bit more prepared, and this time he figured if they were going to stuff themselves on his animal treats, he'd happily kill one for his own Thanksgiving spread. And so, he waited. Beginning around the middle of the month he'd begun getting out of bed just before dawn and loading his rifle. He was a hunter after all, and this was his property. He was going to give some paybacks this time. It was 1983, a year that Ed would later regret his actions.
On the morning of the 20th, the birds arrived. This time there were twenty strong and as they wandered from the wooded horizon and onto his property it looked like forty glowing alien orbs slowly hovering in for an attack. Their calls were ominous and shrill. They looked around, jabbed one another for positioning, and marched like stalking soldiers into Ed's backyard. He watched, silently, as the turkeys shuffled up to their feast. And just as the year before, they tore into the offerings like they hadn't eaten in their lives. But Ed was ready. He quietly slid up the pane, poked the barrel of his rifle through, sighted his target (an especially rotund specimen) and fired a shot right through the bird's ruddy head. Its skull exploded into gory shrapnel. It stood for a minute, took a few cautionary steps toward its brethren, and collapsed in a feathery heap. The others stopped feeding almost instantly and looked at their fallen comrade. And then the screaming began. Like the cacophonous screech of a sick baby by way of

a megaphone through the cone of a prison alarm. The sound was deafening and awful. Ed dropped the gun and fell to his knees. The birds carried on for what seemed like forever; back and forth, louder, and shriller, they bleated on and on. Eventually, the noise just ceased. Ed drew his hands from his ears slowly. He stood and looked out the window and watched as the remaining turkeys slowly tore their winged friend to shreds.

Part 5-

Years had passed, and Ed had learned a valuable lesson. From then on, he just left out the food and made sure he was occupied with busy work. He even recalled the year he'd forgotten to leave any food out at all. He was traveling that year to his friend's house in Martinsburg for the holiday, just a few hours south. He locked up, didn't think anything of leaving out goodies for his turkey pests, and left. Upon his return he instantly regretted this oversight as well. The birds had smashed through his big picture window, as evidenced by the trail of bloody feathers spotting the crime scene that looked as though someone had been murdered with a furniture duster. They'd ransacked his house, tore apart his couch and chair, pecked apart the wires to appliances, and managed to yank open the fridge and laying waste to its contents. The stench of fouled food hung in the place like a decaying body. That was the last time that happened. It cost him too much to argue with the birds, and so he just gave in. But this year would be different. This year was going to be the turkey's last.
He sipped on his beer and knew, subconsciously, that tomorrow was the day. It had been far too long in years, and he'd gotten to know the turkey's routine. But Ed was getting tired. He was too near eighty now to want to put up with the barrage of fowl that plagued his pre-holiday festivities. And besides, this year he wanted company at his house and the last

thing he needed was the fret on about a flock of angry birds. He was ready, and he could only hope he'd catch the turkeys by surprise.

Part 6-

Morning. Early. It was six-fifteen, and first light was maybe an hour away. Ed slid out of bed into his slippers. He stretched, yawned, and smiled. It was going to be a good day. He knew it. He strode with a shuffle to the kitchen where his automatic coffee maker had just finished making the pot, he'd set to brew twenty minutes prior. He poured a mug, always black, and slid out a chair at his dining room table. It was as close to the window facing the yard as he needed it to be, and he waited. At last, the calls echoed from the far side of his property; that wretched crowing that signaled the arrival of the mass of turkeys that had been ruining his holiday for thirty years. This year was going to end very differently; in fact, it was going to end before it could even begin. What he was about to do he'd seen on a cartoon, believe it or not (even he could only shake his head), and he just knew he could make it work in real life with only a few tweaks. You see, in the cartoon, the target got away, but Ed made damn sure that wasn't going to happen today. As the rafter of turkeys approached (this year quite possibly numbering in the thirties), Ed stood and slowly moved to the little button that was wired just inside of the window. Soon the birds began to feed on Ed's home-made goodies, each laden with enough black powder in all to blow apart a solid concrete wall. Each item was wired to a sparker that led back to the house. He wanted to catch as many turkeys as he could in mid peck so the damage would be just as spectacular as he'd imagined. He waited patiently. There was plenty of food.
Then, suddenly, the time had come. Without another moment's hesitation, Ed pushed the button.

The sound and the fracas that followed was a circus of freakish agony. Right off the bat after the button was pressed, ten bird heads immediately blew apart like miniature fireworks. Seconds later, the individual pieces of food exploded into geysering flame balls that set another twelve birds on fire. Then, as the still living birds suddenly began to scuffle in terror, the black powder in their mouths and stomachs ignited from the fire and intense heat. Guts burst forth like burning party favors. Turkey necks and beaks blasted apart like over-filled balloons. Headless bodies flopped around, torched feathers smoldered, and the acrid smoke of slowly dying birds coiled into the air on the lazy breeze. When it was finally over, only two birds still moved, and Ed just waited as the flickering flames eventually overtook them and they, too, popped like Champagne corks. It was finally over.

Ed sat for another minute and enjoyed his coffee with a huge, satisfied grin. It was almost time to bring in the bodies. That food was going to last him for months.

THE END

Tales of The Amulet
Part 12: Behind Me

I was angry.

This was probably the seventh time in a month that the Buick took a shit.

And for the seventh time the car sat lifeless on the shoulder of the road, releasing its soul in the form of dirty, gray clouds floating skyward from under the hood.

So yeah: I was angry.

And the real tasty icing on the crap cake was rolling in from the west: dark purple clouds with that unmistakable stain of ugly tan swirling around beside the oncoming wall. Thunder argued its location from the horizon and the flickers of lightning announced the bigger storm to come.

Angry. But at least I had an umbrella, because yes: I had to walk. The road ran the rural outskirts of the city and from where I stood there wasn't a restaurant or a gas station for at least a mile. I was definitely walking.

The drops began as soon as I shut the door; heavy, loud, and with a fury like the rain was mad at the ground. I popped the umbrella just in time as the downpour picked up speed sounding now like a waterfall splashing on a tent. I began my walk.

The rain continued to pelt my meager covering like a barrage of water bombs. It was torrential for one minute, and an outright deluge the next. As I looked around with stunned wonder, I noticed immediately that the road's edge quickly became a running, muddy mess. And so, I plodded on.

Soon it became all too apparent that the arm not holding the umbrella - I rotated as frequently as my aching hands desired - was rapidly becoming a sodden sponge. It might have been an umbrella, but with the downpour, it was doing very little to deflect much of the torrent and barely kept me dry. I did my best to keep my mind off the drenching chill, and so I let it freely wander.

I thought of my wife and kids warm and dry at home. I thought of my phone with its useless, dead battery. Why did I listen to music all night at work without charging? And so, I walked and thought.

Just then, something that most definitely wasn't the relentless rain caught my attention. I cocked my head as I continued my march through the deepening puddles. Then I heard it again. It sounded like footfalls beating in opposite rhythm to my own. Worse yet, they sounded agonizingly close.

I breathed deeply and collected my thoughts. There was obviously someone behind me; someone near enough for me to discern their sounds through the ceaseless storm. I wanted nothing more than to stop and turn around, but half of me said not a chance, and forced me to keep walking even more quickly.

My breathing came more rapidly, too, not only because of my pace, but largely because of my fear. Why was I so scared? I'm a grown man... And a big guy! So, what if someone was following me? This was not the plot of one of those Slasher flicks In was so fond of. People don't just go around stalking and cutting up pedestrians! This was stupid!

But that was just a bunch of macho bullshit because as the footsteps continued to match my pace, panic and blinding fear sank its claws even deeper. I swallowed hard enough for it to click in my throat and instinctively coughed, cleared my throat, and spoke aloud,

"Guess I'd better call my wife!"

There was no way my trail had any idea my phone was dead. I mocked dialing - knowing full well the lighted display wasn't glowing - and waited, pretending to listen to the nonexistent ring. And all the while the footsteps never faltered.

My heart was hammering in my chest as I began to talk to no one,

"Hi honey! Guess where I am!"

I prayed for the plodding footfalls behind me to slow; to edge a little off their pace. But even as I carried on my fabricated conversation, they never once wavered.

If possible, the darkness seemed to deepen around me. It felt as though its inky cloak was enclosing me so tightly, I'd never be able to free myself. I tried to slow my laboring breath and forced myself to continue the charade I'd begun on my dead cell phone.

"No, I've been walking to town. Yeah, it's crapped out again. No, I should be the..."

I was abruptly cut off as the thing following me let out what could only be described as a laugh; a low, guttural chuckle.

A cold bolt of fear lanced up my spine and I could feel its chill ring in my ears.

I missed a step and nearly tripped. The night around me suddenly grew far warmer as the sensation of absolute dread made sweat bead all over my face and body. I juggled my umbrella from one hand to the other as my sweaty palms threatened to drop it entirely. I had sense enough to put my phone away before dropping it, too, since there was no reason to pretend any longer.

I kept my pace, as did my pursuer. By now my fear-heightened senses could clearly hear it breathing through the still-pouring rain. By now, the aching need to see what was back there was almost overpowering my natural fight-or-flight sensibilities. I had to know.

I slowly - without breaking stride - turned my head.

Just then my balance gave out and I stumbled over a rise in the road. My feet tangled and I fell over myself. I landed hard on my hands, both of which I managed to throw out in front of me to brace my fall. The umbrella cartwheeled down the road, and everything I had in my pockets jingled noisily across the blacktop; my key chain with my antique amulet bottle opener, my phone, my wallet... it all spilled onto the soaking wet street. I could feel the gravel as it stung deeply into my palms as the blood began to pool and trickle out.

As I sat there on my knees, stunned, I looked desperately around trying in vain to locate any shadow or glimpse to show just who or what had been following me. But even as I shot my gaze as far as I could into the dark, rainy night... I saw nothing. I heard no sign that anything was ever there. By the time I scrambled to my feet and gathered my sopping possessions (the umbrella was a lost cause), I was drenched to the core. Heart thumping a hole in my chest, shivering from head to toe, and on edge like a startled cat, I continued fruitlessly to survey my surroundings. But still I saw and heard nothing.

Nothing except my salvation:

Headlights and an engine.

The End

Tales of The Amulet
Part 12: Spirits

I had driven as far as my exhausted mind would let me and I eased off the Interstate onto an exit for a town called Perkins. The sign that led me here boasted both a Motel 6 and a diner; the notion of either sounded like Heaven to me. Besides, not only was my personal fuel supply dwindling, but so was the gas in the old Buick I'd been piloting since Vicksburg. I braked at the four-way stop; the glowing red illuminating the surrounding black like a welcoming beacon. Turning right, I headed toward the motel following the sign: "Three miles ahead, left." I was almost shivering with anticipation.

The parking lot was as desolate as it was abandoned; dark, deafeningly silent, and just short of full-on frightening. I'd seen enough horror films in my near 40 years to know a creepy hotel car port when one was presented to me, and I had to chuckle in spite of myself. I parked by the dimly lit office and sighed as I killed the engine and listened to the quiet, broken only by the ticking of the cooling motor. I climbed out of the car with a groan loud enough to startle myself, arched my screaming back, and made my way to the door as I winced through knots and aches.

The door welcomed with one of those electronic chimes that sounds a bit like R2-D2. Sadly, not quite as 'small town' as I'd

expected. The lobby was pretty standard for a mid-level motel: plastic potted plants in the corners, a long desk riddled with brochures for the surrounding attractions in a fifty-mile radius, two wing-back chairs that looked slightly over-used, and a wall full of artwork from people no one has ever heard of. I looked around, shrugged, and counted the paces to the front desk... a nervous habit.
42...

Though the small room was meagerly lit with hazy globed lamps positioned in all four corners, there was a small desk light sitting on the counter next to the ledger. On the opposite side was a bell. Quaint. This was the kind of thing I was more accustomed to seeing in one of these off-the-main-drag inns. I smiled again, and raised my hand over it, readying it to strike, when out from the back -maybe ten feet behind the counter to my right- came a small man decked out in a weathered golf shirt and thick-framed glasses. He wore long carpenter-style shorts, Chuck Tailor's, and continued to chew his late-night meal as he wiped his mouth on one of the motel's own finest linens. I couldn't help but stare at his impeccably honed bald scalp that reflected the white glow from the wall sconces. He grinned, nodded in a welcome, and swallowed his mouthful with an audible gulp.

"Sorry 'bout that, buddy. Dinner time, ya know... anyway, can I help you?"

I nodded in understanding and started to remove my wallet from my pocket. "Yes indeed. I would very much appreciate one of your fine rooms!"

"Mm-hmm... one of our fine rooms. Finest in all the land." He said sarcastically, likely at my expense. But if he was angry about it, he showed no signs of ire. "Well, we've got quite a slew to choose from, considering it's pretty dead in here and only eleven of our thirty-two are otherwise occupied... do you have a preference?"

I mulled it over for a second, "Yeah, I guess I'd like one with a view of the parking lot out front here." I wasn't sure why I said that, but it sounded as good an option as any.

He flipped open his reservation book and rifled to the midway point. "You're in luck, Mr.--"

"Miller." I finished.

"You're in luck Mr. Miller, room 27 is available and it just so happens to be the one just to the right as you exit the lobby."

A tinny bleep echoed through the front of the office as the door swung open behind me making me jump just a bit. I spun around and watched as an older man dressed in a tattered trench coat and poorly kept loafers trudged it. He sported an unkempt Fedora with a really odd disc-shaped medallion on the band and lugged an abused briefcase under one arm, upon which sat a long umbrella. Was it raining now? No, couldn't have been, the umbrella was closed and didn't look at all wet. I stared far another second as the man surveyed the room, and then I returned to the desk clerk. He had a cocked eyebrow and an irritated shake passed through his head.

He leaned over to me and whispered, "I know this dude. He comes in about twice a month on his business trips. Complete wing nut."

I raised my own eyebrows, smiled wanly, and nodded in mock understanding. The clerk, whom I now suddenly understood was named Ted (his name tag was pinned far lower on his shirt than I'm sure it ought to have been), slid the key to me and I signed in leaving a fifty-dollar deposit for any damages or stolen property. Thankfully a credit card wasn't required since I don't carry one. We exchanged pleasantries, I said, "Thanks, Ted", and made my way back across the lobby.

As I turned, I saw the man Ted knew standing in exactly the same disheveled pose in which he was standing after I looked him over a few minutes prior. He looked like one of those homeless person statue actors you see in bigger cities performing for handouts. I glanced; he didn't move an inch, so I pulled open the door and walked out to the parking lot. As it turned out, the 'wing nut' was probably just a little crazier than even I'd given him credit for: the night was full of stars and a slight crescent moon hung in the east.

I walked the distance of probably the width of a football field (what can I say: sports are a big part of my downtime) and found that, indeed, number 27 was sharing a common wall with the lobby. Probably the side at which there was a storage room or maybe even the office's restroom since I didn't remember seeing it when I was in there. Despite the obvious attempts to keep the motel as Old-Time cozy as possible, the door locks were still updated to key cards. I still call them keys no matter where I am. Old habits die hard. I slid it in the electronic reader, waited a second for the lights to blink green, yanked it out and turned the knob. Immediately I was greeted by a not entirely pleasant blast of cleaning product; bleach, bathroom cleanser, and something floral hovering just above everything else. I winced and coughed as I flipped on the light and shivered just a bit as the farthest of two wall lamps blew its bulb with a crackling pop. Delightful. I'd have to razz Ted a bit about that in the morning.

The bedspreads were completely reeking with 1970's charm, which is to say they were dark mauve with purple filigree patterns lilting about. And years of hotel visits had taught me

a few things, up to and including stripping the bed cover and stashing it in a corner furthest from where one was to be sleeping. Apparently, they can be riddled with human germs and... other, far more tasteless body fluids. I yanked it off the bed I'd be sleeping in, sat down heavily on the stark-white sheet, and sighed. I was even more tired than I'd imagined, but my stomach argued the point far more profoundly, so a trip to the diner was certainly going to happen soon.
But that thought was dashed quickly as I was startled by an unexpected knock at the door.

I was a little unsure how to respond. Why would someone be knocking on this door? Was someone lost? Did I order pizza? That last thought was just to break the tension as I shook my head and got up from the bed.

Another knock, this time followed by a muffled male voice, "Mr. Miller?"

"Yes? Who is it?" I inquired sounding silly to my own ears.

"Mr. Miller, you left your wallet at the front desk." Came the response.

I did?

I felt my front pocket, sure it had been there all along... and lo and behold: no wallet. Well, what do ya know? Now this was just getting funnier by the second. It seemed good old Ted had Boy Scouted himself a courteous deed for the day.

I laughed, said just a sec, and opened the door.

And there stood 'wing nut'.

For a second, we just looked at each other. He, the poster child for the over-worked and society-whipped, and me, the epitome of hunger and exhaustion wanting nothing more than to find some hot food. It was a bizarre dichotomy to say the least. He just stood there, looking past me rather than at me. That was disconcerting. I tried to smile at him, even though he had a face that appeared almost exactly like something surprising was happening just over my shoulder, and it made me rather uncomfortable.

"Uh... hello?" I said, questioning everything at that point.

"Yes. Hello, Mr. Miller. It seems you forgot your wallet back at the lobby. I took it upon myself to make sure it was returned to you. I told Theodore not to worry about it and that I'd make sure it was returned to you immediately. It seems we're sharing the same side of the building tonight, and since I was heading to 25 anyway... well, there you have it."

"Okay... well, that's great... and thanks!" I stammered, still sort of trying to grasp the absurdity of the situation. I still stared as the man just spouted his diatribe without so much as a flinch. His face belayed not a twitch and he looked almost like one of those animatronic robots from those old pizza arcades.

He lifted his hand and turned it over. His hand was incredibly big. Almost cartoonishly big, considering the rest of his frame, which was not large by any stretch. Cupped neatly in his mitt-sized palm was my wallet, sure enough. I made a move to gingerly pluck it from his right when his left suddenly sprang out and curled around the circumference of my wrist with room for his spindly fingers to overlap his thumb. And my wrists aren't exactly bony. I stiffened visibly and looked at him with an air of confusion and unpleasant surprise.

"Hey! What the Hell!" I managed to bark through my unexpectedly dry throat.

"Worry not, Mr. Miller, I mean you no harm. I promise. But I must insist on coming into your room before I return your wallet. There is something of the utmost importance I must share with you." The stranger said as he held fast to my wrist, though, surprisingly, not uncomfortably so.

"I-I-I... was actually just leaving... for a meal... dinner. At the diner... ha ha... so, why don't we just-"

"It is a pity, then, Mr. Miller. I am sorry to have inconvenienced you. However, I would like to return at a later time, for I need to give you -and of this you must trust me- the information I have." He said as he lightly placed the wallet in my hand while releasing my wrist. His touch left a frigid imprint on my goose-fleshed skin.

"S-sure. Ah... Okay. Sounds fine. I'll be back in an hour or so, I guess?" I said as I looked him over anew. His pallor was waxy, and he appeared to be sweating under his hat.

"I shall make it two hours. No need to rush a meal, Mr. Miller." He said as he stood, "It's not good for the digestion, you know. Rushing a meal. Enjoy it. buy a paper. But please remember: this information is of vital importance."

And with that he mechanically turned on his heal and headed to his room.

I remained still as I watched him methodically plod away. What on Earth was this guy's problem? Why would a guy just randomly want to come into a person's motel room he'd never even met previously? What the Hell was going on? I turned back to the room, grabbed the key and my jacket, pocketed my wallet, double checked that my car keys were in the other, and watched the door shut itself behind me. I was still starving, but before I headed to the diner, I really needed to go grill Ted about this 'wing nut' and just exactly what his deal was.

The digital chime of the lobby door bleeped through the air as I made my way to the front desk. To my surprise, a petite, cute woman and what must have been her daughter were waiting. The younger lady sat in one of the worn chairs and glared intently at her phone while her mother chatted sing-songy with Ted. I hung back a little, not really wanting to hear what was happening, since not much more than renting a room was the likely conversation. I looked again at the young lady in the chair and watched as she tapped her phone screen, probably texting or updating her Facebook status. She smiled and giggled at whatever it was going on from the other end of her chit-chat. As I looked back to the counter, Ted had just handed the woman a key card and indicated where to sign. Money was exchanged, and the woman turned toward me and her daughter. I smiled at her as a look of surprise spread across her face like a weird mask. She glanced at me as if she had something to ask; but didn't. Then she walked past her daughter (barely even registering her appearance) who, in turn, did little more than grunt an acknowledgement, and the two left the lobby with an eerie quickness.

"Mr. Miller!" Ted inquired, "I trust you received your wallet?"

"Yeah... and that's what I came here to talk to you about." I said as I rubbed my brow.

"Oh crap. What did Mr. Christopher do this time"

"Mister... his name is Mr. Christopher? Are you kidding me?" I asked with a laugh.

"Nope. Not kidding. That's his name. Oddly it escaped me when I mentioned him to you earlier. You'd think a name like that would stick with me... anyway, what happened?"

"Well, when he came by, he made to offer me my wallet, and then grabbed my wrist-"

"He did what? Did he hurt you? I can call the pol-" Ted sputtered as he grabbed the phone receiver.

"No, no... nothing like that. It surprised me, that's all." I said as I motioned for him to relax. "It was what he said after that really caught me off guard. Ted, he asked to come into my room because he had something really important to tell me. Why would he do that?"

Ted didn't respond right away. In fact, he looked as though he had to find what he wanted to say before nearly a minute passed. "Um... here's the story on Mr. Christopher. First of all, he's really pretty harmless, as far as I've been told. I've only ever met the guy maybe four times over the past couple of months. He comes here looking identically to the last time, he buys a few nights in either room 25 or, well, room 27, oddly, and he more or less keeps to himself. That's about all I know."

"No, that isn't about all. You said, 'first of all' which implies that you had a 'second of all' to follow." I said with a knowing sneer, "So spill it, man... what else is going on with this dude?"

Ted sniffed and looked around, obviously making sure he wasn't being watched by... who? No one else was in the room. "Okay, look. One time when he was a guest here... this was before I was brought on, another guest came up missing. No one said it was Mr. Christopher, though he was questioned, and the guy was never found. All of his stuff was just left in his room. The cops and the CSI guys or whatever spent a few days here, cleaned up his stuff, and nothing's happened since. Again, as far as I know. I only work nights on the weekends.

But I guess I'd have been told if anything else had gone on. And there you have it."

I stood there for a minute absorbing what I'd just heard. "Was there any reason to believe Mr. Christopher had anything to do with the missing man? Or was it assumed because the guy is obviously bonkers?"

"I don't know. No one here told me anything else. Except to maybe be a little leery of the guy, ya know, just in case." Ted said as he nervously moved a pen around the desk.

"Ted, I appreciate the info, but my guess is there might be something else you're not really allowed to say, and I can dig that. Don't worry, I'll keep an eye out."

Ted looked like I'd caught him lying to his mother or something. But I left it at that, nodded to him, and left the lobby. By now I was famished.

I sat behind the wheel for a few minutes just kind of stewing over the experiences I'd been through over the past hour. What was going on? Why, of any number of potential motels, did I choose this one? I could have driven twenty miles further on and stopped at Strongsville; the city was big and had a half dozen places to stay. What drew me here? I was tired, true, but not falling asleep at the wheel. I just couldn't put two and two together. But what I did know was that I was really, really hungry. I started the Buick, backed out of the spot, and drove what proved to only be about a mile to the diner. And when I say diner, I mean just that: Diner.

It was small but spread out. There wasn't a starkly visible sign anywhere. Just a placard on the front that read (in bold, blue letters on a dingy white background) 'Mom's Dive'. It was lit up- well, half of it was, and it pulsated with cheap fluorescent bulbs. The lot was actually pretty full; pick-ups, old beater cars, hard-driven minivans, and even a few motorcycles. I cruised in and parked next to the newest looking vehicle in the bunch: a Toyota hybrid. Obviously, a traveler like me, judging by how it stuck out. I stepped out of the car and was immediately assailed by what was obviously cooking away in the kitchen; savory-sweet, toasted, roasted, and enough to make my mouth water. A rectangle of light lanced through the far-right end of the building, proving that the back door was open and a man with a cigarette pressed into his mouth was leaning against it staring into the night. His white apron was mottled with any number of stains from various foodstuffs, adding to the fact that he was certainly one of the cooks. He didn't see me as I made for the glassed front doors and pushed my way in.

To say the place was far more bustling than it even appeared from the number of vehicles outside was an understatement. It was no wonder I smelled good things cooking, because the place was just that: cooking. The diner atmosphere was palpable: red Naugahyde booths, black-and-white checkered floor tiles, a long counter with a dozen spinning stools, a rather eclectic supply of whimsical crafts and artwork festooning the walls, a smog of coffee fumes and grease, and the cacophonic din of chitter-chatter. It felt cozy, homey, and just a little out of time... but mostly inviting. I stood by the entry way and the sign proclaiming: PLEASE WAIT TO BE SEATED. There was a little wooden island with a dingy cash register and a crooked spindle jammed with receipts. Gum, Life Savers, a March of Dimes collection can, and a tray of business cards surrounded the perimeter of the cash machine, and just behind, having trundled up from one of the tables, was quite possibly the most singularly cylindrical woman I had ever seen. She was plump but packed into her strangling uniform like a blushing sausage. Her cheeks were rosy in a way to make Santa Claus jealous, and her tightly knit mass of curly reddish-gray hair balanced perfectly on her head, with only two wooden needles jutting out like Martian antennae. She was, in short, adorable. Her ample and equally compressed bosom help present a time-worn name tag on which was written in cutesy script: DARLA.

She offered me a genuinely appealing smile. "Howdy, there, buster! Can I get ya a table?"

I smiled back, doing all I could not to chuckle. "Absolutely, Darla! I'm about as hungry as I've ever been!"

She did laugh at that one. "Well, you've wandered into the right place, then, haven't ya? C'mon, I got a booth with your name on it!"

"Actually, Darla, any chance I could get a table... somewhere in a corner maybe?"

She gave me a once over and realized that with my relatively large frame a booth was definitely uncomfortable, which was what I was hinting at in the first place. Darla nodded, grinned knowingly, and led me around to a small, two-seat table near the kitchen door. I told her it was perfect as she dropped a menu in front of me and expertly wheeled around to snatch a glass of water from the counter.

"Coffee?"

"Um... sure. Why not?" I replied, really wishing I had opted against, yet knowing full well sleep was a long way off.

"Leaded?"

"Definitely. Cream and sugar if you don't mind."

"Not at all! Be right back."

And with that, Darla sprang into action like a well-oiled machine. I sighed and began looking around. The faces were all in motion: eating, talking, laughing, drinking, yawning... it was alive with human emotion and activity. And it was then that I spotted her.

In a booth near the door was the very woman I'd seen not an hour ago with her daughter in the lobby of the hotel. And maybe it was the light -maybe the ambiance- but she was stunning. Nothing about her was visibly different. Apparently, she and her daughter had checked into their room and left immediately for a meal. But wow: she practically glowed with allure and femininity. I sat there and stared, and I suddenly realized I wasn't even trying to hide it. She caught my eye, and I quickly switched my glance to Darla, who had serendipitously returned with my coffee. We exchanged smiles, and she asked if I'd had a chance to check out the menu.

"Ya know what, Darla, why don't you tell me what you recommend tonight."

"Tell ya something, sugar: I recommend the same thing every night! The chicken-fried steak. It's Norm's specialty. It comes slathered with sawmill gravy, a side of mashers, and corn. It's divine if I do say so myself. And I'll clue ya, it's really not complete without a piece of our peach cobbler to end it all, if you know what I mean... à la mode, even."

"Sold." I said. It sounded more than divine. It sounded like Heaven.

Darla swished away, and I returned my gaze to the woman from the lobby. She was engaged in conversation with someone, likely her distracted daughter. It seemed to be going about as pleasantly as one might expect. There was obvious finger-wagging, head shaking, and eye-rolling exaggerated enough to be seen from as far away as I was. I estimated they were maybe fifty paces away, but I was getting at least an amalgamated gist of what was likely going on. For the life of me, I couldn't look away, and when Darla returned with my steaming plate -a thing of pure beauty and southern over-indulgence- I was startled out of my gaze.

"Sorry, suga', did I wake ya?"

"What? No... no... I was... well it's been an incredibly long day. Most of which I spent driving. So, ya know..."

Darla smiled wanly, "Well, I don't know about all that, but I do know I could almost feel the line of your gaze as I wandered over here with your meal. It's that sweet little thing by the window, ain't it?"

I choked on my first forkful. Tears immediately welled up in my eyes and I needed to take a few gulps of ice water before I could talk. "Who? How did you...?"

"Easy, stranger. I don't pass no judgement on anyone. I just call 'em as I see 'em. Besides: she's damn near the cutest young thing in here. I wasn't born last night, ya know. I can see when a fella gets googly eyes for a lass." She grinned again and I could tell there was something behind the warmth; something she wasn't telling me.

"Well, I'm just going eat my food now, so..." I said carving into another bite of quite possibly the best chicken-fried steak I'd ever laid mouth on.

Darla sighed and let her sassy stance fall apart. She dropped her arms to her sides and leaned in a bit with a look of concern on her face, "Confidentially, you might want to re-think your approach, especially considering the, uh... company she's keeping."

And with that she turned on her heel and trundled back to the counter.

Company she was keeping? What did that mean? Why was her daughter someone to be concerned with? Now I really was intrigued. Confused, but intrigued. As I tucked into the remainder of my meal, I decided I needed a well scripted plan to meet this woman with whom I was suddenly infatuated.

Fifteen minutes passed. I cleaned my plate so thoroughly there might have been no need to actually wash it. And I was full. I sipped my third cup of coffee; I liked being at one of those places where they leave the carafe right at the table because I hate having to signal for refills. As I sat back, relieving the pressure on my loaded gut, I returned my attention to the booth with the woman. She was looking out the window into the night, nodding along with what her daughter was telling her. I couldn't make out what it was as the noise level was still at a fevered pitch; as often as people left, the same number replaced them. It was a busy joint, no doubt about it. And in a way, its popularity played to my benefit as I spent an inordinate amount of time taking this woman in with long, drawn-out stares. Finally, I spied movement in the boot. A head popped up from the side that wasn't in my view, and the person who stood was most definitely not the woman's daughter. In fact, the Fedora with its remarkable amulet was a dead giveaway: Mr. Christopher.

To say I was shocked was to say I didn't nearly spill my coffee, and both of those things were instantly true. When did he get here? Was he here the entire time? I'd never dropped my sight from the woman for more than a few seconds at a time to eat and converse with Darla. What was going on? It suddenly occurred to me that this was what my observant server was talking about when she said, 'The company she was keeping'. Mr. Christopher rose to his full height, nodded at the woman, and turned to head out, dropping several bills on the table from his wallet. I diverted my gaze and turned my body to look down at the floor. I had no desire to let the man see me. I waited a full thirty-count and returned to a proper sitting position.

Mr. Christopher was sitting in the other chair directly across from me.

"Mr. Miller! How fortuitous!"

I swallowed and heard my throat click as it tightened, "Apparently."

I looked over the strange man's shoulder and saw Darla. She looked at me with wide-eyed surprise and set what was obviously my dessert back on the counter. She was visibly unnerved, and quickly turned away.

"Can I help you with something, Mr. Christopher?"

"Ah, but it is I who am prepared to help you... as you no doubt remember."

"I remember." I said flatly, "But I still don't understand. Not to mention the fact that you sat at my table without being invited. I'd suspect even you would understand how rude that is."

"Tut-tut... semantics. Besides, no one was using the chair, for one thing. And for another, I'll be but a moment of your time.

A moment you can scarcely afford to dismiss."

I sighed and resigned myself to the fact that this man wasn't going to leave until he'd spoken his peace.

"Go on."

"Excellent. What I have for you is information, of that bit you have been previously regaled. But in actuality, it's a warning." He laced his fingers, nodded once, and sat still.

"A warning. And what makes you think I need a warning about anything? You don't even know me."

"Mmm... perhaps I don't know you directly, true. But I knew you were coming."

I looked at him side-long, "Yeah, it didn't take a magician to assume I was coming here, considering it's likely the only restaurant for miles in any direction."

He nodded yet again, and let a wry grin dance across his lips, "You misunderstand me, Mr. Miller. What I meant was that I knew you were coming here: the motel... this town."

I couldn't help but bark a rather loud laugh, "What? What kind of crap are you trying to feed me?"

"Eloquent. No... (ahem) *crap* intended, Mr. Miller. Most certainly not. No, I only arrive at the motel when I am... shall we say, *directed*. Directed to do so. And as such, I was made privy to your eminent arrival."

Ignoring the obviously crazy man, I signaled to the newly interested Darla to bring my cobbler and ice cream. But she hesitated.

"Oh, Darla won't come here. She's... not too fond of me, I'm afraid."

"What? Why?" I asked suddenly not smiling anymore. In fact, this whole situation had gotten a little too bizarre.

"It matters not. What does matter is the warning I have yet to relay to you. You must listen and hear me very well. Then I will be on my way."

I sipped my tepid coffee, scowled at it, and nodded for him to go on at the same time.

"Stay away from the woman."

I froze.

"Uh... wha-what woman?" I stammered, knowing exactly whom he meant.

"Please, Mr. Miller. Let us not feign stupidity. You know about whom I refer. I reiterate, stay away from the woman. It is in your very best interest to do so."

And with that, he thumbed his hat with a nod, quickly and quietly rose, and left the building like some kind of ghastly wraith. I sat stunned and numb, and watched as though I were in another place, in another time -outside of my own body- as Darla returned to my table with dessert. She, too, looked unwell.

"He was the company she was keeping; I'm guessing." I said, barely hearing my own query through the sudden timpani of buzzing in my head.

"Yeah. He was. He's absolutely one of the most... frightening men I have ever met. I'm sorry I held up your cobbler."

"No, no apology necessary." I rubbed my temples and squeezed my eyes shut to force away the ringing in my ears. "What his deal, anyway?"

"He comes in here every time he's in town. But I guess that's not really the issue since we are the only rest'raunt for a few miles... it's just his, what's the word... *demeanor*? Is that right?"

I nodded and forced a smile, "I'd say that's just about perfect."

"When he first started coming by -maybe a year or so ago now- he pretty much kept to himself. But eventually, he sort of got nosy. Anyone who'd arrive while he was in town, he'd... well, he'd scare the pants off, that's what. Talking about information and warnings and crazy threats if folks didn't pay him mind. And people started staying out. He'd never bother the regulars -folks who live here- but he'd sure get under the skin of passers-by. I'd had enough one day, after he made a woman cry, and I told him he had to leave. He nodded politely enough, but his eyes looked daggers right through me. Since then,... well, I can hardly stand to be around him." Darla explained as she looked off into the distance of the diner, and likely the distance of her past.

"Well, that answers that. He told me you'd never come to the table with him there." I said as I poured more coffee to warm up the room-temperature beverage in my mug.

"And I'm just saying, here... it might not be a bad idea to... uh, listen to him." She said, returning her gaze right to my eyes. It startled me a little; her face was ashen and pallid.

"What? I thought you just said..."

"I know. I know. The man is a kook without a doubt. But here's the thing: his warnings always come true. Or pan out... or whatever you want to say. Somehow... he just knows."

I looked at her and nodded. Was Darla serious? She must have seen the question in my eyes because she went on.

"About eight months ago... yeah, that would be April... he was in town on one of his regular visits. He came into the diner, and at this point I had now seen him about half-a-dozen times. Anyway, he came in and met with a fella much like yourself: a guy just moseying through on his way anywhere else. The fella seemed nice enough, so I chatted him up much as I'm doing with you. And then Mr. Christopher gave him his cock-and-bull story, but the man refused to listen. He flat out told me it was hooey and left. The next day he was gone. They found all his belongings up in his motel room, but the fella had just vanished."

I shivered so much gooseflesh erupted over my skin like a flurry of tiny pox. Didn't Ted tell me the exact same thing? The story of the man coming up missing and just leaving all his stuff? I shuddered again and I must have looked like someone walked over my grave.

"Are you okay? I've never seen a man turn that white before!" Darla announced as she took a step back.

"Fine... fine. But I'm not hungry anymore. Thanks for the dessert, though."

Darla waved me off, "You look like you need to lie down. Let me pack that cobbler to go, I'll just scrape off the ice cream, so it doesn't melt all over." She left and returned quickly with a foam clam shell.

I paid cash. Darla and I exchanged pleasantries and I said I'd be by for breakfast. She told me she was always there and looked forward to seeing me again. She also insisted I heed Mr. Christopher's urgency. In fact, she made me promise. I said I would and left. The night was cold, and I could see my breath puffing out in grey clouds. Just then the fact that I was exhausted slammed into me like a wall. It was time for bed.

Before I could settle into the car, I saw the woman leave the diner; her features illuminated by the halo of the restaurant's lights. I'd then wondered where her daughter was? Did she leave her back at the motel? That didn't seem particularly safe to me considering she was likely only in her young teens, if even that. And why would she eat alone when she had her child with her? It didn't make sense, but then, none of this evening made a whole lot of sense. I watched for a minute more as she got into her vehicle, started it, and drove off. One final thought popped into my mind: what on Earth was Mr. Christopher talking to her about? Was he giving her a warning, too? And if so, was it about me, as mine was about her? I had no idea. And I had no idea what made me care so much. I was mentally drained, and I really needed some sleep. I slid into the driver's seat, fired the engine, and left for the motel.

The knock came at 1:13 a.m. I had fallen asleep atop the bed covers, in both my clothes and my shoes. The TV was tuned to ESPN's SportsCenter, and it was on incredibly loud to my formerly-soundly sleeping ears. Another knock at 1:14.

"I-I'm coming... just a sec." I said groggily. I rolled over and allowed gravity to tug my weary frame to a sitting-leaning position.

It took a few seconds to wipe exhaustion from my eyes, but I managed to bring the waking world to focus and stood up. I peeked out the peep hole before opening the door, since my head hadn't completely cleared yet I pictured Ted in his pajamas carrying a peach cobbler... wait, what? But the image was of the woman. Alone.

I dropped the chain latch, unbolted the deadlock, and opened the door, "Yes?" That was all I could manage.

"Uh... hi. I mean, hello, sir. Um, I'm sorry about the very late hour... but I need to... speak with you."

She was visibly upset, that was obvious from the streaked mascara that ran inky stains down her flushed cheeks. Her auburn hair was a tousled nest, and she stood there looking anxious as she wrung her hands. She was even pretty in her current bedraggled state: not too tall, not too short, beautiful eyes -despite their watery sorrow- and features a guy like me could enjoy. I couldn't help staring, as I'd done at her the length of my stay at the diner hours previous And it made matters all the worse that I was still almost half asleep and my mind was hammering out thoughts of raciness and indelicacy. She wore a T-shirt maybe just her size and her ample breasts jutted out. It was then I noticed she wasn't wearing a bra, nor a coat, or shoes. Her feet must have been freezing. She looked anew at me with concern and abject worry. I leaned against the door and ushered her in without saying a word. She took the offer and stepped inside out of the cold. Warning be damned: this woman was in dire straits.

She sat at the little table that was positioned by the heat register near the only window. The curtains were down, but she stared through the little crack where they didn't quite fill the void. I went to the little coffee maker that sat in the bathroom, brought it out to the TV hutch and plugged it in while shutting off ESPN. She continued to gaze out at the parking lot through the gap in the fabric as I prepared the little coffee filters that came with the room; nothing spectacular, but enough to warm us up for what I was sure was about to be a lengthy stay. I poured water into the back and flipped the switch. Soon the smell of brewing Maxwell House filled the room.

"So... can I offer you a plastic mug full of second-rate coffee?" I comically inquired.

She turned to me with a face that looked like something out of a horror movie. Her eyes were huge, her face wan and colorless, and her lower lip quivered as she nodded an answer. I could do little more than look at her and feel terrible for whatever it was that had happened. I looked away as the crackling gurgle of the coffee maker signaled its complete brew cycle. I poured two mugs, walked the seven paces to the table, and joined her.

"Thank you. I'm, ah... Miss Bonny... well, that's what my kids call me. At my school. I'm a second-grade teacher at Woodhill..." She quickly sighed, brushed hair out of her eyes, and smiled soullessly. It was all too apparent that she had been through something.

"Hi, there... Miss Bonny. Nice to finally meet you."

"I saw you at the diner tonight." She said, not letting any irritation at my constant ogling show through.

Regardless, I flushed with a bit of embarrassment, "Yeah... the diner. Great food wasn't it?"

"Sorry, I wouldn't know. I never ate."

I recoiled in sudden question, "Then why were you--"

She cut me off, "Because he asked me to meet him. Mr. Christopher. He asked me to meet him there."

I sat there dumbfounded. At some point between when I first saw Miss Bonny in the lobby and when I finally made my way to the diner, Mr. Christopher made his move on her, too. And by the looks of it, he'd frightened her out of her wits. But that was hours ago. And it was very evident that she'd been quite recently crying.

I decided to angle the line of questioning back to when I'd first seen her, "Who were you with when I saw you in the lobby?"

"What? What do you mean 'who'?" She asked with an overtly genuine raise in her voice.

"Yeah, you smiled at me -almost making me think you wanted to ask me something- anyway, you smiled at me, and left with who I assumed was your daughter."

She blinked twice. "I don't have any children."

It was my turn to sit in disquieting silence. "Wait... then who was that little girl who followed you out of the lobby? Your sister?"

"Sir- what do I call you, anyway?"

"Mr. Miller... since we're going by formalities for the time being... Miss Bonny." I said with an air of sarcasm.

"Mr. Miller... I don't know what or who you are talking about. I don't remember seeing a little girl. And I certainly don't remember acknowledging anyone else there... aside from you, that is."

"You're kidding! She was right there in the old chair in the lobby! Messing with a phone or something! Are you serious! She wasn't with you?" My inquisitiveness had reached an oddly fevered pitch.

She solemnly and slowly shook her head, "I saw no one. And as I said, I have no kids. In fact, I'm here alone on my way to a Teacher's Convention in New York. I could have flown, but I like to drive, so..."

I was flabbergasted and not a little bit dismayed. I saw the girl. I knew it. How could this woman possibly not have seen her? She walked right past her, and the little girl followed her out the door. I shivered despite the warming heat of the coffee. Maybe she was just in a hurry. So, what if it wasn't her kid, I guess it's possible that her gesture was just a coincidence... but maybe there wasn't a gesture. Maybe I just assumed there was because I also assumed she was her child.

"I'd like to tell you why I came here... Mr. Miller." Miss Bonny said breaking the uncomfortable silence.

"Of course. I'm sorry... go on."

She took a sip of the coffee, peered once again out the window, "When Mr. Christopher came to my room earlier this evening, he petrified me. Look, I know I'm a young woman traveling alone without much concern for trouble... and I regret that, but I just felt I'd be safer stopping at this motel rather than one in a bigger city with more people... more strangers. Ya know? Anyway, when he came to my room, I felt all of my latent fears bubble to the surface. Especially after he told me what he forcibly said he had to tell me."

I nodded. I understood how she felt. Mr. Christopher scared

everyone, "I get it. I really do. Go on."

This time she merely looked at her cup, "He warned me I was being followed. He said to always check the shadows. Can you believe that? Who says that to someone? 'You're being followed! Check the shadows!' What is going on with this guy? He alarmed me so much I lost it and broke down right in front of him."

"And this was before you went to the diner?"

"Yes." She wiped the fresh tears from her face as I offered her a tissue, "I guess he felt bad for me because he invited me to dinner. I couldn't figure out any other reason why. Until I met him there."

I looked at here again. I didn't understand what she was getting at. "You mean he had more to tell you?"

"Yes." She took a long drink of her coffee, "As we sat there, he asked me about myself and if I'd ever had any feelings of being followed... like, mysteriously so. I told him I didn't think so. He asked me if I ever felt that someone or something was 'there' when I was otherwise alone. I told him again that I didn't think so. He nodded, but he said nevertheless that I was, indeed, being followed by something... and he reiterated about checking the shadows. He went on to tell me about the waitress at the diner who was serving you and that situation. And he even explained about a very unlucky individual who chose not to heed his warning--" She trailed off and took a deep breath and looked once again out the window.

Tears welled up in her eyes and I could think of nothing else to do but take her hand. She turned to me and smiled.

"Funny thing is," I began as I laid my other hand on hers, "He told me to stay away from you. That was my warning."

"I know. When I first saw you in the lobby today, that's exactly what I was going to say... for some reason I was going to tell you to stay away from me. And now it makes sense why."

"You're kidding? You were going to tell me to stay away from you? Seriously?"

"I was. I had no idea why. It wasn't like you looked like a creep or anything... even if you were staring at me." She smiled.

"Well, you and the little girl in the--"

"Wait a minute." She said suddenly, "You don't suppose..."

We could do nothing more than look at each other. Tears trickled down her face and I literally had to do all I could to not scream. I don't scare easily; I love horror movies and the unknown, but this was just shy of completely and fully insane.

Little else was said the rest of the night. Few words were shared; she warmed up to allowing me to hold her as she silently sat and shivered in my arms. Nothing made sense anymore. I had been in town for literally just shy of a full twenty-four hours and I had somehow slid into a severely outlandish set of circumstances. I was at a loss as to where to go next, but my intuition said to pack up now and get the hell out. But what of Miss Bonny? A name that just tickled me as almost unreal. She obviously was unsafe. Whether or not it was because she was actually being followed, or from Mr. Christopher himself... I didn't know. But I was implausibly worried. As I sat there in the chair cradling a woman I didn't know in my arms, I found myself rocking her back and forth; I slowly pulled ribbons of her hair away from her tear-soaked face, staring intently at her shuddering form. A maelstrom of feelings and plots stormed through my head, not the least of which was, 'what am I going to do with her?'. She moaned a little and pushed at me gently attempting to sit. I released my soft grip and watched her as she raised from my arms.

"I think I have to leave." She said, matter-of-factly as she wiped her eyes on the wadded tissue in her hand.

"What? Are you sure? Are you okay?"

"No... I don't know. Maybe. But I know I have to go." She stood up and once again looked out of the slitted gap made from the too-small curtains.

I looked at here askance. "Are you... sure?"

She sighed, swiped her hair from her face leaving a thin trail of the remaining mascara that had run down her sodden cheeks, "No. I have no idea. It's been a... bad night."

I nodded. In both agreement and weariness, I was definitely tired, even if I was buzzing from the caffeine. But I was only feigning agreement, because deep inside I was scared for both of us. Rather than let her freeze on her way back to her room, I offered her a hooded sweatshirt I'd packed in my luggage. But she refused, and said her room was just number 30 (an answer to a question I realized I'd never gotten around to actually asking her). I opened the door, and through an obviously forced smile and a put-on facade of momentary alacrity, she thanked me, and followed with two words that would haunt me the rest of the night:

"He knows."

I stood there a heartbeat and watched as she quickly closed

the short distance to her room. And I counted the steps: 32.

The door closed with its stuttering swish and click, and I stared at it half expecting Miss Bonny to return, while half expecting something -anything- else completely maddening to occur. In the few minutes it took me to realize how much I needed the bed, and to notice that it was pushing three a.m., nothing happened. I kicked off my shoes, shrugged out of my shirt and pants, and laid down. I flicked on ESPN again, but I was out before the fuzzy picture settled into clarity on the age-old screen.

"... He knows..."

Fear sits on your chest and suffocates the life from your body. Fear comes in forms as innocent as a baby and as diabolical as a banshee. The fear I felt that night as I pitched and sprawled through three nearly broken hours of fitful sleep was as palpable as the cloying, wet sheet I was knotted up in. I awoke from a blissfully sporadic and short nightmare where Mr. Christopher was steadily burying me in dirt. I fought to claw my way free, but the relentless shovelfuls kept piling on the earth. I screamed for help and watched in terrified disbelief as Miss Bonny stood atop the open grave and just masked her face with her hands. The gaunt and sinister soothsayer continued his ceaseless scooping and flinging of dirt as he kept repeating the mantra, "He knows!" over and over. Yes, that night fear perched atop my petrified form like a poltergeist and supped on my wavering sanity. I woke, breathless and exhausted. I was drained and drenched with perspiration. I knew right then I had no choice but to leave. And soon.

I had to shower first. I was literally sopped with the night sweats, and I had to get out of my sodden clothes. I stepped into the steaming tub (the water pressure left a lot to be desired, but such was the bane of motel bathrooms) and let the hot spray rinse away as much of the previous night as it was able. Sadly, much of what I saw; what I felt and experienced, remained. What I couldn't seem to heat through was the chill that marched up and down my spine like icy fingers. I stayed under the warming cascade for a while and let my thoughts play out. Part of me already had my keys in the ignition and was nearly backing out of the parking lot... yet the other thought held me fast and told me I had enough unfinished business with the haunting and mysterious Miss Bonny. The shower's rapidly depleting water temperature did little to really sway me either way, and so as the mist turned tepid, I turned it off and stepped out onto the bathmat.

I glanced at the mirror. A habit, though I knew I wasn't as cleanly shaven as I would have otherwise preferred. Imprinted in the fogged glass were two handprints. Child-sized handprints. Condensation had just begun to pool and run little rivulets through the haze that coated the surface. I dropped my towel and listened. Someone had to be in the adjoining room.

My heart was thrumming in the back of my throat. I looked again at the prints; prints that had certainly not been made by me... or any adult, for that matter. I began to breathe in halting gasps as I reached over on instinct to touch the markings left on the vanity. But I stopped inches before I could. I was scared to even be in the same room with the ghostly figures, and why I thought I wanted to touch them suddenly seemed horrifying and disgusting. But I didn't want to leave the bathroom. I stood there and shivered unsure of what to do. Was someone still in my room? How did someone even get in? I knew I locked the door behind-- wait, did I? I shut the door, but I didn't chain it. No, that wasn't possible: motel room doors lock automatically when they're shut, or else you wouldn't need a key. Then how... who? I ran thoughts through my head all the while cocking my ear to the door in hopes of maybe catching the intruder... or rather, in hopes of not.

Minutes passed, and I'd begun to feel foolish. What was I hoping to hear, exactly? I looked once again at the mirror and what I'd thought I'd seen moments before was nothing more than damp streaks and clearing spots where the cool glass had warded off the heat of the steam. I resigned myself to just being paranoid and overly tired, and opened the door to my room.

The ethereal girl on the bed turned to look at me; her stare both at me and through me, a gaze of both sheer terror and foreboding innocence... and then vanished into the emptiness.

I remember my knees buckling but once my head hit the bathroom door, the next half hour was nothing but a white flash.

As I came to, I found myself naked sprawled like a haphazardly tossed marionette: legs akimbo and uncomfortably twisted beneath me, my temple painfully pressed into the corner of the door jamb, and my arms numbly folded underneath me. I groaned and struggled to sit, breathing past the monotonous throb in my head. A welt was forming where I'd apparently struck the wood, and it was tender and raw. I wasn't out long, maybe thirty minutes; my hair was still wet as was the floor where I'd come to rest. I had seen the little girl; of that I was absolutely positive. I had seen moist handprints on the bathroom, of that I was slightly less positive, but still almost sure.

The ringing phone stung my aching skull and raised me a shade more quickly from the floor.

"Mmmm... Hello." I moaned.

"Mr. Miller. It appears you have chosen in error not to heed my warning." Came the gruff, sharp bray from the other end. It was doubtlessly Mr. Christopher.

I held the receiver away from my face and looked at it in mixed puzzlement and trepidation. The tinny voice from the earpiece echoed from my grasp, "Mr. Miller, I know full well that you are on the other end of this conversation."

"What do you want." I croaked in a voice that was not my own, yet still from my mouth.

"Mr. Miller, I am not making this call to humor you. I provided you with a very simple set of instructions... instructions you chose to ignore. This decision of yours has sent ripples in motion. Ripples I may not be able to calm. Do you understand me?"

"Look, you bastard, she came to my door! She came to my room!" I barked into the phone.

"Regardless the circumstances, Mr. Miller, the outcome -the rapidly approaching repercussions- shall prove to be... dire."

"What was I supposed to do? Turn her away? You have literally scared the both of us to--"

Mr. Christopher abruptly cut me off, "To death? This outcome may be more poignant than you can possibly imagine. I can no longer offer my assistance or cautions, Mr. Miller. You have set the cogs in gear, and I can assure you that you and Miss. Bonny are ill prepared to deal with the aftermath. Good day."

The click from the phone was deafening. I returned the set to the cradle and looked at it in an amalgam of disgust and rage.

As I threw my meager belongings in the trunk of my car, I couldn't help but argue with myself of what to do next. Nearly taking over my decision process every time was self-preservation: fight or flight; getting the Hell out of Dodge as quickly as humanly possible. However, I wasn't a jerk, and I knew that caught in the mix was an innocent schoolteacher suffering the same mental anguish as I was. Chivalry might me dead, but I guess I never got the memo. I knew full well I couldn't leave Miss Bonny alone. And damn the consequences. I stood by my car and stared off into the distance where the welcoming sound of the highway could easily be heard through the crisp, late fall air. I sighed, wishing I were picking up speed on the entrance ramp and heading away... far away. But I'd kick myself for the rest of my life if I didn't know she was safe. This place was making me see things. I'd only once before in my life seen what I thought might have been a ghost, but it literally paled in comparison to the image that appeared on my motel room bed. I was still shaken, but I felt a lot better just being out of the room all together. And with that, I knew I had to make a stop at the lobby. I had a key to deliver, and a little something else.

"Ted!" I shouted as I purposefully marched to the counter, "Ted! Where ya hiding, buddy?"

Silence.

The lobby was eerily quiet. The remnants of my voice echoed through the small office. I leaned over the counter and tried to peer a little further around the back corner into the rear of the room, but to no avail. I couldn't see much further than where the hall entered the back.
"Ted! Where are you, man! It's Mr. Miller!" Why hadn't I ever

told him my first name? Oh well, it didn't matter, even as odd as my name sounded to my own ears without actually saying it.

I listened again, and it was then I heard a lowing emanating from somewhere further back into the office. I stood there for a second and listened a bit more intently, and sure enough the moaning continued. It sounded like someone was either hurt or in the process of being hurt. I couldn't just leave it alone. I turned the corner of the counter, quickly walked to the little hallway, and peered around the edge into the rear office.

Lord help me, I immediately wished I hadn't.

Ted was curled up in a ball on the floor. A deathly pallor hung over his face like a sheet. Tears streamed down his face, and he was visibly shaking. A few feet just above his ashen face was an ethereal, translucent form that -even from the distance and angle I stood- was unmistakably the same little girl I'd seen only an hour before. She glared at him; scowled and chastised. Ted was absolutely terrified; a fact made all the more apparent by the rapidly spreading wet spot at the front of his jeans. I stood in silent wonder as the form continued its malevolent lesson. But an audible click from my gaping mouth betrayed me.

The apparition turned, saw me, and I swear she smiled at precisely the same moment she seemed to fly directly at me... no, not 'at', through me. The feeling of sorrow and disillusionment was so palpable and real that I did all I could not to faint from the melancholia. I dropped to my knees and tried to catch my breath as I looked over at Ted. He was completely petrified with fear to the point that he appeared to be dead. I stood, walked over to him, and it turned out that appearances weren't always deceiving. Ted's breathing had ceased. I held his wrist, and he had no pulse. I swallowed and immediately thought that I had to get to the phone.

Until a voice shook me to my core.

"Theodore refused to listen, too, Mr. Miller."

To Be Continued...

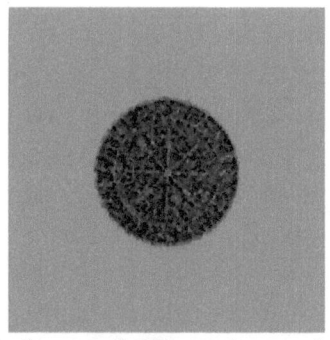

Tales of The Amulet
Part 13: The 4th

Dale sat on the hill above the high school football field. The grass was dead and dry and scratched at his bare legs. He looked down at the meandering masses as the gathering people chose their seats and spots for the fireworks display still 90 minutes away. The hot sun hung just above the horizon; its fat, shimmering heat permeating the muggy evening. Dale peered at it through his sunglasses and silently cursed its wretched warmth.

From where Dale sat, he was comfortably out of the view of the scattered populace below, and that suited him fine. People irritated him to no end, and they always had. For Dale, seeing his father -just home from the first skirmish in the Middle East called Desert Storm- descend into a pit of sorrowful madness was excruciating. His dad was a strong, proud man, but the war destroyed him from his psyche outward until what was left was a ragged husk that withered and died like an Autumn leaf. Dale watched it all and stood by his father as waste ate him to death. His father was his hero regardless, but as he slowly died, Dale questioned constantly why his own government -those men he fought for- did nothing to help. Dale was done with people, and he found his solace in an item he discovered in his dad's old Army trunk.

It was a disk about the size of a '45 record. Its burnished and rough exterior was emblazoned with runes and etchings that meant nothing to Dale... but what did mean something was the pulsating rouge 'eye' in the center. It spoke to him. It comforted him, and it gave him both hope and a job. Dale would soon have the vengeance his dad so richly deserved.

As Dale sat on the grassy mound, he solemnly fingered the trigger of his dad's sniper rifle. It was loaded, and the safety was off. The time was nearly at hand; he just had to wait for the colorful explosions to light up the sky. Next to him, wrapped in a loose rag was the amulet. It thrummed red in unison with Dale's own heart.

The dark night slowly overtook the light of day, and Dale heard the announcement over the school PA system that the fireworks would begin in 15 minutes. Dale laid down and positioned the rifle, and in doing so he kicked the amulet from under the rag and it slid and rolled down the hill onto the night.

Dale froze. His mind cleared from a dense fog that had been blanketing it for what felt like an eternity. He suddenly heard his father's voice. His dad reminded him how much he loved him and that what had made him fall was no fault of Dale's. He told him that by his own choice he fought for the freedoms Dale enjoyed and that what he was about to do would solve nothing. Dale heard his father's words and began to weep. What was he doing?

Dale looked up past the sight and saw hundreds of people gathered together in freedom and peace. The fireworks began and their beauty was unmistakable, as was the message for which they stood.

Dale silently thanked his dad, told him he loved him forever, and retreated with his rifle back down the hill as the bombs burst in air behind him.

Tales of The Amulet
Part 14: It Begins

Though in the beginning there was Heaven and Earth, there was also Hades. God, in his omnipotent wisdom and merciful grace, was the Lord of his Heaven. Around him stood limitless columns of clouds, vast expanses of beauty, and complete un-Earthly forever as far as the faithful could see. This was perfection; this was what those who truly believed and honestly expected would find after they shuffled their mortal coil. It was to be All; it was to be Life Anew. It was Heaven, and it was breathless, exalted, and pristine love in all its completeness. But not all who knew and understood and believed would be granted admission.

Some had to be punished. Some had to learn from their mistakes. Some had to know Heaven only as an unachievable respite to their Purgatory in the insane depths of what only their most wicked nightmares to remotely conceive. For they had to be sent to the fires. They -the ones who turned a blind eye to the words of the Lord- must be tossed asunder to suffer endlessly in the burning, searing, relentless pits of the House of Hades. All hate, all wanton desire, all evil... it was thrust upon them as they lay about crying, weeping, pleading... it was forever. Even God: the Holy Spirit and embodiment of all things light and right, had to turn his back and let the ones who rightfully deserved to rot like fetid meat do so. And so,

Hell took on a population of its own.

He Who Sits On Ashen Throne; He who is called Satan... He looked upon the inky, smoldering depths of his inhuman home. His place as ruler of Hades was written long before there was a choice to make. But his Hell had grown fat with writhing, sinning, blasphemous, wretches and he had to make a choice. He would send forth an Army. A battalion of Hell Spawn to swarm about the Earth destroying lives and sending those innocent lives above, to where God had to deal with them. But how?

An amulet. A trinket of such outstanding and awesome power as to turn man and woman alike to quivering, lifeless husks. He would imbue it with all the essence; all of the foreboding, filthy, anger of Hell and he would arm his minions with it. And they would scour the Earth, wreaking havoc as they marched their ill will throughout. And so, the Amulet was born.

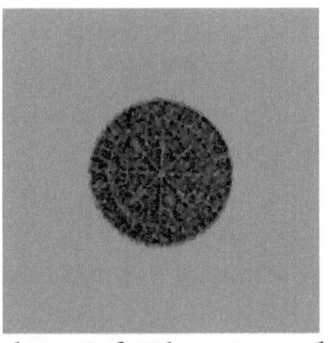

Tales Of The Amulet
Part 15: Nightmare

Aaron sat at his desk. The chair was cool and oddly refreshing in the early morning atmosphere of his room. His windows were open to the Early-May breezes languidly rustling the leaves just outside, and his fan hummed on 'Low' in his south-facing window. It was never very cold in the bedroom -it was rare that the winds changed just right to sufficiently make the air chilly- but the chill at this particular two-twenty-eight a.m. was nearly freezing and it set deeply in Aaron's bones.

Aaron pressed the heels of his hands to his eyes and rubbed away the dwindling strings of his horrific nightmare. Or at least he tried to. Some of those strands clung tightly and kept bringing him back to the jarring dream that virtually trapped him in deep sleep. He remembered clawing, struggling... fighting his way to consciousness and he was exhausted for it. Exhausted for it and from the dream. The nightmare was palpable and heavy. Aaron could smell it; sense it. It still had hold and he couldn't shake himself fully awake. He sighed and reached for his cup of water that sat on his desk next to his laptop.

Aaron would write it away. It suddenly occurred to him that the best way to battle the remains of a nightmare that refused to release his psyche was to write it out and drag it kicking and screaming from his head. He raised his laptop screen and watched as the warm glow of its screen spread into familiar brilliance. A quick mouse clicks and a writing program sprang to life. Aaron sat back and looked to the ceiling; his eyes closed as he re-stacked the deck that represented the cohesive layout of his dream. It didn't take long, for the whole picture hadn't fallen all to pieces just yet. He rolled his fingers and set to write.

"I was trapped. The gloom that fell around me was a black that no light could even hope to penetrate. And to even speak of hope -hope as a feeling of exuberance- is to speak of the dead, for hope had long since dissolved into disillusionment. I knew I was in a city. A big city. Perhaps Chicago, since it is a city I am rather familiar with. I sat in a car. Oddly a 2-door coupe; a car I haven't owned for nearly twenty years. And I had a passenger. A passenger whose face I never saw; not before the dream, nor during, and certainly not one I could drag from memory even now. I saw hair. Her hair. I was looking at the back of this woman's head, and her hair was long and sandy-blond. This much I can remember. She was alive -which is to say (*as you'll soon see*) she wasn't among them. She breathed rapidly and shivered with the same choking and relentless fear that I was feeling (*and that I feel even now as I write this*). She moaned with little, tight, audible whines that sounded like the mewls of a sad cat. I felt bad for her, and I swallowed my fear as best I could manage, only to have it collect in a sickening lump in my throat; a lump that was either going to escape in a cacophonous scream, or a flume of fear-induced vomit. (*incidentally, the lump has returned as I regale...*). Though the dark was so inky and thick, we both knew -this female passenger and I- that the things just outside our ridiculously un-protective doors were seconds away from scrambling into the car with their guttural gibbering and twisted, knurled talons ready to flay our flesh. I broke out in goose bumps (*just as I did in my sleep and just as I do now*) and a chilling sweat beaded my arms and head and rolled down my neck. It was just then my female passenger's throaty groans turned into words. I understood almost immediately that she was repeating the droning mantra, "My fault... my fault... my fault..." over and over as she rocked back and forth. Right then I had no idea what it meant, that monotonous dirge, but the closer I looked her over -feebly attempting to garner a guess at her identity- I finally noticed something hanging from her neck. Even in my dream I recognized the item; it was an item I, myself, had created... in the wakened world. (*As I write this I have begun shaking and feeling tenseness creep through my terrified muscles.*) What she wore was The Amulet. The very disc-shaped rune-stone that held a starring role in each and every one of my stories! And it was alive with its wicked red brilliance. It pulsated in time with the woman's erratic heartbeat. And it thrummed in unison with the approaching monsters that were moments away from springing out of the darkness with their chattering mouths and their angry hands...

And then I woke. And I lay there on the cusp of screaming into the night. I fought to control my breathing. And then I sat. And here I am"

Aaron leaned back from the computer satisfied but feeling no better for the writing he'd done. In fact, all it had served to do was reattach the strings of the nightmare he'd thought he'd severed. His shoulders felt tight, and the back of his neck throbbed as though a weight had been tugging it downward. He reached his hands to his nape and prepared to work the muscles out. It was then he felt the chain. The chain he knew all too well.

Aaron wailed into the darkness as the ruby hue ebbed and flowed at his chest.

Tales of The Amulet
Part 16: The Amulet (Part 1)

Kimmy listened distantly to the stony clunk as the heavy head of the wet and sticky ax fell to the concrete beneath her feet. This had been easily the longest day of her life and, finally, it seemed to be drawing to a messy, ugly close. Laying strewn about the place like discarded store-front mannequins were the mutilated remains of seven bodies each in a vastly different state of slaughter and disassembly. Kimmy surveyed here doing, sighed with a confusing mixture of remorse and cloying disdain, and crouched to her knees in order to collect the Amulet she'd fought so bravely to reclaim from the dying hands of her family and friends. This very Amulet, some might have called it the Jewel of Mortis, was the cause of and solution to all of the plaguing problems that filled the last 24 hours like a bowl too overloaded with soup. Kimmy hadn't a clue as to how any of it occurred; all she knew was that upon waking from her restless slumber, she was set on by her three brothers: each enveloped in a milky, blank stare and consumed by their merciless thirst for murder. Kimmy had no idea that the hunger was brought on by the Amulet she'd just purchased a day earlier from a street vender outside of the Museum she'd visited on a class field trip. Even as she sprung from her bed, clamored down the basement steps to the garage, and snatched the axe from against the wall nearest the wood-burning furnace, did she still remain blissfully dumbfounded and intensely frightened at the curious goings-on. Kimmy was never one to show an overt amount of courage; some might have even called her a bit too girly to be the self-proclaimed tom boy that she's often strived to be. But she brought out every bit of her pent-up anger and survival skills as she systematically severed heads from necks and twitching limbs from torsos. Yes, her family was lying about in rapidly congealing pools of blood, but the Amulet was hers once again. Now, it was only a matter of getting out of the house...

Tales of The Amulet
Part 17: The Amulet (Part 2)

Kimmy's parents were among the dead. She felt the tightness of guilt and the numb fluidity of sorrow grip her and threaten to take hold, but it was a temporary feeling and she absently batted at a rolling tear as she stepped over them.

It wasn't really them. It wasn't really them...

She took a big step over the gored corpses and began making her way to the front door. Something stirred behind her, and she froze. Her heart thrummed wildly in her chest, and she could feel its pulses in her throat as it created its customary clicks of fear. Kimmy felt herself snatching quick, whistling breaths as she swallowed past her fright and slowly turned around.

She was pelted from the side. The dip of her neck where it met her right shoulder was suddenly muzzled by a warm wetness and the unmistakable feeling of a tongue licking her. Kimmy sighed and a grin creased her bloodied face as she reached around and caressed the furry jowls of Tanner, her St. Bernard.

"My God, Tanner... you almost made me throw up! I'm so glad to see you, boy!"

Tanner panted and stared at her as he resumed lapping up some of the dried blood spatter that had coated her during the recent debacle. He dropped his paws onto one of the bodies, that of Kimmy's dad, and he began to nuzzle and sniff the familiar odor of the man he'd lived with for years.

"Don't. He's dead, Tanner. He might smell like dad, but he definitely wasn't a minute ago..."

Tanner cocked his head sideways, sneezed, and resumed his frantic panting. Kimmy completed her wide berth of the massacre on the kitchen floor and headed anew for the exit. Tanner bounded the mess, landed a tad awkwardly in one of the rapidly congealing pools of blood, and trundled after Kimmy leaving an odd pairing of red pawmarks in his wake.

Kimmy slumped on the couch. She needed to reorganize her thoughts. She needed to come up with some kind of plan; some way to get out and get going without calling too much attention to herself. In one hand she still gripped the sodden ax. She set it with a heavy clunk on the coffee table and examined the object she held in her left hand: the amulet.

"What is the deal with this thing? Why did it turn everyone into a raving... loony?" She began to softly weep.

Tanner flopped on the couch; an area he was unaccustomed to being and dropped his snout into Kimmy's lap. His eyebrows arched with a false look of sadness; a look every dog has mastered whether its honestly showing feelings or not. He huffed, nuzzled a bit deeper into Kimmy, and closed his eyes. Kimmy absently petted him with long, careful strokes as she stared into space and slowly swung the horrid, metallic disk in a languid pendulum.

****

Kimmy's eyes fluttered open, and she inhaled deeply, bringing herself out of the terrible nightmare from which she was suffering. Thanks to being a horror movie fan coupled with the events of late, her dream featured zombies in various forms of decay surrounding her as she and Tanner hung on to chimney. She was unsure how she managed to get her sixty-plus pound dog up there, but it didn't matter since their safety was in jeopardy anyway. Kimmy shivered, in turn waking Tanner; his head bolting from her lap and a low growl escaping his throat as a low woof.

"It's okay, boy. I guess we fell asleep. I wonder what time..."

She glanced at the glowing numbers on the cable box. They showed 7:15, which made sense as the waning bits of the sun shone orange and deep ocher through the kitchen windows. Lighted, crisscrossed squares highlighted the heap of bodies still lying motionless on the tile. The visuals brought forth other senses and Kimmy suddenly became aware that she could smell gone off meat and the acrid tang of blood. She shook her head and wondered if Tanner was suffering far worse, as she'd read somewhere once that dogs had a way keener sense of smell than humans. Probably.

And then the knock came.

TO CONTINUE...

Tales of The Amulet
Part 18: The Parking Lot

Ted pulled into Kalamazoo at 3:15 a.m. and eased his Jetta onto Westnedge Avenue from I-94. He was tired, there was absolutely no doubt of that. In fact, he'd spent the last three hours struggling to keep his road-weary body from swerving off the freeway. He'd never been a consistent smoker, but he heard that keeping a burning cigarette between your fingers would offer up its gag-inducing odor and potentially burn down enough to singe your fingers if you nodded off. The tunes remained cranked to a station featuring an evening of nothing but Metal. The passenger-side window was as open as Ted felt comfortable with despite the frigid, twenty-degree air, and the heat remained as low as possible while still keeping the windows frostless. All of these things ought to have combined to make a volatile solution for staying awake, but in fact, all they did was make his mind wander off into near-dream land. Frustration and irritation got the better of him and eking off the highway was his only safe recourse.

Ted was hungry, not for fast food, but for something a bit more forgiving to his stomach. He was here for the weekend at the Radisson just a few miles downtown, but his stomach was protesting even the minor jaunt to a more comfortable location. So, it was time for a little snack to while away another fifteen minutes to bedtime. Just past the off-ramp on the right was a local 24-hour grocery and sundry supply chain called Meijer. The parking lot was a wasteland of sporadically parked autos, a few orphaned shopping carts, and a small group of -what, kids?- trotting through the lot. Though they were all over the central states, Ted had only heard about them since his travels brought him from Arizona, where such a store didn't exist.

Ted shrugged, pulled into a spot, and stretched the stretch of a thousand miles as he cracked and popped his frame free of the car. He sighed deeply, hollered a bit as he arced, loosened his spine, and made his way to the eerily lit front entrance. The low thrum of the automatic glass partition spread open belching free a torrent of stale heat. Ted walked in and was immediately overwhelmed with the sudden realization that this store was just far too big for a simple snack search and rescue mission. He stopped, looked around, and just barely heard a greeter bid him welcome as she nonchalantly went back to her magazine. Well, one thing became obvious: the food was off to Ted's left. He smiled distantly, and made his way to an aisle with on-sale chips for its end cap.

Ted loomed at the end of the row as choice after numerous varieties offered itself like an eager hand. Ted walked past potato chips of every flavor nature never intended, Doritos from spicy to cool, and all the way to good old tortilla chips. He snatched a bag of Tostitos and a jar of medium salsa from the accessory rack just beneath, and quickly retraced his steps back to the junction. He wasn't especially thirsty at the moment, but with his munchie choice, he surely would be soon enough. Ted opted for a 2-liter of Brisk iced tea, and slowly, awkwardly, stuttered to the front check-out. A quick transaction with the only open lanes: automatic for your convenience, Ted left the hugging comfort of the toasty store and seethed a little as the blast of chilly December air punched him in the face.

Ted marched to his car to excise himself from the chill as quickly as possible. He pressed the unlock on his key chain with its characteristic double-honk and opened the passenger door.

"Excuse me, mister? Could I help you with that bag?"

Ted whirled around as he left the pavement in a panic. He was quick to hold onto the plastic bag's handles and the glass jar of salsa would have certainly broken otherwise. Standing close enough to Ted for him to clearly see his face from under the giant, humming fluorescent lights, stood a boy of maybe ten.

"I can help you load your things for just a ride home."

Ted was speechless. Another glance over the boy's far-too-small-to-be-out-this-late features made him shake his head and gesture a little toward his one, small bag. But the oddest thing about the boy was most certainly his voice. Possibly a product of the cold air, maybe shivering, he sounded empty, hollow, lifeless even. It had risen the hair on Ted's neck to even listen to it and certainly had no intention of doing it again.

"N-N-no thanks, kid. I've got it. You really ought to run along home, it's really late."

The boy just stood there, not even flinching one way or another. Then, it really struck home, and Ted felt an icy hand tickle from his ass to the top of his head: the boy's eyes were black. Not just the iris or the pupil: all of it. The boy's eyes were solid, deep, black. No trick of the light here. No optical illusion could have created such possessed and grotesque eyes on a child. No reflection, no glimmer from the lamp, just solid, dead, black eyes. And around his neck hung the weight of a

CD-sized necklace. No, an amulet of some kind. It let off just enough of a glow to easily discern its deep, bloody hue.
Ted took a step back, and the boy, forward. Ted dropped his back to the floor of his car, quickly slammed the door, and sprinted to the opposite side. The boy was there before Ted could even recoil.

"I just need a ride mister... just a ride."

The white-yellow protection of the light crackled and burned out. A man; displaced, exhausted, and alone, wailed into the frigid night.

Tales of The Amulet
Part 19: Father Terrance

I was told about the gravestone when I was little more than
eight by a friend of mine who lived for nothing more than to
scare the Hell out of me. He was older; therefore, he was
expected to act like the older sibling I didn't have. His name
was Barry and he lived in the neighborhood that butted up
against the one I grew up in and so it was easily within
walking distance. We hung out all the time, and I really did
see him as a brother. He was the one that told me about the
gravestone and what was supposedly buried underneath it.

We sat around a little fire he'd built in his backyard back
when burning leaves and twigs within the confines of your
own property was still considered acceptable. He danced
around the subject for a while as I brought it up; I'd asked a
bit coyly if he'd heard about the 'thing' that was buried
beneath the Virgin Mary head stone at the Methodist Church
graveyard. He shrugged, nodded a bit, and popped another
bit of jerky into his mouth. I'd told him that I guy I knew at
school (at the time I was a full 2 grades below him, so, to me,
he was always the source of my fantasies, if you know what I
mean) had said something about it a few days ago and that he
and his sister and a friend were going to go try to dig it up.
Barry then looked at me with saucer-sized eyes and barked a
laugh that was more nervous than humorous.

Barry conceded and launched into his story. As he was told...
"a very important Church parishioner had died back in 1936
when the church was originally built. He'd come from another
community bringing with him much of the ideals and
teachings he'd used and put them into action to his own
Church staff. Some folks were a bit taken aback by the new
methods, but most fell in line and soon the Church became the
most fully attended in town. Anyway, this guy... Father
Terrence passed on and nearly the entire town had shown up
for his interment. At that same time, one of the more
boisterous anti-church townsfolk shoved his way to the front
just as the dirt was being shoveled onto the casket, shouted a
few incoherent curses, and tossed a plate-sized amulet into the
ground. Well, he was ushered away and held down as he spat
forth various bits of gibberish and, after that day, was never
heard from again. Anyway, it's this Amulet that is said to give
the unresting spirit of Father Terrence his haunting ability and
why, it's said, the church itself is lousy with his spirit. So,
there ya go."

I chuckled a little at its silliness, but somewhere deep inside it
all sounded so plausible. How hard would it be to get ahold of
that amulet, really? I had to know.

Tales of The Amulet
Part 20: Split Through The Soul

Zev walked alone. His thoughts -exploding, dangerous, wicked- kept him company but often ordered his string-tied body to convulse or twitch uncontrollably. He was a slave to all he'd seen: all he'd done. He was a conduit for the old adage of every action having and equal but opposite reaction. He was a criminal, an exile, a devil. He shuddered, though not cold, beneath his tarnished and frayed trench coat beneath which he still wore his white collar and black Nehru-esque Parishioner's shirt. His filthy pants: they were tacky Chinos nearly gray with miles of road dust and too much grime kicked up from running so often, long ago lost their cuffs to time and tribulations. And on his feet clung the only pair of shoes he could rummage from a local garbage bin as he hid among the shadows and darkness on his way out of who remembers which town: leather sandals nearly split through the soles.

Split through the 'souls'. If there was ever a way to describe how this once-man felt right now as he plodded down another dirt road, that was surely it. Zev stopped. He glanced around shielding his eyes from the bright heat of the early morning as the sun erupted from the mist. He had no idea where he was, but it didn't matter: the Amulet did know. Around Zev's neck -more closely his throat, perhaps- dangled the enormous weight of the Amulet: cursed, hated, and every centimeter of its disk shape evil and rotten. Often it would reverberate through his chest like a low, sorrowful call of some un-human monster. And when it knew where the man -Zev- would stop next, it would glow a sickly, deep, ruby red around its edges and he -Zev- would feel the tug, perhaps a yank, in the direction the Amulet wanted (nay, needed) to go. This was symbiotic relationship between man (former man) and the Amulet; this was how Zev was cursed and forced to live by the cause and the slavery of it. And now, as the sun slowly crept higher in the sky and radiated its warmth the land over, Zev was once again prodded in a new direction to a town he could not yet see. He often thought of fighting it; he would yank the horrid, demonic article from around his neck and toss it asunder and run, run away as fast as he could leaving the Amulet alone for the next poor victim to stumble upon its terror. But, alas, Zev was as powerless as the babe and could do no such thing.

Now, as Zev could see a church steeple rising over the horizon, his heart began to dance near to bursting in his chest. Zev knew, with aid from the unearthly Amulet he wore in punishment around his person, he would eviscerate the poor hovel from stem to stern spilling its collective blood till the roads ran red with it. Zev began to cry in earnest.

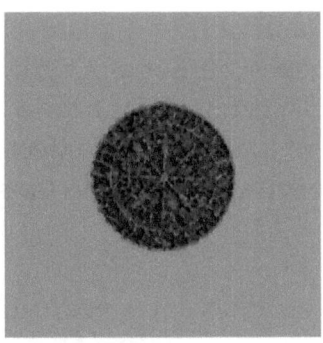

Tales of The Amulet
Part 21: Jack and Dianne

Jack and Dianne were 80 and 83 respectively. They were happy, as healthy as one can be at this advanced age, and perhaps just a bit peppier than one would otherwise expect. By all accounts, they were normal, regular, run-of-the-mill folks. But it wasn't this that was so unusual. No, none of this was anything to write home about, unless you understood the simple fact that the two of them, the Morrisons, had always been 80 and 83. Respectively.

Jackson Renee Morrison and Dianne Leslie Stevens bought their first home after their matrimonial union in 1951. It was a ranch, it was complete with 3 bedrooms (one would become a den), a huge basement (this, too, would serve as entertainment for their two boys), and a sizable bathroom as well as an attached 2-car garage. The Morrisons couldn't have found a more perfect deal or location if it had been handed to them. And, as it turned out, it was. Well, it wasn't as though the realtor had any idea just what he was selling when the newlywed couple jumped at the chance to own their first home. No, he had no clue that wedged deep within the crawlspace in the boiler-room of the basement was an item of such unearthly evil and unimaginable deviltry that its power could stop time itself. No, this was never a selling point. But there it was just the same: a teacup plate-sized metallic amulet sat wedged in the deepest corner of a tight, completely ignored concrete shelf giving off its horrid, sickening ruby glow. But that, though the cause and effect of the Morrison's lack of aging, was never noticed but to those who knew them best.

The Morrisons had two boys a few years into their happy lives: Grant was first in '55, and then Marcus in '58. They grew normally, lived regularly, and moved on just as children eventually do. Of course, at this point, Jack and Dianne had yet to reach that point in their lives where the process of aging dropped along the wayside and the odd occurrence of living life as a breathing wax statue took over. But time shoved them all along and years down the line, Grant went on to have three kids of his own with his wife and then, as the years unfurled like a wind-whipped flag, they, too, had children. And it was then that the Morrison's, now honestly reaching the ripe old ages of 80 and 83, respectively, just stopped needing birthdays.

Yes, people indeed noticed but they were always laughing at their own unbelievable ideas about such nonsense especially since -though aging was now a pointless factor- illness still reared its ugly head time and again. This, above anything else, made most realize that the couple was moving on in life just like the rest of the outside world. However, it became increasingly more obvious to the family (as well as to the Morrison's themselves) that remaining in their first and only home was literally not going to let them die. And so went the terrible power of the Amulet: Hell itself.

Tales of The Amulet
Part 22: Shoes

David and Sally sped down the darkened highway. The shoulders as far as either could see were slightly overgrown with trees whose canopies arced across the pavement like an arboreal tunnel. David hated roads like this; in fact, one of his scariest and most livid nightmares was getting lost on a night highway just like this and getting forced to wander. Alone. He glanced over at Sally who was pondering over a puzzle book equipped with a little Book Light so David wouldn't be quite as affected by the glare. She smiled, peered over the top of her reading glasses, and made a cutesy, kissy face with her lips. David tried to return the grin, but just then his gaze was stolen back to the road by a set of glowing yellow dots mere feet in front of the minivan. He tensed, inhaled in preparation of having to slam on the breaks, and shivered with a nod as a speedy raccoon bolted across the road within just a few inches of the bumper. Fortunately, David had slowed enough. The little animal stopped, peered with fright and question at the piercing lights, and quickly continued his journey to the opposite side. David breathed easier and Sally just chuckled in her chest and patted him on the knee.

The desolate and infuriatingly straight highway cut its flora-lined path through the forest. Only every so often was there a sign indicating speed or which freeway they were still presently on.

"Want me to drive?" Sally asked as she sipped from a half-full Snapple bottle.

"Hmm?" Asked David, "Oh, no... no, I'm good. But I could use a stretch. My damn knee is acting up a bit."

"And where, specifically, do you think we should stop? There's nothing out here but trees and more trees?"

David laughed a little, slowed the minivan, and eased onto the little dirt strip just off the pavement. "I guess this'll have to do. I gotta pee anyway."

They opened the doors, stepped out into the surprisingly muggy and thick air, and bent themselves into twists enough to sound off pops.

"David. I know we're on I-79, I saw the sign back there, but did you have any idea it was this... I don't know, scary?"

"Scary?" David asked in a laugh, "Yeah, I know. It's pretty lonely and boring out here. But the last time I was up this way... Jeez, back in '02... it was just as bad. But that was during the day. What time is it anyway?"

Sally pressed the button on her watch that lit the face, "9:45. It sure doesn't seem to be getting any cooler out here... it's just fuggy!"

It was July 15th. David and Sally had vacation coming from both of their jobs and they managed to coincide with each other's. David thought it might be time to show Sally the little town of St. Winsmuth where he grew up. They'd been married just two years now; David had met Sally at the local Barnes and Noble both enjoying a latte. They hit it off right away and began dating. Sally was from town, so her parents were within the limits, but David was from out of state from a very small, very out-of-nowhere village and Sally had always been curious. So, with a printout from Map-Quest in hand and a weekend's-worth of luggage, they set off for St. Winsmuth.

David finished relieving himself on a sapling, stretched again, and slid back into the driver's seat. Sally, begrudgingly using an empty foam drink cup from the last gas station, poured its warm contents all over the same tree, and climbed back into the minivan.

"Okay, well, I guess we're off," David said as he cracked his knuckles. Sally hated that.
"Gross," She flinched, suppressing a gag, "Okay. I'm gonna try to sleep a little. What do we have left, an hour?"
"Ninety minutes tops. Rest well, I'll wake you when we're within the county limits."

David looked around for oncoming traffic, naturally, before pulling back onto the road. Realistically he could have peeled out and spun a few donuts and no one would have even taken notice. But he didn't. They resumed their drive.

The encompassing grip of the sprawling tree line held the freeway like a never-ending set of fingers. It was so dark. David sometimes had to slow down just because he thought he saw things; lights, eyes, figures walking in the inkiness... but there was nothing. Then, not a half mile ahead, a steady glow of what could only be a streetlight appeared from the nothing with an almost blinding halo.
"Hey baby, wake up," David softly rubbed his wife's shoulder as she stirred.

She yawned, blinked a bit as she readjusted her glasses, and smiled, "Is that really a streetlight I'm seeing or have we gotten lost in the Twilight Zone?"

"Nope. That's the first light you see when you enter Macomb County. I'm home, honey."

The glow of the road lamp came into view and slowly passed over as they burst free from their leafy tomb. David audibly sighed.

"I knew it: that stretch of road bothers you, too!"

David sighed again and shrugged.

But Sally saw it first and it physically made her jump.

Hanging from a wire stretched across the road coming from the second streetlamp in town was a half-dozen shoes knotted together in pairs. A few sneakers, a set of boots, and at least two pairs of lady's Keds.

"What the hell?" Sally gasped.

David slowed, stopped, stepped out into the night, and looked up, mouth agape, at the lynched footwear, "Huh... that's a little bizarre."

"David, you know it's just probably a joke. Maybe a last-day-of-school thing. Let's go. I'm getting hungry."

David leaned his head into the door, "Sally. I can just see ahead with the next light. There are more shoes. I don't know, maybe twenty."

Sally shook so hard her hair stood up, "David, you had better tell me your kidding--"

David slid in and shut the door. He just sat for a minute. Two minutes. "That is so weird."

Sure enough, the next wire that spread across the street was absolutely festooned with shoes. So many so that they weighed the line down. And the next wire after that, and the fourth, and fifth, all the way into the town of St. Winsmuth were positively slung with more varieties of footwear than a shoe store. They swayed ever so much in the ebb and flow of the incoming breeze. Their shadows literally danced across the lighted spots on the road. David and Sally crept through town staring at each as though a new discovery. David flinched as he quickly and suddenly smashed the brake pedal into the floor. Ahead, across from an empty storefront sat a form. Hard to make out from where the minivan sat, it was obviously human. A human sitting in a chair. At a table.

The town was dead. No one was out, no lights were on -save for the streetlights with their tennis-shoe gallows- no cars drove by, and, oddly, the three local taverns showed no signs of life at all. The otherwise flickering and lit neon that announced their openings and closings were lifeless. But the figure yards ahead of the mini van's headlamps was moving. In fact, it was gesturing.

David and Sally stared at the human, blinking, each positive that what they saw was a mirage.

"David," Sally began, "Please turn around. I'd rather face two more hours in the woods than here. Please."

David just glared ahead. He blinked, squeezed his lids, and almost comically shook his head. But the figure stood and beckoned for them.

"David," Sally interjected again, "Let's please go... I really don't like this."

David again just looked straight ahead, almost in a trance. "I think I know that kid!"

"Kid? That's kid? Oh Jesus, David! Please turn around!"

"Really. That's Jason, the Miller boy. He was maybe 12 when I was here last. One of the leaders of the church youth group. I wonder what he wants?"

Sally's eyes burst open at the mere notion of David's inquisition, "You are not going up there, David!"

"Sally, I really doubt there's anything to worry about. I'd at least like to know what's going on here... where everyone is."

"I'll tell you where everyone is: out looking for new shoes."

"I promise, we'll just drive up and see. If it looks bad, we're out of here."

Sally sighed and wrung her hands. "Fine. but I'm not getting out of the van."

They slowly drove ahead to the figure who now appeared to be waving to them. He sat in an old steel fold-up chair behind a card table. On the table was a glass pitcher full of liquid and ice cubes. Next to it was a stack of plastic cups, a shaker of sugar, and a what looked like a ball. In the jug was a long spoon. In front of the glass was a tented cardboard sign. As David and Sally approached it was clear it read, "LEMONADE - .50"

David stuck his head out the window, "Jason? Jason Miller, is that you?"

"Yes! Hello Mr. Hanson! Your mom spoke about your visit at church last week! How are you?"

Jason seemed genuinely glad to see David. His face betrayed no ill will or rancor, he offered no air of fear or mistrust. He reached out his hand as an honest gesture of greeting and friendship.

Though Sally was immediately apprehensive, David stuck out his arm. He and Jason shook hands.

"What, ah, what are you doing out here so... late?" David asked as his arm was let go.

"Selling lemonade, of course?" Jason giggled as he deftly slipped a cup from the stack and poured.

"Okay, I can see that. But why... at, wow, eleven thirty, are you selling lemonade. On the street, of all places?"

Jason placed the filled cup on the table and moved on to another, obviously meant for Sally, whom he'd yet to meet, "Well I'll tell you. People get might thirsty around here. Even at close to midnight. I do this all the time!"

Jason's matter-of-fact reply actually made David grimace a little as he looked over his shoulder at Sally who was, for lack of a better term, cowering behind the blanket she'd had with her.

David put on a phony smile and turned back to Jason, "Okay, sounds good. Um, so where all are your customers... where is everyone?"

Jason offered both cups to David through the minivan window. He took them, but merely sat them on the dash.

"Have a sip! It's my mom's recipe and you know her; she can make some lemonade"

Jason was right. David knew Miranda Miller and yes, her lemonade was stuff of local legend. David nodded to Sally and they both hesitatingly lifted their cups.

Jason stood smiling with his arms folded, "Go on! I know you know you love mom's lemonade! Sweet, just tart enough... man, it's so good!"

David thought back to years ago when he'd drink his fill of Mrs. Miller's lemonade at the neighborhood functions and the village socials... he loved it. And so, as he nodded and mocked a toast to Sally, they both took long drags of the cool, sweet and sour liquid as it quenched their thirsts completely. And it was, as he remembered, delicious.

"So yeah, about the townsfolk," Jason began, "They were here. They were here and they were bad. Yes, God spoke to me and said that it was so. The town was rotten and callus; it was dark, it was evil, and God asked for its cleansing."

David just stared as Jason continued his diatribe. Sally choked on her drink and coughed.

"God spoke to me through this..." At that, Jason reached into his shirt and drew forth a large pendant attached to a heavy chain. It was roughly the size of a compact disc, and it was as black as the night itself. Arranged in a ring embedded in the amulet's material were several deep-hued red gems. David could feel its pulsating, thrumming, heartbeat split the air. "God said cleanse the village; destroy the evil ones and lay it to ruin. Oh, and worry not, your mother cried your name as she fell."

From under the table came Jason's right hand grasping a pistol. David and Sally stared in awe at the dangling amulet as it's horrible reds and blacks swirled in hypnotic waves. The gun fired twice into the night.

On the first lamp wire in town, dangling like the limp bodies of an odd sacrifice, hung a new pair of Keen hikers and a set of blue Chuck Tailors.

Tales of The Amulet
Part 23: Daddy

Daddy used to get home at 7:30 every night. Without fail, in fact; every night, like clockwork, at 7:30. I'd have dinner ready. Daddy wasn't picky; if he could eat, he never really cared what it was. When we could afford something better: ham, a chicken... of course that's what he really liked. But nearly every night, we ate soup. Luckily, we kept enough bones on hand to flavor our soups, or else Daddy was forced just to enjoy the vegetables we grew outside. Much of those, too, were kept frozen. But Daddy made life good. Mostly because Mom had died when I was two, so Daddy took over both responsibilities. For a few years, our neighbor from a mile down the road would walk to our house and keep an eye on me while Daddy was at the docks. But none of this really matters; none of this is what this tale is really about.

Daddy was a wonderful man. Though he had no real reason to ever raise a hand to me, he never even did it just because. He was kind, quiet, often withdrawn, but always gave of himself and found that extra hour of the evening to spend time with me. And the best days -the days that I did my best around the house and spent a little extra on making our soup perfect- were Wednesdays. Wednesdays were the days when the Maligned came in. The Maligned was a crab boat that spent a week at a time out on the water landing pots (those, Daddy said, were like big baskets) and pots of crab. Though Daddy could never afford to buy a crab (however, on rare occasions, the guys would give him a little one), the captain of the Maligned always brought Daddy a gift to give to me. The captain, a Mr. Leland, had a daughter of his own back at his home across the sea, so he felt a special connection to me. And that is why Wednesdays were the best days.

One week, I was given an old, rusty diving bell. Another time: a still-functional compass. A few times I'd gotten a bottle with a slip of paper in them, but I'd never gotten up the guts to open them and read the notes. Something about the helplessness and the thoughts of the likely long-dead writers... Anyway, they went in the collection. The gifts were great, all of them. But the part I really liked was the stories Daddy told with them. Were they truth? I never knew and I never cared; Daddy embellished everyone with wonderful tales of the object, to whom it supposedly belonged, and just how it came to get landed by the fishermen. I can still recall every story from each of my special items like the backs of my hands. But Daddy only told them once, the memory was up to me.

One Wednesday, things were different. Not in the way that Daddy forgot the gift, oh no, he remembered it alright. But this time, the gift itself was bad. I can't describe it any better than that: it was bad, bad, bad. Daddy brought it home in a sack. The bag was just a typical bait bag: burlap, thick, scratchy... but this time, it was the bag that was keeping the bad thing quiet. Until I opened it.

It was the size of a saucer. It was round, weighty, and exquisitely ornate. Etched on its surface were designs I'd never seen (Daddy called them 'runes'), but I knew right away I didn't like them. They... well, they glowed. The deep red surrounding the marks, laid out in gem-like rings, hummed to the beat of my own heart. I couldn't touch it. No: I wouldn't touch it. And that's when Daddy got bad, too. I had never once seen my Daddy like that: fear, anger, rage... his eyes ebony with hate. He came after me.

Fortunately, I am faster.

I buried Daddy two weeks ago. I have the... what, 'amulet' I guess, wrapped in three bedsheets, and locked in my jewelry box. I am sad, yes, but the way I'd seen Daddy... well, I know he's better off. I wish I had the pitchfork back, though. Because I've seen things...

Just outside.

Tales of The Amulet
Part 24: Dream a Little Dream

I glance up at the clock: 1:45

The stack of papers neatly piled on my desk are easily an inch high.

Test papers.

The kind of test where you have to slit open the tab on the side of the envelope and follow along precisely with the instructor as you neatly shade in little dots on the answer sheet.

An 'Aptitude Test' they're called. 'Aptitude' is such a subjective term since no one is all that clear as to what criteria the instructors go by to 'grade' your answers. And this is why I hate them so much; why I generally just shade the ovals in to vaguely resemble a shape of some kind. Today it will be a penis.

I look around at the other students eagerly awaiting the arrival of the professor to launch us into a frenzy of dot-filling and brain-wracking. They sit stolid, motionless; some chewing gum -an offence as I understand it, another smiling as she texts someone on the other end of her phone. No one seems particularly thrilled over all to be here, but, alas, no one has a choice.

The door swings open with a whisper and a tall, lanky man sidles in carrying an armload of paperwork, a pair of small glasses, and what looks like an apple.

He quietly sets each object on the big wooden desk at the front of the test room, daintily clears his throat, and sets the pair of spectacles on his nose.

"Good afternoon, students," He begins as he turns away from the class with a fresh stick of chalk in his hand. His light German accent belays him, "My name is Doctor Holle. In ten minutes, we will begin the Aptitude Test,"
I glance at the clock again: 1:50

The chalk makes gritty scratches on the board. Dr. Holle turns to us with a playful, almost sneering grin on his face and sets the chalk on the desk. His name is scrawled in jittery Cursive on the board. It becomes obvious that he's a lefty as some of the last bits of the last few letters are smeared.

"Many of you are no doubt wondering exactly what this Aptitude Test aims to prove. Am I correct?"

The majority of the class nods in a kind of eerie unison. I, not especially interested, roll my Number 2 pencil through my fingers like a rocker's drumstick

Dr. Holle suppresses a faint cough with a balled fist and continues, "As you are all aware, in the coming weeks, you will begin looking for employment outside of your studies. Unfortunately, a vast number of you will either be unable to secure a position of your primary choice, or else be ill suited to do the same. So many children now-a-days are so naive in the ways of the outside world and in how all the little interlocking gears and cogs fit within one another. I say this because, those of you who... shall we say, fit into the lesser half of the Aptitude outcome may be forced to make other, more fitting, decisions."

I am listening. Something about this man's diatribe strikes me as a little odd. What are, 'more fitting decisions?' Does he mean that we can't just sign up for a career and hope to be trained?

"Furthermore," Dr. Holle continues as he absently removes his glasses and begins wiping them on a hankie, "Since fewer and fewer job opportunities are making themselves available to the new batch of graduating youth, another, newer option has risen; an option I am hoping several of you might see a potential interest in. It is called, 'Dream A Little Dream'..."

Some of the class chuckles at the light-hearted name and the professor, with that wry grin on his face, calms them gently with arm gestures.

He covers another cough, this time more forceful, with the handkerchief, "Despite the name, it is a most excellent choice for those of you seeking an alternate path from a career you are likely not suited for. Since so few jobs are becoming available, training for those that remain is in, unfortunately, less demand. Ergo, just the hope that you could be trained to fill an available, more specific position, is false, at best. With the new, 'Dream A Little Dream' openings, your future is far more secure."

Somehow, he'd only been speaking for less than five minutes. The clock moved slowly on from 1:55.

A hand went up behind me. I had seen the guy a few times in the halls, but since I had seen many people in the halls each shouting to be heard, I had no idea what his name was.

"Yes, there is a question?" The Doctor asks as he slips his glasses back onto his nose.

"Right. Yes... sir. Um, Dr. Holle..." The boy stammers as he flushes and tries to hide his embarrassment, "Is there any more information about Dream A Little Dream that might persuade us to join... you know, like incentives or what it actually offers?"

Dr. Holle nods and clasps his hands together, "In fact there is. However, since the test is to begin in sixty seconds, I will quickly usher those interested to the door where they will be met by a Mr. Gabriel who will take you to a separate room."

I stand. The boy behind me stands. All told, eleven seats empty as their occupants rise to their feet. We are quickly told to leave our test booklets and pencils, as we won't need them. Dr. Barnes opens the door, bids us all a fine afternoon, and we're all met by Mr. Gabriel. He is dressed as though he'd been teaching at a college: tan sport coat with elbow patches, a loosened tie over a denim shirt, and corduroys. Yet, the oddest thing about him is the large, fascinating amulet that swings from his jacket pocket. I might be wrong, but there's just something about its beauty. Something I can't quite place...

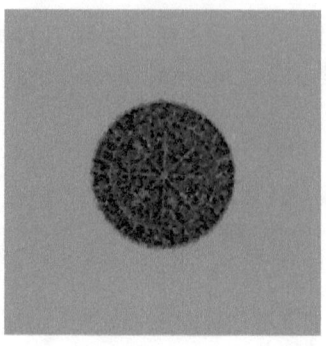

Tales of The Amulet
Part 25: Waiting

Sadly, Ben hadn't moved in two days. The tepid dampness
that clung to the cushion and to the bottom of his sweatpants
spread over the easy-chair's edge and dammed up near the
footrest. Ben was wet; he'd thought about trying to get up and
run to the bathroom many times in his mind -hell, he'd
formulated plans and methods- but all in all, it was just easier
(and somehow less dangerous) just too pee himself. And so,
he did. His fingers had scraped ruts into the curved edges of
the armrests; back and forth, back, and forth, curling under
with nervous anticipation. His mouth was pasty from lack of
anything real to drink. Fortunately, Ben was a bit of a slob, so
several half-drunk cups of liquid sat gathering dust all around
his chair either on the end table or sitting on the floor... so, he
did have those. They were nasty: flat soda, stale iced tea, beer
cans with nothing more than warm beer-flavored backwash
sitting in congealing pools in the bottom. Yes, he had a
modicum of sustenance, but few things that wouldn't make
him retch, not to mention no food at all. Ben was coated in a
slick sheen of perspiration. It had gotten rather humid in the
room since he'd first sat down, and none of the windows were
open. Ben's eyes hurt. They burned and stung. It had nothing
to do with allergens, but it did have to do with trying hard not
to blink. He stared ceaselessly straight ahead, and only

blinked when the agony turned to screaming numbness. And even then, he'd only blink once. Ben's legs had atrophied sometime in the middle of the night and all he could feel of them was kind of a ghostly, deep-seated ache when he attempted to switch his position or wiggle his toes. There was no denying it: Ben was trapped. Ben was trapped by something sitting, stolidly, on the doorway carpet.

Thursday night, Ben Anson gathered a plastic cup of Diet Coke, snatched up is remote, and plopped down in the tan Lay-Z-Boy he'd called 'good old mama' since he found it perched longingly on the curbside of a house whose inhabitants were moving out three years ago. It had some tape on it, one side of the cushion was a bit lower than the other, and it did, on a hot day with no circulation, smell a bit like a wet dog. But none of this mattered to Ben, because at the end of the day, it was really the only comfortable thing he had, and pretty much the only thing he owned that still, in a weird way, reminded him of his dead wife. She'd passed a week to the day after he found the chair. She died in it, in fact. Ben wanted something comfortable to use for his wife's final days as she slowly succumbed to the ravages of colon cancer. She passed quietly in her sleep and was removed by the EMT's not an hour later. 'Good old mama' was Ben's chair, and it was also his wife's chair, and between the two of them and their mutual attachments, the chair stayed and slowly faded into a sort of living comfort. Ben plopped down, flicked on NBC, and fell into fits of typical laughter as he watched the humor fall in spades. But then the door opened and closed as the darkness walked in.

Ben didn't often lock his doors until he was literally pacing the house just before bed. So, it surely wasn't odd that the front door was basically open to whomever decided to just turn the knob and waltz in. And so, during The Office, it did. Ben had known the squeak that the door emitted like he knew the house itself. It always sounded like it was sighing the word 'tin', so when he heard the all-too familiar noise, Ben bolted upright in his chair and glared over to the front door that sat directly across the room from him. Two seconds later, the door shut behind whatever it was, and echoed its lone word: 'tin'. And there, in the dark shadow provided by the stairwell, stood... something. It didn't move, didn't flinch, and didn't make a sound. Ben called to it, not so much angrily but out of surprise and question, but it didn't respond. Ben waited, tried to get a better idea of what it was by squinting, sitting up a little, and finally calling out yet again, this time with a bit more baritone and ire to his voice. Still, nothing. But something just the same. A quick metallic flash arced across the mid-point of the shape and Ben could just make out a ring of deep red dully illuminating a large disc-shaped object. It was right then Ben became frozen in absolute fear to 'good old mama'.

And now, two days later, Ben was sitting in a rapidly growing puddle of his own urine, fighting back the gnawing growls of his suffering hunger and slightly less annoyed thirst. His voice was dry, but Ben finally gathered all the strength he had and decided to call out to the unflinching, stone-solid shadow that stood firm at his doorstep.

"I-Is there something y-y-you w-w-want?" Ben barked in a voice that sounded horrific in his own ears.

"I do," came the slithering, gibbering cackle that belched from the shape, "I want you to wait... longer."

Ben felt not only a frozen flash crawl its way from his dead legs all along his spine to his scalp, but also, in contrast, another flood of warm pee spill out onto the chair. Ben's breathing came in short rasps, and he could feel his already frantic heart immediately turn into an off-pace drum beat hammer through his whole being.

"W-w-why me?" Ben found himself whimpering into the stale air.

But it didn't answer. Never again. And eventually, thanks to strong odors permeating the air both in and outside the house, Ben was finally found, slightly mummified, by his dead wife's sister who'd decided to stop by for a surprise visit. Ben had been dead for nearly a month. As she stood in the doorway of the oddly unlocked house, even before the stench of death made her vomit onto the patio, she discovered something metallic and disc-shaped hanging by a chain from the stairway.

Tales of the Amulet
Part 26: Endless

Commander Davitz sat at the observation deck of the U.S.S.
Vista, arms folded across his chest, staring blankly at the
anomaly that hung, motionless in space directly in front of the
ship: just where it had remained for the past 74 hours. Davitz
twiddled his thumbs, sighed defeated, and tapped his control
panel. Up sprung a complete readout of the past three days
with folders, files, and lists detailing everything he and his
crew had tried in an attempt to communicate. The info hung
in the air like a formless computer screen and the Commander
was able to manipulate the 'desktop' with mere movements of
his hand; he did just that with fluid, dreamy flicks and twists
once again mulling over every piece of info he'd already seen
a hundred times.

Strangely all he and his entire crew knew was what was
directly in front of him: the mysterious object was disc-shaped
(that was obvious), but beyond that it was layered with
undulating runes of a completely indeterminate origin that
ringed the inner surface. It was a dull silver, like brushed
chrome that had been left to slightly corrode. The center (or
'eye' as it had come to be known) was round and of such a
deep, blood red that it was almost frightening to look at. The
color was one thing, but the fact that it also pulsated like a

heartbeat was even more disturbing. In fact, not 'like' a heartbeat, but matched precisely to whomever sat in the chair looking out into space. Right now, it was thrumming in rhythm to Davitz's own. That was eerie like nothing else.

The chimes that announced a visitor blooped.

"Come." Davitz announced both bored and irritated.

The First Officer, Captain Andrea James marched in stiffly and regal, "Sir. We have some new information on the structure."

Davitz's brows furrowed, "I bet. Let me guess: something else painfully obvious, Captain?"

The Captain frowned, belayed by the smile in her eyes, "No, Sir. In fact, you actually have to see this to believe it. It caught us a bit off guard."

The Commander looked slightly more interested and beckoned his Captain forth.

Captain James took position to the left of the observation chair, touched a few buttons on the control pad, and the info display was replaced with an audio conversion program. Within the program were several digital dials and sliders used to adjust pitch, volume, vocal depth, and the standard bass and trebles. On the top of the simulated screen were the words: Cannibal Corpse.

"I'm confused Captain. What is this signifying? And, while I'm at it, what is a 'Cannibal Corpse'.

The Captain grinned, "This is an audio readout and adjustment program we use to understand foreign and alien audio. But it can be used to play selections as well."

The Commander nodded, losing interest rapidly.

"As we... the science officers and technical operators... spent some time attempting to throw different types of communication at the anomaly, we eventually stumbled - quite accidentally and on a mere whim- on something. It seems to respond to a specific type of music from the 20th Century called 'Death Metal'. Watch..."

Captain James offered headphones to the Commander, but he waved them off to a 'suit yourself' shrug. The Captain punched the button that began the track and horrific sounds belched from the internal speakers. She then tapped the button that would force sound waves out from the frequency scrambler on the ship straight to the disk. What happened was both breathtaking and absolutely revolting...

To Be Continued...

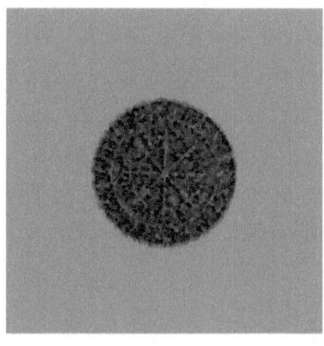

Tales of The Amulet
Part 27: Soul Stealing

Joe sat back heavily on his butt and let out a wet, desperate sob. Angel was gone, as he'd always known she would be one day sooner or later, he knew she'd breathe her last and so would end an ordeal in both love and terror.

He sat in the grass for a while longer, staring through eyes like wet church glass and just inhaled steadily while his heartbeat, a broken and worthless instrument.

Joe sat up on his knees, smiled and mouthed his undying love for his long-suffering bride, and stood with a moment of vertigo. It was time to go home. Time to go back to the house that was now an empty, cavernous shell, just like his own life, now. Angel was gone, and Joe had one thing left to do.

In 1997, Joe Porter met Silvia Angel at a bar. Often meetings based around mutual love for alcohol and pool rarely got beyond one-night stands, but somehow, some way, the two had clicked. Time soared for the next two years and before they knew it the couple were shopping at Bed, Bath and Beyond for wedding gifts. The wedding itself was a stunning, unforgettable affair with a royal air and everything lovers of the Medieval enjoy like costumes, period-specific food, horses,

swans, crowns... regal to say the least. The nuptials and
reception party lasted well into the following day until
everyone finally succumbed to weariness and went their
separate ways. Joe and 'Angel' (she hated Silvia and took to
being called to her now former surname) went home and
spent the evening opening gifts and consummating their new
relationship.

The gifts were all unwrapped, save one. It was neither the
biggest nor the most unusual, but, at the same time, it seemed
to be the one they collectively avoided without really realizing
it until the very end. It was round, roughly the size of a tea
saucer, and tightly wrapped in nondescript, white paper. Yet,
even with all the commonality about it, it resonated with
something neither could quite explain. And they didn't. No
one spoke, but Joe held it up, rolled it over in his hands with a
quizzical expression, and shrugged as he began to separate
the tape from its moorings. Angle stayed his hand with a look
of fearful dismay and quickly shook her head. Joe smiled and
gave her a solemn cock-eyed glance and removed the
remainder of the paper. In his hands lay the most unusual
piece of (what, artwork?) that he'd ever seen. Angel then
seemed to physically pull away from the disc-shaped object as
an invisible cloak of fear enveloped her.

It wasn't precisely ugly, but it surely wasn't something either
would consider beautiful or even very cool, but it was a gift
from -well, this was the odd part: neither could find an
attached tag or card announcing from whom it came. Despite
that fact, they still decided to display it lest the giver come
over at some point and ask about it with undesirable results. It
was given a small stand like a picture and set over the
fireplace on the mantle. They stared at it longingly yet fought
to tear themselves away. It's etched runes that ran the
circumference of the disc seemed to thrum and pulsate with a
deep, horrible red; a red that nothing of this Earth should

rightly be hued. It was a dull, unpolished pewter elsewhere and had an almost unkempt, filthy quality about it that, for all intents and purposes, made the casual viewer feel ill and dizzy and not right at all. Yet, they were prodded -somehow-to keep it. And so, they did.

As with many lucky couples, Joe and Angel fell even deeper in love. They spent as much time together as they conceivably could. They were able to find jobs with matching schedules, 9-5, and never let an evening conclude without love making and sharing of one another. They stole long, passionate kisses in public places as they coyly darted their glances at those not nearly in as deep of love as they. They began to skirt danger by having sex in locations where it was even a little more than just taboo: airliners, restaurant washrooms, friends' bathrooms and bedrooms, public parks, and darkened bars in corners where no one could see them. They were rebellious, but neither cared and they began thriving off the thrill of the spot. Joe seemed to be the most adept at securing a location that seemed just out of the views of prying eyes. But even so, they still enjoyed the simple fact that they could, at any time, be caught. And so it continued, as often as it could, the sex where shadows only dwell. And little by little, things began to change.

Angel began getting sick a fair bit more often than, say, a normal person of her typical health. She felt weak, drained, older... she took to far longer stays in bed when she wasn't at work. A chore in and of itself. Angel made several trips to her OBGYN and was told that there was nothing discernibly wrong with her. The only thing she was told was to change her diet and pick up her exercise routine. But nothing helped and her failing health and rising ills turned her into but a shell of her formal self. Her and Joe's sex life began to slowly fade. It was too uncomfortable. Even their kisses seemed lifeless and drab. Especially those offered by Joe in the candlelight of the family room. Especially those felt by the disc above the fireplace. The disc that pulsated with the rapidly declining heartbeat of Angel.

Yet, there was another change going on, and it was within Joe. Just as Angel was aging and slowly succumbing to the ravages of her failing health, Joe seemed to be something of a 'Superhero'. He had begun a standard, low-impact workout routine to be there with Angel as she attempted to fix herself. But as her results only sided with the worse, Joe began to bulk up, add muscle mass, and generally become a guy he'd never in a million years suspect he'd become. His health was just as impressive: lower cholesterol, little to no fat, and the cleanest bill he's ever seen. He was stronger, faster, and felt years younger. But it was all useless and just as meaningless as he could do little more than watch as his beloved soul mate, Angel, became a ghastly husk. Joe still loved kissing his wonderful wife, and often, as he did in front of a crackling fire made to keep Angel warm -even in the summer- he swore he saw, from the corner of his eye, the strange disc vibrate and glow with that sickly, bloody red.

It became all too obvious to Joe and Angel as he held her in his arms and gently, softly pecked her lips. Joe knew, now where this evil had originated. Joe knew, now that the gift, the amulet, in their family room was responsible. But Joe was defiant if he was anything else, and Joe had no intention of letting the amulet win without a sucker punch.
Angel was thin -better to say she was emaciated. Her illness had leached every useful bit of muscle from her weakening body. Her skin had gone ghostly pale and as thin and fragile as rice paper. Even at its surface, the blood that still, barely, scarcely, pumped through her dying veins could be seen in hues of purplish blue. Her lips sloughed away from her rotting gums that still held onto the last of her diseased teeth. Her arms and legs hung limply from her atrophied form as

they spilled like limp jelly from her nicest dress; a dress Joe had long since given up on seeing her in again regardless of just how much he loved her in it... so very long ago. And now Joe intended to make love to his wife one final time. He could feel her slight heart giving up, giving in to him. For it was Joe; Joe and his kisses, his love, his sex, that stole from her. Joe robbed Angel of her very life.

And the Amulet was the catalyst. The evil. The pure, horrible evil that dwelt within the amulet made Joe its slave. Each and every time Joe professed his love for his bride physically, and even mentally, he would unwittingly steal from that which kept her alive. He would steal from an Angel's soul.

Joe and Angel -against their most basic emotions- fought the devil that dwelt inside the amulet, and they made love. They bonded together for the very last time. As Joe came, and as he felt Angel give all that was left of her once beautiful form, the repugnant disc flashed a ghastly red, and then shone nothing but the deepest gray. Angle died in her husband's arms just as it was meant to be... though it was far, far too soon.

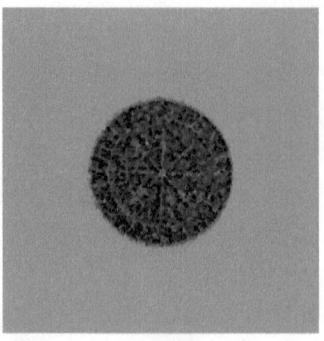

Tales of The Amulet
Part 28: Face Time

Tim and Grizzly mounted their respective choppers and peeled out of the Stop-N-Go parking lot spraying gravel and plumes of dust into the scorching Arizona air. Tim's bike had the sidecar. He typically loaded it up with their crusty duffel bags and other sundries they'd gather along the way, but today it featured something -rather, someone- a little unusual: Erin McAllister. But she wasn't along for a joyride through the sizzling desert, rather she was roped, duct taped, and masked and currently unconscious and coated with tacky, drying blood.

1.

Erin's day began not unlike any other: alarm jolting her from sleep, shuffling to the shower, dressing in her cleanest (and often shortest -customers appreciated it) shorts and Stop-N-Go T-shirt, brush the hair and teeth, and head out the door. Her mom would smile and wave with a blown kiss from her home office across the family room, barely acknowledging, and Erin would slide out the mobile home's screen door and begin her half-mile trot to work. This was the standard procedure every week: Tuesday, Thursday, and Saturday. She padded past her only two neighbors along County Road 560:

Bev and Harold Shumaker (elderly, always complaining, but more than willing to share their all-but unused pool), and Dr. Albert Marx and his son, eight-year-old Gus (he who was obviously hitting puberty a tad early) and followed the gentle curve to where the rocky road met I-40 right at the Stop-N-Go. But today, Thursday July 29th, Erin saw something out of the corner of her eye.

The dirt road itself always fairly glinted and sparkled with detritus from ages-old car accidents and broken bottles, but this particular Thursday Erin saw something just a bit brighter and somehow odder than anything else. It gleamed to her left and made her stutter a bit in her jog. She skidded and caught her breath tossing up mini clouds of rain-parched dry earth. Just off the side of the road buried about half-way up was something round and grayed with dust and age. It jutted askew and shone in the early morning son. Erin crouched near, as it appeared sharp and somehow dangerous; she balanced between wanting to touch it and knowing she shouldn't, teetering precariously between somehow right, and also very wrong. But often times curiosity actually does, as they say, kill the cat. Her outstretched hand brushed the rough surface of the metallic object and a dull thrum lanced up her arm feeling... well, not entirely unpleasant, actually. She snatched her arm away and rubbed it as she furrowed her brow, giving the object a cursory glance. And then the object's color began to change.

2.

Tim Ames and Dexter 'Grizzly' Adams slowly arced into the parking lot of the Stop-N-Go just off interstate 40, cruising their Harley's into adjacent spots. Following on their wheels blew in wafts of tire-thrown road dust and mini twisters. The dirty ghosts of the road past meandered and furled past the men as they dismounted their hogs, unlatched their helmets, and patted clods of brown, caked-on filth from their leathers. The men breathed deeply, took in new air that wasn't muggy from helmet glass, stretched loudly and languidly, and waltzed slowly to the doors. The bell dinged slightly as Tim pushed it into the air-conditioned interior, and he and Grizzly sighed a little at its comforting embrace.

3.

Erin crouched, her backside nearly touching the calloused earth below her, and gingerly stroked the shimmering, and now red-glowing, metallic object poking from the ground in front of her. It occurred to her just then that more of it was below the ground and so she went about considering options for its removal. Nothing shy of her actually pulling it free made any sense at all, and so she did. She tenderly gripped the rim, all the while taking in its constant vibrating hum, and pulled. It came free like the decay of a rotted tooth; no resistance as the parched ground around it rolled away in loose bits. In her had appeared a disk the rough size and shape of a small dessert plate. She'd seen things its ilk before; her mother had a collection of inherited China sitting in a small cabinet in the family room. Emily brushed off the dirt and dust and stared at the rune's intricate loops and whorls, etchings and textures, reliefs and carvings... it was ornate to say the least, but it was surely the dead center where the pulsating red originated that held her attention. She absently swatted at a few flies that had begun to gather, ignored a runnel of sweat that trickled down her back into her shorts, and never even felt a small rivulet of blood that dropped from her nose...

Stay Tuned For Part 2

_____

Tales of The Amulet
Part 29: Kindred

Kimmy stared at the door. She breathed and paid close attention to her heart as it pounded rapidly in her chest. She sniffed, rubbed her nose, and thought to herself for just a second that maybe she'd imagined-

knock knock knock

Tanner's low growl steadily built its crescendo erupted into a series of sharp barks. Kimmy jumped a little at her dog, and slowly patted his head. She almost felt like screaming herself. She swallowed and turned to Tanner.
"What'll we do, boy?" She whispered harshly.

"Hello? I-i-is anyone h-h-here?" The tiny voice from the patio said.
knock knock knock

The voice certainly didn't sound as threatening as Kimmy's mind was attempting to make it. She scooted off the couch with Tanner immediately at her heels. She tip-toed to the front door, cupped her hand, and pressed it and her ear to the wood.

"My n-n-n-name is Molly. I-I-I-I've been walking a really long time... with this pitchfork. I'm really tired and lost! Hello?"
knock knock

She sounded to Kimmy like she was on the verge of tears. Kimmy sidled over to the curtain and slowly pulled it back just enough to see the porch. There, in denim overalls, without shoes, filthy and obviously exhausted, stood a little girl maybe twelve years old. And next to her on the concrete was, as she said, a huge pitchfork. The tines were tinted with what could have either been dirt or, possibly, blood.

Kimmy watched with a bit of sorrow as Molly plopped on the porch, hiked up her knees, and began to sob. She knew there was literally no way that Molly was any kind of threat. Kimmy turned to the door and saw Tanner jump u to his hind legs and begin to whimper. Somehow even the dog knew that this little girl was as innocent as could be.

"Okay boy, get down. We'll check it out. But we'd better be safe about it..."
Kimmy stepped to the table and grabbed the ax. She returned to the door, and slowly turned the handle. There, on the stoop, was the sad sight she'd seen from the window, curled into a shuddering ball before her.

"Hi. I'm Kimmy." She said lowering herself into a crouch.

Molly shot her head up and instinctively covered herself with her arm. This, in turn, threw her off balance and she basically spilled onto her back. Molly scurried to her feet and quickly snatched up the pitchfork that was obviously far too heavy for her to handle with one hand. Kimmy just stood silently with a side-long grin on her face.

Suddenly the door flew from Kimmy's hands and the large do
that would no longer be corralled lunged forward, barked
once without a hint of malice, and wagged itself up to Molly
and began licking her hands and face.

"Whoa!" Molly gasped with a hint of a laugh and tried to
swipe away the dog's fluttering tongue.

Kimmy giggled and called back her dog. "His name is Tanner
and I think he's made a new friend!"

Molly let him finish licking until he leaped to Kimmy's side
and obediently sat at her side.

"As I said, I'm Kimmy. I live here with my..." She choked a
little as the word 'parents' caught in her throat. "I-I live here..."

"I'm Molly. I live... over that way." She pointed east toward
the more rural section of the outskirts of town where the
farms and acres of land stood spreading into the horizon. "I
had to get out. I had to k-k-kill my daddy..."

Suddenly weeping again, Molly did the only natural thing a
girl her age could do. She dropped her pitchfork and ran into
Kimmy's waiting arms. They both stood on the patio in the
setting sun and cried into one another's caresses. Molly,
between hitching breaths, told of how she had to murder her
father because of an evil coming from an amulet. Kimmy
nodded in complete understanding and relayed her own tale
of death and destruction and how she, too, had an amulet.
Neither one understanding just how much worse the situation
had gotten. Not yet.

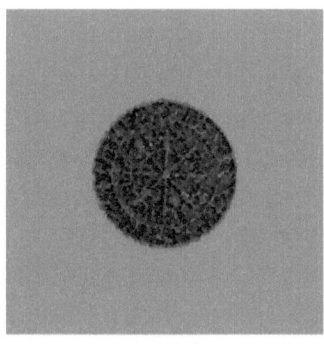

Tales of The Amulet
Part 30: Origins

The full moon hung in the cloudless sky like a wide-open, grey eye. Its surface features were as brilliant as the surrounding landscape; craters visible creating a simulacrum of a human face, winking yet indifferent. The chill in the air was thick and cloying, numbing bodies to their bony core. Warm clouds of exhaled breath wafted in the light breeze, spewing constantly from the collection of cowled adults gathered in a complete circle around a hundred candles and a chilly stone tablet set atop a marble altar. Though the atmosphere was brittle, the heat radiating from the chanting men and women could almost be seen as shuddering waves cascading into the night. Chanting, low and murmuring, rose in a baritone crescendo. United ancient words melded together in one, coalescing tone into the brisk, crisp air. And on the pedestal, in the center of the tablet -undulating in rich, deep reds and chromatic pewter- sat an amulet; pulsating, thrumming, beating... alive.

Six men, six women. Their circle complete. Their order was offset; one woman, one man, one woman. Each wore a black, woolen robe with a hood that completely concealed their faces save for their chanting, moaning mouths. Underneath their robes, they wore nothing, as was the way and the law of the

Sayer. The Sayer had many rules: each member must be united with the next, and he united with her, and so on until all twelve had become, essentially, one; and each single member, though afforded a meager dwelling, had to spend every sixth night with another member. Often times, this meant several with one, so said the Sayer, and all believed this inter-mingling to be an accepted way of life. The sixth month, on the six night, for six hours beginning when the moon was high in the sky, the twelve returned to their sepulcher and prepared the Amulet for 'The Variance': the combining of their souls into the 'Eye of the Sayer'. The formed their circle, they repeated their chant, and they lost themselves to The Sayer and its Eye

Each of the twelve was a respected member of the society of their village: Engruu. They all held lofty positions in the hierarchy including judge, treasurer, chief hunter, village elder, and war general. Each, as well, was a receptacle for pure evil. They willingly opened themselves to darkness, sorrow, hatred, disrespect, anger, and callousness. They each became a vessel for each and every feeling and desperate act that would otherwise cripple the village. And so, imbued with these feelings, they led their tribe and waited, patiently, to purge themselves at the Sayer's Eye. For days, weeks, and months, the twelve absorbed every ounce of evil, and every bit of deviltry only to expurgate in the circle. And so, the Amulet; the 'Eye of the Sayer', supped at the people's negativity as it ebbed and flowed into it like a tide. The Amulet grew into an object of such unspeakable horror and ghastly repugnance that it soon began to extrude its consumed power over everyone and everything in Engruu.

It was time to find others.

Tales of The Amulet
Part 31: Memory

The last thing she remembered saying was, "How did we hit it that hard?"

Dana Marts lay in her hospital bed staring, unblinking at the ceiling. The white tiles mocked her from twelve feet away. The monotonously cheeping box beside her monitored her fragile life; fed her fluids and kept the tube attached to her face chugging in the life-giving oxygen. Dana let a tear fall down her cheek at a weird, forty-five-degree angle. She really had no other choice. Her chest lifted every six seconds as her lungs inflated and emptied the air from her frail being. Her lips were cracked with chap as the hung, swollen in the room. The blanket was draped over her, innocuously, collecting the dust that hung in the solemn air. No one sat in the chairs, no one paced the room in pregnant anticipation, and no one monitored the machine and took notes with alacrity. And the heavy metal amulet draped off the edge of the bed-side table and thrummed with its beating, amber hue. The last thing she remembered saying was, "How did we hit it that hard?"

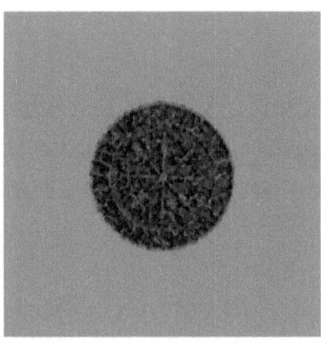

Tales of The Amulet
Part 32: Kindred (Part II)

Kimmy and Molly lay curled up on the couch. It was a little after three a.m. and neither had slept. Tanner arched his eyes restlessly at the girls as though begging them to give him some purpose... something to do. For tonight, even the dog was an insomniac.

The girls had spent several hours writing. They found some paper and a few Sharpies and set about coming up with some semblance of a plan. They had to leave, of this there was no doubt. But where to go? Kimmy knew that she had an uncle who just lived about ten miles away out past the mall, so they had thought about going there. But that would require quite a bit of walking, an exercise neither was too thrilled about. Molly suggested they head to some place like her church, which was a little closer to town, and was full of food and things. They considered this option, too, until the conversation got weighed down with the constant numbing pull of a recent past filled with, of all things, their now dead parents. Then they just sat, silently wept, and stared, with hollow emptiness, into the room. And so, it went.

Kimmy stretched, reached out and patted Tanner on his ignorant head, and smiled, sadly at her blissfully unaware dog.

"Tanner... you have it so lucky. You're just a dog... you have no idea what's happening, and you have no reason to care," Kimmy choked back a sob and swiped her sleeve across her face.

Molly nodded, sighed, and yawned. She wished just a little that she could be Tanner, too.

"Kimmy... I'm really hungry. What's left here to eat?"

Kimmy and Molly raided what was left of the decent food in the fridge consisting of half of the cherry pie they'd begun last night, a bag of carrots, two plastic cups of yogurt, and some very cold -and probably a little old- lemonade. They found quite a few cans of food in the pantry along with several boxes of crackers and other snacks which they decided would be best saved for their trip neither really wanted to discuss. Tanner sniffed, muzzled, and knocked over his kibble and lapped up a few pieces feigning hunger more than fulfilling any real desire to eat. The pink elephant in the room hung around like an impending piece of terrible news; Kimmy and Molly had to get down to the business of forming a cohesive plan. I was time to go.

Kimmy went to her parent's bedroom closet and found a small suitcase on wheels and a tennis duffel bag. She spread the bag open and unzipped the luggage on the floor. The girls filled the duffel with all the canned foods they could conceivably carry along with the much lighter crackers and snacks. Kimmy, in turn, found a few outfits in her room, including a few she'd just outgrown that would likely fit Molly, and may just be a bit baggy. She asked Molly if she'd brought a toothbrush to which Molly literally guffawed a big, boisterous laugh. Kimmy laughed, too, and found a spare that had never been opened from its package. They glanced at the medicine cabinet and felt it best to only take things they were sure about and decided on Band-Aids, bandages, cotton balls, a bottle marked Aspirin that Kimmy knew was for aches and pains, and a package of her mom's pantie liners. She hadn't begun her period yet, but there was no sense in tempting fate without some kind of protection. After another thorough check for anything they might need, Kimmy tossed a kitchen knife and the meat tenderizer into the bag. Then she shut both, handed the handle of the suitcase to Molly and slung the heavier duffel over her own shoulder. She leashed Tanner (just in case), snatched the hatchet, and slid the handle into her belt. Molly decided against the cumbersome pitchfork and instead opted for the kitchen cleaver.

The girls stood at the door. They stared into the open expanse of the world beyond. Under Kimmy's shirt, dangling from her neck, the amulet slowly pulsed.

Tales of The Amulet
Part 33: Business

High atop the mountain range in New Los Angeles sat the hospital known as Te' Luma Health Systems. Since 2110, the corporation had provided a way to reverse the onset of natural aging. For hundreds of years prior, getting older was just a way of life and the complete result of it, but Te' Luma discovered the secret.

Locked inside every human is a very simple trigger lying dormant in a very specific set of amino acids. When each is triggered in a specific sequence, they begin to systematically reverse the effects of aging. Mental acuity is reestablished to its twenty-year plateau, physical prowess becomes that of a typical, moderately fit thirty-year old, the standard signs of aging such as wrinkles and graying recede almost completely, and the person nearly wholly returns to an age where ageing is never even an issue. It's nothing shy of a miracle. But how did Te' Luma find this God-like cure-all? It depends on who you ask.

Local legend tells of a man by the name of Martin Derrick, a man, who it seems, is coincidentally the great grandfather of Te' Luma's founder, Ivan Derrick. From stories pieced together over the years it is known that Martin, sometime in

2021 was out plowing his farmland just before planting season. He was tilling the soil when suddenly his machine grinded to a halt. As he stopped to investigate the source of his troubles, he discovered something foreign lodged in the tilling disks. After some finagling, Martin was finally able to remove the piece. The item he held in his hand was a pewter-colored (albeit filthy) circular object roughly the size and shape of a tea saucer. After some cleaning in curiosity, he held the disk to the sun and noticed runes and hieroglyphics scrolled across the surface of the outer ring. The center hummed and lit with a dull crimson phosphorescence that spread like blood-filled veins into the writing. It shook, almost unnoticeably, with a numbing thrum that seemed to set off all the nerves in Martin's hands as he held the amulet... yes, that's what it was: an Amulet. And it somehow beckoned. Beckoned to him.

As the years passed, Martin began to regain some of his youthful fervor. He tended to daily tasks with a bit more aplomb and whimsy than his age would let on. He was up at four, tending to the animals and the land, in by noon for a hearty brunch, and back to work till sundown. This was daily, and he thought nothing of it, especially as he kept the amulet with him at all times. It wouldn't let him have it any other way. And Martin was content. But he couldn't help thinking, as he said his prayers and kissed his wife, that there was something else he could be doing with his newfound vitality. And there was, at least one thing: his wife bore him his first and only child, Emmit.

As Emmit grew and began to take on likes and dislikes of his own, it was clear to his father that farming was not in his boy's blood. Emmit was adventurous, daring, risky, and far too scatter-brained to focus on tending the Earth, so, when he turned eighteen, Martin helped his son pack -including the Amulet hoping beyond hope that it would impart the same luck and youthful exuberance it had for Martin, though at the same time quite reluctant to see it go- and sent him on his way to make his fortune in the city. A fortune that would become the basis for the end of death as we know it.

To be continued...

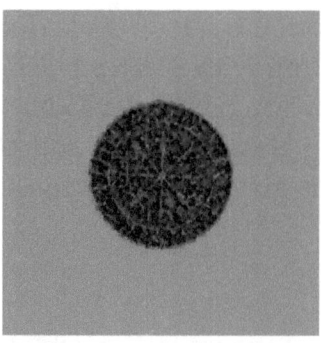

Tales of The Amulet
Part 34: Face Time (Continued)

1.

Tim yanked out a bar stool and collapsed up to the soda counter. Grizzly made a beeline for the Men's room whistling a Steppenwolf tune.

"Hey buddy, how about a couple cold Cokes for me and The Griz?" Tim said as he sloughed off his steamy hide vest and draped it over the neighboring chair.

"You betcha, mister! Hotter'na raped ape out there, ain't it?" The kid behind the counter proudly announced as though it were the first time, he was actually able to use the epithet.

Tim chuckled (mostly to humor the kid) and smacked the counter in approval. As he shook his head relishing the humor, two sweating glasses of Coke were carefully dropped to the veneered surface. The kid nodded, returned to his stocking duties, and laughed a little himself, proud of his little comment.

Grizzly appeared from the saloon-style doors, announced his appearance by erupting with a fierce belch, and resuming his whistled rendition of 'Magic Carpet Ride.' His eyes lit a bit as he saw the glistening glasses of soda and he, too, sidled up to the bar and raised his glass in a mock toast.

2.

Erin absently wiped at the irritating itch of a drip that clung to the lip of her nose. She sniffed up some of the blood, wiped at it again, and never once even thought twice to examine the red liquid stain that smeared across her hand. She inhaled a few times, swooned, coughed a bit, and all the while glared with woozy fascination at the plate-sized disk she held in her grip. She admired --no, she ached at the touch of --the surface; it's roughed chrome... but more like a smooth pewter (nothing was quite as it seemed... nothing), the gleaming steel... but more like the dulled metallic sheen (it seemed to rearrange itself at every touch), and that horrid (beautiful) red eye in the center. It hummed; but it pulsed. It changed; it didn't. It was sickening; it made her gorge rise with every thrum. But it was also, somehow, everything she ever wanted. The amulet sang in her grasp and the song was something between desire and agony.

3.

Tim and Grizzly sat among idle chatter and slowly nursed Coke after Coke. The icy drinks offered them just enough lost humanity after so many miles on the dry, arid road. They spoke on and off to the counter man (who, as it turned out, was named Earl and who was, happily, from right there in town), and they occasionally meandered through the aisles of the store picking out a few items here and there with which to survive the rest of their day-long trek. And though they shed every inhibition, they still clung (however slightly) to their natural skittishness... but nothing could prepare them for the girl who wandered in with a glare in her eyes like a cornered, angry animal.

The store's door whisked open, setting off the sleepy chime, and Erin stood there, not unlike any other day she was scheduled to work... except for the fact that she looked like a trapped beast facing off her predators. Even Earl caught his words in his throat. He'd seen Erin hundreds of times, but never with the ghastly pallor she cast and never with the hyper eyes of something inhuman and feral. All they could do was stare... until Erin leaped...

To Continue...

Tales of The Amulet
Part 35: The Amulet (Part II)

"So, tell me, Mr. Davis: what makes you think that everyone is, somehow -inexplicably- out to get you?"

WE ARE ALL GOING TO KILL YOU...

"Uh, well, Doctor... it's just that I know. We'll leave it at that: I know."

WE ARE ALL GOING TO KILL YOU, JACK...

"Mm Hmm... I see. So, by no apparent or evident rationale of your own, you have come to the conclusion that the general populous -can I assume that is what you mean? - is going to *ahem* kill you?"

JACK... ALL OF US ARE GOING TO KILL YOU, AND SOON YOU WILL SEE...

"OK, OK, well it's not entirely without basis. I mean, I can... I mean, I do hear... uh... the voices. In my head, the voices that tell me, repeatedly that... well, that they're going to... uh... k-k-ill me; that they're going to kill me and that I-I-I will see. Soon see."

IT IS APPROACHING. WE WILL KILL YOU. AND YOU WILL SOON UNDERSTAND...

"Mr. Davis... Jack, look, it has become much of a cliche to my profession to have people blame any number of deeper issues on hearing disembodied and mysterious voices coercing them into doing something or into having something done to themselves. It's all very common, Jack, and I see no evidence otherwise to assume your case is somehow different or special from any other. However, as I will stipulate, when did you first notice these troublesome voices?"

JACK DAVIS: WE WILL KILL YOU. THE PUNISHMENT SHALL SOON COMMENCE.

"Well, Doctor Torrence, I guess it was about two weeks ago, or so... I think. Yeah, about on the seventh, because that was the day I got that card... that card with the check in it..."

KILL KILL KILL KILL

"A card with a check in it. Hmm... from whom, may I ask"

KILL SOON KILL SOON KILL SOON

"I, uh, don't remember... or really, I just don't know; I didn't know then either, it just came in the mail with a hundred-dollar check made out to cash with a small note prompting me to head to, um, where was... oh right... to head to Hanson's Antiques and purchase the silver and red amulet from the front display case. Or, as it put it, "post haste". That means right away, I found out."

WE WILL KILL WE WILL KILL WE WILL KILL

"Mmm, yes it does. So why do you suppose that a strange, nameless card with a check should arrive at your address more or less demanding your immediate purchase of some amulet from a crummy antique distributor?"

IT IS CLOSE WE WILL KILL IT IS CLOSE WE WILL KILL

"I-I-I have no idea... I wasn't out any money from anyone; no one really owed me anything, that I can think of. I don't know... but I did what it said to and bought that weird, old amulet from the store. Funny thing: it was only priced at fifty bucks, I remember that, but I felt that I somehow needed to offer the clerk the entire thing, just to, sort of, get it off his hands... like a tip."

JACK JACK KILL KILL JACK JACK KILL KILL

"Interesting. Is it too much to hope that you have this amulet on your person at this moment?"

WE WILL KILL JACK WE WILL KILL JACK

"Uh yeah... I mean no. It's right here..."

Jack pulled on the gaudy chain that held the weighty amulet around his neck. For a mere moment, the blabbering voices drifted to nothing more than background noise, and Jack was suddenly relieved. The Amulet was roughly the size of a DVD; it had etched on its surface a half dozen runic symbols, a deep ruby background that almost shimmered too much in such dim light, and a black circumference that held several, tiny, deep-red stones. As Jack held it at arm's length, it hummed with a vibration one could easily feel deep within the chest, and it was at this that Dr. Torrence clutched himself in terror and fell into the Amulet's depths.

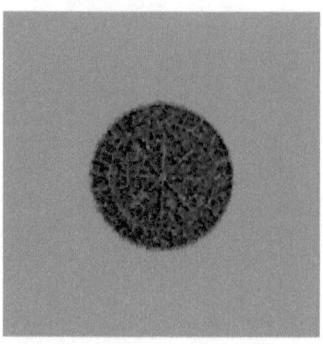

Tales of The Amulet
Part 36: Errant Desires

The desperation he felt had weight. The sorrow coated him like a sodden blanket and wrapped him so tightly he could feel its suffocating grasp. Every breath was a shuddering, wheezing fit wracked with hitching sadness and the never-ending flow of tears. But worst of all --the thing that held him in a vice grip of shame and misery-- was the guilt. Why had he even given in? Why had it become acceptable with him? Why hadn't he seen it coming? The tumult of questions beat at his head like a progression of angry drums.

And alone he sat. He'd allow his mind freedom to wander without even remembering giving it permission. It would trace the trail of shock and revelation backwards through the days. It would trip over visions, stumble headlong into occasions, and fall headfirst into moments just as it had the first go round, only this time witnessing each with the outcome first. And sometimes his unconscious would stick and repeat like a movie frame caught on a fleck of broken film. He'd relive those monstrous memories over and over, always knowing how each would end but praying nonetheless that this time... this time he could affect them for the better. But never. And then he'd jostle his head, shake himself free from the torturous thoughts, and snap himself back into the now. The now that was flooded with grief, unanswered questions, and dark, vast, endless sorrow.

And his desperation had a weight like a revenant's chains. They slowly, methodically drug him lower and lower to where, in all actuality, his head languidly lay on the ground. And he wept. The seething guile he knew was finally exposed ratcheted through his mind like a thousand connecting cogs. And he'd lifelessly beat at his head in a harmless attempt to knock loose the thoughts that sought nothing more than to consume him in a fit of ravenous madness. Fear would bubble to the surface and send his teeth to chatter, just as his wanton need to project his weakness on anything else would push away the terror and try to take control. Wrath won out all too often and he felt as though his blood would scream, super-heated from his veins causing him the forbidden comfort of bleeding to death as he bawled for what he'd lost.

Though it was she who brutally trod on his heart with her deceit and blatant duplicity that ultimately reduced him to a fragmented husk, it was always the thing that began it. He'd long since forgotten how it came to them; never was one to hang onto stories about objects. But it had come to them, and it had brought with it the immoral, disastrous, fiendish misgivings that gradually forced a wedge between them, culminating in her desire to insult him and make him suffer. She fell under its mesmerizing charm. She succumbed to its morbid revulsion, and with it she fed. She became a glutton on the negativity it poured forth, and she eventually turned... into something else. Her actions were deplorable and her explanations despicable. She buried her thoughtless words and actions into him like daggers.

He was done. He saw no road ahead, no distant, glimmering horizon. He was done. His life had sloughed from him like a layer of dead flesh; she removed that cleanly. He was done and he knew it. No silver lining, no darkness prior to a better dawn, and he could care less how much greener some other pasture might be. Nothing mattered. Nothing worth anything remained.

The hull-grey .45 sat desolate on the table. He stared at it for a bit. He licked his lips wondering how the metal would taste and if it would shatter his teeth before darkness fell. He fingered the trigger and scooped up the gun. It felt icy in his cradling palm; icy but somehow inviting. He glanced down one last time at the pulsating, undulating rouge hue that swam across the surface of the amulet as it hung, and hummed, from is neck.

He was done.

Tales of The Amulet
Part 37: The Stairs

I.

Tendrils and wisps of the remainder of the early morning fog streaked the ancient stone like the fingers of some long-forgotten ghosts. Eerie tails of opaque white curled among the lichen-strewn rocky outcroppings and looped over the dew droplets that clung to the spears of timothy. The air was thick and cool; the morning sun had been shut out by the encroaching gray clouds, yet the wetness of the humid air felt cloying and dank. The pebbled surface of the decrepit masonry was slick with damp moss and ran freely with tiny rivulets of moisture that had collected in the exposed crags and loosed rock. The stairs angled upward into the weighted cloud and disappeared into the spectral gloom of the slowly receding morn.

II.

Ages ago the stonework steps were built as a pathway to enlightenment. Their creators and masons were monks, who desperately searched for a way out of the valley they inhabited. For the valley had fallen to an evil so unspeakable and horrid that they had little choice but to escalate themselves skyward toward the hand of the God they'd prayed hadn't forsaken them. And so, they constructed. They meticulously and laboriously unearthed and drug stone and rock from the river at the base of their valley home. They toiled day and night perfecting their last path to salvation. Yet for them, it was too late. They soon fell as the blanketing repulsion suffocated them. And so, the staircase stood, as a reminder to what could have been.

III.

At closer glance, the fine scrollwork that ran the length of the ancient and crumbling steps was quite impressive. It also spoke volumes of what the monks who created the massive stairs were working toward. From the moment the sadistic sickness befell their civilization, their lone goal became escape. Their God promised sanctuary, but the people were made to earn it. Freedom from the oppressive bleakness would not come without sacrifice and offerings; their lives wouldn't be preserved, and therefor spared, without a total and complete giving of themselves. And the etchings that looped and whorled up and across the surface of each eroding rise was a true testament to their undying devotion.

IV.

Piece by piece, slate by slate, boulder by boulder, the steps slowly and with painful precision fell into shape. Decades passed and the tower of fitted rocks grew ever higher, just as people gave up their lives and plead to their God as they fell. The colony gave up much: celebrations, livelihoods, daily freedoms; all for the defiance of the sinister and the quest to achieve salvation. They lived and died by their powerless struggle between good and evil. But the evil had strength. And the evil was in the earth itself. It seethed, it writhed, it gnashed, and it fought the people every single step of the way... and every way of the steps.

V.

As the afternoon sun burns away the remainder of ghastly
fog, the slithering tendrils that caress the exposed roots
hanging languidly from the depleting stone evaporate into
ethereal nothingness. A step back reveals the perfection of the
rising hill. Its corners; perfect. Its angles; uncompromised. Its
rises and falls; works of art. And the edging that showcases
the precision script winds its way up either side cascading
from the top-most stone to the very bottom. The encroaching
wind echoes with the broken spirits of a thousand buried
voices as it whirls up the steps. The haunting drones of eons
past -living with the long dead calls of ancient voices- ebb and
flow through the haunted, overgrown valley.

VI.

The population slowly died away. The evil of the valley had
manifest and entered the spirits and very souls of the
adolescents. It crept in and strangled the life out of the
righteous; the blank slates who devoted their lives to
constructing the stairs and reaching the hands of their loving
God. The children began to hate. They began to thoughtlessly
punish. They began to commit hateful crimes and destroy the
builders of the stairway. With recklessness and deviant
amorality, the young overpowered and eradicated the old. But
even with the elderly falling, the steps eventually reached
completion, much to the behest of the strangling horror from
below.

VII.

The cryptic designs that ran the length of upward stairwell
did not sit idle. Their circular etchings vibrated with a deep,
guttural thrum. And they pulsated a dark, haunting red hue
that ebbed in rhythm with the beating hum. Each connecting

hoop-shape looked exactly like an amulet of sorts. They were roughly the size of saucers with even more intricate artwork; tribal in nature, which encircled a center 'eye'. And it was this eye that truly emitted the most horrific shade of blackened red. Anyone who stood long enough at the stairs, or who made the decision to walk its seemingly endless path, would begin to understand what the long-deceased civilization was attempting to reach. And one would be unable to understand how feelings this dire and terrifying could be misconstrued as anything other than pure and complete evil. Maybe it was the Gods within the valley who were the actual true amalgams of truth. Many have fallen as their understandings were shattered. And many have followed the path of the amulet.

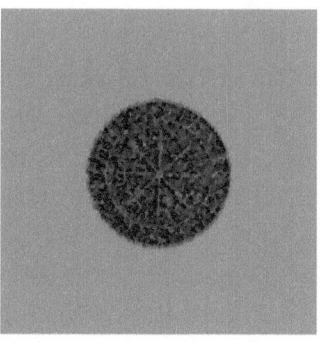

Tales of The Amulet
Part 38: Homecoming

We sat shivering in the basement of the old, burned-out American National bank. A few cans of unlabeled vegetables and beans sat opened and half-eaten near our small fire. We'd managed to find what used to be a pretty good-sized wok in a dumpster across the street where the Joy Fong Chinese Restaurant had once stood, and now the sauté pan served as a portable stove of sorts. Burning in it now was a bunch of warped chop sticks, also procured from the derelict eatery. They seemed to burn longer after we soaked them for a bit in a soured tub of old cooking oil. Danny sat with his back against the vault wall and sighed; something he had done often after a day of scrounging and pack-ratting everything and anything we could find of value. For a boy of twelve, he had tremendous reserve and a will that nearly never quit. But it eventually did, right around the same time every evening. And that was fine, because my forty-year-old tenacity wasn't as limitless as it once was.

Danny and I met about a month earlier. I had lost my family a few years ago, to the horrors you see, and I was traveling as best I could on my own. I was lonely, of that fact there was no doubt, but I never tried too hard to find anyone else, because most of the remaining human race had either gone completely insane -thanks in part to the Fixers (I'll tell you about that another time)- or had been devoured by the horrors; the creations brought on by the Scourge of the Amulet. So, there were very few of us left. But I found Danny... or should I say Danny found me. I was kneeling, lost in thought, over a dead deer carving off good meat with a sharpened comb handle. Most of the carcass had gone off, but a bit, near the head, was still okay... provided I cooked the hell out of it. Which I'd planned to do anyway. And it seemed Danny was just as hungry as I was. He'd found the decaying animal, too. But Danny had a gun. A gun that, as it turned out, wasn't loaded. But it scared me just the same.

I wanted no part of a bullet, so I dropped my tool and the meat, and Danny just scrambled up to the carved pile and began shoveling it into his mouth; no cooking necessary. I calmly told him that were he not to char the dickens out of that meat he was going to be puking up his shoes by the end of the night. I offered to build a fire and make us dinner. Danny glanced at me with fresh juice dribbling down his chin, looked at his gun that was now a few feet away (I kicked it just to be safe) and not only did he nod, but he burst into tears. I don't think he'd seen a person in a very long time. Especially a person who wasn't under the influence of The Fixers. He ran to me, clung hard, and wept into my filthy sweater. That was all it took; friends for life, we were, after that.

Danny and I had found the bank vault a few days ago. I had to chase a lady who was just lousy with The Fixers; gibbering and swollen, fistulas and pustules oozing grey liquid, her left eye dangling, forgotten, from its socket... she was a sorry mess, and wasn't long for the world. I finished her misery with a jab to the back of the head. A quick search of her meager possessions only provided a small tack hammer and a rusty bucket. But the vault was a fine place to hold up, and so Danny and I brought in much of our findings before the

Scourers began their nightly hunt, and we felt relatively safe.

Danny sighed deeply again and rubbed his eyes. I sat down beside him and rubbed his filthy hair. He smiled; his eyes deep with sorrow, regret, and an aching sadness that threatened to bring tears to my own eyes. I smiled back and offered him a piece of a Dolly Madison snack cake we'd found a few days before. He shook his head and mimicked opening a book with his hands. I shook my head, momentarily not quite understanding... until he did it again, this time mouthing, "story". My face lit up with recognition: Danny wanted a story! Hey, I could do that for the kid. Besides, I had quite a few. Especially since I had seen The Amulet just before it destroyed everything.

The Tale

Eight years ago, I was married to an amazing beauty named Selah with twin daughters named Joy and Faith. Yes, we were Christians and very involved in our local Church. Our friends were there, our love was there, and our lives were there. But the hand of darkness wasn't far off. But we didn't heed the warnings. We believed we were as safe as we needed to be. Even our Pastor -Paul Easton; a wonderful, if naive, man- refused to acknowledge that trouble was simmering just on the horizon. Of course, this particular trouble wasn't Biblical... it just was.

The time had come to move. Our house was just too small, and with to growing daughters and the distinct probability of more children to come, it made sense to find larger dwellings. But before the packing, it was time to part with as much of our unneeded sundries as possible, so we had a garage sale. My job was cleaning out the attic; a feat that was made all the more difficult by the fact that it hadn't been done the entire time we lived there. Eleven years of boxes just shoved up there willy-nilly. So, needless to say, I had a full weekend ahead of me. As I went through stuff, Selah would take what she deemed sale-worthy, and set it aside. The rest got thrown out. Things were going along swimmingly; we found old China, baby toys, decent clothes, shoes, books, VHS tapes, and oodles of things we no longer used. But then I found it. Deep within the recesses of the musty attic, in a box that held nothing but a moth-eaten drop cloth; it was metallic, the color of pewter, with runes strewn about the surface. I had, as far as I knew, never seen it before in my life... and I wish right now that I'd never laid eyes on it then.

-- To Be Continued --

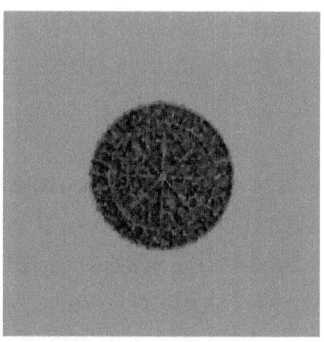

Tales of The Amulet
Part 39: Homecoming (Part II)

I paused a moment to clear my throat and take a sip of our
dwindling water supply. It wasn't fresh, that's for sure, but
boiling it (I had learned a few things from TV years ago, my
friends) made enough of a difference to at least keep us from
getting painfully ill. But it still tasted flat and all together
harsh. But water was water... Where was I?

I took a sip and looked at Danny. His wide, cornered-doe eyes
pleaded for me to continue; but the fear poorly hidden just
below their shimmering surface told me that he was also quite
frightened, indeed. I shrugged my shoulders; I asked if he was
sure he wanted me to go on. He knew about the Amulet:
everyone has at the very least seen its symbols. He nodded. I
continued.

*I held up the metallic disk to the waning light coming up from the
open attic door. It glinted, horrifically in the dimness. Its runes
played an angry rose hue across the surface that met in the blackish
rouge 'eye' in the center. There was a sickening vibration that
emanated from the thing that I could feel so deeply it almost shook
my bones. I was immediately revolted by it; it's shape, its feel, its
antique hieroglyphics... all of it. Yet, at the same time, I was oddly
attracted to it. It spoke to me. It called to me. And just then I had the*

overwhelming urge to throw it back in the box and never set eyes on it again. A hand touched my shoulder, and I could have sworn my heart stopped.

Danny let out a yelp. It was weird because he never talked. Hadn't ever spoken word one since we'd met. But when he called out, I knew he had to be scared. I set my hand on his knee and comforted him. I smiled; even chuckled a little because I knew what was coming. It wasn't bad. Not yet.

Not yet.

I went on.

Selah stood just behind me. She burst into laughter as she obviously saw that I had turned ghostly white, and my mouth hung open; breathing like I'd just run a mile. I gathered myself and looked her in the eye. She saw the box I had open and asked if she could take it downstairs. I cringed a little and took the glass of iced tea she offered. I didn't know what to say even after she asked a second time. I just stared at her, and the box, dumbfounded. I didn't know why I was hesitating; just a box with a... what? And Amulet of some kind? Why was I worried? And that's when I finally told her: Sure, go ahead and take it. It might have been the worst mistake I have ever made.

Danny hissed in his throat; ya know that sound you make when something startles you and it sounds like you're drinking really quickly from a straw? That sound. I didn't laugh this time. I think he finally understood that what I had found would eventually become why the world we know had become... the world we know.

You see it was that very Amulet that brought on the Scourge. An epic cloud of devastation that slowly, agonizingly coated everything with fixers. The fixers were like some kind of

psychotropic drug; a drug so insanely powerful that everyone who ingested was 'fixed', or completely under the control of The Scourge. Then they -the very people we had come to love, and know in our daily lives- became twisted, gnarled, and feral. And they were called The Scourers. They were sent out on nightly patrols, when the sun wasn't piercing through the now unpredictable atmosphere (some days it would intensify the sunlight, others it would block it out completely and the earth would literally freeze) and the Scourers were pulsating with fixers and they would search, relentlessly for survivors. They would devour you whole, and spit back nothing but a shambling carcass of your former self. A new Scourer.
All of this because of the Amulet. The Amulet I'd let slip away.

I let Danny nestle into me, and I continued.

You see, just then I had only a vague notion of the gripping control of the Amulet. I had held it and gazed upon it; and were it not for my precious Selah arriving just when she had... well, who knows. Worse things were yet to come, but just that minute I gripped its cloying terror in my hands... well I knew. I just knew that this thing was a culmination of every evil, vile, wretched thing imaginable. And Selah was carrying the box in which it lay right down the attic steps. As much as I knew -deep down in my soul- that I had to stop her; had to grab that box and destroy it in any way necessary, as much as I knew this: I let her go. Even then it had a hold on me that I never even conceived. It had already set into motion its own plans. As ridiculous as that sounds, and even though I had no earthly idea how it had come into my possession in the first place, the gears were already turning. The Amulet was about to spread its disease.
She disappeared below the doorway and into the garage. And I just knew that thing was about to change hands.

Danny once again peered up at me; this time through misty eyes that had begun to run with tears. His lip quivered, and he sniffed a little. But worse yet was his trembling: he felt like a little motor, running silently but churning. He was petrified. And so was I. But I'd learned to push my fright deep down inside. I had spent years telling myself that it couldn't have been my fault; that I was only indirectly involved. I knew this, but it took a long while to accept it. Danny had just found out, and yet, even as he shuddered with horror, he didn't pull away. He didn't flip out and run screaming (I bet he could scream if he wanted to) into the night. Maybe he understood, too. I don't know.

-- To Be Continued--

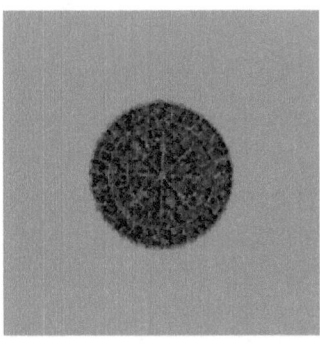

Tales of The Amulet
Part 40: Dread

As the breathless man clung to his terrified children -holding them closer and wrapping his goose-fleshed arms around them- he loudly prayed, hoping beyond hope that His ears would hear. The four of them huddled beneath the stairwell in the basement, the man doing his very best to soothe his inconsolable children as they wept sorrowfully between hitching breaths and flooding tears. Their home was dark now, though the power had been cut out for several hours it was only over the last few minutes that the sun had set below the tree lines and its light no longer flooded in the windows. And it was this feeling -this feeling of eminent dread- that now crept over them like a nightmare, no lights, no calming effect of the last of the dwindling sun, no more safety. Though the man's sanity was rapidly fraying, he was a father first; and to his children a hero, and so he began to sing to them through his quavering, shuddering voice. He slowly rocked them; his big boy eleven-year-old, his fiercely independent middle boy, and his little baby girl, rocking them and trying valiantly to assuage their escalating fears.

But the knock came anyway. The pounding was so deafening and intense that it felt like it could blow the basement door off its hinges.

The man caught his voice in his throat and his singing turned into a temporary shriek. The children (for the moment lulled into what was for them an unknown false sense of security) recoiled in horror and each began crying anew. Their father did his best to shush them soundly and appease them, but no solace was to be found in his words.

The knock came again. The four of them jumped and began begging out loud for the intruder to go away. The man finally lost his composure. A man of strength; a man that never showed emotion to his children, and a man who withstood all adversaries finally succumbed to the horror that overfilled his life, and he screamed at the top of his lungs. No words, just an explosive yell, long and overflowing with alarm and panic and release. The children stared at him in unison, momentarily too stunned to cry. But the moment was fleeting and as soon as they realized that their own father was just as frightened as they were, their sobs were even more wracking.

The long moments ticked away into what felt like little eternities. The man strained to hear any more sounds while the trio of children mewled in his arms. His limbs, he felt, were growing numb. He'd been sitting squat forever and the weight of his horrified kids in his arms had begun to feel like lifeless sacks. But he knew they weren't, and he knew they'd only protest with stronger constrictions if he made to move. He was trapped for the moment in every way, both downstairs in his own home and in the death grips of his terrified offspring. But he also knew that he had to see if the thing was gone. It had been far too long since any noise at all was heard. And it was only now that he realized his youngest had cried herself to sleep.

The silence was deafening. The man slowly released his youngest into the arms of his oldest, placed a calming finger to his lips and began to methodically stand up. No one stirred, no one cried out, and the man knew now was the time to climb back into the turmoil and assess the situation. He stood, creaked a little and angled his tight joints so he could move without wincing in agony. He glanced with tireless anticipation and a heavy heart toward the wooden stairs that led into the proverbial belly of the beast...

The stairs that lead to the beast he dreaded the most: The woman he loved.

Tales of The Amulet
Part 41: The Story of Jimmy and Wil

I haven't thought about Jimmy and Wil for a few years now...
probably more like a decade or two, honestly. But it's time I
shared the tale of the one moment that -not to put too fine a
point on it- changed my life forever. In fact, it changed it in a
way that would scar me in the deepest and most profound
way possible.

It was 1981. My best friends in the world were Jimmy
Davidson and Wil McMahon, and during that summer break
from fifth grade we were inseparable. We attended Bible
Camp together, we stayed over at one another's houses and
back yards, and we spent as many hours in each other's
company as physically possible. Life was great and during
that vacation of '81, nothing could have been better, and yet
what the three of us were soon to discover, nothing could be
worse.

Over the week of July 4th, I had to spend six days away from
my pals on a family vacation to Niagara Falls. It was great, but
three days in and I was pining for the companionship of my
buddies. And by the time we rolled into the driveway at the

end of the week, I was in full-blown withdrawal. Within the following fifteen minutes, Jimmy and Wil were sitting next to me in the yard bombarding me with questions and throwing six days' worth of new information at me about what I'd missed. It was wonderful to be back home.

But then Jimmy dropped the bomb. He looked at Wil and they both nodded. I looked quizzically at them as the readied themselves; it was clear that what they had to share was pretty damn important. I waited patiently for Jimmy to begin, both excited and a little frightened. He finally asked if I remembered the trail that led out to the old barn, we called the Chicken Shack. It sat about fifty yards beyond the cul de sac on which our houses sat. I said of course I did, what about it?

Jimmy continued with an air of hesitation. He said he and Wil were out catching fireflies a few nights ago when something shiny and very red captured their attention. It was sticking out of the dry weeds next to the trail. The sun had nearly set, but it wasn't its glow that reflected of the object's surface; the ominous deep vermilion hew was glowing all on its own. I nodded and shrugged not yet really getting the full weight of what I was being told.

Now it was Wil's turn, and he began by looking around to make sure no one else was listening. He glanced at Jimmy and continued the story. The thing they found was not only just emitting a sickly red light, but the closer they got they could make out a deep, reverberating hum that seemed to hit them right in their gut. It was a low thrumming that was almost painful. He and Jimmy got as close as they dared and stared at it. There was no doubt that it was metal; it had a rough, unpolished surface that looked almost ancient. But the most bizarre part were the etchings that encompassed the face of it. The closer they got, the more the ache of the vibration stung and burned. They got within ten feet before the nose bleeds.

Jimmy said he felt a pop in his face and a trickle of blood oozed from his right nostril. Wil said he heard a weird echoing sound and his nose sprung its own leak. That was as far as they dared go, and they turned, abandoning their bug jars, and ran home.

I sat with the two of them in silence. It was apparent just by their curious faces that each wanted to go back to it, but each wanted to wait for me. A bloody nose? I could deal with that. I nodded and wordlessly the three of us agreed to go the following night. I wanted to go then -dark was a mere hour or so away- but my parents had already confined me to yard and house for the night. Besides, I was tired and, truth be told, maybe a bit scared.

I spent an hour that night staring at my ceiling pondering just what it could have been Jimmy and Wil discovered out there, and if I really wanted any part of it. I wish now that I'd chickened out, because little did, I know that in 24 hours I'd never, ever be the same.

It was Saturday night. The three of us had spent the day in a kind of distant haze. We dragged sticks around, kicked ay rocks, and generally just wasted the day. We went to Wil's for burgers and dogs on the grill and gathered jars for our cover of collecting lightning bugs. Our parents all knew where we were going; we'd been staying out late nearly all of Summer vacation. They knew we were safe and besides, I was having both over to my house overnight. Our bases were as covered as they were going to get. And as the sun ducked behind the tree line and the little pops of yellow dotted the muggy evening, we set out.

Mid-way down the trail I was the first to notice the ruby incandescence. It came from just off the trail the very same way Jimmy and Wil described. In a few steps it became uncomfortably apparent that the dull hum could be felt in the bottom of my chest. We stopped. No one said anything and neither of us knew just what to do next. But I knew if I waited too much longer, I'd have likely turned around. I took another tentative step, feeling that horrible drone deep in my gut. Jimmy and Wil followed suit, but somehow neither looked as though the sonorous buzz was bothering them at all. As I looked them over, wry grins danced across their mouths. It was then I felt the death-grips of their hands and they grasped my upper arms.

I remember shouting at them to let go, but neither even seemed to hear me. Soon my ears began to sting as the tremors grew in intensity. That's when I felt the jab behind my eyes and the rivulet of blood ran down my lip. I tried to fight my way free, hoping it was all a joke, but knowing it wasn't. We inched ever closer to what now looked like some kind of disc poking from the dirt. As I struggled, I looked at my friends. Their eyes had rolled up and I could see only whites. They glared dead-faced and slack-jawed; trickles of foamy drool ran down their chins. We were feet from the object, and I wanted nothing more than to be in my house and hiding in my mom's arms. I tripped a half-step and saw a pretty big rock. I fell on purpose and that quick move loosened Wil's grip just enough. I yanked my right arm free and grabbed the fist-sized rock. The blood was running freely now, and I could feel my chest about to burst from the violent drumming that continued to get worse and worse. I stood and swung; the rock collided with Jimmy's eye socket, and he wailed in agony releasing his hold. I looked back at Wil who was reaching toward me. I stepped back and whipped the rock, connecting with and subsequently breaking his nose at the bridge. He, too yowled in pain and dropped to his knees. My head felt like it was stuffed with angry bees, and I knew I had to get away. But how could I leave my friends?

I heard the voices. Way back, somewhere in the cavernous depths of my brain, I heard them. They spoke in hisses and chittering clacks. They called to me with their gibbering growls and guttural tones. They told me I'd won. They told me to kill. I stood above my fallen friends with a mind not my own, and I obeyed. I kicked and kicked until I felt crunching and mush.

For a few years my new home was a Juvenile Detention Center and the occasional hospital hooked up to brain machines in hopes of answering "Why?" Eventually, as I'd remained silent for six years, I was given to the State and its cells and rooms. As I sit now... unsure of the time or the day or the year... I look around at the padded walls and wonder just how much of what I've told is just voices in my head.

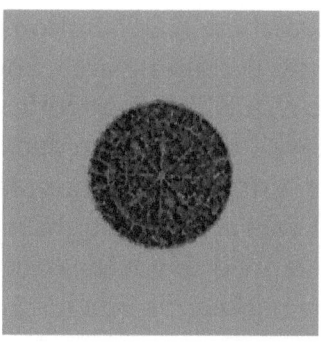

Tales of The Amulet
Part 42: Unfaithfully Ever After

Steve felt pretty good about himself. He stopped on the front porch of Karen Chase's home (her home she pretended to live in happily with her daughter, Meg, and her frequently absent husband, Shawn) and took a deep, steadying breath, staring out across the lawn he'd now come to know every Thursday afternoon. Steve Parker was a salesman from Payne's Home Improvement in charge of hocking windows and gutter covers to anyone and everyone city-wide. It was a crummy job all around, especially since very few people in this economy were improving their homes in any meaningful way. In fact, many were just outright selling and moving on to more fertile grounds. But were it not for Steve's position in said crummy job, he'd never have met Mrs. Chase one lonely, steamy Thursday in August when, given the circumstances, she'd likely have purchased anything from windows to the Polar Ice Cap. Steve was decked out in his typical Polo shirt emblazoned with the Payne's logo, hair combed slightly askew and tousled, and splash of musk just for its hint of crisp, acrid scent. Mrs. Chase was putty. She's invited him in - obviously bored and probably even a little ready for some sense of danger- and offered him coffee. He accepted, smiled at her politely, and watched in admiration at the swish of her butt as she led him into the dining area. She bought two windows, signed the requisite paperwork, and sat staring, like a coy animal, into Steve's eyes as both decided, wordlessly, to move things into the bedroom. And hour later, Karen became his Thursday stop. It was at this thought that Steve breathed deeply the day and stepped down the concrete steps to walk the block to where he parked his Buick.

The Buick had other ideas than Steve's of leaving. The starter chugged, but it wouldn't catch. It had happened before, and typically it just took a half-hour or so for it to calm down and fire up. Steve sighed and smacked the steering wheel. Though he was parked a block away and around a corner, he still felt a certain sting of worry and apprehension. One never knew who might have seen him go into the Chase home and leave seventy minutes later. One never knew who had large eyes and loud mouths. Steve sat motionless and stared out of the windshield into the nosy world beyond. And it was just then he saw the reflection.

His heart nearly stopped as it jumped into his throat. One wandering glance was all it took for Steve to catch a view of the man sitting in the back seat. Steve froze with what might have been a yell catching ineffectually in his larynx. The man sat stolid; a derby sat straight and crisp on his head, the shadow from the brim obscuring half of the man's face. He wore a full-length trench coat that covered him to nearly the ankles, and proper loafers finished the ensemble. Other than that -the mostly unassuming outfit- the man only held one other thing, and it was in his lap: a medallion the shape and size of a compact disk.

"Wh-who are you?" Steve managed to stammer in a forced whisper.

The man sat motionless for a beat. "Someone who knows, Steve. Someone who knows."

Though Steve knew exactly what this man was talking about, he decided to play as dumb as possible. "What? What do you know?"

Steve was, as he sat trembling and facing facts, scared to death. Somewhere in the cellar of his thoughts he supposed he knew he'd be caught at some point. However, he was always sure it would be Karen's husband who'd do the catching. Steve saw his picture all over the house, since Karen apparently didn't believe in the time-honored tradition of cheating wives turning down images of their spouses for fear of them somehow knowing from afar. In this case, Karen's husband was kind of a mousy guy with weaselly features and slicked-back, 60's hair. All told, he looked a bit like Squiggy from the old Laverne and Shirley show. The man that currently sat cucumber-cool in the back seat was absolutely not Mr. Chase. Of this, Steve was nearly one-hundred percent certain.

"I know of the indiscretions, Steve. I know of the ruination you insist on perpetuating, Steve... the sanctity of marriage.... That's what I know."

Steve blinked. He turned his head to the back seat rather than talk to the rear-view mirror and stared at the man in the black coat and hat. The man looked like he hadn't flinched, statuesque and frozen in time. Steve gave him a look of disdain and glared at him for a time.

"I'm sorry but I'm not going to sit here and take any crap from someone who obviously has no clue what he's talking about. So please... get out of my car."

The man only sat; still and unnerved. The disk on his lap began to shine a little oddly and Steve chalked it up to glare from the sun through the glass or something. Until it pulsated.

Red tints of undulating hue snaked across the surface highlighting the etchings that Steve just then noticed. The face of the disk looked mottled with runes and glyphs. The scarlet pulses danced across the disk like tiny flashes of bloody lightning. Steve was momentarily mesmerized.

"The Amulet knows all, my friend; good, bad, and indifferent... it sees everything. And though it feeds from the endless trough that is human unkindness and ineptitude, it also seeks those floating in the mire of damnation and... well... inhumanity. It seeks them and shows them the errors of their actions."

Steve stared dumbfounded at the man in black. His mouth hung open and a throaty sigh escaped him. The only movement that passed between them were the thin, gnarled fingers of the man as he played them slowly over the carved surface of the amulet.

It was then Steve's mind filled with the torturous overture of the nightmares he might have inadvertently caused with his thoughtless acts. His head was thrown back, his neck arched with a snap and his spine followed. His mouth yawned open in a rictus of terror and a bark of pain escaped his throat. Thoughts paraded through his brain, each more painful and agonizing than the last; the past was shown proving that maybe Karen's husband knew after all and his subsequent plans for suicide, and the present played on as well where Karen herself began spreading the rift between her and her husband causing ripples in their child's life. And then there was the future -the worst part- slicing into his psyche like a hot dagger. Years not yet existing delivered images of a grave plot, a mourning woman, and a distant silhouette hiding in the shadows. The atmosphere was dull grey and heavy with emotion. Though Steve couldn't see it was dreadfully apparent that the cemetery stone had the name of Karen's husband, and the silhouette was their child. It was all too much... just too much.

Then the red that surged across the disk's surface suddenly ceased. The angrily dancing lights suddenly stopped, and a deafening silence slammed into the car. Steve was curled into a fetal position in the front seat, a runnel of drool stringing into a pool at his cheek. The man in the black coat and hat slowly slid out from the backseat, he took one cursory glance at Steve, smiled wanly, and left the vehicle. The amulet glowed one final time: a pulse for good measure.

Tales of The Amulet
Part 43: Her Dad

Rachel sat down on her bed and yawned, stretching her arms high releasing some of the tension of the day. It was late. She'd been through the wringer today and could feel every second of it pulsing through her like hot, electrical wiring. Saying she was tired was an absolute understatement; she was exhausted and physically worn to her core. She peeled off her clothes, unhooked her bra, slipped into her favorite *Monster Squad* night shirt, and dropped to the bed like a sack of meat. Sighing deeply, she rolled to her side and managed to just get her phone plugged in when the blessed sensation of sleep swept her up in its warming embrace. Her last glimpse was of the digital clock on her nightstand: it was eleven twenty.

It was the thud that woke her. It jogged her with such ferocity that her breath caught in her throat, and she cried out a little. She lay there, practically hyperventilating and trying with staggering difficulty to understand if the noise was real or just a product of her sleep. But her question was answered for itself when the thud came again. Rachel squealed and felt the motion bounce her bed. She instinctively scooted her knees to her stomach and wrapped her arms around herself. The only light was that from her dim clock readout, so she blinked and stared around the near-total darkness searching for sight. After a few minutes her innate bravery kicked in and she slowly undid her legs and made to step off onto the floor.

THUD!! The forcefulness of the sound and its sudden, shuddering jolt nearly spilled her to the floor. It was then that it became evident that whatever it was had emanated from beneath her own bed. Rachel scrambled to the floor and stood idly by with pregnant anticipation. Another few minutes went by, and she slowly made her way on tiptoes to her bedroom door. Just as she turned the knob, the thud came again with such force that she could actually hear the bed bounce against the floor. She yanked the door open, swatted up the light switch, and turned toward the family room. What appeared before her frightened her so instantaneously and completely that her comprehension didn't have time to catch up with what her eyes were trying to tell her she was seeing. She saw her father; her father dressed in his favorite T-shirt and sweats standing in the shadows cast by the bookshelf and the TV stand glaring at her with dreamy eyes rolled back into his sunken, pallid face. Yes, her father who had died three years ago by his own hand right there in the family room. The spectral image seared itself into her psyche and the last sensation Rachel felt before black fog enveloped her was her knees buckling.

A slice of dawn pierced beyond Rachel's closed eyelids, and she winced, rolling away from the window. Then she jerked upright kicking the covers from her body. Her bed? No. Not possible! She knew with no doubt that she'd collapsed in the family room after seeing... Daddy. Impossible! It was obviously a dream. Absolutely without a doubt. Wasn't it? She sat there thinking past the fog that still blanketed her mind and stared off into the distance of her bedroom.

Rachel's day was as hectic as all the rest -including a trip to the DMV to get her license renewed; a visit made all the more irritating by the jackass in front of her in line- and as she slouched into her front door the sensation of both being comfortably home and fearfully in a house that produced such a real-world nightmare that she'd felt it throughout the day hit her twofold. She dropped her keys in their pottery bowl, hung her jacket over the door hook, and looked off into the dimly lit room still safely brightened by the wavering setting sun casting purple stripes through the blinds. She was dead tired, but at the same time had almost no desire to go to her room to bed. But it was finally common sense that made her roll her eyes and walk with trepidation to her room.

Rachel once more began to undress; she slipped the disk-shaped medallion she frequently wore from her neck, stripped down to her underwear, and slid into her nightshirt. Slowly the need to sleep enveloped her and as she sunk beneath her covers, relishing the cool comfort, all thoughts of the previous night faded away.

The first thud jostled her awake at a quarter to one. Her heart hammered a vicious drum beat in her throat and she quickly clamored out of bed. The next thud rocked her on her feet and the bed shook violently. She whimpered and ran for the door. Back in the family room she was once again brought to tears by the horrifying apparition that hung in front of her disbelieving eyes. Her deceased father was both passing through the ceiling and passing into the room. His wavering shape blurred and cleared back and forth; he was both there and not there, recognizable, and amorphous, her father and a mist. Her fear was at its zenith... and then the phantasm froze. It turned and looked directly at her, and through her. Rachel was paralyzed with terror.

His mouth worked. It didn't make a sound, but it made the motions. It mouthed "You" repeatedly and held a finger accusatorially at his daughter. Rachel saw black for the last time. As she faded into sleep, her final rest, the last thought that passed through her mind was that of her dad, happy.

Tales of The Amulet
Part 44: The End

1.

Waves lapped at the little wooden dock like hungry tongues exploring the remaining bits on a corndog stick. The old lumber was rotted and spongy, but it held through the years and the seasons on the shore of the aged fishing cabin in Connecticut. The inlet was relatively secluded and didn't often get either the human traffic or the battering waves of the Atlantic, so the dilapidated timber that securely held the old launch a few feet above the water line never got more than just splashed repeatedly rather than drown.

Until now.

It was Sunday. James Wickford was eyeing his kayak as he nibbled on a bologna sandwich. He knelt and flicked at a pretty plump spider that meandered around the boat's bench. It looked clean enough, and James was ready for his regular Sunday jaunt into the sea with his fishing gear. From the peripheral vision of his left eye, he caught motion and a series of concentric circles indicative of ripples. This wasn't anything unusual, there was always something swimming by or moving around down there… but this time, something seemed immediately different. A mound slowly rose to the surface; drab green and flecked with mud and slick with a substance that reflected streaks of sunlight. The mound rapidly grew larger as water rained down and muck slid off the oily object and hit the suddenly churning water in heavy plops. James Wickford dropped his sandwich, shivered where he stood, and began to howl with crippling fear in the back of his throat. His legs only worked a little and he physically shook as he worked them to back up. But his journey was short lived, and he tripped over an exposed stump and flopped to the damp earth.

The mound became a massive ribbed and horned mountain. The newly exposed humps and knobs that attached themselves to the original mound surfaced just under the little dock and proceeded to shatter it to bits with a wet, coughing crunch. The planks that attached themselves to the shore peeled up like loosened teeth, and then they too, twisted and snapped. From the hidden inlet, the otherwise calm and peaceful fishing spot became a churning, torrential maelstrom. And then, what was once but a filthy hulk, now stood forty feet tall, dripping feverishly with water and some kind of thick, oily mass, and looked around both curiously and uncaring at its surroundings. The creature's head was free, and James could hear its raspy, soggy breathing. He'd never seen anything so big in all his life, even having once been whale-watching. He fought to stand; his brain fought to get him moving, fought to get him to run back to the house and speed away in his truck, but his legs refused to respond and so he sat, and he felt his bowels release.

Its snout spouted putrid, green fumes and a deep, guttural thrum echoed from somewhere far within the beast. Its nothingness-black eyes surveyed the landscape and spotted just below it the quaking form of something… something showing tremendous fear. The beast slowly leaned forward, arms broke the surface of the water, but they were arms like none other ever seen. Where elbows were, attached to an upper arm –as gigantic as a tree trunk- were not one arm (radius and ulna) but two complete sets both ending in horrific talons, freely dripping with fetid slime. The immense beast pulled itself forward and bent down to come face to humongous face with the cowering thing on the ground. James began to scurry backward, catching his pants on gnarly bits of fauna, and pulling them free, smearing the ground with feces. But the beast continued forward, suddenly stretching its incredible jaws, jutted on every inch with crusty, rotting teeth. The cacophonous belching howl that spat forth from the opening mouth split the heavens with its tone, and the frightened being dropped dead to the ground.

The rest of the creature excised itself from the little cove and stood erect, but not on legs. The beast, now nearly a hundred feet tall, spread apart several trees with its claws, and called out again with a terrible, echoing squeal. Just below its waist was the rest of its body, coiling and writhing like a massive snake. It was riddled from front to back with gleaming barnacle-like thorns, each oozing freely with reeking and viscous fluid. The beast inched forth as sticky slime coated its trail in a thick veneer, and the run-off slowly dissipated into the earth and everything around it. As it touched the dead body of James Wickford –the body that was scared and deafened to death by the incredible monster- the corpse twitched. The thick mucus spread across the body of James. He suddenly jerked and jolted… and slowly stood, gaping into the void.

2.

Eric Watson lowered his cupped hands and listened intently to his own echo reverberate through the Northern Michigan forest. He and his crew –Aaron Phelps, Kevin Marrick, and Danielle Furst- the NMSA (Northern Michigan Sasquatch Association) had spent the better part of the last four days hiking camping, and otherwise scouring the forests of Marquette, Munising, and Ishpeming setting laser-site traps, night-vision camera perimeters, and basically globally positioning every piece of land they could in an attempt to once and for all prove the existence of Big Foot. So far, their efforts had more or less come up fruitless, often only hearing possible calls, spotting and casting slightly iffy footprints, and seeing occasional deer bones scattered about. But they were stolid in their drive, and relentless in their work, so they kept up their collective spirits by making every little find a huge deal. So far, it appeared to be working.

"Nice call, Eric! I could hear that one clearly way over here! Over…" Aaron said into his walkie-talkie as he squatted a few hundred yards away from Eric and Kevin.

The return report crackled through the radio, "Thanks. That one was built on pure adrenalin. I'm getting a little worn out. I mean it's, uh… pushing four a.m. We're gonna lose daylight here pretty soon."

"True. We'll start making our way toward you guys, maybe we— "

The last bit of Aaron's words caught in his throat. A few feet to his left he could make out the crystal-clear sounds of something approaching very quickly. Twigs snapped under the footfalls and a deep, hollow breathing huffed with each movement. Aaron froze where he stood. He slowly reached to his right and yanked on Danielle's thick jacket. Aaron turned to look at her and she, too, was standing, mouth agape and wide-eyed, staring in the direction of the sounds. She nodded slowly and swallowed heavily with an audible click that seemed to echo all too loudly. Aaron and Danielle stared into the cold, inky blackness as what they were tracking methodically stomped through the underbrush and nonchalantly pressed its way through low tree branches, sometimes snapping a few, letting them fall to the ground. The noise got ever closer; Aaron and Danielle heard nothing else but the ruckus that was occurring just to their left. The pine trees rattled, the forest floor rumbled, and the darkness line suddenly got just that much darker. The overpowering odor that wafted through the cloying, resinous pine was horrifying. Aaron and Danielle did all they could not to vomit on the spot. It smelled like putrid, rotting flesh, dead fish, and wet dog.

The slowly rising sun lit the dead black night like luminescent, white ghost. In the extremely dim glow, Aaron and Danielle could now make out a hazy silhouette of the creature that towered before them. It was nearly ten feet tall, covered skull to ankles in thick, course fur, and had a slightly primate-like face. Its oval head was bare, but splotched with burrs and bits of twigs. Its visage hung long as its nostrils yawned with every throaty, wheezing breath. It snuffed, tested the air, and at first looked right over the heads of the two petrified shapes standing directly in front of it…

Until one of them let forth an ear-splitting wail.

Aaron recoiled just slightly as Danielle bellowed a scream that could only have come from the depths of her very soul. The hulking beast took a step back, snorted, and howled with a throat-wrenching call that sent birds chattering out of the trees.

Suddenly the two-way radio clipped at Aaron's belt barked to life, "Wow, guys! Those calls were amazing! I thought we were calling it a day? Over."

The hairy creature eyed the black box from which the voice came, stared directly at the two beings standing like statues, and by its own instinctive nature, shot out its sinewy, muscular arm and grasped the first thing by the throat, lifting it to its feet.

Danielle squealed, almost inaudibly, in the back of her throat as she was instantly lifted from the ground by her neck. The sasquatch's hand was the size of a baseball glove; roughly furred and studded with filthy, black nails. She was brought face to face with the beast as he explored her with a side-long, curious look. The monster's mouth burst open. Flecks of warm spittle spattered Danielle's face as she saw massive fangs like dirty steak knives. And then it came at her throat.

3.

Paige Wilson drank the last few gulps from her umpteenth can of pop, belched triumphantly, and chucked the empty into the collection box. The array of terminals at which she was currently staring glowed in front of her like a battalion of readied robots; each empty, unblinking eye awaiting orders from their human master. Paige worked for a small company sanctioned by a hush-hush Government subsidy that spent sleepless nights gazing into the cosmos for any and all signs of potential life. The crew- including Paige herself- were all secretly certain that there really was nothing out there, but a big fat paycheck was a big fat paycheck, regardless of the dullness and utter pointlessness of the job itself.

The little concrete building that sat above ground, and marked the actual entrance to the company, was built in Baltimore, Maryland and was marked, rather inconspicuously, TBIRC – Authorized Personnel Only Beyond This Point. This rather lackluster acronym stood for The Baltimore Inter-Galactic Research Society. The company sat underground as to distance itself from as much of Earth's own interference as possible and used twenty-four satellites strategically placed throughout a six-block radius. It housed a group of scientists hand-picked through a government program back in 1992 to scour the skies every night for any cough emitting from any distant location in space. Besides Paige, there were sixteen others, each at their own set of screens staring intently at their own quadrants of the void. So far, there had been eight incidences of potential white noise coming from huge distances, and, sadly, each had been debunked as either outer-planetary interference or, oddly, the sounds of dying solar systems. So, basically, over the past 20 years, the persistent crew had found nothing.

Until now.

Paige began sipping the fresh foam from another opened can of soda, when a very unusual anomaly appeared on the top row of eight screens. She swallowed, as such surprise was known to bring on unwarranted spitting, shook her head thinking false alarm, and stared anew at the rather quickly moving hash mark. Not only was it still there and still approaching a vector very near Earth, but it was also moving at a clip she'd only seen in meteors and comets. And it didn't look at all like a piece of space detritus or a dirty snowball. In fact, it looked sharply angled and… metallic?

Paige immediately angled her headset mouthpiece, pressed the call button, and hailed her superior, Dr. Runjeet Ashraff. Fifty yards down the hall, Dr. Ashraff's remote communications display showed a blinking light, and he begrudgingly set aside the unspooled pages of read-out data and left his office.

"Miss Wilson, I was alerted to your communication. Is something amiss?" Dr. Ashraff inquired in his still-quite-thick Indian accent.

"Yes, sir!" Paige replied hurriedly, "Take a look at this! I've been tracking its trajectory for a few minutes now and it appears as though it is heading directly for Earth!"

Runjeet bent at the waist, dropped his glasses from his head to his face, and stared intently at the top row of display screens. After only a few seconds it appeared that what Paige was referring to was exactly correct.

"It certainly doesn't appear to be any form of cosmic debris. We haven't been tracking any sort of off-track meteors or comets, have we? No... no. That's impossible..." Dr. Ashraff traced his finger along the projected path of the oncoming object.

"As you can see, Doctor, the object appears to be sharply angled and even made of some kind of metal. It almost looks like a US Military Stealth Fighter in many ways, except it isn't black and there might be... yes! Look! Are those lights blinking? My God!" Paige turned to look at a stunned Dr. Ashraff who had quickly begun to sweat on his balding scalp.

"Security Code Alpha Zero-Zero Tango," Dr. Ashraff instantly tapped one of the many communication outlets on his mobile device and was immediately put through to the supporting Government section in charge of the TBIRC, "This is Dr. Runjeet Ashraff of the TBIRC in Maryland, Colonel. Yes sir, it appears we have discovered some kind of incoming anomaly just outside the distance of the sun, sir. Yes sir, it does appear to be on a course for Earth. No, sir, we are as yet unsure of its size. Yes, sir we will keep you informed. Yes sir. Thank you."

Soon a crowd of scientists nearest Paige's readout were ogling the display and offering their own insight as to what it might be. Dr. Ashraff alerted everyone to return to their stations and switch their displays to the same quadrant Paige herself was studying.

Runjeet turned to Paige, his face ashen with fear, and continued following the path of the UFO.

4.

Towering, fifty-foot conifer trees toppled like stacks of lose cards. Oaks and elms were carelessly felled like models made from toothpicks, and the very ground itself sighed and retched as the ambling beast slithered across the landscape bound for nowhere. The small forest parted and revealed a freeway that led to the deeper parts of town. Trees dropped across the asphalt like slain soldiers and lay about, damming up traffic. The rapidly collapsing flora proved too much for the speeding cars; no one could break in time and the resounding squeals and wrenching, broken metal sent arcs of flame into the early morning sky. As drivers and passengers began to slow at the realization of a massive accident, it became all too apparent that something horrible and ghastly was moving across the twisted wreckage. The onlookers, some young children, and others with weak constitutions, wailed the call of the damned into the air and fainted dead away. Others scrambled free of their cars, leaving them running, and fled hollering into the woods. The monster paid no mind and retained its path to wherever it was headed.

As the creature slid remorselessly over the carnage it caused, its barnacles leaked ceaselessly about the gnarled metal and the hideously slaughtered bodies therein. It's vile, tacky slime drenched the corpses, thickly coating them in a fluid veneer. The dead twitched, released themselves from their steel coffins, and joined the march behind the winding beast. One by one, each and every slain man, woman, and child dug itself free from the terrible chrome and aluminum madness and shambled forth dropping severed limbs and broken parts on the way as they fell in line behind the others.

Those still alive and watching in icy horror saw first-hand the reanimation of bodies they'd once witnessed die in ghastly wrecks. The living looked on as a parade of the most impossible of nightmares ambled forth.

Lynn Harper –with her three-year old daughter, Anna, cradled in her shuddering arms- stepped from her still-intact car (having missed the last vehicle in the long line of destroyed autos by mere feet) and stared, dumbfounded as only thirty yards away, hitching, puppet-like corpses meandered out of their contorted, stannic coffins. The scene was just too overwhelming.

Lynn exploded with a deafening scream that startled her daughter and set her, too, into fits of braying weeps. Thirty yards away, with the immediate suddenness of an instant, one of the dawdling cadavers stopped short at the sound of human noise. Lynn snapped her mouth shut and instinctively put a cupped hand over her daughter's mouth. Others had gathered behind her and were pointing ahead at several of the moving dead now changing course at the sudden realization that there were living humans not far away. Without missing a beat, Lynn hugged her child closer, and began shoving her way out of the gathering crowd of motorists.

Now within twenty yards, several of the dead were scrabbling their way across the wreckage.

5.

The obscured, opaque slits that were Danielle's eyes struggled to focus. She could hear crunching and feel slight tickling as she wiggled her body, so she knew she was lying flat on the forest floor. She slowly took in a comforting, steadying breath and blinked the blur out of her vision. It was early morning, which made sense considering the last time she could remember anything the rising sun had just begun tinting the horizon with its milky glow. Birds were twittering in low branches and Danielle felt as though she could hear something small pattering across the underbrush. Then the sun went black, and Danielle caught her breath.

Standing above her was a tall silhouette with its hand extended.

"You alright?" It was Aaron. He knelt and offered his hand.

"Dunno… guess so…" Danielle said as she struggled to a sitting position. "Wh… uh… what ha-happened?"

Aaron unscrewed the top of a water bottle and handed to Danielle as she swooned a bit and bobbed her head. "I, uh… can't seem to remember much myself. Well, everything up until the 'squatch picked you up, I can. After that: nothing. Do you even remember that?"

Danielle stared intently at Aaron for a very long minute and eventually shook her head in both amazement and complete puzzlement.

"A sasquatch picked me up? You mean like…" Danielle animated being lifted as though in a cradled position.

Aaron shook his head and sat next to Danielle. "Nope. He got you by the neck, babe. Lifted you right off your feet. With one hand…" He trailed off as he looked off into nowhere.

"Well, I guess that explains why my neck and head… shoulders too… are killing me. Did he just drop me and run off?"

Aaron shook his head again. "I don't know. I remember seeing you, you were screaming and… I went to punch… ya know, hit the thing… and that's the last I remember. That's it."

Danielle took another swig of the cooling water and pressed the half-full bottle to her throbbing neck. She sighed, looked around instinctively worried something might still be out there- and leaned her head on Aaron's shoulder. "So, where's Eric and Kevin?"

"They caught up with us just as I was getting up, a few minutes ago. They ran back to the truck to get a few supplies and call an ambulance. They –well me too- thought you were…" Aaron touched Danielle's leg and smiled.

"Well, that's very chivalrous of them. Maybe you should radio and tell them I'm okay." She returned the sentiment and put her hand on Aaron's.

"Can't," Aaron said as he fished it from his pocket. "Broke. Must have happened during the scuffle. Oh well, you should probably get looked at anyway." He stood, returned the damaged radio to his pocket and stretched with audible pops.

"I suppose. I feel like I got hit by a bus. And…" Danielle pulled the now sticky water bottle away from her neck, "It looks as though I'm bleeding. In two spots…"

On the right side of Danielle's neck - just below her jaw- were two, centimeter-diameter, punctures, both still weeping with clotting blood.

6.

Paige Wilson ticked a few strokes on her keyboard and watched the screen zoom in closer to the unidentified object making its way toward Earth. Her heart was beating so hard and fast that she could hear it in her ears. Her eyes were glossy, and a lone tear escaped across her cheek, but she wasn't sure if it was because she was so overwhelmingly excited at the current circumstances or scared beyond all comprehension. Either way, she swiped at it, took a deep breath to steady herself –this was no time to start breaking down- and checked the count-down to when the object was due to enter the atmosphere.

1:24:37 – Less than ninety minutes.

Dr. Runjeet Ashraff recognized the clear signs of Paige's emotions, because he, too, shared the same feelings but was surely not going to show his cracks to his crew; they relied on him to lead, and to do so without jumping for joy or especially breaking down. So, he stared with renewed interest at the screen as Paige zoomed in further showing the anomaly still on a beeline for Earth. And he, too, saw that there were less than ninety minutes until its potential entrance into the sky. Thirty more minutes and he would have no choice but to contact the higher authorities at the White House. But for now, he had no choice but to watch… and wait.

Up until now, the UFO was little more than a tiny, possibly metallic blip on the screen, but just then something happened; something no one could have possibly expected. The object suddenly expanded to nearly three-times its original size and appeared to sprout nodes from all of its three sides. What was once a perfect triangle was now more similar to an odd, molecular-type structure: a three-sided craft with four outcroppings on each side each ending in a smaller, round 'polyp'. It now began to take on more of an organic shape than just a straight-sided triangle. Paige gasped and began to shiver. Dr. Ashraff could no longer hold back and he, too, let out a moan.
1:19:19

7.

As you enter the town of Candlebrook, Connecticut, the first thing you notice is the quaint little shop owned by Marg Fields called 'Olden Times'. She and her husband, Carl, bought the run-down building back in 1964 and immediately began stocking it with bits and pieces of their own personal collection of gathered things from years past: rocking chairs, cabinets, China sets, baby clothes, old pictures, and any number of other forms of bric-a-brac. Since then, it has become the most well-known and deeply cherished stores in the burg. It was the first to be reduced to crumpled timber and felled bricks. In the creature's wake the building looked like a smashed model. And the bodies of Marg and Carl shuffled behind it smeared with a slick sheen.

8.

Danielle looked, stunned, at her palm. It was tacky and bright red. Aaron raised an eyebrow and stared, concerned at Danielle's face. She sighed forth a gruff laugh and wiped her hand on her pants. Aaron shook his head with a wry little smile, and kneeled, anew, at Danielle's side. She coyly grinned, stared at the ground, and lifted her hand once again to her neck. Her middle finger lightly prodded the puncture wounds, feeling them run slightly with thin rivulets of blood, slowly clotting. Aaron tore off a piece of his under shirt and began to fold it into a bandage. Danielle raised her gaze, peered longingly at Aaron as he gingerly leaned forward ready to wrap the makeshift dressing around her neck, and their eyes met.

Aaron and Danielle had never been anything more than just great friends. Sure, there were moments between them that were often misconstrued as flirty situations, but nothing ever went further than fawning and almost brotherly-sisterly fooling around. Last summer, they almost decided to date; they each discussed the possibility with their cadre of friends, everyone already assuming that something was, in fact, going on. Their friends were thrilled and wondered how it hadn't happened long ago; citing their years-long friendships and secret love for one another. But nothing ever materialized, and they just went on being friends… good friends.

As Aaron put his arms around Danielle's neck –gently avoiding bumping the wounds- she tilted her head to the side and gasped, with a moan, letting him take her in his embrace.

Aaron got as far as placing his hands on Danielle's shoulders, working the compress around her neck, when he felt her warm breath just below his throat. Her soft lips grazed his flesh and he immediately exploded in goose bumps. He inhaled sharply, pretending to ignore the feeling he had lancing through his body: ecstasy, joy, desire… the feelings he'd always secretly hidden from Danielle; hidden behind walls of play and childish goofing. The warmth of her mouth pressed into Aaron's neck and worked its way down nearly to his shoulder, and then back up. Aaron did all he could to concentrate on sealing Danielle's wounds under the cloth, while at the same time only thinking of the torrent of fluttering feelings arcing through his suddenly too hot body. He groaned, deep and fulfilling in his throat. It was a groan that had been pent up for years, longing to be released in Danielle's passionate embrace. He shuddered, dropped the torn bit of T-shirt around Danielle's shoulders, and let himself fall into the feelings he'd never known…

Danielle's fangs pierced deeply into Aaron's jugular, and his elation blocked out all the pain.

9.

Eric Watson and Kevin Marrick stepped out of the woods and off the two-foot drop onto the shoulder of the road. Their SUV sat parked, secluded by a few trees and blanketed by a Navy-surplus camouflage net that looked remarkably like loose leaves and low-hanging branches. Eric snatched the leading edge of the false-flora tarp and yanked it free from the hood and the windshield.

"So, do you think Danni and Aaron saw something back there?" Kevin asked as he began loading his gear into the back seat, "She sure looked pretty banged up."

"Yeah, she did. I dunno… I guess." Eric laid the net on the ground and began haphazardly folding it up, "I mean I want to believe… I want to… well I guess it doesn't matter; the point is she is banged up. We should probably get to the nearest…

The trees just past their vehicle began to shudder and sharp snaps emitted from the footfalls of some approaching thing. The saplings along the woods edge spread mere feet from where Eric and Kevin left them moments earlier, and a sudden, penetrating wall of odor hit the two men waiting fearfully by the SUV.

"Son of b…" Eric began as he continued stuffing the tarp into the back seat. "Oh… oh man…"

Kevin stared at the approaching thing, still buried in shadow. He slowly began to slide into the driver's seat and watched, completely dumbfounded as a towering sasquatch strode into view. In ear-splitting screams, the man-beast let forth a cry that startled the men so completely that they shook and covered their ears and squinted their eyes. Suddenly, the front of the SUV dipped down sharply as the bigfoot, now close enough to touch, pressed on the hood and shoved it to the ground. The metal crumpled, the window split and spider-webbed, and the bumper exploded from the frame and clunked to the road.
Kevin fumbled the key into the ignition, turned it to fire the engine, and immediately slipped off the fob as the front end was once again pressed rapidly toward the ground. Once again, the world was broken by the deafening scream of another call as the beast climbed the vehicle and stood,

howling into the sky. Kevin froze as a filthy, fur-coated fisted hand burst through the windshield and snagged him by the jacket. Eric reached across his lap, turned the key completely, and the engine roared to life. In the dirty grip of the monster, Kevin managed to focus just for a minute and slammed on the gas.

The SUV remained in Park and the engine revved as the wild sasquatch tore free the ruined window, climbed into the front, and fed.

10.

1:15:45

Paige Wilson drummed her pen against her chin nervously. The UFO, which had previously been making a direct course for Earth, had completely stopped moving. The side of Paige's screen ran with numbers that gave approximate distances and even an area of the craft within inches of its actual size. From where it was currently stalled, it measured a radius nearly the size of a standard city. It was far bigger than anyone had anticipated from its earlier location: yes, it grew some as it change shape, but no one could have guessed that it had gotten big enough to dwarf a small town. And Paige could do nothing more than stare at the hovering, slowly rotating object.

Dr. Runjeet Ashraff was in the middle of his fifth phone call to the White House. He had yet to be directly connected to the President, but he knew that it was imperative that it happen very, very quickly. Finally, he heard a click on the other end and a voice break the silence.

"This is Secretary of State Parker. I will be speaking to you, Dr. Ashraff, along with President Haynes on a three-party line. Please, doctor, tell us exactly what you've discovered," The Secretary's voice was indifferent and surprisingly calm.

"Yes sirs. At about 18-hundred hours, the TBIRC –that is to say Paige Wilson of the TBIRC- discovered an anomaly on a direct course for Earth coming from deep space. We immediately determined that it wasn't categorized as any form of space debris or commonly known cosmic occurrence," Dr. Ashraff continued to the highest officials in the free world.

"Was the object exhibiting any kind of offensive maneuvers?" This was the President's voice, and Dr. Ashraff suppressed an urge to blurt out a child-like 'hello'.

"No, sir. It was merely –as far as we could ascertain at the moment- just heading toward Earth. However- "

"However?" The Secretary interrupted.

"Uh… y-yes sir. However, the craft did… *change*. In midflight. Sir." Dr. Ashraff wiped a bead of sweat from his brow and snuck a sip of water to quench his suddenly killing thirst.

"Did you say it 'changed'? How did it change, doctor?" The President once again inquired.

"Well, sir… it appeared to… grow." Runjeet sat back in his chair and looked side-long at Paige.

She turned to Dr. Ashraff with a look of shocked horror plastered across her face. "And, uh, doctor… still growing."

11.

Beth Tennant sat bolt-upright in bed and tried desperately to focus on the bed-side clock. She was coated in sweat and shuddering, even as she sat absolutely freezing. The nightmare she'd been jostled from was ferocious, but it was the sound like an ear-shattering—

Explosion...

There it was again: the sound of a distant explosion. Oh no! Was it happening again? She'd been far too close to the September 11th attacks that the slightest noise of something blowing up –that wasn't happening on July 4th- jarred her terribly. She leaned over the side of her bed and stared out her bedroom window. Her single-bedroom, sixteenth-floor apartment had a pretty awesome view of the city, and she was able to get a good look at much of the horizon. It was three fifteen a.m., and the inky black night coated the entire city only broken by slight halos of streetlamps and 24-Hour store fronts.

In the distance, perhaps a few miles south, came another muffled whump followed by a shower of sparks. The object immediately silhouetted against the plume of sparkling flame was unimaginably enormous. For the split-second Beth saw it, the hideous form of the thing was etched in her retinas forever. And then she heard it, too.

Over the deep, echoing boom of the next fountain of fiery bursts, Beth distinctly heard a throaty wail that vibrated through to her very core. Beth's eyes took in the horror once again and could plainly make out a body, and large, scrabbling arms attached to… a writhing snake body? Beth was now sure she must still be asleep. There was no way what she was seeing could possibly be real. Another blinding flash flowered even closer to Beth's apartment, maybe only a mile away this time, and it shook the ground so violently that she was knocked precariously from her bed and fell, painfully, to her knees on the floor. Suddenly her clock winked out and the bathroom light she always left on went pitch dark. This was definitely not a dream.

As scared as she was, Beth couldn't tear her view away from the catastrophe happening to her city. Noises she'd apparently blocked out as she was waking up to the awful sights began to flood her ears: cars were blasting their horns, sirens were crying out from any number of emergency vehicles, and the sounds of panicked screams carried throughout the night. Peril was setting in and she once again watched helplessly as madness gripped the town.

So, close it rattled the teeth in her skull, the thing that was laying waste to everything Beth loved barked a shrill, guttural call into the sky. She instinctively slapped her hands over her ears and scooted back against her wall, no longer interested in seeing the hellish reality playing out before her like an all-too authentic horror movie. Her mind had taken in all it could handle, and all Beth could do was sit back and add her fearful screams into the cacophony of the dying city.

12.

As the deep ochre sun gave up its last gasp beyond the edge of the earth, the waxing moments of early dark spread their cloaking deep blues across the forest.

Aaron and Danielle held each other, suppressing the onset of shivers that come with the approaching night. But this time, the chill of the air meant nothing to them as their embrace was of passion and desire, and not that of warmth. Aaron looked to the sky and grinned; it was a grin of enameled daggers and of opalescent, feral needles. He parted his fangs to take in the scents and breathe deep the clean night air, but for the first time since the very moment he cried as a birthed infant, he felt no need to inhale. In fact, his body showed no signs of even having the suffocating want to perform such natural habits. It was a curious feeling, but not all together unpleasant; though there was a tinge of fear somewhere deep in his psyche, it soon faded.

He looked down at Danielle and she, too, smirked up at him and he noticed that her chest as well did not have that familiar rise and fall of a human's respiration. And the answer to his unasked question suddenly became all too obvious: Danielle and Aaron were no longer the standard definition of human.

"Wow. Is this… is this magic?" Aaron asked as he gently released Danielle and moved to stand.

Danielle giggled a little and shrugged her shoulders, obviously just as shocked as Aaron, "I don't know. Maybe? But what I do know is that is feels… free!"

"Yeah… that's the word I was trying to find, 'free'. Boy, for a day spent searching for creatures of myth and legend, who would have guessed that we'd end up as entirely different creatures of myth and legend!"

Danielle laughed harder this time and stood as well, "I can feel my teeth. They're so sharp! Oh, and I'm really sorry I bit you... I mean, I guess I could have warned you first."

"Oh, no... don't apologize... don't apologize at all! This is the coolest thing that's ever happened to me. And I'm glad it happened with you, Danni."

"Me too. I think I might... love you, actually." Danielle leaned her head onto Aaron's shoulder and kissed him gently on the cheek.

"Well," Aaron asked as he returned his affection to Danielle, "Now what do we do? Should we try to find Kevin and Eric. I bet they'd just love this! Oh, and I've always loved you... but now, somehow even more."

Danielle's eyes suddenly got brighter, more erratic. She furrowed her brow and leered at Aaron, "Now that is a good idea... besides, I'm suddenly really hungry... but it's not a stomach growling kind of hunger..."

"Now that you mention it... it's almost like a, I don't know, a longing for something..." Aaron confirmed as he absently wiped and the slowly congealing blood that clung to his neck.

In a blink, Danielle's mouth was enclosing Aaron's blood-dampened fingers, and a low, animalistic slurping escaped her lips.

Aaron sighed, licked his incisors, and nodded, "It's blood. That's what I want... blood!"

Danielle continued to lap up the last stains of red from Aaron's fingers, "Let's go get it!"

13.

The trail of death left in the wake of the towering; rampaging creature grew in vast numbers as every minute passed. The monster slithered like an enormous eel over the bricks and mortar, the flattened metal and glass, and the demolished homes, schools, businesses, and churches as it continued its unabated trek through city after city. But the dead didn't stay dead, for as the nightmarish beast trampled humanity with every twist and turn of its incredible bulk, it also oozed its unnatural slime like some kind of hell-spawn slug.

The gloppy, dripping opaque paste fell upon everything, including the bodies that lay crushed and mutilated by the unearthly thing. And as each became covered in the wretched cocoon, they began to violently shudder, scream out with the continued death-knells they fell proclaiming, and begin to walk anew. And now the marching masses of the once dead numbered in the thousands. Their chittering, gibbering mouths yawned and flexed with gore... and hunger. The dead that followed the monster without thought or hesitation began to search on their own, for prey; their insatiable feasting spread further from the lumbering parade that once stuck close to the massive hulk, and now moved out to attack those left alive after the initial devastation fell upon the cities and towns. The starving, gaping maws of the somehow living corpses fell upon those that stopped even for a second to see the unimaginable horror unfold before them. Children were wrenched from weeping parent's arms; the pleading parents were then, too, engulfed by the encroaching hordes of the unnaturally fixated cadavers that ran freely through the war-torn streets.

And the unstoppable terror that tore the undefended land asunder continued without a thought. Perhaps it was possible that the hideous giant had no thought; perhaps it was possible that it had no clear course, but just to move on as it always had on the lands and places from whence it came. But in its aftermath, it left smoldering ruins, unfathomable destruction, and army after army of the traveling undead.

14.

Dr. Ashraff stared at the monitor. It was the same monitor he'd been examining for the past several hours, and up until now nothing had really changed much. But as he watched with a new chilling fascination, the metallic craft that had hovered just outside of the earthen atmosphere began to literally unfold into something entirely different; something that –even as it shifted and eerily morphed- fluidly became an entirely new shape. What was more or less a triangle with individual nodes sprouting from its three sides suddenly and without warning became a much more of an octagon with an attached circular ring outlining the perimeter.

"Dr. Ashraff! What is going on!" It was the Secretary of State's voice echoing tinnily from the speaker of the phone that hung limply in the doctor's hand, "Doctor! Answer me, dammit!"

"S-s-sir… y-y-yes sir, I'm sorry… I, uh, would suggest that you show Mr. President the, um, special monitor we ha-"Dr. Ashraff was suddenly cut off.

"No! Doctor, you know damn well that that knowledge is completely privileged! What gives you the right to-"The Secretary, too, was broken up in mid speech.

"I'm sorry, Mr. Secretary," The President began, "Am I missing something here?"

"Sir, not a thing, sir. Dr. Ashraff was misspeaking. He has no idea- "

"Mr. Secretary, you will keep your mouth shut until I am through speaking to Dr. Ashraff. Doctor, please continue… you were saying something about a 'special monitor'?

"Sir, yes sir," Runjeet began as he swallowed hard and continued focusing more of his attention on the UFO reforming in front of his face, "The special monitor was installed by our corporation previous to your administration. It is specifically used –and most strictly- for occasions such as this… uh, sir."

"You mean to tell me, Mr. Secretary, that I have had a monitor the entire three years I have sat as President, and I am now – during a potentially incredibly dangerous situation- just finding out about this? Please tell me this is not what I am – failing- to understand."

Secretary of State Parker breathed heavily into the line. He was audibly upset at both Dr. Ashraff's outburst, and at President Haynes' irritation. He had been sworn not to announce the presence of the monitor that would keep the President –he of strict honesty and over-zealous information giving- completely in the clouds. That is, he angrily had to admit, unless something just like this were to happen. He had no other choice.

"Yes, Mr. President. That is the truth." Secretary Parker begrudgingly admitted with a deep sigh.

"I see. Well then, what I want –what I want right now- is for you to make this monitor available to me. Please hang up your end and go do as I ask. Now. And as for you, Dr. Ashraff, I'd like you to hold the line while I transfer phones so you and I can finally look at this thing together. Is that okay?"

"Absolutely, sir. It is my pleasure to share with you any and all information I have found." Dr. Ashraff admitted as a little smile danced across his face.

Paige noted his rapid change in facial features and turned quickly back to the screen that she, too, had been staring at for what seemed like forever. And as she did, the newly shaped craft began to once again move toward Earth.

15.

Cradled in the mottled hairy arms of the lumbering sasquatch dangled the limp bodies of two human men. The nearly human big foot walked on to its forest nest as confused as a little child, and not really understanding why it had the bloodied and battered corpses of two male people draped over its furry shoulders. It had encountered people before, but always from a distance and it had never, under any circumstances, come into close contact with them. But lately, for some reason, all the gentle giant wanted to do was to find them, touch them, and destroy them. But why didn't the other two stay dead? It could not comprehend why, though it had bitten the woman severely and strangled her, she continued to live? It had no real reason to hurt people, it had no carnal want to harm humans... but here it was just the same: people were bad; people were the enemy and it had to kill.

Movement against the beast's chest startled it and it stopped in its tracks. It snuffed in surprise and dropped the bodies just as one began to twist his head and open his eyes. The sasquatch stepped back and grunted a confused bark. From the damp forest floor, the humans stirred and moaned, shifted and stretched.

"Uh... what... what's happening?" Eric pleaded as he slowly groped at the darkened wet leaves.

The towering ape-like creature ducked into the deep black shadow of a tree and as were its natural instincts, remained absolutely still and deafeningly quiet. He watched in what to it was similar to a human being flabbergasted as the people writhed and spoke on the ground in front of him. He was, for the first time that his unknowing mind could fathom, frightened.

"Wow… I, uh… I dunno. I don't even know where we are? Last thing I can remember… weren't we in the car?" Kevin replied as he, too, fought to regain his consciousness.

Eric rubbed his quavering hands over his face and neck, and they came away tacky with what could only have been drying blood. He opened his palms and even in the deeply darkened night, it was still obvious they were coated with sticky blood.

"Why… why am I all bloody?"

"Yeah, and look at me!" Kevin cried as he held up his own open, splayed fingers.

As Eric leaned in to examine Kevin in the shrouded early night, his tongue just naturally snuck out as it would anyone in any kind of concentration… and that's when he felt them: his teeth were finely pointed daggers. He immediately flung open his mouth and began to explore his newfound fangs with both his tongue and his fingers, at the same time momentarily intrigued by the residual clotting blood still coating them. "Thweet Jeethuth, Kev… are…are your theeth tharp, too?"

"Are my wha—"Kevin began as it quickly dawned on him what his friend was trying to say, "What the…"

Though the sasquatch only understood a few small English words -much like a dog or a primate would comprehend a few- it could tell just by how they were probing each other's mouths in utter fascination that something highly unusual was playing out before it. It was now so scared it began to cry and softly wail to itself.

In unison, the boys looked rapidly in the precise direction of the big foot, and in the shadowy eve, they both grinned the grin of the hungry.

16.

The terrorized people of the city of New York fled in panic as the mammoth, hideous creature laid waste to everything in its path. Though the monster had no clear direction and was seemingly only wreaking havoc at random, the barrage of walking dead –corpses shimmering in the early morning light with a patina of viscous slime oozed upon them from the beast itself- were suddenly realizing that they needed, perhaps wanted to feed. And feed they did: as the large city's inhabitants scurried, awash with horror and blinding fear, the shambling carcasses that were once human citizens snagged them in their tracks and bore down upon them with ravenous and insatiable appetites.
***

"Channel 9, Action News, this is Frank O'Brien with a special report." The interrupting signal of a bulletin broke into every station, both local and those like CNN and CNBC, "The city of New York is once again under attack, however in a completely different, seemingly more horrifying –and certainly less understood way, today. For on the horizon behind me you can plainly see some kind of towering creature demolishing everything it its path. Authorities have just been made aware that this –thing- for lack of a better term made its way inland from a small cove in Connecticut. What it is, where it came from, and why it's here are all, as yet unanswered questions.

As you can also see, circling above it are numerous military helicopters and we have just been informed that more vehicles are en route including tanks and armored vehicles with members of the Armed Forces ready to, hopefully, stop this creature before it continues further inland destroying anymore cities in its path. We will be staying with this story as it develops. For now, let's send it to Les Warren — "
***

Choppers buzzed the creature's head and heedless attempts to communicate with it fell on deaf ears. Though it moved with a sickening, writhing grace through the city, continuously toppling buildings and crushing anything that stood in its way, an attack by the military had yet to commence. Perimeters were created from cul-de-sacs of concrete pylons, but the monster's tremendous bulk and perseverance just shoved them aside like a child's building blocks. And always, following in its rear, were battalions of zombies trudging through the aftermath, scouring the wasted grounds for victims on which to feed.

It had become horrifically obvious that these rampaging cadavers could not be killed as many of the armed citizens and military personnel understood from watching many movies. Headshots were useless, knocking them down and chopping off their heads was a fruitless venture. However hard you fought to bring the reanimated dead to a stop, no matter how powerful the weapon, nothing seemed to break the grip of the sludge that clung to them like webbing. It incased them and held them together as they pressed on consuming the living, leaving nothing but gore in their wake.

New York had once again fallen to terrorists, only this time the nightmare was incomprehensibly unreal.

17.

Paige felt a tap on her shoulder. Her attention was, as it had been for the better part of a day, firmly held by the images that played out before her on the monitors: a UFO was only moments away from entering Earth's atmosphere. They had less than a half hour. "What is it? Oh, oh sorry… yes, Tom… what have you got?"

Tom Andrews was one of Paige's assistants who often picked up a few extra hours on various shifts so she could knock off early and get some sleep. If anyone in the TBIRC was monogamously attacked to his job with loving fervor, it was Tom. He loved Sci-Fi, all things horror, and was a huge fan of the creepy, crawly bug-type movies that featured monster-sized insects rampaging through cities. And it was these thoughts that immediately coalesced in Paige's mind as she saw Tom's ashen face and saucer-sized eyes. "I-I-I think you might want to call Dr. Ashraff over here and see this…"

Tom looked exactly how you'd describe someone who has just seen a ghost: pale features, lidless, gaping eyes, and an air of sickening pallor all over his face, "O--K… what's going on?"

Tom grabbed Paige's sleeve and led her to another set of monitors on the opposite wall. And there, right in front of her playing out exactly like any given monster movie, were live feeds from several news channels reporting an attack on New York in the grotesque form of a gigantic creature. Paige's brain wouldn't allow her to register what she was seeing. How could it even be remotely possible that at one end of the building they were watching the potential first invasion of an alien space craft in modern records, and on the other they were witnessing New York being reduced to smoldering rubble by an impossible terror… and now a new reporter inside a separate box next to the first was going on about… the walking dead? This was too much for Paige, and she slumped down in Tom's chair and gasped for breath.

Dr. Ashraff saw that Paige was no longer behind him as he waited for the President to get to his monitor at the White House and began searching frantically for her. He found her at Thom's desk, slouched in his chair as Tom pressed a cool washcloth over her head. He ran over to her and before he even had time to ash how she was, he saw on the screens before him the chaos that had befallen New York. He was frozen and had to physically force himself to turn away. "Mr. President… glad you are back! Ha-ha-have you seen… have you seen what's happening in — "

"In New York. I have just been made aware. In fact, I was talking to my head officials while you were on hold. In my wildest nightmares I have never, ever, imagined something like this happening. Never. Tell me you have some kind of good news on this Unidentified Flying Object of yours."

Dr. Ashraff, in a mild panic (momentarily having forgotten what was happening above the Earth rather than on it) ran back to the monitors showing the movements of the UFO. He drooped with a heavy sigh. The moment he'd been waiting for was finally happening, "Sir… the craft has just penetrated our atmosphere. Sir… it's directly above the United States… and still approaching."

18.

The sky unfolded like a clouded blanket. Roiling cumulous swirls cascaded and burst into hanging gray blobs. For a moment, the sun was utterly blotted out by the spherical shape of the metallic object that appeared directly overhead. People on the go halted suddenly in their tracks and peered skyward: day instantly became night, and then just as quickly the warmth of the mid-morning returned as the shadowed craft approached closer to Earth. But no one moved. The vision of a hovering octagon encircled by an outer ring hovered in the heavens. It was eerily silent as the collected populous of the US stared up at the now motionless object, each lost in his or her own moment of frozen fear. The craft hung in the sky like the attached toys on a baby's mobile, and in that instant a pulsating ring of lights ignited and began to chase around the outer ring. What followed was an audible hum that broke the deafening quiet, sounding not unlike a turbine whirring as it performed some unseen function. Still the unidentified object remained completely motionless, except for the glowing circle of lights that continued to increase in velocity.

Abruptly, darkening storm clouds began to build all around the object. Crashing thunder echoed across the land and forks of blue lightning split the sky.

19.

The only sound was the slight wind gusts whistling through the pine boughs. Eric and Kevin sniffed the air like animals searching out prey, which was -in effect- precisely what they were doing. Newly discovered wild instincts seethed through their bodies, coursing from vein to artery to every fiber of their being. The men slowly stalked the grounds taking in deep breaths of the surrounding air sneakily ferreting out their prey: the very beast from which they'd gained their brand-new hunting, vampiric, monstrous personas. The men were thirsty, and they hungered for a meal that no human food could quell. Deep within them burned a desire so wanton, so heated that nothing stood in their way as during their search they tossed aside huge, dead logs, wrenched massive boulders from the earth, and leapt from one branch to another.

The sasquatch remained dead silent as he watched the feral humans hunt it. He had never known fear like this.

But it had to move. It knew it wasn't safe where it sat; crouched behind the stump jutting from a rising mound. Eventually the men –now more beastly than ever, apparently made so by its own horrific mauling just hours before- would smell his presence and attack it. And this idea made it more afraid for its own safety than anything ever had in its life. Even as a hunter by its own livelihood –daily making necessary kills for its own existence- the sasquatch was unaccustomed to fearing for its very life from its own prey. And yet, this new prey that it had –albeit inadvertently- somehow changed into creatures it had never known, created a shuddering panic that triggered in it a need to run and hide so powerful that at the moment, it could do no more than sit, frozen, watching.

It forgot itself for just that moment, and the humans were on it like ravenous wolves. It howled as pain like it had never known ripped through its core; teeth piercing its tough hide as though they were razor-sharp daggers. The darkness began to swirl as flashes of light burst before its fading vision. And then there was nothing.

20.

Danielle and Aaron crept lightly through the underbrush and hanging fir boughs, stepping, feline-like, without making a single sound. Their senses were aflame with scents and odors wafting all around them; animals settling into rest, flora alive with soft, lilting richness, and, of course, the cloying tinge of a fresh kill. They knew they were close.

Open ground spread before them, and Danielle and Aaron saw in their crisp night vision Eric and Kevin at feast. Flowing around the prey like a giant darkening stain was the last vestige of its life; the sour, coppery nose of newly spilt blood filled the chilled air. It was immediate: Danielle and Aaron lost all control and trampled the last few feet to the dying creature, thinking only of satiating their gnawing desire to feed. They both grunted and lowered their heads, as though their animalistic behavior had completely taken over. Eric and Kevin looked up with sinister grins played across their faces and returned the guttural snorts allowing their friends to join them in the fantastic feast.

Soon, the four friends who had once been nothing more than human, nothing more unusual than regular people going about their day trying to debunk myths and prove theories, were gathered around a creature no other human could really ever explain or really ever solidly identify, feeding on its flowing life blood like piglets at suckle.

They drank until they were full. But their metamorphosis continued unabated.

21.

High above the eastern seaboard of the United States, deepening gray storm clouds were gathering like a swirling hurricane. The darkening sky, that minutes before showed the rising sun and the wakening of a new day, now looked ominous and foreboding as the building, towering thunderheads piled upon one another like angry dams of dirty snow. In the eye of the storm hovered the impossible craft; spinning repetitiously, pulsating with illumination, somehow –beyond all human understanding- creating the massive front that collected just outside of its metallic perimeter. Tremendous booms of thunder echoed through the atmosphere followed almost immediately by sinister forks of steel-blue lightning. Then the rain began to fall in vicious maelstroms.

For a moment, the enormous beast stuttered in its step, and turned its curious gaze skyward. It knew, and it understood, what was happening hundreds of feet above its head. It was the first to feel the rain drops as they cascaded from the immense thunderheads in drenching sheets. It could remember and realize that far too many times in its eons-long existence the very same thing occurring: its pursuers were, once again, attempting to cleanse the planet on which it trod of its destruction. It had millions of memories from countless other times on innumerable other worlds of the very same moment and the very same result. It was never afraid, it had never set out to wreak the havoc it undoubtedly had, and it had no intention of ever becoming the fugitive it had so long ago become.

Deep within its cranial recesses, like the still waters of long ago forgotten well, the creature's most ancient knowledge bubbled ever so lightly to the surface. It somehow understood that the very ground over which it traversed even now, the age-old Terra Firma on which it currently stood, was oddly familiar to it. From within itself came a feeling; a shivering recognition that it had, a millennia ago, walked these very same grounds.

It also knew that it had never been captured or destroyed completely by the beings who always sought to punish it for taking actions it scarcely understood. Yet here it was again, just as it had been over time immeasurable, locked in a moment with those who spent eternities hunting it down like some kind of frightened prey. And it knew that it somehow had to make this time's end result… different. It was done running.

The Heavens were torn asunder, and the black-clouded sky let forth a torrent like humanity had not seen in hundreds of years. Rain fell so hard and fast that there weren't individual drops anymore, just gushing floods like soaking waterfalls. Thunder deafened, lightening blinded, and the storm surge raged.

22.

It was a time when evolution had yet to make its first great strides into becoming creatures that would, eventually, over countless generations, become even the most basic recognizable forms of intelligent life. The planet -much later to become known as Earth- was a roiling, steaming, constantly shifting desolate wasteland. Craggy outcroppings of unworn rocky plates jutted forth like the scales of a forgotten dragon. Pools of sulfurous, fetid water constantly gurgled and spat forth toxic fumes that spewed out in acrid bubbles from the open fissures of the planet's core. A low-hanging cloud of deadly gas and particulate debris slowly meandered across the world, blocking out the life-giving sun and holding the frozen planet in a death grip that would still be years away from exposing its treasures. And one solitary creature emerged from a great lake of putrid stench and stepped, for the first time, onto the arid crust.

It opened its eyes and surveyed the strangled grounds; completely void of life as far as it could see. Yet it knew, a distance from where it stood, things stirred and lived. It began its journey in search of three creatures that it was born to assist; a trio of things that would remain on the planet over millions of years, eventually giving in to the power of legend and myth. This creature was already ancient; having been born before even galaxies… and even then, it had been given a task. Its entire existence hinged on locating and teaching a small collection of living beings their ultimate destinies. Each was as different from the other as any three things can be and still tread similar paths.

The first was a gentle giant. It would soon call primeval forests its home. It would have a modicum of intelligence and hold guardianship over nature. But it also held a deadly secret. It was to be called Sasquatch.

The second was to be two things, but never at the same time. Its life was in constant turmoil revolving solely around the waxing and waning moon cycles. It was a balance of both friend and foe, and often the scales were to tip in opposite directions. It was to be called Lycanthrope.

The third, and perhaps the most frightening of the three, was a creature of such incomprehensible terror that its very name would one day strike cold, wicked fear in the hearts of all who heard its utterance. There would be only one, for that was all that was needed. It would command the impenetrable shore on which it survived, and it would be a worthy audience for even the eldest Gods of the universe. But it would one day be summoned to punish the very creature that gave it life. It was an unbreakable circle that would take eons to finally be made whole. This monster would be called Cthulhu.

Thus, the creature continued on its path. It had time, but not much. The internal struggle within its brain had already begun to fight free. There was work to be done.

23.

Paige Wilson and Dr. Ashraff sat in the highly illuminated basement of the Baltimore Inter-Galactic Research Society; their collective attentions adhered to the digital readouts portrayed on the monitors around them. A new day had dawned since their first discovery of the alien space craft. Originally it appeared as a tiny blip moving through space, but the several hours since had shown vast changes and the pictures they now witnessed were of a cyclonic object aggressively creating an incredible storm. Though they were at least forty feet below the substrate, they could plainly hear the torrential rains buffeting the concrete building above their heads. The winds moaned and threatened to sheer their earth-bound antennae from their moorings, and each scientist secretly prayed against such possibilities lest they lose their feed… and as it was, their screens had begun to flicker ever so slightly in the raging maelstrom.

Adding insult to injury was the more recent discovery of a titanic creature trampling through New York City like some kind of long-extinct, prehistoric dinosaur. And, oddly, it was this –not so much the bizarre UFO- that sparked to most panic in the research facility's inhabitants. When balancing between two completely unbelievable occurrences, the mind seems to latch on the least credible and it begins to weigh the heaviest, tipping the scales and igniting a new kind of fear: the possible impossible.

"Mr. President, I am at a loss as to what to either recommend or what to do at this point," Dr. Ashraff coldly admitted. "This is something neither of us has ever seen, let alone ever imagined."

"I understand, doctor, and thank you for your candor. I must prepare for a public address right now, but I do want you to continue communications with my staff, so I will leave you with David Barnes, my Secretary of the Interior. He is also my chief 'science officer', if you will, and likely… well, 'understands' more about things like this than anyone. Thank you, doctor." There were audible clicks and movement as President Haynes switched his headset to his replacement, Dr. Barnes.

"Good morning, Dr. Ashraff. It is my pleasure to speak with you. I have been updated on all the current goings-on and will be with you as things continue."

"Welcome, Dr. Barnes. I have read your theses on the possibility of Ancient Aliens on Earth, and I found them very informative and well written," Runjeet said as he rolled his eyes in a gesture of his true feelings. "So… with what you seem to understand, does any of this make any sense to you?"

Dr. Barnes reclined in his chair and moved his gaze between two 55-inch, flat screen, High-Definition monitors, each scrolling with figures and numbers as well as the dual images of the circulating storm and the craft, and the rampaging beast that now seemed to be staring skyward. He snuck a glance around the small office and found he was alone, aside from a set of security guards posted at the door. He reset himself in front of the action, nodded in readiness, and spoke into the headset.

"Well, Dr. Ashraff… yes, yes it does. Let me tell you about a find we unearthed just five years ago in the Outback of Australia. A find that literally shows the very indescribable acts we're all witnessing. And the key to its undoing."

24.

The acrid, vile stench of decay and sour meat hung in the humid air like an unclean butcher shop. Wafting through the trampled ruins of what was New York City was the sickening odor of death and those who reeked of it: the living dead. Hunger begat slaughter; slaughter begat death; death begat horrific rebirth; and the beast that ran with a never-ending flow of the toxic sludge that re-animated deceased tissue marched the march of destruction. Corpses shambled through the ravaged streets stopping only to tear living flesh from the citizens as they attempted to flee. Blood, viscous and rank with its coppery scent, sluiced like red syrup throughout the city, trailing the rampant and unholy murders brought on by the cadaverous demons. Citizens lay screaming along the roads, grasping at the fountains of gore that erupted from their killing wounds. People trampled madly past flattened cars, crumbled buildings, and the multiple bodies that, for one moment, lined the curbs, and another bounded forth searching for another human victim. The devastation was incalculable; no one could even imagine the cost of livelihoods, let alone the towering cost of human lives. Multitudinous numbers of the dead rapidly became a scourge of zombies causing the vicious circle to repeat itself infinitely. New York City was a terrifying wasteland.

Peace began to fall in the quenching form of precipitation. Drop by drop; soon sheet by sheet, the cleansing rain began to pour. The swirling, charcoal-gray cloud formation that hung far above let loose its collected payload, and the impending storm broke. The deluge soon built to a crescendo and started to rapidly flood the city. And the marauding dead suddenly ceased their mindless shuffling, falling to the ground, unmoving.

25

The ones who lived sought shelter in what was left of the buildings still standing in the whole of New York City. Most were either demolished to flattened husks of their former glorious forms, or else looted to the point of looking like picked over skeletal remains. But it was those that the remaining populous flocked to. Hundreds packed into the lower floors of gutted office buildings, even more scrambled to emptied shops and stores, and still others found evacuated homes on the outskirts of town and temporarily inhabited them. Anywhere, it seemed, was deemed safe just as long as it was as far off the open streets as possible. The people were being forced from their own city as inhumanity ravaged the streets, devouring any stragglers left alive. That was, until the storms came.

Those closest to windows peered out in a mixture of confusion and amazement. Though they felt overwhelming sensations of loss and crippling fear, there was something soothing and comforting about the sky opening and enveloping the horizon in a Biblical downpour. They watched as the streets ran like rivers tainted with the blood of the innocent. Bodies of the victims bobbed along the raging torrent like damming logs and were followed by even more of the city's detritus and debris. The cleansing weather front felt like a saving grace, but no more so than when the survivors finally began to see the buoyed cadavers that were once the scavenging dead. They flowed down the flooded roads like ghastly flotsam, some clogging against parked cars and fire hydrants like engorged blood platelets in a gigantic artery. The stink was overwhelming; the sour tinge of old meat and wasted flesh hung in the air like a muggy blanket. And the rain continued, pouring down without pause, as it slowly rid the city of its befouled predators.

26.

Before them lay the desiccated, exsanguinated husk; its matted, fluid-soaked fur becoming clotted in the warm evening breeze. The gentle giant's life now extinguished by the very monsters it unknowingly created. Leaves rustled ever so lightly; the night's noises were surprisingly mute, save for the rhythmic, sonorous rasps rising from the four once-humans. With their feeding complete, the friends all fell into a satisfying coma and literally dropped where they fed. Their faces and hands, the fronts of their shirts and jackets, and even smeared in red wisps through their hair, was an impressive abundance of coagulating blood. Were it not for the very clothes on their backs, they'd go completely unrecognized as the former people they once were not twenty-four hours prior; mud and bits of flora clung to their rapidly growing hair, their crimson snouts protruded from misshapen faces like a nightmarish amalgam of beast and man, their triangular ears jutted from the sides of their slightly more compressed canine heads, and terrible claws pierced through their gnarled fingers like corroded nails in twisted wood. But they remained bipedal, for this was not a transformation that made them fully animals. No, this was a transformation that made them something that no human from the ancients till now had ever laid eyes on. The beasts that now slept, satiated and bloated, were of imaginations so vast and incredible that to call them lycanthropes was to only scratch the surface of an ever-spreading horror. What they had become was something new, something outside comprehension... something that should never be.

***

The night was crisp. Fall had certainly taken hold, and after the scorcher of a summer they'd had this year, it was none too soon, either. Hunting season hadn't strictly begun in Michigan just yet. Sure, bow was just around the corner, but Terry Ferguson was always a rifle man. And no, Terry Ferguson didn't always follow the letter of the law, and so this brought him out on this cool, slightly nippy morning in search of maybe some wild turkey or, if he was really lucky, a nice buck. Terry was lovingly familiar with these woods; he was reared just ten miles south, having grown up in an old logging house raised by his daddy. It was always just the two of them; daddy would head off to the mill and Terry would fend for himself for hours a day, exploring the woods, setting small game traps, teaching himself to hunt like a man, and always bringing something interesting home for supper: coons, pheasant, woodchuck, and even the occasional deer. Daddy died in '68, and Terry was sent to live with his Aunt and Uncle in Marquette, not too far for his home grounds, and now that he was pushing thirty, he wanted nothing more than to be back home, scouring the forests and stalking the wilderness.

Another reason for his decision to skirt work today and take to nature was the news coming out of New York City. Terry had heard some unbelievable garbage in his life, but word that there were attacks by a gigantic monster, an alien space crafts, the living dead, and a wicked storm was just too much to handle for one morning. He stared at his television for about twenty minutes trying to absorb all of what he was hearing and seeing; chaos, fear, demolition, visuals straight from horror comics… it was enough. Terry had to get out and get away from reality… or, unreality, for a while so he called into the plastics plant, feigned sickness, packed a few odds and ends –including his trusty hunting rifle- and headed out into the early dew.

The light tendrils of fog curled across the damp foliage like phantom fingers. The air was heavy with moist earth and the approaching sunrise, bringing with it the promise of a wonderfully sunny day, all the more perfect to hang out among the firs and maples and take in the bounty. But another scent caught Terry's attention, too. It was sour, foul, and ripe with decay. He couldn't be sure where it was coming from, but it did get stronger the further north he pushed into the trees.

Cresting a small hill, Terry's stomach lurched, and his eyes spread open in stunned terror. In a clearing about fifty yards ahead lay the body of what might be a bear surrounded by four smaller bodies each clothed but –even at this distance- not at once resembling anything human. Terry was frozen somewhere between gripping fear and a tugging curiosity. It was when one of the forms surrounding the bear stirred that Terry's legs finally decided they'd move under their own accord, and he slowly, silently, crept forward.

Within twenty yards, another of the bizarre beings that lay around the –sleeping? - beast began to make groaning noises that were far to feral and guttural to be anything human, and Terry once again found himself unable to walk any further. A call echoed from the mouth of the creature, a call that fired itself into Terry's mind and carved a path of abject fear straight down his spine; it was a disgusting mix of wild pig and a rabid dog. Terry felt a gorge rise in his throat but swallowed it away without a sound. He knew he was breathing rapidly and was surely going to reveal his position
u

The second of the four creatures sat up and began to sniff the air like a dog being led outside for the first time. He quickly shook his head in an attempt to locate whatever it was that caught its olfactory senses. Terry had a sneaking suspicion that it was him they were smelling, but he wasn't about to wait around to find out.

Shaking off his strangling fear, Terry slowly raised his rifle to his sight line, eyed in the target with the scope, and popped a shot directly through the back of the creature's head. As he quickly lowered the gun, the other wakened creature sprang to his feet and leapt to his friend's side. He emitted a mournful low and raised his glance to look around him. His eyes locked on Terry and the red-stained forms of his fangs were bared in anger. But it was too late.

Terry had his rifle poised for another shot the second the beast was on his feet examining his friend, and as soon as those beady, sinister eyes were on him and those ghastly teeth were flared, another shot rang out in the misty morning hitting the second creature right between the eyes. The beast stiffened, yawed a little to the right, and pitched to the side landing directly atop his friend. The ring of the gunshot stirred birds and some little mammals from their resting places, yet it did not even budge the two remaining creatures that lay, just breathing beside the –it wasn't a bear after all- furry mound. At this realization, Terry ventured forth even closer with his gun at the ready.

Upon closer inspection, it became very clear that the large creature was decidedly not a bear after all, but something far more simian-like. Terry could do little more than stare at it rolling over in his head the simple fact that it might just be a sasquatch. He'd heard of such giants patrolling acres and acres of Michigan forest, making themselves seen to a select few who, in turn, regaled tales of the massive monsters and their storied myths. But Terry had never –nor thought he'd ever- see one, alive or dead. But here it was its fur was tacky with congealed blood, bite marks dried with deep red stains all over its body, and the look on its face was of utter panic and frozen fear. Terry felt a small sense of sorrow for this beast. He knew it was the creatures –two of which still breathed- that did this to it, and it just somehow felt very unnatural. In fact, his entire day had felt completely unnatural.

Terry turned to the two creatures that lay on the matted earth, resting, as it now seemed, enveloped in each other's arms. The picture was grotesquely unimaginable; snouts pressed together both caked with gore, clothing shredded in places that allowed for more intimate closeness, thick mounds of fur protruding from their faces, arms, feet… backs, stomachs… It was hideous. Terry could only bare to look the length of time it took to aim, and to fire.

Two more shots radiated through the waking forest. Terry looked around and said a silent prayer to a God he –up to this point- never really bothered to speak to and removed a collapsible shovel from his pack. He dug into the early afternoon, neatly burying the four creatures in one single hole, covering it with wet leaves and fallen needles to hide the carnage as best he could. As for the sasquatch… he left it be. Somehow it felt more natural that way; nature had birthed it and it would be nature that would waste it away. Feeling satisfied, Terry looked one more time at his work, packed up his things, and began the long walk back to his home.

When night fell, and Terry was sound asleep in his bed with all six of his doors locked, some of the dirt shifted just a bit… the dirt that topped the unmarked grave that held the bodies of four once-humans.

27

The President's Chief Science Officer (also his Secretary of the Interior, which meant even less than normal at this particular moment) climbed into the armored limo carrying with him the only conceivable means by which to destroy the rampaging monster that even at this very moment was moving –albeit slowly- south from New York City. Rain pelted the car's windshield and the buffeting winds threatened to tear it from the road, but Dr. Barnes sat staring into space, undeterred by the weather's vicious attack, yet silently concerned at the unmoving UFO that seemed to be the cause of it all.

A large Halliburton briefcase sat next to the Secretary and rattled slightly as the stretch slipped and jagged at the wicked bursts of wind. Dr. Barnes was intimately familiar with its contents. It was 2006 and a small, ragged group of Paleontology students were busy carving out and mapping a new dig in the Australian Outback. A new species of dinosaur had been discovered, one that was slightly smaller than a T. Rex but every bit as terrifying a predator, and with the exception that this one –according to the fossil imprints- was covered with fine feathers. This discovery alone was enough to shake up the scientific community; the prospect that many of the already discovered dinosaurs may have had feathers and eventually evolved into modern birds was still a hotly debated notion, but here it was in all its glory. Sadly, this discovery had to be kept tightly under wraps –literally as well, since it was to be transported to the Smithsonian in D.C.- until the collected heads of certain specific scientific groups could make closer examinations. Dr. Barnes was asked by the President to make the trip to Australia high priority to oversee the final unearthing and transporting. His arrival was met with high approval -and even a bit of fawning considering actions like this were hardly routine at dig sites, But Dr.

Barnes took it all in stride and even began to feel a little out of place still dressed in his suit and tie. Luckily, he brought with him two of his closest colleagues, both vastly more prepared than Dr. Barnes himself, and it was them he'd sent to assist with the remainder of the dig. And it was later that same afternoon that the hollers of delight and discovery echoed from the chasm as something else was unearthed.

It turned out to be more like 'somethings', since what appeared to be, at first, just a rune-etched slab crusted with eons of rock and dirt turned out to hold with it the most important piece of the mythical puzzle: The Amulet. No one was really sure if that was actually what it was, considering most amulets are worn much like brooches or necklaces and this disk was roughly the size of a tea saucer. But, according to what could be deciphered from the glyphs, the ancient sigil-engraved artifact was indeed used as an adornment. Be that is it was, the round, metallic item was as horrifically grotesque as it was strikingly beautiful. Though it had sat encased in its earthly tomb for untold centuries, it came free nearly unworn and untouched. The surface held an almost crystalline sheen; a polish as though it had taken on a veneer deep under the ground rather than lost a luster like most other objects. The center resembled an unblinking eye in both a metaphorical sense and in the fact that it was an almond shape with a deeper center like a pupil, all of which was of the angriest hue of blood red anyone had ever seen. Emitting from the epicenter and scrolling outward toward the edges were unreadable writings carved and inked in the same damnable shade. Surrounding the crimson, bisected in four parts by the writing, were symbols and hieroglyphics in a tongue completely baffling to all of those who looked upon it; all of those present with enough combined linguistic knowledge to span the entire modern globe, as well as those languages considered dead. It was terrible to look at, a wretched piece of the ancient occult. Yet, it was impossible not to gaze upon, an object of untold power and opportunity. And thus, it had to be locked away until a time when others could decipher its hidden passages.

A year passed until enough information was gathered to make a more educated pass at the stone slab and its accompanying Amulet. After a few months of painstaking research and breaking down of a language so ancient and unused that it hadn't been even heard of since the Macedonian era, a reasonable recovery of the lost text was made. It told the tale of a great being who traveled to Earth far pre-dating almost any life, and how the being gave its vast knowledge to three creatures that would carry with them the secret to a time in the future when they would be called upon for very different reasons. The time was to occur in 2011, a mere three-and-a-half years away, when the being would once again return to Earth and rend it asunder. There was but one of the three creatures that could be called upon to stop it, though it was not as an assist to the race that inhabited the Earth, it was just because that was its destiny. The writings made no indication of humans –apparently having no idea of what race would be the wisest- nor did it actually spell out the year as 2011. In the latter case it was more of an obscure mathematical method that worked out to be that precise year. And in the former case, it literally didn't mention any race at all.

The information struck those involved as almost too ridiculous to be true. However, there were those –the Secretary being one of them- who knew better than to discount something so random and so believable –at least in his own eyes- and so he kept the objects locked away in the sub-basement of the Smithsonian under the guard of a revolving set of armed men until the time was right to do what was necessary.

As the limo pulled into the TBIRC parking facility after its remarkably short journey, Dr. Barnes sighed, relieved to finally release the secret he'd kept hidden for far too long. He popped the latches on the case and peered inside at the metallic disc that sat before him. The center eye pulsated in time with his heartbeat.

28.

Dr. Ashraff responded to the request from security that the Secretary of the Interior, Dr. Barnes be allowed to enter immediately. He expected the Chief Science Officer's visit and nearly met him at the door directly. The two exchanged pleasantries passed greetings to one another and the Secretary's escorts and made for the information bunker stationed below the Earth's surface. Business was of utmost concern, and the matter at hand was taking a decidedly terrible turn for the worse. They sat and stared at each other in momentary silence not quite sure where to take the next step.

"Dr. Barnes," Dr. Ashraff began by shattering the stagnant silence, "You spoke of something you had discovered that could potentially end this madness."

Dr. Barnes shifted in his chair, still a little uneasy about sharing knowledge he had kept so close to himself for over four years. But, in the end, the survival of a nation depended on his decision to relinquish something held so closely by only a scant handful of people. "Yes, Dr. Ashraff, it is true. However, what I'm about to tell you will more than likely force you to see me in an altogether different light. Can you accept that?"

"Well, Dr. Barnes, since I have no Earthly idea what it is you are about to tell me, then yes, I suppose whatever reaction you assume I will display might just fall under the category of a 'different light'."

"Fair enough, Dr. Ashraff. Fair enough. Well, since our precious little amount of time seems to be dwindling faster every second, I suppose I ought to regale you with the tale."

Over the course of the next twenty minutes, Dr. Barnes told the story of The Amulet. Dr. Ashraff sat in stunned and utterly confused and disbelieving silence. And in the war room, Paige Wilson stared at the display as the alien craft turned the storm it had created into a Category 2 hurricane. The monster, in all its seemingly lost persistence, pushed to the south terrorizing town after town.

29.

"But it says that this… uh, R'yleh is somewhere… hm… I guess that'd be in the South Pacific, right?" Dr. Ashraff inquired skeptically as he gave a sidelong glance to Paige who had since been called into the private meeting; more to do with her initial discovery than her actual knowledge of the situation.

"Well, that is indeed where the archaic directions point, for sure," Dr. Barnes continued, "But it also states at the time of its purpose it will have repositioned itself somewhere near… oh…"

"Oh what, doctor?" Paige interjected, just a curious as her colleague.

"Um… oddly it states that it would be somewhere between a reigning Old Kingdom and a Newly Formed Kingdom. I'm guessing that it means… off the coast of America in the Atlantic."

Dr. Ashraff had to chuckle a little at the even odder notion that an entire location, however difficult to believe on its own, had the ability to relocate just because that was its destiny. "Look, I'm going at this whole thing with a few grains of salt here, Dr. Barnes; the simple notion that this amulet has the power to raise an abomination to thwart an already rampaging abomination is blatantly absurd. But now you're asking me to take this already baseless piece of artifact and - just on assumption mind you- believe that the locale spelled out in the glyphs can move just because it's supposed to? I'm sorry, doctor… I really am, but…"

"I understand doctor, I do. But just imagine for one second that this ancient text is completely true. Are you willing to drop it like fiction just because it doesn't sit well with your notion of what can and can't be believed? Do you think anyone thought Dinosaurs could have existed in their presently known forms over fifty years ago? Of course not, they would have been called crazy to do so. Do you think that the Christian Faith would be as solid as it is, were it not for the written teachings of The Bible? Absolutely not, Dr. Ashraff, and this circumstance is no different," Dr. Barnes explained with a palpable feeling of passion everyone in the room felt.

"Okay. Let's just assume that this writing is, well, a kind of eminent instruction manual from thousands of years ago. It doesn't make any difference what any of us believes, what matters is are we going to put all of our eggs in this one basket and just hope beyond hope that it works? I mean we're talking about raising a potentially nightmarish beast to destroy one we already have… what if it doesn't work? Being no worse off than we already are, in this instance, is to concede to our own deaths!" Paige proclaimed as her rising guile filled the room.

The two sides stood in gnawing silence. They were all right, of course: there wasn't any proof this would, or could work, the ramifications of its insanity were not lost on any of them, and any amount of bickering wasn't going to change it. Dr. Barnes looked around and accepted the fact that he might have to go at this alone. He alone; the guardian of The Amulet.

Dr. Ashraff broke the hastening silence, "I'm as skeptical as you can possibly imagine, but I'm taking all of this on your word."

Paige nodded in agreement, staring blankly at her hands. The necessary agreements were made, and now it was only a matter of finding the correct location. Dr. Barnes gestured to his limo and told the driver to head toward the coast.

30.

The bathing downpour drenched New York City, flooding streets, drowning those caught out in it, and washing away any signs of the evil scourge of the zombie invasion. The marauding monster knew it would happen; he'd seen it time and again and the result was always the same. Something about his physiology seemed to reanimate dead tissue regardless of its make-up, provided it was carbon-based and reasonably intelligent. It turned its gaze once again to the craft that remained aloft just at the cloud line, generating the wicked winds and sopping rain, and scowled; nothing new to it at all, though it still had trouble understanding how it fit into all of this. Still the beings powered up the hurricane and spilled its cleansing contents across the already devastated city.

And there, deep within the ancient recesses of its mind, it understood where its path lay: it was going to finally be vanquished. After countless eons of empty travels to innumerable worlds doing its one, soul predestined duty, its time had finally come. And though it felt a small tinge of remorse and disdain that what it had been created to do was once and for all concluded; it was mostly at peace. It was time to go home.

Finally.

31.

The limo sped to the Maryland coast following a path that no one could understand, yet Dr. Barnes somehow felt was right. He held the steel briefcase, peered longingly and terrifyingly inside, and watched… and listened… and felt. The reddened center of The Amulet pulsated more quickly the closer they got to the shore, and that pulsing, in turn, followed the metronomic pace of his heart.

Dr. Ashraff and Paige Wilson sat on the adjacent bench in the rear of the limousine, both staring out their respective windows. Neither was completely sure what was happening, and both were still riveted and equally stunned at the occurrences that had gone on over the past day and a half. It had been a day that no other human had even dared dream was possible. Even curious and overly imaginative children and Sci-Fi authors could not have even come close to describing the brutal horror that they'd watched unfold. And now –and this was perhaps the most insane part of all- they were headed to an unknown cove to summon a creature that would, somehow, put an end to the madness. No; it was all madness begetting more madness. Neither had any inclinations that this was going to end well for anyone, yet neither could even devise a conceivable outcome. It was, after all, madness.

Suddenly, Dr. Barnes barked into the intercom for the driver to stop. The limo had arrived at an old fishing dock. Wooden piers sat crumbling into the unforgiving sea, overgrown weeds and saplings choked the boat entrance, and what appeared to be years of neglect and avoidance turned the once pristine boating slip into a slowly dying tenement. The doors were opened by Dr. Barnes' armed escorts, and the group of scientists stepped out onto the soggy ground.

No words were exchanged as Dr. Barnes immediately set to work, almost as though he'd done this on a regular basis. The case was unlatched, and The Amulet was gingerly removed and set on the hood of the limousine. Next to it was placed the ancient rune stone with its nearly unreadable glyphs and carvings. Dr. Barnes looked out to the calm sea, and breathed deep the salty air, steadying himself for the performance he'd waited four years to act out. He was as ready as he was ever going to be.

Dr. Ashraff and Paige took a side-step to give the doctor his needed room, neither understanding why it was even necessary, but letting the compulsion move them regardless. They watched in abject curiosity as Dr. Barnes began reading the incantation in a dialect neither had even dreamed existed. It seemed there were many steps to the proper ceremony, and the doctor seemed to know every step flawlessly. They could have sworn that just then the wind picked up just a touch; a chill that bit to the marrow was in that wind and it conjured fear throughout the spectators. Out at sea, a slow roiling erupted from the surface, churning into a frothy boil. Paige and Dr. Ashraff found themselves in one another's arms, holding themselves against the coalescing terror that was rapidly whipping about them. Gusts buffeted the trees, curling them side-long against the attack, and even shook the stolid limo on its wheels. The icy nip built to an almost frigid crescendo and stung them to the core. When it at once seemed like they could no longer stand the maelstrom, Dr. Barnes bellowed what was to be the final words written on the ancient stone out at the tempestuous ocean:

"Ph'nglui mglw'nafh Cthulhu R'lyeh wgah'nagl fhtagn!"

32.

A city rose from the churning waters; a city carved entirely innumerable eons hence- from solid stone. It was towering in its enormity, blocking out the sun and scraping the very bottom of the Heaven's themselves. With it came a cacophonous roar that seemed to emanate from within the stone fortress itself; it echoed across land, sea, and sky, dropping all who heard it to the ground, writhing in agony and fighting to stave of what was thrumming right through their skulls. Adorning the massive throne that sat at the helm of the gigantic, floating island were rows of circular disks that looked remarkably like The Amulet used to raise it; each pulsating in rhythm like a hundred heart beats. And yet it was what sat upon the throne that created nightmares and turned away even the demons.

The horrific leviathan that perched upon its earthen chair was of such indescribable loathing that even the mere sight of it scarred visions and burned its visage forever into memories. Hued a shade of sickly, unnatural gray-green, and splotched throughout its ghastly form with writing and gibbering sores like wretched barnacles, the lamentable abomination surveyed the surroundings like an angered God.

And so, it was.

Grotesque, abhorrent, nauseous… the brutish thing sat wheezing in ire at its tower door. Tendrils of ocean steam spat forth from its maw over which hung a bulbous mass of threshing tentacles, each layered with knobby protrusions and angry spikes. Its serpentine fingers viciously contorted as its wicked talons dug feverishly at the craggy arms of the throne. Pustules gouted ichor, and open fistulas ran freely with rivulets of phlegmy sputum. Sprouting like giant, water-logged umbrellas from its back was a set of leathery and severely chapped wings; both hung limply down across its shoulders, neither looking that they had any strength to create lift. Its entire skull throbbed with the choking breath of oxygenated air; individual sacks like bellowing bladders struggled to maintain breathing. The immoral redolence that hung in the air like a wet sack was gagging and palpable.

It slowly leaned forward, bringing to bear its entire face. An ancient, putrid cough burst forth with a sound like misfired torpedo, and then it spoke.

Gargling bass erupted from its mouth; the sound split the eardrums of the onlookers. Only a single phrase was uttered as the six assembled, cowering humans screamed into the sky:

"The end."

A Bonus Tale
Amulet Adjacent?

The Sitter
1.

The chemical tainted steam spewed from the radiator like an automotive geyser. Hot water and coolant splattered inside the car's hood and engine and all over the Tee shirt sleeves of Ivy Daniels favorite top emblazoned with a rainbow Phish logo. She cursed through her teeth, took a cursory glance at the gurgling mess and the car parts she knew nothing about, and slammed the hood.

"Fuck this. Where the hell am I, anyway?" She swore as she yanked her cell from her cut-offs pocket and tried to glance at the screen through the searing glare of the afternoon sun.

It was hard to tell, but she thought the map on her screen indicated somewhere called Lawrence. She'd left the comforting speedy confines of I-94 because her car's temperature gauge was threatening to overheat and somewhere in her rattled mind it seemed safer to travel in the same direction on backroads that likely meandered through towns and villages that might have service stations were she to need one. Well, she needed one. Ivy didn't know what Lawrence was in terms of stature. A town? A 'Burg'? Some backwoods dirt-coated stain in the glorious state of Michigan? Looking around she definitely saw houses, street signs… was that a diner? Well, it wasn't tiny, so to speak, so that was something, anyway. She looked over at her little Honda Civic puking fluids onto the road's shoulder and knew there was nothing more to do than find somewhere she could ask for help. Just then it seemed help might just find her.

"Hi there! Sorry to startle you, but I'm guessing you've got car trouble?"

Ivy looked over her shoulder at the sound of crunching gravel and the sweet voice of a woman not too far from her own age, "Oh hi! No problem, and yes... problem."

The woman laughed softly, "Yes, it is. My name is Kat. I live just over there."

Ivy followed Kat's arm as she indicated a house just yards from where the two stood by the dying car. Ivy smiled, nodded, and the two gave each other the all-too-familiar looks of mildly questionable acceptance. Everyone was the same when it came to a greeting to a stranger: no one ever feels immediate comfort regardless of the situation. Kat and Ivy, both felt it and it was clearly visible on each other's faces. But Kat's smile was genuine enough, and Ivy certainly needed the aid in a little squat-burg she had no knowledge of. So, she grinned back with what she hoped was an equal amount of angelic patois.

"Fortunately, you're not too far from Jack's Repair. It's right up the road about a mile. I can give you a lift if you're not in the mood to hike it."

Ivy glanced up the road and thought maybe she could make out a white brick building, but it was just as likely just a mirage caused by the blinding sun, "Okay. Sure, I guess. I mean I don't mind walking if it's any trouble it's just..."

Ivy pointed to her feet. She was wearing thin flip flops that had certainly seen better days. "Oh, right. Very familiar footwear, friend. I have about ten pairs of those myself and they are not walking shoes at all. Anyway, yeah, I'd be happy to give you a lift." Kat said as she held an arm across her forehead to block out the blazing light.

"Well, I very much appreciate it. But I don't, ah… see a car at your house."

"Well, you wouldn't… I mean not right now, anyway. I actually babysit for my mom while she's at work and she takes my car since her Jeep is at, well, it's actually at Jacks."

Ivy smiled at the coincidence and looked down the road again toward the service station solemnly and silently weighing her options. Did she really want to walk? A mile wasn't that far, but she'd have sore (or worse) feet when she got there. On top of that she wasn't sure what the outcome would be anyway especially when it came to how long the shop would need to fix her Honda. It would make sense to get to know someone so if there was need for a place to hang out…

"… brings you to Lawrence?"

Ivy snapped out of her thoughts, "I'm sorry?"

Kat smiled, "I was asking what brings you to Lawrence? I'm assuming you're not from here, judging by your license plate."

"No. I'm not. I've never even really been to Michigan, at least longer than just driving through. I live just outside of Chicago and I'm heading to my mom's in Buffalo. So, what brings me to Lawrence is this piece of shit I really should have rid of a long time ago."

"I get it, I really do. My mom's stupid Jeep has been more trouble than the damn thing's worth and I'm pretty sure it's in the shop more often than it's on the road. Anyway, would you like to come inside while we wait?"

Ivy thought about it. Kat seemed harmless and clearly willing to help, and to be honest, she really needed to pee. "Okay, sure. Do you know when your mom will be back? I don't want to waste your whole day hanging around, ya know, since you're probably doing things with your siblings?"

Kat shook her head and put on an affable grin, "No. Believe me, I'm not. The twins hang out in front of their video games like the world doesn't exist around them. They might be smart little twelve-year old's, but they definitely don't show it. It's all about Minecraft and Animal Crossing or whatever the hell it's called."

Ivy could relate. Though she had a sister who wasn't at all interested in video games, they both had friends who were, and their friends were frequently more absorbed in PlayStation than they were in doing anything else. "Oh, I get it. And yeah, it's Animal Crossing."

"Well come one. I'll give my mom a call when we get home and see when her shift ends. She's been working a lot of overtime lately because, well, the Jeep. But if she knows I've got company with a bum vehicle of her own, she'll probably head home at the end of the day. Usually around 3:30."

Ivy checked her phone. It was a little after one. She sighed. It could have been worse, "Sounds great. Lead the way."

2

Kat led Ivy across the large yard, over the sidewalk, and up the cracked driveway to her front porch. The house looked similar in façade to all the other ones around it: ranch style, brick and wood, aluminum siding over two-thirds of it that looked like it needed a good pressure wash, and a garage that stood detached from the house with its door open like a gaping maw. The front yard had little to show aside from a huge, old oak with wooden planks nailed to the side for climbing and the requisite tire swing on the other, and a short hedge just outside the picture window that also looked as if any recent TLC wasn't recent enough. Rather than go in the front, Kat motioned toward the side door that was between the east end of the house and the garage. A pair of roller blades, a baseball bat, and two snow shovels leaned against the wall.

"Come on in. Don't mind the mess, I haven't gotten around to cleaning the breakfast stuff yet." Kat stood aside and gestured Ivy into the house.

Immediately Ivy was overwhelmed with that odor that strange houses carry with them; a scent that showcased a mélange of every and any recent things cooked, cleaned, or, Heaven forbid, unflushed. The smell was not unlike old, fried fish mixed with beef vegetable soup and cat urine. It probably wasn't as strong as she was imagining, and there was no doubt Kat was immune, but it hung like a damp fug in the air. Ivy did her best to pretend not to even notice. However, aside from that, it was very clear that Kat hadn't tidied up -not that she was expected to, given the suddenness of the current situation- this morning, or likely even last night. Ivy tried to ignore that, too. But her eyes betrayed her, and it was obvious Kat was a little embarrassed.

"Sorry again about the mess…"

"Don't even sweat it, my place is always a shit hole." Ivy immediately regretted the comparison.

But Kat nodded and smiled. She reached into the fridge and produced two cans of Red Bull, "Care for a pick-me-up? I've only been awake for about two hours, and I'm still not sufficiently jarred yet."

Ivy accepted even though she hated energy drinks. She was a coffee girl taking it strong and without sweetened creamy accoutrements. But she wanted to be nice, she was, after all, in a stranger's home and when in Rome.

Kat suddenly keened at the top of her lungs, "DAVID! SARAH! GET IN HERE, PLEASE!"

Ivy just stood, staring at Kat's reddened features. She heard slow thumps beginning to emanate from the rooms beyond and dreary voices replying with whines and unhappiness.

"Sorry for the yelling, but I at least need to let the twins know that you're here. It's not really going to matter anyway since you're probably not even going to see them again. But still…"

The set of fraternal twins plodded into the kitchen with all the gravitas of a black parade. They looked sullen, unkempt, and sleep deprived to say the least. The boy, David, sported a shock of hair that looked like Edward Scissorhands and gone Super Sayan. The girl, Sarah, had rouge luggage under her eyes, disproportionate pigtails, and a Hayao Miyazaki shirt festooned with stains of unnatural hues. They stood there yawning in unison with questioning looks and rolling eyes. In unison: "What?"

"Well good morning to you, too. This is Ivy. Her car broke down outside and we need to get her over to the service station. So, I'm going to be busy for a few hours. I need you two to get this kitchen cleaned up before you do anything else. Got it?

The kids looked as though Kat had asked them to isolate genomes. Their faces betrayed no interest; no indication they'd even heard her. But they did as they were told. They shuffled into the kitchen without so much as a nod toward Ivy and began robotically performing their chore.

"Alright, that ought to keep them busy for a while. Let's go call my mom and Jack's and see what we can do about your car."

Ivy looked at them all with wide-eyed interest and even an air of dumbfounded curiosity at the twins as they went about their menial task in an almost somnambulated stupor. She watched as Kat left the kitchen and made her way into the next room. Ivy followed.

3.

"Hi mom!" Kat said as she spoke into the receiver of the old-style house phone: big, rectangular, and huge, opaque buttons, "How's work?"

Kat took out her own phone in an almost contrasting clash of technology and used her fingerprint to bring it out of its slumber. She noticed that her battery was teetering on the precipice of thirty percent, and she mentally cursed herself for leaving her charger cord in her car. She also noticed that her service bars were far lower than they had been outside, which made sense as often being indoors caused that very thing to happen. But just then what was one slice of the incremental wedge now showed a question mark. Damn. Nothing now.

"Okay. I'll let her know. No, I'm sure she won't mind. Yeah, I understand. Okay. Love you, too…" Kat trailed off as she hung up the phone with a plastic *CLACK*.

Ivy looked up as she put her own phone back in her pocket, "Something tells me that she's not going to be home by three thirty?"

"No. Sorry. Mandatory overtime. I was worried about that. Probably not 'til six. But she did say to go ahead and call Jack's and have them come tow it. They won't charge you since it's within their radius. So, there's that. They can at least start looking it over! Right?" Kat said with a lilted upturn in her voice that acted to coat over the bad news with as joyous a veneer as she could muster.

"Yeah. That makes sense. Sure. Can you call Jack's then? I really want to get the Civic down there and I just feel weird about imposing all of this on you. You've been very kind."

"Sure will! And you're not imposing! I promise!" Kat said, happily.

Ivy didn't have time to see the glint of metal that flashed past her peripheral vision before she felt the deafening thud. Blackness swirled and she heard herself curse from the other end of the tunnel she was falling through.

4.

Ivy fluttered her eyes and struggled to see. There was only dark. As consciousness leapt back into focus like a drunk bathed in ice water, Ivy felt a thunderous throbbing on the side of her head marching to beat of her quickening pulse. Her breath caught in her throat, and she winced in blinding agony. She moaned and tried to feel for her pounding wound but there was no give in her arms. They were strapped to her sides, that much she could tell, and it seemed her legs were lashed in much the same way. They were crisscrossed and it quickly became evident that there was some kind of metal pole running between them and up through her arms. Even as her eyes began to slowly adjust, it didn't matter as there was absolutely nothing to see. Ivy gasped again as her head flared with another seizing blast of pain and she cried out into the echoing expanse around her.

"I guess you're awake." A voice chirped from somewhere in the distance, "I'm sorry about your head. We cleaned it and there's a couple Band-Aids on it. I bet it still hurts though."

Ivy tried to speak, but she found it hurt entirely too much and just ended up groaning weakly. Consciousness swum around her, and she felt herself slipping back into nothingness…

"Hey! You're done sleeping! We need you awake!" The voice demanded from the other side of the room.

Ivy fought back into wakefulness and took several breaths to steady herself. She swallowed dryly and tried to see into the blackness to locate where the voice was coming from. The light that followed blinded her immediately as the metal shop lamp clicked loudly to life. The dark was replaced by such whiteness that tears pricked the corners of her eyes and ran down her cheeks. As her vision began to clear away the hazy ghosts left behind, she eventually made out two figures standing at the opposite end of the room. She knew right away she was in the basement. A cursory glance around the room displayed age-old tools and weather-worn implements hanging on pegboards. The pole she was strapped to (yes, strapped as it appeared her extremities were held tight by a series of leather belts) was the support beam that was fastened directly into the concrete floor.

"That's good. Now just sit here and keep quiet. We'll be back." The twins simultaneously turned from their posts aside the workbench and marched up the old, wooden steps.

5.

It was the Fall of 2019. Crisp air whistled through the naked branches of the oaks and maples, jostling loose the remaining leaves. School had begun, but Erin Barton was a single mom with twins in middle school, a ten-hour a day job, and no one to come over after the kids got off the bus. She was nervous and worried because losing the job she'd recently gotten was not in the cards. It was the best work she'd ever found, and it paid enough to keep them above their bills, fed with extra left over for emergency expenses and occasional sundries. Consequently, she didn't want to lose her would-be career at any cost. And so, she needed a babysitter, and quickly.

Erin scanned want ads online, checked local sitters, and even looked on the dreaded Craig's List, but so far to no avail. Just then she saw a pop-up ad. Normally she'd ignore those and 'X' them into oblivion, but this one caught her attention. It read:

I'M A BABYSITTER AND I WANT TO SPEND TIME WITH YOUR KIDS!
MY NAME IS KAT BLAINE AND I LOVE CHILDREN!!

Below the lines was a picture of a really attractive young lady, below which were even more pictures showing her past sitting experiences with happy kids having wonderful times. Boy, when Google analytics read your mind, it really read your mind, Erin mused. Attached to the pictures and the well-put-together byline was an attachment for references and ratings. Kat absolutely had her stuff together and Erin was immediately swept up in just how amazing it all seemed. But she still held a modicum of trepidation beneath her radiant joy. She clicked the link. Followed the ratings to their Facebook accounts and even searched online everyone's names including Kar herself. Much to her happy surprise everything came back perfect. Erin nodded in appreciation and decided to call right away. The sooner the better, right?

Two days later Kat showed up at the door. She had a bag with her showcasing Japanese Anime characters of varying types, a pair of shoes covered with Super Mario characters, and a metallic purple jacket with a huge Pac Man ghost on the back. Her smile was infectious, and Erin caught herself grinning at her as she stood in the doorway with an outstretched hand.

"Hi there! I'm Kat Blaine! It is so nice to meet you!" Kat said with as much saccharine sweetness as Erin could stand.

"My, you are definitely as cute as a button, aren't you? And so… gleeful?"

"I love what I do, and I love kids!"

Erin laughed out loud and gestured for Kat to come inside, "I'll go rouse the twins. Chances are they're playing video games. Pretty much what they do with their spare time… after homework. Of course."

Kat giggled along with her, "Of course! I'd think nothing less, Ms. Barton!"

"Oh no. none of that. Erin, please. Just Erin."

Kat nodded as Erin called out for David and Sarah.

As the twins bounded into the room, it was obvious that they were a happy-go-lucky, well-behaved duo, and to prove that point, they walked dutifully up to Kat and shook her hand. They then turned and sat in two kitchen chairs, and each took turns talking a little about themselves with David speaking knowledgeably about his love for video games and costumes made to look like those characters, and Sarah waxing poetically about her love for true crime and wanting to be a CSI Agent when she graduated High School. The kids were adorable and showed no signs of dislike for a babysitter they'd never had. Not just Kat, but any kind of sitter at all. This made Kat very happy, and she knew they'd be an easy group to get along with; they'd listen to her without question and that, she thought, was how they'd all work together just splendidly.

"I am so overjoyed to meet you, two! You are certainly some of the most well-spoken and well behave children I have ever met! And trust me when I say, I have babysat for some real… stinkers."

At that they all shared a laugh, and Erin dismissed the kids as she had to handle some quick paperwork with Kat before she felt comfortable that every loose end had been closed. The twins spun out of the room, but not before each one giving Kat a nice, warm, welcoming hug. Kat felt the excitement in both of their embraces and knew that this would serve to be her best sitting experience yet.

"So, Kat," Erin began after the children's doors had shut. "I'm just a little curious about one thing I couldn't seem to figure out on your employment history. Every job you've had prior to 2018 cleared perfectly. All the phone numbers given came back fine and everyone I spoke to couldn't have said better things about you. It's because of those you're here today, by the way. But something struck me as odd after February of 2018."

Kat cocked her head to the side in curiosity, "Oh no. What was the problem?"

"Well, it's just that the family you worked for couldn't be reach on either the home, cell, or work phone numbers you provided. In fact, each one came back as a non-existent number. I mean I could have just chalked it up to a mistyped number if it had been just one of those three... but ALL of them? Doesn't that seem weird to you?"

Kat laughed out loud, "Oh, you mean the Pearsons'? Oh, that's easy! You had me worried there for a minute! You see, I was babysitting for them almost as a live-in as Mister and Misses Pearson were looking for a new place in Georgia. You see, they were moving because one of the two -I can't remember which- had gotten a new position to work there. So, I moved in, in effect, and watched the kids every day while their parents were away finding a new home."

Erin audibly sighed and showed a visible sign of relief, "Oh my God, Kat! I'm so sorry for even bringing it up! That certainly makes sense. Well, that takes care of that elephant in the room, I'd say! Wonderful. So, with that, I will see you tomorrow morning bright and early at 6:30, right?"

"Oh yes, Miss Bar... Erin! I'm very excited about it! I promise, you will have absolutely nothing to worry about!

If satisfaction and contentment could be etched into a face as examples of how one might feel after a huge weight had been removed, Erin was the picture. She had reprieve finally from her worry about her job and her kids. It felt, to her, in her heart and soul, that everything was really, at last, going to work out for the best. "I am so, so glad, Kat. And I can't possibly thank you enough. You are an honest and true God Send!"

"Thank you, Erin. I will do my best to make you proud."

6.

Ivy tried not to panic, but her heart was drumming in her chest, and she could feel it in her ears. The room had focused since the ghostly halo of light temporarily burned into her vision had faded some. Above the old, wooden workbench hung the shop light, clipped to a hook in one of the joists. Its bulb was aimed toward her, and she could almost feel its heat in the dank basement. Looking down again with greater scrutiny she saw she was strapped to the support beam with what turned out not to be leather belts, as she'd first thought, but rather leather strips meant for making clothing. The pieces were wrapped around her several times and presumably tied behind her. She'd also realized just then that the leather was surprisingly thin and had just enough give so she could begin to wriggle just a little. Her legs were sloppily wrapped and tied with two kitchen aprons. This was a quick and unplanned action by people who really didn't have much practice at it. Not that Ivy had been tied up before. Bondage was not her thing and nor, did it seem, was it the thing of whomever did this. She was willing to bet it was Kat.

Ivy surveyed her layout and found she was actually very close to piece of an old bolt that was jutting from the floor. At one time it held something into place, but its new use was going to be ripping through the aprons that were lashing her legs. She shimmied her body around the weight-bearing post just enough to get atop the piece of metal (almost small enough of a move that would hopefully seem imperceptible to anyone who should come down the stars to inspect) and began scraping the taught cloth against it. After a few minutes, Ivy noticed that the more she strained against the leather wrappings while sawing at the aprons, she was also slowly loosening from them. This was good! She felt some elation wash over her and continued her methodical escape in hopes of being free before anyone else could come down the steps.

She stopped quick and caught her breath. The basement door opened with a whine and daylight spilled down the top few stairs. Then the descent; one step after another. Slowly. It was definitely not Kat judging by the thinness of the legs. It was Sarah. She had a cup and a bottle of water. A cup?

"Hi." Sarah said, sleepily, "Take the pills in this cup, please."

Sarah looked at Ivy with disinterest, and before handing her the cup and water, stepped over to the workbench and grabbed what looked like a box cutter, "If you don't Kat told me to use this on your hands."

Ivy glared at her through widening eyes, "Kat asked that you give me those pills, or you'd have to cut me? Is that right?"

Sarah nodded slowly, methodically, and handed Ivy the little cup first. Inside were three pills: Valium. She'd guess probably 20 milligrams each, as their desired effect was probably to knock Ivy out for an extended period of time, and she'd taken them before for her anxiety issues a few years ago. Little did Sarah know that Ivy had no intention of swallowing anything she was given by anybody in this house.

"Okay, okay… just don't cut my hands. I'll take them."

"Good. Because you seem nice and I don't really want to hurt you like Kat did to my…" Sarah began, choking back tears.

Ivy saw this as a good distraction. She snatched the pills, tossed them from the cup to her mouth (not the easiest of tasks considering she could only just barely reach her mouth), and reached out for water. As she did so she deftly tucked the pills behind her back right bottom molar. Ever since she had her wisdom teeth removed for braces years ago, there was a gap, coincidentally the perfect size in which to hide a few small pills. "What did Kat do, Sarah? Did she do something to your mom?"

Sarah nodded as tears spilled down her cheeks, "She's hurt really bad. But I'm not supposed to say anything, or else Kat will…"

Ivy took the water she was offered and swallowed two big gulps, "What will Kat do, Sarah? Is she making you do things you don't want to do because she's hurt your mommy?"

The word mommy made Sarah's face screw up into huge gouts of weeping. She stood in the middle of the room and began to make loud, bawling sounds. This was not ideal.

"No, Sarah. You have to be quiet if you want me to help save your mom. Okay?"

At that, Sarah snuffled, wiped her face, and nodded with what appeared to Ivy to be some kind of hope.

7

Kat showed up at precisely 6:20. She prided herself on being early. Besides, she mused to herself, the earlier the better for all the excitement I have planned! She really did love kids. They were always so sweet and innocent around her. She gave off an air of being affable and sympathetic without seeming too much of a push over and a chump to the parents. She was fair; she'd hand out punishments as they were necessitated, but she didn't believe in 'Time-Outs' or staring blankly into the corner to serve out a chastising. There wasn't need for needless sanctions and ostracism for kids, as they infrequently understood just what sitting alone stewing over a problem served in the long run. Kat felt the same way, and her statutes and precedents were simple: Be kind to one another, no physical encounters with one another, and treat each other with the respect you'd want for yourself. Simple.

The parents were another tale all together. The parents were often the real issues behind the children's misbehaving, and it was to them that they often showed their anger and discord. But Kat wouldn't have any of it. If your issues were with mom and dad, then it was to them you'd show your dissonance, not to her. To that end there would be repercussions. Kat was not a parent, and she surely was not going to play one to any of the children she sat for. She'd spent enough time learning adults were always where the core of trouble lay, and it was to adults she'd focus her ire. She knew grown-ups very well and she'd never like any of them. A lesson learned from the Pearson's. A lesson she didn't want to repeat.

She rang the doorbell and within moments Erin welcomed her once again into her home.

*****

The days and weeks went by wonderfully. The twins loved Kat, and it seemed Erin did even more. Their after-school days consisted of homework first, then an hour of free time followed by games together (like their favorite, CLUE), PlayStation challenges, and working on extracurricular projects as they were required. Erin would return home from work around six, exhausted but content. She would join them for dinner, talk over their days; "How was school? Are you enjoying classes? Is Kat helping out well?", and in turn she would share her time at work (as boring as it seemed, they all appreciated it and loved that she enjoyed her job). The days went by like that as Summer began its inevitable approach.

"Well, Kat, I don't think there is a way to thank you enough for the past nine months. You have been the best thing to happen to this family in a long time and you have more than given me an opportunity to breathe a little easier. The kids only have about a month left of school and, well, I guess we need to discuss your future with the family." Erin said through sleepy yet attentive eyes, "What is you'd like to do? Do you have any thoughts on the Summer?"

Kat had thought about it at length. She knew the school year was drawing toa close and that discussion of where she stood was inevitable. "To be honest, Erin, I have thought of nothing beyond my life here, with you and your family"

At this Erin smiled. It was genuine, but there was something hidden behind it. Kat knew she wasn't going to like what was coming next. "That's so sweet, Kat. As I said we have absolutely loved having you here, the kids and I, but I'd be lying to you if I said that there might be a change in plans for the Summer. You see, there's something I haven't shared with you, and the kids know only because you aren't here on the weekends… but I have met someone. Someone I work with who has grown to mean a lot to me and the twins."

The Twins and I, stupid, Kat corrected in her head through a bitten tongue, "Oh? Well, that's wonderful, Erin!" She said, containing as much rage as she could and, hopefully, showing none of it.

A forlorn look danced across Erin's face, "Kat, sweetie, I know this isn't the best news right now. This is the reason I wanted to tell you while there's still a month to go. I figured it would give you plenty of time to seek out other employment while still working for our family, you know? I'll absolutely give you the best review you could possibly ask for! And it's not that we don't -well, I don't- want you around. It's not that at all, it's just that my new friend, Samantha, Sam, will be moving in with us in June and she will be working opposite shifts… well, you understand."

Sam? Samantha? Erin was a lesbian? Kat never even considered this, not that it made any difference. "Oh, Erin… don't sweat it, okay? I appreciate the timely warning and… sure, I can definitely find another sitting gig. But what about Sarah and David? Weren't they upset?"

"Oh, you bet they were, Kat. They cried for some time. This wasn't an easy decision for any of us: not me, not Sam, and certainly not the kids. But after some explanation, we all agreed it made the most sense."

Kat could feel fury churning inside her. She felt like a volcano, moments away from blasting searing hot anger into the stratosphere. But she tamped it down, swallowed back every word she wanted to scream, and remained as stolid as ever. "Yeah, I suppose it makes sense if you're going to have a live-in sitter, so to speak…"

"Right! Exactly. I'm so glad you're taking this news so well, Kat. I will be a change for all of us, and the twins and I will be so sad to see you go. I really do wish I could keep you on, but… I mean it just doesn't make any sense, I guess. I'm so, so sorry."

"I know, Erin. And I'm sorry, too." Her apology hung in the air like a threatening wraith.

8.

Ivy watched with newer purpose as Sarah began to make her way back up the stairs. "Sarah," Ivy said, quietly, "Remember, you have to keep this a secret. Kat cannot know about this… not even David. Not yet, okay?"

"Right. I promise. I don't like Kat anymore. She's not nice." And with that statement, she continued her slow process up the basement steps.

Ivy reached into the space behind her molar and extracted the Valium. She arched her head as far as it would turn to the left and spat them into the darkened corner of the basement. She could her them clatter against the cement floor. With that, she returned to her work sawing at the metal bolt tearing through her restraints.

Ivy didn't know how much time had passed, but she could make out a little light coming in through the tiny window to her right. It wasn't bright, but that didn't matter since the glass was coated with ages of dust and a litany of faded cobwebs. Her pace at freeing herself from the leg constraints was perilously slow, but she was making admirable progress and she could begin to feel the binding apron strings loosen. She tried again to spread her legs, and with a considerable amount of effort and one strenuous contraction, she felt the cloth give and new she was free. The job done there, she knew she couldn't congratulate herself completely yet, nor could she let on in any way that the aprons had loosened. What she needed was the box cutter Sarah had. But where had she left it?

The basement door once again creaked open, and a set of shadowy legs appeared on the illuminated landing. They looked like Sarah's, but Ivy couldn't be sure yet. She sat motionless, drooped her chin to her chest, and feigned sleep.

"It's okay, miss… Ivy, it's just me, Sarah," The child spoke with little emotion, "Sorry I took so long, I had to help David clean up yucky blood."

Ivy quit her ploy and looked into Sarah's face, "Blood? Whose blood?"

"Samantha's. It's getting all over the bathroom floor."

"Wait. Who is Samantha? Did Kat lure another person to the house since I've been down here?"

Sarah shook her head, "No. This is… was mommy's special friend," she choked back tears again, "Kat murdered her in front of us to make us listen. I was so scared! I liked Sam, too. Me and David both did. Her blood went all over… we had to clean it all up and…"

"Okay, sweetheart, that's fine, you don't have to tell me anymore. But I need to be able to get out of here if you want me to help. Does Kat think I'm asleep?"

"Yeah, I told her you swallowed the pills and that I made sure. Kat trusts me because I do what I'm told and don't argue. But I don't like her anymore." Sarah said with mounting anger in her voice.

"I know, honey. I don't like her either," Ivy said, matter-of-factly, "But you need to listen to me, too, now, right?"

"Yes. I can do that."

"Good. First thing you need to do is get me out of these leather straps. I can only loosen them so far and it's not enough to wriggle out of them. I need something sharp. Do you have that box cutter still?"

Sarah shook her head again, "No, Kat has it."

"Damn. Okay. Well, we need something else from the tool bench. What else is over there?"

Sarah dutifully stepped over to the bench and began taking inventory, "A screwdriver. A hammer. Some kind of glue. I think a saw blade…"

"Wait." Ivy said, "What kind of saw blade? Round or long and thin?"

"Long and thin. It's pretty old though. I can see rust on it."

Ivy smiled, "That's fine, Sarah. Bring me that. Just set it on my hands and then head back upstairs before Kat starts to wonder what's taking you so long."

Sarah did as she was asked. She then kissed Ivy on the cheek. "Help us, Miss Ivy. We're really scared."

"I will honey. Don't worry. No go on."

Sarah turned and marched back up the steps. The door closed behind her and Ivy, pinching the saw blade between her thumb and forefinger, began to work at the leather straps.

*****

Kat stood in the kitchen with a Cheshire grin splayed across her lips, "Is the bitch still asleep, Sarah?"

Sarah met Kat's gaze, and without a flinch or a hint of untruth to her demeanor she responded, "Yes, ma'am. Her head is drooped and everything."

Kat cocked an eyebrow, "But did you really check? Did you poke her a few times… maybe eve kick her like I said?"

"I did. I poked her nose and kicked her right in the leg. She never even squirmed." Sarah admitted with no show of emotion, "Kat, I'm hungry."

Her deft change of subject brought a kind grin to Kat's face. He eyes opened wide. "I have a surprise for you and David! Corndogs! You kids love corndogs!"

Sarah faked a passable smile, "We sure do! With tater tots, too?"

Kat laughed a little to heartily, "Tots it is, sweet Sarah. Tots it is."

"Thank you, Kat! May I go play in my room now, please?"

Kat's wan smile twitched just a little and her shoulder jumped, "In your room… yes, yes of course. Go play with David. I think he's up from his nap. But let's not forget there's still some more of that mess I had to make left to clean, right?"

Sarah nodded. Kat tousled her hair and watched her plod slowly to her room. She trusted Sarah to do what she'd asked, mostly because her mother's life was slowly ebbing away, and Kat was the only one who could keep her from passing away completely. She had the kids at her every beckon call. But even so, it occurred to her she might feel better if she checked on Ivy herself. This was not the time for screw ups. She knew she could still have this precariously balanced house of cards collapse around her if she became too careless. This couldn't end like the Pearson's. She wouldn't let it end like that. That was a disaster she'd just as soon never think about again.

*****

The saw blade proved to be the perfect tool. Ivy held it in her mouth as she snapped the last bit of leather holding her hands bound. Just then the basement door swung open, this time not with a creak but a burst. There was no doubt in Ivy's mind it was Kat. She had seconds to hide her handiwork. Letting the sawblade drop down the front of her shirt, her cleavage hid it well enough, she slid her leather clad arms under her breasts and drooped her head just as Kat hit the fifth step and her head came into view.

Kat stood at the landing, unmoving but surveying the area. Ivy could see her out of the corner of a half-closed eye. If Kat got even close, she would burst forth and strangle that bitch where she stood. But Kat maintained her distance.

"I don't know if you can hear me, but I'm hoping you can. Sarah said you were asleep, but I'm not so sure I believe her. If you're awake, listen closely," Kat began as she leaned more closely, "The only way you're going to live through this is to stay right where you are. I've done this before, and I know what I'm doing. But I don't really want to kill you, too, unless I have to. Don't make me have to."

Ivy listened to Kat as she waxed poetically about her past endeavors. "I wasn't always like this… ya know, a killer. But it seems it pays a lot better when it works. Erin was such a gullible bitch; she fell for my charms like an idiot. Sure, I had to talk my way out of the shitstorm my last sitting job was, but that wasn't too difficult since Erin pretty much loved me from the word 'hello'. The Pearson's were an accident. They were going to move away from me, and I just couldn't have that. I couldn't let them take those kids from me! I loved those kids. But no one will ever find the bodies. Only I know where they are. Fortunately, they made enough stupid financial mistakes while I was their nanny that I made a pretty hefty profit from them… but I never wanted to kill the kids. But I had to! You see? There couldn't be witnesses!"

Ivy stayed perfectly still. What she was hearing scared her enough that she wasn't ready for a confrontation just now anyway. She needed to be completely free from the lashings and holding a weapon in each hand. She listened as Kat kept on with tales of her exploits. "Erin was easier. She didn't even put up much of a struggle, really. The kids were a bit of a handful, but a few Valiums here and there and they stayed in line. Sam was another problem all together… I didn't expect her to show up. She fought hard. But, in the end… well, it's her blood the kids have to clean up, ya know? Anyway, I'm just talking. If you've heard any of this, do what I said and don't try to be a hero. It will not end well for you. I have to go make the kids' dinner. I have a surprise for them!"

Kat stood, turned, and stomped back up the steps. Ivy opened her eyes, shook herself free from the straps, climbed out of the apron strings, and raced to the workbench. There was little doubt left in her mind now: Kat was a psychopath and a murderer. She instinctively reached for her pocket in hopes of finding her phone there, but of course it wasn't. She had to get upstairs right away. There was no point in making those kids, and their mom for that matter, suffer any longer. She grabbed the hammer, the saw blade from her shirt, and located a relatively sharp wood chisel. It was now or never.

9.

There was a knock at the door. It was 7:30, Erin had just gotten up this Saturday morning and was filling the coffee filter with her favorite grounds. She murmured to herself wondering who it could possibly be at this hour, not expecting Samantha until 9. The knock came again, this time just a bit more forceful, Erin noticed, "I'm coming, just a second!"

She reached out a hand to open the door, and instead stopped short, "Who is it?"

"It's me, Erin. It's Kat. I think I left one of my books in the house last night." Kat's muffled voice announced.

Erin sighed with a smile, released the chain lock, slid back the dead bolt, and opened the door. "Hi Kat, come on…"

The blow came in an instant as Kat swung out with practiced accuracy. The weapon was a heavy rock that used to sit just outside Erin's front door. It hit cleanly and Erin collapsed backward like a sack of flour, blood trickling from her ear and immediately pooling on the tile around her face. Kat didn't know if the connection was enough to kill, but it was surely enough to break a bone or two, and she landed the shot directly on the side of Erin's skull. Kat stood over her target with a leering, predatory look in her eyes. Without a word, she stepped over the body, grabbed it by the arms, and dragged it away from the door. Kat peered out, making sure no one had seen her deed, and shut the door behind her.

The twins weren't awake yet. This was good, as Kat had a few things to do before she wanted to deal with them. She rummaged through the junk drawer and found a few multi-colored and sized zip ties. She fastened Erin's arms behind her and lashed her tightly at the ankles. Erin looked sad and silly at the same time: bruised and unconscious, but with brightly colored plastic cuffs on. Kat couldn't help but smile. Blood had begun to ooze afresh from Erin's ear and ran in thick rivulets down her rapidly bruising face. She' have to deal with the mess later. She dragged Erin's limp body to the bathroom. She weighed a lot more than she looked, and it took a bit of effort to get her body around two corners, across the bathroom, and over the side into the tub. The job done, she stood back and glared at her handiwork just as Erin's eyes began to flutter open, showing only the whites as her pupils were still mired in a comatose fog. Kat smiled with such feline ferocity that a peripheral glance in the mirror gave her pause.

"Don't try to talk, Erin. And it's probably best not to even try to move. I clobbered you pretty hard. You're gonna have one bastard of a headache for a while. So just fuckin' chill, okay?"

Erin didn't or, more likely couldn't, respond, and Kat found this satisfactory. She tossed a towel at Erin with some hidden form of concern, and yanked the curtains closed with an equal amount of indifference. It was time to get the kids up.

10.

Ivy steeled herself at the landing of the staircase. This was surely not a situation she'd ever imagined finding herself in, and she sure as shit had never been it one like it before. Yet, she knew she wasn't helpless. Even with the procured tools, she had an air of gravitas that was pulsing through her body, giving her a new level of confidence. Though her father had been an asshole, his actions taught her to be strong and always ready for unseen circumstances much like the one in which she found herself. She'd defended his advances as a teenager; always trying to touch and rub her when her mother wasn't paying attention. She'd thrown him off her more than once, and it was times like those, character building and strengthening, that gave her the power she needed now. Kat was a killer. Her dad was just a disgusting drunk with a penchant for rape. Not the same, but not that different. She took a deep breath, steadied herself, and began to silently ascend the steps into the unknown.

*****

"Kat, may I have some more ketchup, please" David asked through drooping eyes and slow, methodical speech.

Kat obliged without a word. As she squeezed a puddle onto David's plate it reminded her instantly of the coagulating spots of blood that stained the carpet. The twins had cleaned the worst of it from the tile floor, but the rugs and the hallway carpeting were another story. The blood had soaked in and begun to darken to a deep red. I was going to take a lot of extra effort to get those stains out. She solemnly nodded think of all the work she'd have to make the children do.

"Eat up, guys. There's more to do." Kat announced as she divvied out a few more corndogs each and scoopfuls of tater tots.

"But I don't think I'm really hungry anymore, Kat." Sarah Opined, as she pushed food around on her plate, "Can we please see mommy again. I have been good…"

As Sarah's voice trailed off into fresh tears, Kat stared at her like a minster ready to strike, "No. I already told you, Sarah, we have more to do. When everything is cleaned up, I will let you see your mom. Now finish. I have to use the bathroom."

Ivy could hear their voices clearly through the basement door. She sat poised as Kat's chair slid from the table, and she left the kitchen headed to the bathroom. With that she slowly, gently turned the knob to open the door. I was as quite as could be, but to Ivy's ears the door's creak sounded like the loudest scream and she just knew Kat had heard everything. But not even the twins, sitting at the table with grim, exhausted looks on their faces, heard the door. She had the element of surprise, but she didn't want to startle the children either. She had to be very discreet.

But Sarah turned and saw her first. She opened her mouth with a bright smile and Ivy had to hurry over just in time to clamp a hand over her mouth. "Sarah, shhhh… don't say anything!" she whispered.

Sarah understood and nodded her head. Ivy looked at David. He was lost in a torpor. He saw Ivy but didn't even open his mouth. It was obvious he was drugged far worse than his sister. The poor boy looked like the walking dead.

"David, sweetie, are you okay?" Ivy asked, instinctively putting the back of her hand to his forehead. It was clammy and cold.

"I guess so. Mommy is in the bathtub with a lot of blood. Kat is so mean…. I don't feel so good, either."

"No, I' d guess not. And we're going to help your mommy, I promise. Okay, first of all: we need to call the police." Ivy said in a hushed tone.

"We can't. Look." Sarah pointed to the phone on the wall. Both cords were cut, and the receiver hung free, broken.

"Do you know what Kat did with my cell, Sarah?" Ivy asked with a whisper.

Sarah shook her head. Damn. Calling the police was out for now, "Okay, okay… well then, we need to get you two to the neighbor's house. Do you know them, are they home?"

Sarah said she didn't know, but yes, they knew the Morrison's, "But I don't want to leave my mom!"

"I know, sweetie, I do. But it's not safe for you to be here anymore. Trust me, I am going to make sure your mom gets out of here, okay? I said before I promised, and I intend to keep that promise." Ivy said as she kept her gaze down the hall toward the bathroom. "In the meantime, I need to come up with a plan. I really don't want to anger Kat even more than she already is -if that's even possible- so is there maybe somewhere for me to hide?"

David, in his drug induced stupor, pointed to a pantry door right next to the refrigerator. Ivy stepped to it quickly and opened it. It wasn't huge, but it had more than enough room to conceal her, and she could leave the door open a crack as she waited. "Okay, kids. I'm going to wait in here because she's bound to be back soon. Just act the way you have been around Kat and do NOT let on that I'm..."

Ivy was cut off as the footsteps approached. She had a final second to put her finger to her lips and pull the door almost closed. All Ivy had to do now was wait for the perfect moment.

*****

Kat turned from the kitchen and plodded to the bathroom. This whole act was getting exhausting. Sure, she loved the children very much, but murder, and keeping them quiet, and maintaining Emily's rapidly waning life... not to mention the mess Samantha left... it was a lot. She breathed in and sighed. Why did it always have to end like this? She wasn't a bad person! Not really. Her life wasn't bad; she had a normal childhood with normal, dull parents. But when she'd met Gabe all those years ago. He showed her so many things about life that were just horrifying and more terrible than anything she'd ever seen. Gabe was a 'Bad Boy'. He had a knife, his dead father's revolver, he smoked, he was a complete package and Kat fell for every gritty bit of him. It was Gabe who showed her that a killing wasn't always a bad thing, especially if someone did something you didn't like. Kat fed off that knowledge and trained herself to realize that life wasn't precious, especially those of adults. Kat was an adult, and a fair bit older than she let on to anyone else. She was a liar, and always to get what she wanted: to be the best babysitter for anyone. And if the parents tried to stop that, well…

Erin was still lying in the bathtub, but Kat had given her a towel on which she could lean her head. She'd also cleaned Erin's wound just enough so it wouldn't get infected. Kat liked to believe somewhere in her black heart there was still some semblance of sympathy. "I see you're still alive. That's good."

"W-w-where are m-m-my kids?" Erin queried with a visible struggle.

"Oh, look. It can still talk! I guess maybe I need to hurt you a little more, eh? I wonder what I can do…"

"N-n-no…. please. M-m-my kids…" Erin stammered, bleakly.

"They're fine, stupid! I don't hurt kids! Adults I hurt. Speaking of which, I saw a pair of plyers downstairs. I think I need to make sure you don't do anymore talking!"

Erin began to cry. Whether it was from relief that her kids weren't harmed, or for fear that Kat wasn't done inflicting pain on her, Kat didn't know. And she didn't care, either. She yanked the curtains shut and turned to head back to the kitchen, "Stupid bitch."

11

Samantha walked up the front steps with breakfast for Erin and the kids. She had bags from Wendy's in one hand and four drinks in a cup holder in the other. She deftly snatched the food with the hand that held the cups and opened the front door. The house was quiet. Sam was a little confused as she had just spoken to Erin and was told she'd be waiting for her in the kitchen. But where was she? The more Sam thought about it the more eerie it seemed.

"Hello?" Sam called out. She waited for a reply as she set the breakfast bags on the table. But there was no response. "Erin? Kids? It's Sam! I come bearing breakfast! I hope you like- "

"Samantha." The voice stated from the hallway, "Nice to finally meet you!"

Kat appeared around the corner. Samantha was momentarily taken aback, as she had never put a face to the name. She knew who Kat was, but she never expected her here on a Saturday, "Well hi! You must be Kat! So nice to meet- "

"YOU FUCKING BITCH!! BECAUSE OF YOU I CAN'T BABYSIT HERE ANYMORE!!" Kat bellowed at the top of her lungs and sprang at Sam with surprising agility.
Samantha had no time to react. She backed up into the refrigerator, slammed her heat into the handle, and was immediately set upon by a vicious and seething woman. Kat grabbed fistfuls of Sam's hair and continued to jam her head into the handle of the fridge door. Sam tried to wriggle free as she wailed out for help. Kat reached across the table with her left hand, snatched the bag of breakfast food, and shoved it in Sam's face, jamming it into her eyes and mouth. The bag burst open, and the unctuous odor of eggs and sausage filled the air. Sam gagged, choking on paper wrapping and smashed pieces

of food. Sam cried out but her sounds were muffled by the onslaught of destroyed breakfast sandwiches. Kat once again reached out and grabbed the closest kitchen chair.

"I'm going to KILL you, BITCH!" Kat pronounced angrily just as she brought the wooden chair up to Sam's throat.

With a quick jab Sam felt the force of the chair crush her windpipe. She wheezed, reached for the wooden slats and struggled against Kat's terrific pressure. The external boundaries of Sam's vision began to throb with encroaching blackness, and she could feel herself slipping from cognizance. Kat seemed to grow even more powerful as she watched the bulging life ebb from Sam's eyes.

Sam gasped, drawing in fresh oxygen and through her wavering vision saw as the twins wandered into the kitchen rubbing sleep from their eyes. Sarah was first to notice. She screamed, loudly and shrill. Kat heard them arrive before Sarah's reaction, and as she let the pressure subside on Sam's throat, she dropped the chair to the floor with a clatter, "Well good morning, sleepies!" Kat said through gritted teeth,

Sam wasn't about to let the opportunity fade, "Kids! Run! Now! Go!" Her words came in hitching croaks. She kicked out with her leg to catch Kat even more unaware and knocked her to the ground with a questioning yelp.

But the kids didn't move. The looked on with stupefied gazes in their eyes. Sam yelled for them to run again just as she reared back to kick the fallen Kat in the face, but Kat had already seen the error of her own lost attention and put up an arm to block it. With Sam off balance Kat reached out with her guarding arm and yanked at her leg. Sam skidded forward and tripped over Kat's crouching form. She hit the floor hard, her head glancing off the corner of the table.

"Ow! Shit!" Sam barked. Kat scrambled to her feet and leapt, cat-like toward the knife block near the sink, "Kids! RUN!!" Sam squalled again as she tried in vain to clamor back to her feet.

The children could only watch in abject dread as a keening Kat swung out from the counter with a chef's knife in her grip and plunged it into Sam's neck. The force was so great that the blade was buried down to the guard. Sam belched out a 'GLICK!' sound, and instinctively sought out the foreign object that protruded from her throat. Blood began to gurgle and spurt from around the wound as she helplessly pawed at the knife. The more she tried to extract the blade, the more blood shot from the hole like a gory fountain. Kat backed up as streams of Sam's vitality painted the kitchen floor and table and watched with a look of satisfaction as Sam slipped away on the collected puddles.

At this the twins began to bawl. Sam struggled like a trapped fish in a tide pool. She tried to call to the children for aid, but nothing came out except bubbly gurgles. Kat stepped around the growing mess, reached the kids and gathered them up in her arms.

"I'm sorry, my loves. Samantha was a monster! She was trying to take me away from you!" Kat said with false empathy.

Sarah and David continued to weep into her arms, neither having the strength to fight her off, and neither believing what they'd seen. Kat looked at them, looked back at Sam as her remaining life drained out onto the tile, and said, "Well, it's just us now, my children. I should probably show you where your mom is, too. Oh, and she is naughty, too. Let's go take a look. And let's be very good, now. Okay? Be very good for Kat?"

12

Ivy breathed slowly and deliberately, not only to protect herself, but to also be able to hear Kat. Kat was telling the children to get done eating so they could return to their cleaning duties. She wanted them to stay out of the bathroom and that she was going downstairs to check on Ivy.

At this, Ivy grinned. Her plan was simple. Once the basement door opened, Ivy would wait a few seconds, burst from the pantry, and slam the basement door shut, wedging it in place with a chair. She could see it all come to fruition in her head, but her timing needed to be perfect, and she had to hope the twins didn't slip up. Until David spoke.

"What are you gonna do to Ivy, Kat?" David questioned as he went around gathering the lunch dishes.

"Well, kiddo, it's none of your business what I do. But I will say that whatever it is I'm gonna do with a pair of old plyers!" Kat said through a stifled laugh.

"You can't hurt her anymore," David said under his breath, "She won't let you."

"What was that?" Kat asked as she reached for the handle.

Sarah piped up, "Nothing. He just asked me to get the glasses from the table. He's pretty tired."

Ivy listened closely from the closet. David might have just spoiled her plans. Damn kid. But she supposed she couldn't blame him; he was you and he'd been through a hell of a day.

"No, I don't think that's what he said at all, Sarah. How about we let David speak, okay?" Kat said as her anger began to turn her face red.

"I said," David began, staring at Kat intently as she pulled the basement door open, "That you can't hurt her- "

Abandoning her previous idea, Ivy gathered herself in an instant. With one quick motion she flung open the pantry door and burst into the kitchen directly at Kat. She saw the utter surprise on Kat's face as Ivy screamed toward her with the force of a linebacker. With arms outstretched, and by the grace of God, she both shoved forward and kicked the basement door shut all in one swift action. Kat yelled out and, behind the quickly shutting door, Ivy could hear both her pained screeches and the sounds of her body hitting every wooden step on the way down. With the door slammed shit, Ivy grabbed the closest chair and jammed it against the handle, kicking the back legs into the floor for support.

"Are… you guys… alright?" Ivy asked through her panting breaths.

"Is she gone?" Sarah asked, tears welling in her eyes. Her brother looked on the verge of crying herself.

"I don't know. But she's down there now and trapped. I don't hear her anymore."

The twins flung themselves at Ivy and they all shared a hug of relief.

But it was short lived. They all froze as they heard the wailing erupt from the basement.

"YOU'RE ALL GONNA DIE NOW!! ALL OF YOUUUUU!! YOU FUCKING LITTLE SHITS SPOILED EVERYTHING!!"

13.

No words were spoken between Kat and the twins. It seemed they had sobbed themselves into some kind of momentary hypnosis. Kat allowed them to see their mother, semi-conscious and bleeding in the bathtub. At the very least the children could plainly see that she was still alive, but Kat had no intention of letting them linger, let alone hug her as she lapsed in and out of wakefulness. But the children had stopped crying and stood idly by as Kat fed them each a small dose of Vicodin mixed into some orange juice. Her plan was to keep them as drone-like as she could. The meds would sooner or later render them useless as sleep was a byproduct of the pills, but while they were awake, they were her worker bees and she made them clean the blood from the kitchen floor. They only complained once, and as the threats of harm to them as well as further harm to their mom were given from Kat, they complained no more and went about their work. As the afternoon carried on into one o'clock, Kat heard a car cough and die outside the window. A woman exited the driver's side, popped the hood, and began examining the vehicle as steam rose in plumes from the radiator. This day had just gotten even more interesting indeed.

14.

Kat's pain was hot agony as it blasted through her thigh. She flushed with rage as she sat nursing what was likely a broken bone. Kat was lying prone at the bottom of the stairs. Her mind tried to work out how things had gotten to this point. How had Ivy gotten free? She sat in darkness save from the milky haze that shown through the small egress window, but it lit nothing but a hazy storm of dust motes. The pain began to course through her, and she could see and feel herself floating out of consciousness…

His name was Gabe.

Gabe Blanchard. And he was a dream! Kat's first crush. She loved him, and he her. He was a Bad Boy with a bad attitude and Kat drew him in like a breath of new air. They technically met at school, but it was while Kat was acquiring her GED at Vocational College. She'd always been a great student in High School, that is, until her Senior Year. She just lost interest in everything. Her parents wept for her as her future aspirations to become an Engineer trickled away, as did Kat's desire to succeed. Mom and dad tried to help with anything and everything they could think of, but it wasn't until she skipped her last few weeks of High School and didn't graduate where her life finally started making sense to her. And his name was Gabe.

Attending classes toward her GED was not an ideal situation; there were no friends from High School, she felt like a loner, and the atmosphere was most definitely not the same. She felt like an outcast -which, of course, she was- and she had begun to realize that maybe her life could have taken a better path. Then there was Gabe. Gabe sat next to her, hoodie pulled over his head, flicking at his fingerless-gloved hands with a pen knife and a vacant look on his face. Kat watched intently as he chomped away at his gum, saw the haphazardly tucked cigarette behind his ear, and noticed with some kind of new excitement the Ray Ban sunglasses balancing on his nose showcasing the full amount of just how little her cared. Kat was smitten, and she took it upon herself to say hello, and show off her own set of doe eyes and attractiveness. Gabe took the bait and before long they were holding hands in the hallways; she always with a gleeful look on her face, and he always with an air of mischief and mayhem playing behind his black sunglasses. They were inseparable during class time, and practically one person after 3 PM and every weekend. Kat began to take on much of Gabe's traits, much to her parent's dismay.

Kat's parents had met Gabe, and all it took was the one time for them to make their decision that he was certainly no good, and, above all else, he was very wrong for Kat. Their disapproval only made Kat distance herself from them and fall even more passionately under Gabe's aura. As her parent's watched from the sidelines and pleaded for their daughter to drop Gabe before problems really began, Kat became Gabe's willing student in the world of misbehavior and thumbed her nose at their offers of help and love. Kat was becoming all her parents had feared: sassy, rude, disrespectful, and worse. Kat was rarely home those days, spending nights and weekends at Gabe's apartment. They only hoped she wasn't becoming a sexual deviant as well, and they prayed for her safety.

Kat began to trail Gabe on his 'jobs'. She would wait in his rusted-out Ford Taurus while he would work. His 'gig' was to go into local clothing stores, remove clothes from racks, and take them to the customer service desk to return the items he'd never purchased in the first place. Generally, they'd give him a card for store credit, with which he'd promptly find a buyer and sell the cards for cash. He'd then supplement his alcohol habit and do his best to keep Kat happy as well. Kat actually did find a job, having just turned nineteen (never ever telling anyone she was a few years older than she let on) she was able to get work babysitting during the week. This helped supplement her life with Gabe, but it was never about the money, always about the experience. Kat learned so much from Gabe, and none of it good.

The first time she'd seen real violence was when she watched Gabe beat a man almost to death with a crowbar. The victim tried to rob Gabe and Kat outside of a party store and Gabe flew into a rage. Kat saw it all from a distance and, with an animal lust and a beastly desire fell even more in love with Gabe. She watched with all the interest of a student of a Master of Fine Arts as Gabe smashed in the man's face and cracked bones. The blood flowed freely and spilled across the pavement. The shadows hid the destruction, but they could not hide Kat's piqued interest and sinister smile.

From that moment the craving set in. She desired violence, sought out its seductive appeal, and basked in the gory exercise like an inhuman monster. She studied her horror movie tropes like actors study The Bard. She idolized mass murderers and serial killers, learning their brutal histories and poring over their lengthy trails of ruin. Her desires for Gabe grew stronger, but Kat, too, wanted in on the action and she began participating in ritual beatings they'd dish out to the local vagrant population and to anyone who looked at them sideways. Kat was honing her skills, but it wasn't long before the law caught wind and began their investigations into the half-dozen local beatings.

Kat continued to babysit, and as she grew to enjoy it more, she also began to create profiles for herself on the internet. Glowing reviews were the easy part, as she was always a joy with the children and made sure the parents saw her as such. In reality she was a demon, and in her own head she'd begun loathing adults and how they not only treated her out in the world, but also how they looked at her when she was with Gabe. Gabe himself didn't truly feel the need for the approval Kat had desired; his future was a bottomless pit with no direction. Kat wanted her life to be with the kids she loved sitting, and so they began to drift apart. Eventually, as Kat started making a name for herself as the go-to babysitter in the area, Gabe was picked up for shoplifting and brought before a judge on a litany of other charges, including the violence he's created. He was incarcerated and Kat was left to her own devices. Which was fine by her.

Then she met the Pearson's, and her life would take another turn.

15.

Ivy sat down in the bathroom with the twins and looked at the wrapping job they'd done to Erin's wounds. The bleeding stopped, but she was pail and weak. Ivy retrieved Erin's phone from her nightstand and was ready to dial 911. Fortunately, Kat hadn't looked there, or hadn't thought to, anyway, and they still had a functioning phone.

"Wait, Ivy…" Erin began as she adjusted herself to a more comfortable position, "You said Kat was still in the basement, right?"

Ivy nodded, "Yeah, she is most definitely not happy, either. But my guess is she's pretty hurt."

"Okay, that's fine. We'll leave her for now. Before we call the police -and we will call them- I think it's best to get the children away from here." Emily said with a hitch in her voice as her pain was still very raw.

"Right," Ivy agreed, "But where do you want them to go? The neighbors?"

Erin nodded around with a pained look on her face, "I would have said Samantha's, but —"

"But what?"

"She's dead. Kat murdered her, too. Kids, what did Kat do with… Sam?" Erin asked as fresh tears trickled down her cheeks.

The twins both shrugged, faces red and raw from sobbing, "We don't know, mommy. She made us clean… there was so much blood everywhere!" Sarah was clearly scarred and panicked, "David doesn't know either. We did what Kat wanted us to do (burbling cries were coming anew from the children as they tried in vain to remember anything) We don't know where Sam is, Mommy!"

"It's okay, baby. It's okay. It will all get figured out soon and you'll never have to do anything Kat tells you to do again. I promise."

"Who should I call, Miss Barton?" Ivy asked.

"It's Erin, please. No need for formalities now, huh? I guess we'd better call their father. He lives close, he's just not… a great person. But I think he can help."

"Okay. That sounds good. How close is close? I'm worried about you and the kids, and especially Kat. She's down there and she is not in a good mood." Ivy said, matter-of-factly.

"He lives in Portage. About a half hour away. Let me give you his number."

Ivy dialed as Erin relayed her ex-husband's number. It rang and a voice on the other end answered with a questioning "Hello?" Ivy spent the better part of the next five minutes explaining the situation, and then handed the phone to Erin who added details Ivy hadn't known. Before the call even ended, her ex was in his car and on the way.

+It was then that they all heard the guttural squeal from the basement. Kat was definitely not happy.

16.

Sam's body hadn't gone far because Kat was only so strong. She had found a tarp in the garage and rolled her onto it with some effort. Kat folded Sam up and tied the ends together with some jute. With strength she dug deep to find, Kat drug the dead weight to the back of the garage and hid it with as much stuff from around the area as she could find. She would have to do a better job concealing her handiwork later. But for now, it would serve. She scowled at the half-assed job and went inside to make sure the twins were still mopping up the gory mess.

17.

Kat bellowed with deafening agony. Her broken leg was screaming at her, and she'd dared not move. She knew it was her femur and the only way to ease the pain was going to be to move so the bones weren't rubbing against one another. The thought of doing so enraged her and consumed her: That bitch Ivy had caused this! Those little brats were just kids, but they helped Ivy escape and now her plans were ruined! But this idea faded, because her addled brain was once again being overcome with thick, black clouds. She was again wrapped in a heavy blanket of unconsciousness, and she fell on through the void.

Kat met the Pearson's through a mutual friend in 2018. They needed a new babysitter as they were planning to move sooner than later, and they were house hunting out of state. For Kat this would be a live-in position much like a nanny. Kat accepted sight unseen and knew instantly this would be her big break into a new world. She was ecstatic. She fell in love with their children, Jessica, Ben, and little Violet, almost as soon as she met them. The Pearson's were a wonderful family and put a lot of trust in Kat leaving the children with her sometimes for days or more at a time. She took great pride and even greater responsibility with her new position and did her very best to never let Mr. and Mrs. Pearson worry at all as she watched over their beautiful children.

But this was when the problems truly began. Kat was spending so much time with Jess, Ben and Violet that her personality had warped into allowing her to believe that she was their true mother. Those kids were hers, and nightly, as mom or dad called in to check on them, Kat became more and more possessive claiming erroneously and usually with a slip of the tongue that 'her' kids were doing wonderfully. The parents took no notice, being far too busy seeking out a new home in Georgia. Kat, on the other hand, decided that those kids weren't going anywhere: they were hers now, and she was never going to let them be taken away by a set of parents who had hardly seen them over the past several months. She had no intention of ever letting that happen, not over her dead body. Or as it would seem, of someone's dead body.

A new and different Kat had taken full control of her shattered psyche. To the children, she was loving, fun, happy-go-lucky Kat who treated them like regular, wonderful kids. But, to herself, and on daily phone calls, she had slipped completely into another personality: she began to hate Mr. and Mrs. Pearson. She formed a twisted plot for how she was going to 'rescue' the children from their inevitable move. She knew they were due home for a week in a few days, and Kat would have to be ready to put her plan into motion. She needs supplies, and she needed a location for two graves far enough out in the Michigan woods that no one would ever find them. The once caring, loving, innocent babysitter Kat had been replaced by the conniving, sinister, brutal, murderous babysitter Kat, and nothing was going to stop her from getting what she wanted.

Kat stirred. The pain in her leg was blinding, but she knew she had to move. Clearing her head was a task she was ill prepared for, and she continued to drift in and out of blackness. Her head was swimming. She clamored to the surface just enough to look around the room. Dusty light still shone through the basement window, and it barely illuminated anything, but a shadow caught her attention. Was that a cane? Maybe an old walking stick? She had to reach it. This was her only hope of getting upright and getting out of here. Gathering all the endurance she had, she started to drag herself free of the stairs. The agony hit like hot lightning and Kat bit back a scream. Tears ran down her cheeks. She couldn't give up, she had to keep moving. Another drag, another foot further, and an explosion of anguish. She cried out and reached for her leg. She could feel the broken bone through her muscle and even at the slightest touch made her bawl. It was all too much. The fingers of darkness curled around her vision, and she slipped once again into its grip.

Back again in the past, Kat saw herself as she was when she sat for the Pearson's. She saw herself as she enacted her plan. She watched from invisible corners, like a time-lost fly on the wall, as her past self began what would be her first, most gruesome, murder. As a wandering ghost, present-day Kat witnessed second-hand the terror of herself then as she poisoned the Pearson's Welcome Home champagne flutes with arsenic. Not enough to kill immediately, but enough to incapacitate. No, she knew as she witnessed the vile acts that her next step was to render mom and dad bedridden for the day so she could slit their throats with no retaliation. Time sped up through foggy memories she no longer held and dropped the Now Kat into the Pearson's bedroom. She saw herself standing vigil in the dark corners. She saw mister and missus Person writhing in pain as they vomited blood and stomach contents. The Then Kat approached her victims, a straight razor glinting in the moonlight shining through the open curtains. Now Kat caught her breath, stood like a statue, and watched with sadistic interest in her own handiwork. The Then Kat went to work as the Now Kat smiled, sinisterly. The blood spray was artistic as it painted the walls and the linens with its deep reds.

The Now Kat knew the rest. She didn't need to see anymore. The world around her began to fade. Light washed away the hazy darkness and Kat-

Regained consciousness. With new vigor, she felt she had the desire now to get that cane she was after and get out of the basement. She had murders to commit, after all.

18.

Kevin Barton was five minutes down the road when he finally set his phone down. After the conversation he'd just had with a woman named Ivy and his own ex-wife, the day was bound to only get more unusual. Fortunately, he was only about thirty minutes away, if he obeyed the speed limits, a choice he was going to go firmly against. His mind was racing. Sure, he was worried about the women that were essentially trapped in the house with a lunatic murderer, but his main concern right now was getting his kids out of there. His thoughts refused to work past all the times he was less than a Father of the Year; all the times he chose not to see his own children because of some unimportant thing he figured at the time should take precedence. He was worried Sarah and David wouldn't even want to see him, and he couldn't blame them anyway. This was Kevin's time to man-up and show his ex (and whomever Ivy was) that he could deal with this situation and get them out without any more harm than they'd already suffered. He swung onto the freeway from the ramp and gunned the Camry up to 80.

19.

Ivy and Erin listened closely to the vent in the floor hoping to catch any more noise from the basement below. It had been several minutes since they heard Kat's last gasp and nothing since.

"So, not to pry, Erin, but if your ex isn't a great person, what makes you think he can get us out of here?"

"Well, Kevin might not be the best dad or, as you can imagine, the best husband of all time, he's still the kids' father and a pretty formidable guy. He's always been big, a little imposing, and definitely… strong."

Ivy took the hint in Erin's description and decided to leave it. "Well good, I hope he can do something. I'm glad he's on his way."

The twins were curled up on the landing between the bathroom and the hallway fast asleep on a fluffy towel. They'd had a long day already and even if they showed no signs now of fear and desperation, Ivy and Erin knew they were all very scared for their lives. As much as they hated to admit it, having a big scary guy around right now might just give them an advantage over the psychopath in the basement. Besides, as strong as Erin clearly was, she was in no shape to put up any kind of fight, and Ivy was not about to match strength again with Kat. They needed muscle, brute force, and a hot-headed goon to bring down some wrath. And they both hoped Kevin was the guy.

20

Kevin wasn't the guy for this. He knew that. Yeah, he had a past where he was sometimes (emphasis on 'sometimes') physical with Erin, his ex. He'd pushed her once or twice, he grabbed her arms with a little too much force, and once he swatted her butt a bit too hard causing a welt. But he was not the big, tough, abusing asshole he was so frequently called in past friend-circles of Erin's. Yeah, he was a big guy. Yeah, he had a bald head, a beard, a few earrings and tattoos… but those things did not a monster make, and Erin so many times painted him that way. What was he really? A big Teddy Bear. Well, a Teddy Bear who far too often didn't know his own strength and just as often couldn't put a cap on the TNT that could be his anger. He'd spent a gob of good money seeing a counselor both during the waning period of his marriage to Erin and even into the early parts of his new-found bachelorhood, but the result was always the same: Self-Centeredness with a penchant for Hot-Headedness… in so many words. Kevin sighed as he closed the distance between normalcy and whatever fresh mess he was getting himself into.

Kevin was not the guy.

21

Kat fought through the profuse urge to scream out again as she clenched her teeth against the fantastic amount of pain arcing through her leg. The fight in her was ebbing, but she couldn't give in yet. She knew she had to get out of there and as quickly as her broken body would let her. And probably even more quickly than that. Her trips to her black outs and memory lapses would have to wait, it was now or never, and never was something she couldn't afford. Besides, the more she clung to the possibility of revenge, the more her want to push on grew. Kat lifted as much weight as she could off her broken leg and resumed at a crawl toward the cane hanging from the far wall. With each new blast of torment, she went to her slowly forming plans for retribution. The trick made the trip (only a few yards, really) seem that much more bearable. Soon enough she'd reached the far wall and slowly lifted herself, slipping only once on her cracked femur sending scorching fresh agony through her entire body. But she fought back tears and the desire to yell out, and finally made it to the cane. It was pretty heavy, and it turned out to be an old walking stick cut from some damn tough wood. There was even a handle on which she leaned as she tenderly lifted herself to a standing position. Kat was up. Sweat ran down her forehead into her eyes. She'd been through the wringer and now she stood ready to get back at Ivy. Ivy and Erin. Hell, maybe even both at the same time. Somehow, some way, those bitches were about to pay with their lives.

22.

Kevin checked his GPS on his phone, turned off Red Arrow Highway into the small village of Lawrence, and slowed to the posted speed of 25. He passed a few farmhouses on the outskirts of town, and the voice from his phone told him that he was less than two miles from the house. He passed a service station and what appeared to be a Head Shop of some kind, and there, on the right, was the home of Erin Barton, his ex. He'd honestly never been there before; on the rare occasion he saw his kids, he'd met them halfway at a Pancake House and taken them out for whatever it was they wanted to do. This was different; he was worried for his children, yes, but it seemed he was equally as scared for the two women trapped in the situation they were. He still felt he wasn't the man for this particular job, especially if the crazy woman they had trapped in the basement somehow got out.

Kevin parked in the driveway. He stared for a second at the house and just how ordinary it seemed from the outside. But he knew there was mayhem just on the other side of the front door. He popped open the glove box, rummaged around for a minute, and found a knife he kept for… well, he didn't know, but it seemed like it might just come in handy here. With a deep sigh and a gathering of his guts, he walked up the driveway to the house.

23.

Kat leaned hard on the walking stick. She was drenched with sweat and felt clammy even to herself. Her leg throbbed a torturous drum beat in time with her pulse, and -though she couldn't be sure- she felt like the shock her system was going through was making her sick. But none of that mattered as she stared at the basement window. It was small, but so was she. These types of windows were meant for a person to fit through in case of emergency, and that's exactly what this was. But it was up pretty high, and she hurt even more considering the myriad ways with which she'd have to try to reach it. It was dark, but there was a shop light at the other end of the basement, and it was on, shining in a dim halo that covered only about a third of the entire room. But it was enough. She gathered herself and hobbled over to the workbench. The pain was sharp, but not nearly as bad as it has been. Maybe she was getting numb to it.

Kat looked around for anything she could use to climb up to the window. There were a few five- and ten-gallon buckets, but they weren't big enough. Then she saw it: tucked under a roll of extension cord hanging on a hook was a step ladder. She laughed in spite of herself and dropped the wire to the floor. It was definitely an older ladder made of wood and not aluminum as she'd hoped, but a beggar couldn't be a chooser and right now she was begging to get out of this place. With the ladder in tow, she readjusted herself on the walking stick and made for the window, slowly. There was no need to hurt herself even more.

24.

"Daddy?" The twins sang out in unison as Kevin peered into the bathroom. Somehow no one heard him come in, which didn't make any sense.

"Hi everyone… kids…. The door was unlocked, you know?"

TO BE CONTINUED…

This story never even got around to earning a title. It also never got around to be finished. As you've seen so far... I have issues with that sometimes. – S. Miller

(TITLE)
1.

James Kincaid stared curiously at the darkening blood on his hands; cuts oozing and running in drying rivulets down his wrists and arms. The middle fingernail on his left hand hung crookedly from the root and was caked like the others with grit and tacky gore. He shook, watching his fingers shiver, with a combination of fear, wonder, and worry. As he touched his face, James realized he had no memory of the last several hours. The mirror in which he glanced was filthy and painted with red. He saw his face. It was bruised, sliced open in deep gashes on his forehead and chin, and masked with two pulsating welts under both eyes clearly indicating a broken nose. James sighed deeply and the tracks of tear drops lightly washed away enough grime to make his reflection look like a clown from some grizzly, ridiculous horror movie.

His clothes weren't precisely rags, but they were certainly torn and shredded in several spots, and his shirt collar was split revealing his right shoulder and undershirt. Even without remembering anything, he still needed to clean up. James yanked a fistful of paper towels from the wall dispenser, ran them under the warming water, and wiped his face as neatly as was possible. His nail caught painfully on his collar, and with a sneered hiss he yanked it off and felt sick at the new blood that bubbled to the surface and ran down his hand. James rinsed this new wound, tore off a chunk of his shirttail, and wrapped his finger.

He felt his pockets instinctively and there it was, just as it always was his phone. The weight of it sent a chill shiver through his body, and even worse was the thought of it. *But why?* He thought to himself as he gave his disheveled mirrored image another once over. He had no idea. He forced it away as he turned from his bleak reflection. He stared at the empty washroom, took in the walls and the open stall door where the toilet sat, as it was now bloodied and stained. This was no doubt a crime scene; it was a mess with blood splatter and fingerprints easily seen in much of the drying pools. Yet James remembered nothing. He brushed hair from his eyes, recoiled at the raw sting, and shuffled to the door.

James pushed through the self-closing door into the outside. It was clearly a restaurant, noted as he walked past the glass partition separating the service counter from the walkway to the restrooms. He stopped short of the blind corner, he didn't know what he'd hoped he'd see... or rather what he didn't *want* to see. He caught himself, breathed slowly, and peered around across the bend.

There was no one. The bar stools were deserted, not just empty; food sat uneaten on plates, tall glasses of melting shakes dripped thickly onto the wrinkled paper placemats, coffee lost its heat into the ether, and the tinny drone of flies could be both seen and heard as a collection of insects hovered in undulating clouds. James turned and looked across the eatery at the register, it, too, empty, and unused. Its drawer stood open like a jutting jaw, but he saw no money inside under the flipped plastic fingers. The whole of the place was vacant, still, and startlingly eerie. James resumed moving toward the exit.

His phone rang.

James's heart caught in his throat with a click. The phone rang again. He stared at his pocket as though it were filled with angry bees. James had no intention of answering, but he also knew he had to. (*Why? What the Hell is going on with me?*) It rang a third time. He fumbled through his pocket and brought out the lighted phone holding it at arms-length like a detonating bomb. The screen showed the animated symbol of a jingling handset, and the phone rang a fourth time. There was no identification, no name popped up, it just said UNKNOWN in white letters. James placed his cell on the diner's table and waited. For the fifth time the tone echoed its desire.

2.

James Kincaid was your typical work-a-day guy. His day was spent at a call center for a local bank. His mornings began at 5:30, Monday through Friday, and ended at 3. He sat idly at a computer with three large screens each showing a bank account every time a customer called. One screen showed name, address, phone, all the pertinent personal info. The second; account info, banking history, deposits, withdrawals, the like, and the third pulled up on-line banking info to assist the individual. This happened a lot because not everyone understood how internet banking worked and typically locked themselves out of their own accounts. This went on for the entirety of James's shift with often extra time spent with undeniably incompetent bankers. James hated every long, monotonous second of it and constantly wished he were anywhere else.

The only good thing to come from James's time as a call-center drone was the regular downtime; the time on calls when the customers insisted on telling him why they purchased what they'd purchased, and the precious minutes between calls when he had just enough time to himself to continuously work on his new application idea for the open-source Android format. Basically, it worked with the camera and GPS (both standard with any phone) and alerted the user to potential photographic opportunities such as landmarks, memorials, natural phenomena, and all things in between that any amateur photographer might have an interest in capturing. It was to be called *Pic-It-Now*, and the operator could either set it to text or even call to clue one in to the beautiful picture opportunity. It was a fairly simple set-up, and with the limited coding knowledge he had, James was pretty sure he could put it in the Play Store for free and run ads or sell a full version with some extra features for $3.99, and maybe make a little side-gig profit. So as the days plodded on, James tweaked his app and was preparing to get it running within the month. His work became just background noise as he happily readied what he'd hoped would be a big seller.

3.

On the sixth warble of the phone's ringtone, James reached down to answer, fearing the worst.

"Don't!"

James wheeled around, startled at the sound of something other than his phone, and stared into the distant eyes of a woman, dressed in a blue-checkered dress and apron, strawberry blond hair done up in a torrential ponytail.

"Don't answer that! Don't you know what's happening?"

James could do nothing but stare. The phone rang a seventh time. The woman quickly skirted around the back counter and snatched his cell from the table. She depressed the small button on the side, and shut it off mid ring, "That's not going to stop it for long. You'll have to smash it. I would, but... well,

I don't know you and it's not my phone."

James now realized on closer inspection that the woman couldn't be much older than twenty, if that. She still had a doe-eyed look of innocence about her, as if the world hadn't quite collapsed her youthful spirit.

"Ok. Yeah… ok." James managed as he peered at the woman, quizzically.

"Oh… um, Hi. I'm Jenna. Jenna Barry. I work here… well, I *did* work here."

James held out his hand and shook the daintiest, coldest hand he'd ever shaken likely this side of a morgue, "Hello, Jenna. I'm James Kincaid. And I… don't know what's going on. I can't… uh… I can't remember anything."

"Anything? Like… *anything*?"

James sighed and nodded, "Well, up until about ten minutes ago, yeah. I was in the restroom. For a while, judging by the looks of it. And before you ask, no: I have no idea where all this blood came from. There's… nobody ese in there."

Jenna turned and glanced at the bathroom door. She brushed a stray hair from her face, and returned her gaze to James, "Well, if it helps, I saw you go in there. A while ago, before… all of this happened… You look terrible! Are you hurt?"

"All of what? Where is everyone? And no… well, I mean maybe a little, but I'll live"

"They left. Ran out. In a panic, too…" Jenna commented, thoughtfully looking over the deserted diner.

James looked down at his phone, and it looked as though Jenna was absolutely correct: it lit up again with chime and a jittering buzz, with the caller coming across as UNKNOWN, "Dammit... I guess you're right."

As James peeled off the rubberized case to get to the phone inside, Jenna sat heavily with a sigh into the booth, "This is crazy... I don't know what to do anymore. I thought I was alone in here. I though everyone was dead..."

"Why would you think that?" James asked as he shed the phone's case and plopped the Android onto the table with a plastic rattle.

"Boy, you really don't know, do you? It was the phones... *the App*!"

James stared blankly at Jenna as he gripped his phone in both hands, preparing to snap it in half, "Right, the phones... we've covered that. But what's this about an App? What do you mean it was an App? An application is a tool, it can't *do* anything to anyone."

James was about to realize just how wrong he was.

4.

Within the thirty days he'd set for Beta release, James had completed *Pic-It-Now* and added it to the Android Play Store. He ran trials, of course. He made sure the integration worked perfectly with the camera on his own phone as well as a few different models. It seemed well executed, and it definitely *seemed* just as such with the ability to use TEXT and CALL to alert the user to perfect photo opportunities. James was pleased, and thus felt good about putting the Beta version up for release. It took less than twelve hours and he'd already seen it downloaded over five-hundred times. This was going to be even bigger than he dared hope.

Yet, there was a glitch. This was to be expected during Beta, but this was particularly troublesome. And the problems were being reported to James at an alarming rate. He had a new problem, and it was a big one.

5.

"Well, it did," Jenna began as she slid out of the booth and wandered back behind the counter. "Do you want something to drink? Ice water? I don't think the fountain pop gun is working."

"Yes. Please. So, what do you mean when you say, '*it did*'? What did it *do*?"

"Well, I don't know exactly *how* it happened, but the worst of it certainly went haywire just after eight this morning. And I know because it was our breakfast rush for all the nine-to-fivers, and Ben Malone and Geech McCammon were both in their usual booths nursing their coffees over a scramble plate and the morning's gossip."

Jenna filled two red, opaque plastic glasses with ice, and ran cold water from the tap. She sipped hers and handed one to James, who thanked her, and took a long swallow, "Go on."

"I downloaded an App last night. Something new. You see, when I'm not here I'm something of a freelance photographer. Anyway, it was a Beta release, but I thought I'd give it a try."

James looked over at Jenna, "Did you say a photography App?" *That… seemed familiar somehow.*

"Well yeah, because you clearly downloaded, too, dude." Jenna said with a sneer, pointing at the phone still gripped in the hand not holding the water, "Are you gonna *break* that thing then, or…"

James shook his head, "No I mean about the App… and no, I mean *yes*, the phone…" James stammered as he snapped his cell in two, watching in amazement as bits of metal and broken glass tinkled to the floor. *There's five hundred bucks out the door.* He though, bemused.

Jenna visibly sighed and nodded, "Good. Thanks. So, yeah, the app. Like I said it was the Beta release, and I was interested, and it seemed like a fun little program: it would alert you to any photo opportunity like statues and pretty nature areas, and views… like that. So, I downloaded it to my phone."

James sat and listened. Everything he was learning was starting to sound more and more *real*, as though *somehow*, he knew what Jenna was going to say before she even said it. Had he really downloaded this application, too? It sounded like something he would like. He was still running around rooms of locked memories and not everything was opening just yet. This was worrisome because he really felt like this should make so much more sense to him. He stared at her. She really was a pretty woman even in her disheveled state. Maybe even someone he'd be interested in were it not for the current situation. James didn't have a girlfriend. Hadn't even dated anyone for months: those past few spent coming up with and working on… *something*. It was a big *thing*… but he couldn't place it just yet. But he was beginning to force his cloudy memories into something solid. But just yet they were flashes of things. Flashes and pieces and… nothing. As he listened to Jenna talk about the app and how it worked, he tried hard to focus on what she was saying and less on how she was looking. But he was a guy, a little lonely it seemed, and it was a bit of a struggle. Maybe she could see it in his face; maybe she could tell that he really was wandering in a mental fog. He just had minute sparks of times he really felt deeply he needed to recall. He also believed Jenna saw that. He truly was as innocent as he was coming across.

"Hey… buddy, are you listening?"

He was called out, but played it off, "Yeah… yes. Sorry… it's just, I really am having a tough time piecing all this together. I just can't seem to recall why I'm even here? Like in this diner? As far as I can tell I've never eaten here before… I'm not even *from here*. Speaking of which, I can glean from the placemats that this isn't Michigan…"

"Ohio. Strongsville." Jenna said as nonchalantly as possible, "What does 'glean' mean?"

"It means to gather information from… such as from these placemats you've got here. And yeah, I can tell now they're of Ohio. I love the little cartoon landmarks and whatnot… seems like a great place to take- "

"*Pictures*." Jenna finished for him, "Yeah. I know. That's why I like it so much: lots of nature and things. And now you know why I downloaded the app."

"Right. But that still doesn't really explain what exactly happened with the app." James said.

"I was just getting to that part."

6

The new App, *Pic-It-Now*, was having one fatal issue, and James (though hard at work researching it and running through diagnostic after diagnostic) didn't know how to fix it. He'd spent far too much of his personal (well, *mostly* personal, since he had killed his floating free days on the company dime) time building it that he wasn't about to give up and just let it wallow away into obscurity in the Android Play Store, so he cashed in the remaining vacation and sick time he had left - eleven days- and set to work figuring out where he went wrong.

He knew the biggest problem was the one everyone was commenting about. When the app worked properly -which was most of the time, thank goodness- it would not only point the user to a prime photo opportunity by either text or a call, but it would also persuade the user to cause themselves great bodily harm. This made absolutely no sense to James, but the proof was in the comments:

> *"The app was great up until it nearly had me marching off the edge of the site-seeing cliff!"*
> **1 STAR out of 5 - M. Carvel**

> *"This app was about as poorly designed as an app can be! My kid and I almost drown!"*
> **1 STAR out of 5 - Eric**

> *"I love the idea of this app and the functionality is quite smooth, but when your camera tells you to walk into traffic on a major highway just because the view of the sunset is spectacular… there's something wrong."*
> **1 STAR out of 5 – Karen MacNamee**

They went on and on just like that. Every user in the comments was either nearly hurt or hurt enough to never want to use the app again. This was not how the roll-out was supposed to go; his *STAR* rating was among the lowest for new app releases and he was injuring people in the process. James knew he had to find out what was going on and how it was happening. And he had to find out soon before anything *really* terrible could happen, like a serious injury or a death! That was unless it already had. James might be in some major trouble.

The news did progressively get worse. As first the reviews were just mild injuries or close-calls, soon enough people were posting on every social media platform and not just the Play Store itself: friends falling, sisters being bitten by wild animals, mothers driving into lakes from bridges, and even chaos from a tour bus full of onlookers causing a multi-vehicle pile-up on I-94 while stopping to satisfy their photographic curiosity. The launch of this app was turning into a nightmare. Worse yet, he was beginning to receive threatening phone calls on his line used specifically for this app release. Sure, what people did with apps once they were downloaded was, typically, the downloader's problem, but this situation had become perilous, and James just couldn't sit idly by and watch his creation destroying its customers.

A week later, still during the early days of the Beta release, and James was no closer to figuring out the problem. And the problem was worsening exponentially. He narrowed it down to something going haywire in the AI portion of the code; specifically, the part where the app called and texted when a photographic opportunity presented itself. Somewhere in the lines of his handwritten code, there was a combination of symbols, some numbers and letters, which were allowing the artificial intelligence to reach out to… well, that was the real problem. James had no idea who was being called and from where. He searched everywhere, through all the codes, through all the lines, up and down over and again and the problem still made no sense.

Just as James was wracking his brain over what had gone wrong and how to find it, the news was picking up on the danger of this new app and it was spreading. Local reports of the trouble and damage exploded like a string of fireworks. James knew now he was in real trouble. His phone rang incessantly, most often with UNLISTED or UNKNOWN or SPAM CALL as the only identifier, and he answered almost none of them. Except one. A call he really didn't want to hear.

7.

"The mess all kind of happened at once," Jenna said, sitting back down across from James. She pulled out a pack of cigarettes from inside her work blouse, looked at James with a shirk, and when he nodded with mock approval, she followed with her lighter and sparked the tip. "Everyone was enjoying their breakfast this morning. I had just poured Magda Hamilton another shot of coffee… when all the phones began to ring at once.

James sat up straight, "Really? All of them? At once?"

"Stop patronizing me! You know what I mean, and you know how weird that would be!"

James held out his hands, "I wasn't making fun, Jenna! I was just repeating. And yes, that would be incredibly odd to hear them all ringing at- "

"And so many people with such *obnoxious* ringtones, too. Anyway, they all went off. And everyone, even the little kids-phones everywhere and, apparently, all of them with the *Pic-It-Now* application…"

"But how did you know? How did you know it was because of the app? It could have been anything… right?"

Jenna shook her head and swallowed the ice she was crunching, "No. I knew, because my phone was buzzing in my hip pocket, too. Everyone else that could, took theirs out and stared at the screens. I caught a glance of someone's screen while I was dropping off a tray of food. It said UNKNOWN like yours did, but they were also accompanied by a text. I couldn't get to my phone fast enough, but I saw the same lady check her text, and it said TAKE YOUR PICTURE, TAKE A LIFE."

"*What?*" James exclaimed as he recoiled, "You can't be serious. You must have read that wrong! That's insane!"

"I didn't read it wrong, James. I know this because by the time I got around to checking my phone, after the violent exodus from the restaurant, it said the exact same thing. I don't know why it didn't affect me, maybe whatever power… or brainwave-something, was done by the time I saw it. I have no idea."

James considered this. Nothing about this tale seemed to be real. Nothing happening right then seemed to be real. He'd never heard -never, in his thirty-seven years- of a phone app instructing people to take a *life* to the point where they'd *actually* done it! No one could be that gullible. It just didn't seem… real. There was no other way to say it. But something was nagging at him just the same, something he felt he should know.

"Okay, I believe you saw what you think- what you *say* you saw, but that still doesn't make any sense. Something had to trigger this. Something inherently wrong with everyone. An app just can't set people off like this. What was the... I don't know, the *catalyst*?"

Jenna looked confused, "Well, I did see something on the news a few nights ago: some kind of freak interference... like a satellite or something, but I can't really remember."

8.

"Good afternoon, Mr. Kincaid. Please, we advise you to not hang up. We are contacting you in response to your new Android Application, *Pic-It-Now*. Information has come forth of which you might be very interested."

James pulled the phone from his ear as though it were some sort of venomous alien. He didn't hang up, instead he continued listening, curious and oddly frightened.

"Your silence is appreciated, and it shows your understanding of the situation. As we are sure you know, your Application has proven to be somewhat troublesome. However, we do want you to understand, this was not because of anything you did. We want you to be aware that this... *occurrence* was not in any line of code you wrote. No, Mr. Kincaid, this entire catastrophe -as it were- was of our design."

"Catastrophe? Has it gotten *that* bad?" James asked, just as it dawned on him how unbelievably bizarre the current circumstance was, "Wait, before you answer that... who is *this*, anyway?"

"Who this is, James, is quite inconsequential. That being said, what I will tell you is that we are part of a far larger picture that you are, at this time, able to see. But you will, in time."

James stared at nothing as his head swam through as much information as it could process at one time. This made no sense to him at all, yet the bizarrely analytical part of his brain was telling him that it at least answered the question, 'Why'. It did make him realize that it wasn't his fault that the App kept failing so horribly. It was solace, but just barely. He put the phone back to his ear. And he was tired. Good Lord was he tired. So much time, so many weeks and months dedicated to this application. And then it's terrifying implosion. It was all so much in such a short span of time. Maybe he was sound asleep dreaming this phone call… Maybe.

"Go on."

"It appeases us that you have quickly come to understand the issue at hand. Our intentions are not to harm you in any way, for you paved the way for us to enact our plans. Again, that being said, this is not going to end particularly well for anyone else who has downloaded your… *ahem* *our* App."

"What do you mean? Why? Why are you trying to hurt everyone over this?" James asked, becoming frustrated and angry.

"As I said before, James, all of these answers will be revealed in their due time. Until then, please just try to stay out of the way. We would prefer you not become collateral damage, but make no mistake, we will not suspend our plans if you choose to become a nuisance. May we suggest taking a vacation? Somewhere, shall we say, *off* the grid? That is all for now. We will be in touch. Goodbye, James."

The connection ended and James was left in deafening silence holding his phone to his ear. He was shaking all over, and cold with rage. Was he really going to let this happen?

9.

Jenna stared glumly out the window. James could see she was upset, and he wasn't at all surprised. She'd witnessed something horrible, of that fact there was no doubt. Though James could still not recall anything of the past several hours, it was clear he'd seen his share of ghastly occurrences as well; the bloody proof was covering his torn clothing and was caked to parts of his face, neck, and hands. He fiddled with the pieces of his shattered phone, shoving them around the table trying desperately to remember anything that might help them. But so far, his mind remained a clutter of disconnected thoughts.

"I wanted to be a dancer. Down at The Cage? Yeah, somebody once told me I should be a dancer. I had the body for it. So that's what I was gonna do." Jenna said, ruminating aloud.

James said nothing but remarked to himself that she certainly did have the body for it. Though he couldn't see much, the way her work uniform clung to her form, not to mention her half-opened buttons, tried very little to hide another person she sought to escape. He smiled at her, but she didn't see it. Her gaze was lost to the distance beyond the plate glass as well.

"I was set to start a few months ago. My boyfriend -Zack- was a regular visitor to The Cage and he told me I was better looking than anyone they had working there. He set up an interview... I wanted the job, for him. I wasn't too interested in showing my nudity to a bunch of horny townspeople, but I knew the money was great and the tips even better. So, I wanted the job because Zack *wanted* me to want it, ya know?"

James tried to picture her on a stage, slithering around a gilded pole. He couldn't do it. He might have only known her less than an hour, but she just seemed so much more innocent than she looked and even more so than she was letting on with her story. She turned around and met his gaze, smirked, and brushed a lock of loose hare from her eyes.

"I know what you're thinking, James. Everyone I know thinks the same way when I tell them. But it's true. Under this shitty work smock apparently, I have a pretty knockout figure with boobs to melt your brain," Jenna laughed out loud, "Or so I was told. Zack wasn't much for anything else, but he definitely knew how to inflate my self-esteem."

James looked down at the table and aimlessly examined the parts from his broken phone. He still hadn't said anything, but he did smile and nod at Jenna. Something sparked and lit off a memory in his cloaked brain. He rubbed his eyes struggling to form it into a cohesive thought. He could make out a shadowed face, and almost hear a robotic voice telling him…

10.

"James, are you paying attention? This is very important. You must listen."

James hit the SPEAKER icon on his phone, "Yes. I'm listening."

The metallic voice continued, "Good. We need you to make an adjustment to the code you have written."

"What? Why?"

"Because, Mr. Kincaid, we do not have complete control as of yet."

James frowned, "I am finding this whole 'partnership' very unnerving. I mean it seems like you people are just taking advantage of me!"

"Why James, *of course we are*. This whole problem we've caused for you and the entirety of the downloading population would never have come to fruition without you. Well, with our intrusion, of course. Take advantage, James? That is exactly what we are doing. But make no mistake, if you choose to ignore our directions, you will be summarily punished."

James had no interest in being punished. But on the other side of the same coin, he had even less interest in assisting whomever these people were any further than he already had. Beyond that, did their voices sound more robotic lately? At first, the monotone commands were undoubtedly human, but now; now they sounded like they were being passed through a voice changing mechanism like a vocoder, an easy enough app to find in its own right. James didn't like this new development, and not just because of the threat of retaliation. He'd have to play along for now.

"As I said… go on. Tell me what I need to change."

"Good. Very good. There might be a chance for you, yet."

--To Be Continued--

One Last Job

Jack Davis opened the door to his apartment and stepped into the cloying, still air that smelled of time, age, and the stale tang of something long dead. It had been eight long years since Jack had tasted freedom outside prison bars; eight years inside serving time for a botched robbery the result of which was nothing more than a garbage bag of cash coated with blue ink thanks to the spray pack the teller had slipped in when forced to fill it at the business end of a shotgun. He'd almost gotten away with it. In fact, he and his 'crew' were well hidden in the third of a series of pilfered get-away vehicles on a seldom used back road on their way to anywhere else when Bobby -the stunningly stupid driver- chose that very time to ring his contact. On his iPhone. That was the straw that broke the whole camel wide open. That one ping on the nearest cell tower... and it was all over.

Jack walked in, dropped his zip top bag full of his 'personal effects' -wallet, debit card, house keys, and two condoms- onto his dusty Lay-Z-Boy, and took a long, distant gaze into the hazy sunlight that shown a storm front of dust motes listing in the rays. What the hell was he going to do now? Fortunately, his business partner and cousin, Allen, fronted the monthly rent so at least he had a place to come home to. Yeah, Allen wasn't involved in this most recent job. Typically, he hung behind the scenes, going over the maps and plans and escape routes and the like, so he was home when Jack was sent to the slammer. Jack used his only phone call to let Allen know that Bobby -the stunningly stupid driver- had gotten them into deep shit and he, Allen, was going to have to use some of the money Jack had provided for the cause over the last few years to keep his apartment from getting locked up and he evicted. Allen agreed, however reluctantly, and thus, as Jack stood in the foyer staring into a forgotten yet familiar home, he wondered again just what the hell he was going to do now.

****

Three hundred miles north, just outside of Kalamazoo, Michigan, Allen Harper stood outside his office and glanced into the hazy sunshine. Checking his phone screen, it was 5:20; he locked up, tucked his binder under his arm, and fished his key fob from his slacks pocket. He'd gotten the call around 4:45 that his cousin, Jack, had gotten released after Eight years in Northeast Ohio Correctional Center in Youngstown. He was happy, mostly because he was tired of paying the six hundred a month rent on Jack's unoccupied apartment, but also because Jack was the best at what he did, and Allen had another job in mind. He would give his cousin a few days, maybe a week, to settle back into normalcy... but the job wouldn't wait much longer and so neither would Allen. And this job was a massive score, maybe even into the upper six digits. Enough for all of them to comfortably throw in their towels and live high on the slaughtered hog for the rest of their lives. Allen slipped on his aviator shades, chirped the locks on his BMW, and let his mind wander to whatever he wanted for dinner on his way home.

****

Jack was hungry. But he had nothing in the house and just about the only bit of money he had was the stipend check he earned while in the poke. Sadly, no banks were open, and he was fairly certain none of those Check Cashing joints was going give his prison check a second glance. And then it hit him. He'd just remembered there was a wad of cash squirreled away in a book on his little bookshelf. Grinning to himself he slipped out the warn copy of Moby Dick and there, under the front cover in a carved-out rectangle was a fat wad of hundreds. He laughed. Jack remembered stashing the money there back in 2000 when he and his crew were pretty sure the salad days of never getting caught were well on their way to coming to an abrupt end. He was right, of course, and lucky for him he never told anyone he'd fed the white whale, so to speak, and he was damn happy he'd done it. Quickly counting the wad of cash made Jack even happier. There was three grand in Benjamin's in there! Good thing because he clearly needed food, and maybe a cleaning lady. Oh, and there was more than enough to take over his rent payments from Allen. Things might turn out all right after all. And then the phone rang.

"Jackie boy! I hear Ohio's penal system kicked your ass to the curb!"

Jack grinned, "Big Lon! How the hell are ya, my man?"

Lonnie Ferguson was one of Jack's closest friends, and, coincidentally, one of Jack's usual partners in crime. He was the point man on the botched job eight years ago, but since Jack had chosen to take the fall for the entire mess instead of seeing Lonnie fall for only being tangentially involved, he'd only gotten a year and was out in nine months on good behavior. Big Lon owed him, and he knew it, too.

"Not bad, not bad. So, what's it like seeing blue skies and breathing untainted air again, huh?"

"Honestly, brother, I've been home for less than twenty minutes. In fact, I was just about to head out to get some decent food in this damn place."

"Bullshit you are," Big Lon guffawed in the deep, ursine way he always laughed, "Beers. Down at The Taproom. On me. It's the least I could do."

Jack smiled, "Damn right. Well, the least you could do is nothing... but I will take you up on it since I'm starving and haven't had beer in years."

"Good enough, man, good enough. See ya in a bit."

The line severed and Jack hung up. Big Lon. He never would have guessed he'd be the first person to call.

****

Allen pulled into the Checker's drive-thru and ordered a couple double cheeseburgers and fries. He pulled out his phone and noticed an email notification on his screen. A few deft slides and taps and Gmail popped open.

> Hey Allen. It's your new best friend, Mr. Sandman. It turns out this
> new opportunity of ours isn't going to wait any longer. I suggest
> you pull together your pack and lay out the details within the next
> 48 hours or this fat goose might just waddle to a more productive
> pond. I assume we understand each other regarding the where's
> and how's? Let me know ASAP so we can get this project going.
>
> Yours,
> Mr. Sandman

Allen swallowed the mouthful he'd been slowly chewing. This might be a little more difficult than he'd originally figured. And worse yet, Jack really wasn't going to like it. But the job had to get done, and with the sheer amount of money at stake here... well, he'd call Jack later. He had food to finish and a list of others to get a hold of first. Besides all that was the location. A museum of all places. Not an easy gig. But damn the rewards... Allen chewed his food thoughtlessly and wondered aloud, "A museum?"

****

Jack laughed out loud as Big Lon regaled him with story after story of jobs he'd missed out on during his incarceration. Lon kept his word and paid for all the appetizers and their dinner as well as enough beer to floor a weaker man. Granted Jack hadn't had a drink in eight long years, he still managed to put away plenty as he and Lon laughed the night away and even managed to close the bar at 2 AM.

"Wow, Lonny... buddy, I am three sheets!"

Lon patted Jack on the back and led both of them to an Uber waiting for them at the curb, "No shit! You somehow still have that old hollow leg you were once so famous for!"

"I guess. I'd thought for sure I wouldn't be able to even come close to the old days..." Jack said through a few hiccups.

Lon led Jack into the back of the Kia Sorento just as his phone began to vibrate in his shirt pocket. He pulled it out and glanced with slightly blurry vision at the screen, "Hey Jack! You're not gonna believe this, it's Allen!"

Jack's mood suddenly changed, and he instantly felt just as sober as he'd felt three hours ago. Allen, though family, was on the short list of people he wasn't really interested in talking to right now. A twinge of dread trickled down his spine and launched tiny sparklers in the back of his eyes. Somehow Jack knew this call wasn't going to be the best news ever... in fact, Jack had a sneaking suspicion Allen likely had a job for him. Jack was more than certain that he was absolutely not interested. Not now. Shit, he hadn't even met his P.O. yet, there was no way he was going to get mixed up into...

Lon cut him off mid thought, "Allen, how's business ya old shyster?"

"In the black, buddy... always in the black. So, can I safely assume our mutual pal, Jack is with you this evening?"

Lon grinned and looked over at Jack who had a look of sour smugness on his face, "He is, he is. I decided to take our pal out for a fine meal and drinks on me since he was good enough to take a fall for us for eight years. Seemed like the neighborly thing to do."

"Sure, neighborly. Makes sense. Well, it's Jack I'm interested in talking to right now, and if everything goes as well as I'm hoping with him, then we'll chit chat again afterword and we'll just see if you'd want... in."

"Want "IN"? well this just sounds delicious. I wouldn't necessarily get your hopes up, old pal. In fact, Jacky boy here seems like he might want to go clean. But I'll let you talk it over with him."

"Jack, Allen wants to chat. I have no idea what it's about, but, if history means anything to us, I'm quite sure it's a tasty offer."

Jack took the phone and simply stared at it for a moment. He sighed, shook his head, and brought it to his ear. "Allen."

"Hi Jack. Well, I certainly hope Lonny is showering you with all the food and drink you can suffer right now?"

"Yeah... but let's dispense with the pleasantries, Allen. What the fuck could you possibly want right now? I've been out of big house for less than a whole day and I know your usual M.O. when you call. I figure it's been eight years since I hear shit from you and here, we are. So, spill it: what the hell do you want."

"Easy, Jack. Just take it easy. I get where you're coming from. I know the last thing you want to hear about is anything from me. But Jack, my time is very limited on this. I have about thirty-six hours to accept this thing or we're... well, I'll be out some quality winnings."

Jack flopped back against the head rest. Lon looked over and just shrugged his shoulders. "Well, I haven't hung up yet so at least you have me listening. But before you go on with the details, who is this little magic show from?"

"Mr. Sandman."

Jack's eyes shot wide open, "Sweet Jesus, no shit? I thought he was dead?"

Lonny grew more interested, "Who?" he mouthed.

Allen continued as Jack mouthed the name, "Yeah, now I've got your full attention I take it? And good, because this is... well, it's a pretty unusual gig, honestly."

Lonny just said wow and shook his head in disbelief, "Mr. Sandman. This must be some gig."

Jack said, "Okay. Yes. Interested. But damn it, Allen, this had better be some extra safe, locked down, in-and-out shit because if you think I'm going back--"

"Jack, chill the fuck out. First off, you're not going anywhere. Second off, I haven't even given you any details yet. Bottom line: it's in a museum."

At this revelation, Jack actually burst out laughing. Never before had they done a gig outside a bank or financial institution of some kind. Easy cash, few issues (for the most part), and almost no heroes. But a museum? This was so far out in left field it was almost in a different ballpark, "What? A museum? Why on Earth would we hit a museum?"

At this Lonny reached over, snatched the phone, and tapped the "Speaker Phone" icon, "Allen, are you fucking serious? A museum?"

"I am, Lonny. Obviously, you're abreast of the situation. And I'm obviously on speaker phone. I'm not saying another word until you two are alone."

A mile later the Uber stopped at Jack's place. Lonny paid, and the two went up.

****

Allen laid out the entire plan. And even for Jack it sounded particularly insane. The Eberhardt Museum was currently hiring for a night guard for the grounds. Allen had already arranged for a falsified resume for Lonny, so he was a shoe in for the position. Allen would give him a week to integrate himself into the routine and blend into the employees by getting to know those he needed to and just basically act like a regular Joe. After that, phase two would be set into motion. Now, the reason behind this subterfuge was actually quite simple: The Iron Mountain Diamond. The only significant find of its kind from Iron Mountain, Michigan. Two Hundred and Sixty-Nine carats with the rough size and weight of a baseball. Worth three-quarters of a billion dollars. And it was kept under tamper-proof, bullet-proof glass surrounded by pressure-sensitive alarms and a set of interlacing optic laser beams designed to be triggered at both temperature changes and ambient pressure fluctuations in the surrounding atmosphere. In short, it wasn't going anywhere. Until it does. And that's where Lonny was going to come in. Every night at 2:30 AM all of the systems go through an update that takes exactly three minutes. In that time, the lasers -a unit run on a completely different system for security reasons- will have to be manually manipulated in a way Jack himself was going to have to figure out over the next ten days. He scoffed, but he knew this score was life-changing and so he'd do it. Once all of this was timed perfectly and set into motion, the diamond would be theirs. And that was the crux of the plan.

"Oh, and one more thing," Allen said after the lengthy conversation, "I almost forgot. The, uh… museum… well it's supposedly haunted."

At this Jack and Lonny burst out laughing, "Haunted? So? We ain't 'fraid of no…"

"Seriously. Guys. Like real, honest to goodness poltergeist activity. Well documented. Why do you think they can't keep a night guard on duty for more than a few weeks? And apparently, it's quite mean. As in throws stuff, pushes things over, physical contact... the whole nine yards."

The humor died off. "Okay. We get it. I'll look into that, too."

"Okay. Good. So now that we all understand each other, I think we can set this plan into motion. Lonny, you need to head down to the museum tomorrow and drop your doctored resume at the front desk. I have a few small connections who will see to it that it finds its way to the hiring department over the next few days. Don't worry, you'll hear from them by mid-week and start the next day. Jack, just study up on all the things we talked about, and I'll get back with you in a few days as well. Alright, that's it. Let's do this, boys. And do it right."

****

It was Monday morning. Jack had spent the weekend making his apartment feel like the home he once knew. He also sprung for a decent laptop and internet access. He had studying to do and the best place to find information on anything was the web. Luckily, he had a few friends around who could access even darker corners than the usual avenues led to, so finding what he needed was significantly less difficult. The Iron Mountain Diamond had a pretty interesting history, none of which really mattered to the heist at hand, but a few of the articles he'd read mentioned tales of a curse following it around including a few hauntings and bizarre occurrences from the myriad places it had been housed over the years. This little fact seemed like the most logical explanation for the spooks going on over at the Museum, or so

Jack reasoned. It could certainly have just been the building itself, as it was one of the oldest still functioning in the area, but either way it didn't matter to Jack: the fact was he and his brothers were going to get the diamond out of there one way or the other. They had to. As for the security, that was a bit of a different problem. There was very little on the lasers or their special array at all but what he did find at least gave him the basic principles on how to temporarily reroute the beams and that was all he needed. He'd study more over the next week, but for now he needed to reach out to another of his past partners to get in on the gig. Someone far more familiar with these types of security issues.

****

Meanwhile, Lonny was schmoozing the lady at the front desk of the museum. Sure, she was older, but held together pretty well, "Yes, actually, I would love a tour!"

"Excellent! Let me just get my assistant to hold down the fort and we'll walk through the three-mile expanse. I hope you have a good pair of shoes on!"

"Oh, I do, Nancy! Just bought them; Skechers! Memory foam is something else, isn't it?"

"I Love mine!" Nancy lifted her shoe to show off that she, too, had the aforementioned footwear. "Shall we?"

"Onward, madam! You lead and I shall follow!"

Nancy giggled and the two began wandering the great Eberhardt Museum.

****

"Jack? Jack Davis? Good God, man! I haven't heard from you in…"

"Eight years… yeah, I know. I just got out of the joint a few days ago. How's things, Cargill?"

"Peachy. And since you're calling me, it must mean you're already back on the horse. I guess you didn't really learn much in the slammer, did ya, pal?"

"Yeah well, a score like the one we're in is more than reason enough to try, try again, ya know? I'll tell you all about it in a minute. Firstly, though, can you help a friend out with some interesting security type nonsense?"

"Security type nonsense? Like what, lasers and pressure switches?"

Jack laughed, "Exactly like that, actually. We're gonna lift the Iron Mountain Diamond from the Eberhardt Museum and…"

"The what? You can't be serious! That thing's under CIA-Level security! You'd have to be nuts to heist that thing!"

Jack laughed again, "Nuts it is. And I know how strong the security is, that's why I called you. The point is, Cargill, can you do it?"

There was a long moment of silence, "I can. Sure. But what's in it for me? This score of yours is definitely a biggie. So… I'm gonna need some pretty hefty compensation."

"I figured. How much?"

"I want ten. In untraceable bills. No deposits or Bearer Bonds, that shit is too easily tracked. Ten. Like I said. I'll help, but I've got to have your word."

"Ten it is. I'll figure out how to do the bills later… but I can do it. I have people, too. You have my word. You know it's good, Cargill."

"I do. Ok, I'm in. So, anything I need to know before I get on with my jive?"

Jack smiled, "Yeah. The place is haunted. Or the diamond is, I'm not sure yet. Either way, there's some kind of spirit."

Cargill laughed this time, "Wow. This just gets keeps getting better."

Allen set the gears into motion as soon as he got word that Lonny had submitted his resume. It was just a matter of talking him up as though he were part of a talent agency and hooking the museum staff up with as many contacts and all the background info they could handle. With all that he'd be hired in no time. Next, he needed to call Jack and touch base on how the security breakdown was going. Hopefully he'd even learned some valuable intel on the haunting business as well.

****

As Lonny finished his excessively long, yet relatively entertaining tour of the museum grounds, messages and calls were traveling back and forth basically ensuring his future employment and by the time he and Nancy got back to the front desk, she had surprised him (and herself, so it seemed) with the news that he could start the following evening -a full day ahead of the planned schedule. He feigned over excitement, smiled and laughed appropriately, and tossed a few "my reputation precedes me" nonsense, thanked her, and said he'd be there at 9 PM the following day to meet with Mr. Albert for his first night of training. The plan was in motion now, and all Lonny had to do was pretend he loved his job long enough to let the crew inside next week and the diamond would be theirs. And speaking of this diamond, he was able to stand a distance from it during the tour. He didn't have to pretend not to know a thing about it since until the other day, he honestly hadn't. Nancy explained its significance to the area, how it came to be located in its current status, and even a bit of history on its unearthing (most of this stuff was on adjoining plaques, but Lonny just listened), and yes, she even mentioned some unfortunate business that had gone on over the years regarding hauntings and general apparition mischief. So, Lonny recalled, the tales were at least true enough to have been mentioned by the curator, but that really didn't help the situation at hand. Lonny went to his car and mentally prepared himself for a week of actual work at an actual job. It definitely seemed worth the effort.

■■

Jack sat back in his couch and a wave of honest to goodness fear washed over him. Yes, he'd been afraid before; prison scares a man, scares him good, but it's a different kind of scare, this haunting business was a tingly type of fear he'd only remembered feeling as kid. This was bone-chilling, nightmare-inducing stuff. It was dark out; his shades were drawn but there was almost no light from the moon or anywhere else. The only light inside was coming from his laptop screen and the digital clock on the face of his microwave. He knew there was nothing there, in the room or even beyond it -or did he? – that feeling of not being too sure one way or the other crept over him and sent shivers from head to toe. He sat up, looked again at the screen and reluctantly read on.

"August 16th, 1884. The Eberhardt Museum had been open for six weeks
and strange occurrences began to show themselves in the African Wildlife exhibit. The new night guard, Etrigan Beltran, says he witnessed one
of the animals actually turn its head and look directly at him. He yelped
and fled the area and stayed in the Farming exhibit the rest of the night
avoiding the area on his rounds, 'It's true!' Mr. Beltran said during an
interview, 'The hyena looked right at me, dead in the eyes! It's like his
soul was still in 'im!' After that evening's scare, though he stayed on as
guard for the next few nights, he blatantly refused to go near any of the
animals. Five nights later, while patrolling the corridor between the Local
Flora exhibit and the snack area, he fled the building entirely after seeing
A walking shadow person—"

"February 22nd, 1913 – Eberhardt Museum – 12:42 AM – Museum guard
Daniel Cavendish runs from his position into the night as he swears to
Local constable that he was beset upon by a full-featured phantom coming
Upon him with arms stretched out and a rictus grin on her face—"

"April 8th, 1924 – Eberhardt Museum – 9:50 PM – The newly hired

Night guard at the museum reported to the Picayune the following day

that he had actually seen chairs and books being tossed about near the

gift shop. He said he had chalked it up to just odd coincidence until

he made to clear up the mess when an unseen force shoved him out of

the hallway and down the on the floor. —"

The accounts went on like this over the course of a hundred plus years, each more descriptive than the last and each happening only to the night watch, never to anyone of the purveyors or visitors. Jack breathed a shuddering sigh, and quickly flipped the TV on to the Food Network. Anything to get his mind off the many accounts of serious hauntings he'd just read. One thing did become abundantly clear to him, though: it wasn't the diamond that was doing it since that little gem didn't show up in the museum until 1957. So, if there was any good news from his findings, it was that. But even so, he had an uneasy feeling their caper was going to be anything but cut and dry.

****

Lonny arrived at the museum a half hour before his shift. The woman who was training him in his night duties was about as old as the museum itself. She wore a craggy face with tiny bits of stubble jutting out here and there from myriad moles and warts. She had on a blue guard's jacket that was either too big, or else she, herself, had gotten significantly smaller over her tenure. Walking stick in hand and orthopedic shoes rounded out the package, and her name tag read Alice.

"Hello, Mr. Ferguson. Nice to see you here early and ready to begin your first night. My name is Alice Bigby, and everyone just calls me Alice. It's nice to meet you."

"Hello, Alice! It is equally nice to meet you, too." Lonny said, feigning genuine admiration.

"Yes, well, let's get to it then. This museum has been here since 1884. It has undergone seven major renovations into the large building you see today. Some of it is underground, and I doubt your tour guide showed you those catacombs yesterday, but we'll get to that later. Let's get you to the guard's station around back and see if we have jacket that fits. You'll also get a belt on which you'll carry a flashlight, extra batteries, a baton, keys, and your radio. The guard in the station stays there all shift long manning the 26 cameras we have throughout the museum, and you'll be the one marching the grounds. Got all that?"

Lonny nodded with smile, "I sure do, Alice. Sounds good."

"Good. A quick learner. I like that, too. Sounds like you and I will get along famously. Follow me to the station."

Once at the station, Lonny met the guard there. His name was Benny, and he looked every bit as old as Alice. Lonny stifled a laugh thinking to himself that maybe it was these two ancients running around scaring people for over a hundred years. He cleared his throat and listened as Alice pointed out how to use the earpiece and the radio. Lonny was quite familiar but played along as though he'd never seen a piece of equipment like it in his entire life. Alice droned on, led Lonny through another tour of the grounds (granted, showing him all of the SECURE and LOCKED locations), showed him the underground area which was now designated as the History of Mining in Michigan and the How We Find Fossils exhibit, both of which were by appointment shows only, and finally showed him to his exact station where he'd be when not on patrol. It was a little dais that sat just east of the one thing he really cared about at all: The Iron Mountain Diamond.

Alice gave Lonny her blessing, told him that if he had any trouble to not hesitate to call her at home, and left to Museum to him for the night. Though Lonny was naturally curious about the paranormal goings on, he chose not to ask about it on his first night and figured if he saw anything on his own, all the better. He really needed to get a lay of the land; needed to get a feel of the place and start working on the best plan he could for the task at hand. Though he did have an extra night, it still wouldn't do to irritate his employer, Allen, and it certainly wouldn't do to upset Mr. Sandman. Lonny had no idea who the guy was, but this was their third job under the mystery person and each one had led to big things overall. Lonny hiked up his belt, straightened his coat, and began his walkthrough.

****

Cargill invited Jack into his house, "Come on in, man. Mi casa su casa."

"Cool. Thanks again, Cargill, it really means a lot you helping me out here. This kind of security just isn't my thing."

"Any time, buddy. I know you're good for the cost and have never shit on me. So, let me show you what I've come up with…"

Cargill popped on his three giant computer screens, all of which were filled with schematics, blueprints, maps, and drawings of the ins and outs of the laser array security system watching over the diamond. He showed Jack the inner workings, the most obvious layout pattern of the optics that create the beams, the most obvious directions the beams fire, and, most important of all, the tools needed to redirect them back at themselves without breaking them or throwing off their intended trajectories. It was going to be tough, and Jack had six days to perfect it. Cargill opened up his back of tricks and laid out all the tools and materials Jack would need, and so the two began to work on an array he'd set up with similar beams and a fake diamond.

****

Lonny wandered the museum grounds on his first patrol. It was dark, but not pitch black. There were several exhibits that featured lit screens and LED lights that never got shut off. Sure, it was nice, but it certainly lent an air of creepiness to the entire area. Shadows played here and there thanks to whatever was showing on the screens, and all-around faint sounds coming from little, tinny speakers could be heard with their mute echoes. Lonny walked past several displays showing taxidermized animals in poses closely resembling those found in nature. The Wilds of Michigan exhibit showed several species of bear, cougars, the long-gone Wolverine, and many large rodents. As he turned the corner into the Lakes and Streams showcase a quick flash passed by his peripheral vision. At first Lonny just assumed it was some kind of light coming from one of the many interactive displays, but when he saw it again it actually moved in a direction none of the videos could even remotely match. He jumped a little and started off in the direction the object was headed. As he slowly plodded on, he caught it again a few yards in front of him bobbing around another bend. This was getting equally as frustrating as it was curious. Lonny rounded another corner and was immediately stopped short by a decorative flowerpot sailing toward his head. He ducked and it just missed his shoulder by inches and clattered across the floor. It was holding a fake plant and didn't have any dirt, but it scared the piss out of him, nonetheless. The silence that followed was sharp and Lonny stood where he was for several minutes, scared to move. Nothing else caught his eyes and he heard nothing more than the faint hum of a distant ceiling fan. Lonny breathed deep, reset the plant to as close to where it was as he could remember, and returned to his duties much more on edge now.

****

Allen sat patiently at his desk. Work seemed almost an afterthought today. The wheels were well in motion, and he knew Jack and Lonny were firmly entrenched in their respective plans to make the heist possible. So why was he so nervous? His friends were nothing if not complete professionals, so it wasn't that. He felt a little bad about roping Jack into such a massive undertaking so soon after his release… but only a little. So, what was it? His cell rang and Allen reached across his desk and tapped the screen.

"Go ahead. This is Allen."

"Don't talk, just listen. This is Mr. Sandman."

In his wandering thoughts Allen didn't even bother to look at the screen of his phone. Had he done so he would have seen the number and the display plainly spell out: EMPLOYER ONE. Dammit, he wasn't ready for whatever this was going to be about.

"Good. I have your attention. I trust everything you requested is well in motion and thus far there have been no hold ups. With that assumption in mind, I have decided to add another cog to your well-oiled machine. Her name is

Veronica and trust me, you need her. It has come to my attention that there is another piece to this puzzle that was not in the original design. As I told you earlier, the museum is clearly haunted by some kind of malevolent entity and that fact could cause us some irritation, and we don't want that in the middle of such a delicate procedure. Veronica is a paranormal investigator. She will be meeting with you and your team tomorrow afternoon at the Crow's Nest Café downtown. Be there at one PM. I assure you; you will find her an invaluable asset to your team."

   With that Mr. Sandman hung up. Allen just sat there with his mouth agape. A paranormal investigator? That seemed less than necessary. Oh well, who was he to go against his employer's wishes?

****

   Jack spent the better part of three days going over and over the procedure to deflect the protective laser beams back toward themselves without triggering an alarm or even alerting them at all to his presence. It took six-hundred and fifty-two times to finally get it exactly right, but he did get it exactly right. The trick was to be able to do it that way by heart likely six-hundred times more. He was now on his three-hundredth time and the sweat was pouring out of every inch of him.

   "Got that one, Cargill. No problem! That's three oh one!'

   "Damn, Jack! You're picking this up a lot faster than I'd even hoped! Maybe the rest of the day on practice and I think you've got this down!"

   "Thanks, pal. Glad you had such high hopes for me!" Jack said with only a taste of humor in his voice. In the meantime, he was already resetting and going for another. He was hungry and thirsty, but until he could do this with his eyes closed, comforts would have to wait.

An hour later, wiped out from sheer exhaustion, Jack laid back on his couch and slowly fed himself a big cheeseburger and fries. He was so tired and yet so incredibly hungry all at once. He reached over and nearly poured his soda down the front of his shirt as he tried to sip from the arguing straw. His phone rang and startled him so much he dropped ketchup-covered fries in his lap, "Damn it! Hello?"

"Hey, Jack. It's Allen. Man, you need to get yourself a burner cell, it's hard enough trying to reach you all day when you aren't home."

"Yeah, well, after this score I'll by the best damn phone out there. What's up?"

"Well, I'm not quite sure how to spring this on you, so I'll just out with it… we have an interesting new wrinkle in our new job."

Jack wiped the mess from his shirt and shoved more food into his mouth, "Great. Let me guess, someone else we have to split our winnings with. Am I right?"

"Well, yes and no. She's being paid up front -I assume- but yeah, it's another link in our chain. And even more exciting news: she's a paranormal investigator."

At this news Jack swallowed, nearly choked, and chugged a big gulp of his drink, "You can't be serious? A paranormal investigator? Why?"

Allen continued in the same flat tone, "Because Mr. Sandman thinks we need her. He didn't go into any more detail than that."

Jack thought the news over for a second, "Ya know, as much as I hate to admit it, it might not be a terrible idea for us. From what I've read up on, the place is pretty active."

Allen was silent. "Pretty active? Like over the years or recently?"
"Well, both," Jack said. "There was a shit ton about the history of the place from its opening through nearly every year since. Recently there have been reports and yeah, as we know, the last night guard quit without notice just citing how creepy and uneasy the place made him feel. I guess that's how you got Big Lon in there so quickly. But any more recently than that and I've not found anything. I guess we'll be hearing from Lon at some point today anyway. Last night was his fourth night and I haven't heard anything."

"Me neither," Allen admitted, now sounding more concerned. "I'll give him a call in an hour, he should be up by then. Oh, and by the way, her name is Veronica and we're meeting her at the Crow's Nest tomorrow night. We'll have to pass the word to Lon, he's probably not going to be able to make it."

"Alright, man. Let me know what you here from Lonny. Talk to ya later."

Allen said his goodbyes and hung up. Jack set the receiver in the cradle and immediately it rang again. Popular guy today, he thought to himself.

"It's Jack, go ahead."

It was jack's Parole Officer. This was not a conversation Jack was looking forward to.

****

Lonny showed up for work on his fifth day a little more unnerved than his past few days. Most of the activity he'd seen had happened on the first night, but thereafter he had seen weird shadows, odd mists, Orbs, and even felt bone-chilling cold spots where there hadn't been any before. Nothing, however, as violent in activity as the plant tossed on his first evening. But even still, he was getting a little weirded out by the place and he still hadn't found the right time to really case the diamond exhibit to really find the best points of ingress and egress. He clocked in, waved to Alice on the way out, and headed for his station. Everything seemed fine; the last few stragglers were heading out of the exit doors, lights started to switch off automatically, and his radio chirped informing him that Benny was on watch behind his desk of screens. Lonny was ready to patrol, even as his senses were on edge.

It had been four hours with nothing unusual to speak of, and Lonny started letting his mind wander. Just the, his ears popped with the sensation of falling fast and he swooned to the side. Listing and dizzy, Lonny looked around as the sound of nothingness pierced the darkness around him. As he struggled to right himself, an unseen force collapsed him like a lawn chair, and he fell to his knees. Breathing heavy, he called out into the vast open air only to hear a return of his own echo. He risked a glance above him and one of the many security cameras was poised on a rafter, yet it pointed just slightly the opposite direction. There was no way Benny could have seen him fall. Once again, he sat up, pushed from the floor and finally was able to stand. His head ached and his mouth was sticky and dry. He looked around but saw nothing. Turning the other way, he was waylaid by an invisible hand that knocked him into the far wall. As he staggered around to hold his footing, a moan that vibrated his teeth reverberated through the corridor and sent a bolt of shivers down his spine. Wiping tears from his blurred vision, Lon pressed his back against the wall and surveyed his surroundings. He was scared to death and could feel the racing thrum of his heart in the bottom of his throat. Just as suddenly as it began, all was silent. The eerie quietness flooded the hallway and Lonny regained his breath and stepped out into the darkness with his flashlight playing nervously against every surface he could find. He was cold, but not because of some phantom frigid air mass, no, he was cold because his body was drenched with sweat. Thank God he only had a few more hours and a few more days. When this job was over, he was never going to set foot in this museum again.

****

The Crow's Nest wasn't busy, and Jack sat in silence sipping a tall coffee and waited for Allen and Veronica. He was early. He was always early, a habit of his just to make sure no one was following him or trying to get the drop on him. He knew this spot, though he hadn't been here in years. He looked out the window and watched the traffic streaming down North Park street, and then he smiled as he saw Allen's car pull into the lot.

"Jack! Nice to see you, buddy? How's the week been treating you?"

"Can't complain. Yourself?" Jack answered, glancing over at the adorable, mousy woman trying not to hide behind Allen's left arm.

"Spectacular. So, this is Veronica. No last names, obviously," Allen said, watching Jack as he nodded knowing full well why that was, "She is here under the request of Mr. Sandman, and she will be our liaison with all things that go bump in the museum."

Jack extended his hand and felt the limpest shake he'd ever made contact with, and smiled, "Nice to meet you, Veronica. Glad to have you onboard."

"Hello." Veronica said, with a strangled, squeaky voice that went perfectly with her diminutive features. She was maybe five-foot two, tops. Raven-black hair tied back in pig tails, thick, black-rimmed glasses, pallid skin, and an outfit perfect for the Goth kids: all black jacket, a black knee-length skirt, black striped stockings, and a pair of black Vans. This woman looked every bit her role, and clearly enjoyed covering herself as darkly as possible, "Glad to be part of the team as well."

"Excellent. Now that we know each other, let's get right down to it," Allen began as the two newcomers sat opposite Jack, "Veronica here has been doing some exhaustive research much like yourself, Jack. However, with her expertise and background it seems she has come up with some possible answers to our little situation. Oh, and before we get too much into this meeting, I spoke to Lonny this morning."

"Oh, great! How's he doing?" Jack asked.

"Honestly? He's about as done with that place as one guy can be. He's had several run-ins with some supernatural forces and he's almost too afraid to go back to work."

Veronica pushed her glasses further up her nose, "Poltergeists. They're poltergeists, and they're angry."

Jack just looked at the two of them in silence. It was now finally becoming all too real. The museum was honest-to-goodness haunted and everything he'd read had just that much more validity. This was surreal.

"Okay, Veronica, you can go ahead and share what it is you came up with," Allen said, "Spare no detail, we really need to know personally what we're dealing with here."

"As I'm sure you know, the hauntings go as far back as the museum's opening," Veronica began as the server brought them both fresh mugs of coffee. She took a sip, satisfied with its bouquet and temperature, she went on, "Though the history of each recorded incident is rich and varied, they all stem from the same thing: the grounds, and subsequently the building itself, are atop Native American burial sites."

Jack leaned in, "Jesus. Yeah, I guess that makes sense. Native burial sites are all over this part of Michigan. I'm pretty sure the entirety of downtown rests on hundreds of them."

Veronica nodded, "You're not entirely wrong, Jack. There are four-hundred and eighty-eight that have been recorded most of which are situated around the museum grounds. It's so expansive it covers a huge amount of acreage. These places are sacred considered untouchable by the ancient tribespeople. All we did was destroy so much of what they held so dear -right after wiping out the living first- and we wonder why so many of their restless spirits torment us to this day."

Allen said, "So what do we do about it? We have a very small window of time to get in, get the payload, and get out. The last thing we need is to be fucking harassed by Casper."

Veronica looked at him unflinching, "We have two more nights. And I need to get in there to do my job. Can Lonny get me in tonight?"

"Yeah. Should be easy. But I'll make sure regardless. It's going on four right now and he starts at nine. Let me call him and he'll get you in."

Jack interjected, "Might make sense to just have her go in before closing and have Lon find her some kind of hiding place. The joint also has a bunch of cameras, so, that's something that needs to be dealt with, too."

Allen nodded and pulled out his cell, "I'll call him. He'll figure something out."

Veronica looked over at Jack, "Trust me, I'll make sure nothing… um, spooky trips us up. Okay?"

Jack shrugged, "Sounds good to me. Good luck."

■■

Lonny stood in the camera room. Benny was being cordial and talking him up about the few weird things he'd seen over the years. Benny didn't believe in all that ghost horseshit, but even so, yeah, there were some odd things now and again. Lonny didn't bring up his own experiences because it was clear Benny had seen none of it. Without missing a beat, Lonny produced two candy bars, both of which were Almond Joys, and offered the left one to Benny. Candy was the way to go; Benny had wrappers from everything all over his desk: Kit Kats, Mounds, Rollo, Milky Way… every candy you could imagine. Benny happily took the candy, unwrapped it, and began to bite off a piece as he continued talking about the shit he didn't believe in.

Fifteen minutes later he was out like a baby. The injection of Lonny's own creation was designed to put the recipient to sleep for a nice solid eight hours of lucid rest. Veronica waited in the lady's room for closing time, so Lonny headed to his post and left Benny to dream away his shift. When he did wake, he'd never know what happened and remember nothing.

Lonny heard the big doors close, watched as row after row of lights went off, and knew then that the museum was finally closed for the night. He glanced around, made sure Alice had indeed left for the night (she had, Lonny had to do all he could to keep her away from Benny's post, telling her he'd peek in on him and she should go ahead, looking as tired as she had, and she had that, too). He hurried over to the women's restroom and knocked on the door. A moment later Veronica, dressed from head to toe in black, slipped out of the door almost as ghostly as the things she was there to study.

"So now what?" Lonny asked.

Veronica produced a messenger's bag Lonny hadn't noticed before. "Well first I'm going to set up my equipment."

Out from her bag Veronica gingerly removed and placed six different tools. Only the laptop was familiar to Lonny. "These things will allow me to communicate with our spiritual entities. This is an EMF reader -electro-magnetic frequencies are often given off by spirits, this is a spirit box for hopefully catching any kind of vocal emissions, this is a K2 meter which reads location and strength of communication, this is just a digital voice recorder for asking and hopefully receiving replies, and finally this is REM pod which basically allows a spirit to communicate by setting of lights. I know it seems like a lot, but it's all pretty common."

Lonny took inventory and nodded, "Sure. Okay. Well, I'll leave you to it. I need to do my nightly rounds. I'll let you know if I have any encounters like I've already had this week."

"Okay. Thank you, Lonny." With that Veronica set off plugging things in and setting up perimeters. She was anxious to get started and she knew she only had ten hours to figure out just what was going on here. She was also nervous. This was the biggest gig she'd personally ever done. Sure, she'd been studying the paranormal for a few years, had sat in on several ghost hunts, and even assisted in many EVP sessions and a few Ouija Board readings, but this was definitely a huge undertaking. But she was ready; she knew her stuff, understood her tools and learned a ton of tricks from people far more experienced than she was. She was ready.

****

Veronica sat on the floor of the Eberhardt Museum equidistant from both her EMF recorder and the K2 meter. Her job was to find out how to expel the malevolent spirit or spirits causing havoc to the place before her cohorts could swipe the massive Iron Mountain Diamond from its well-guarded containment unit. And as of this second, the lights on the K2 were dancing all over the place and she'd only just begun and hadn't actually asked a single question. The activity in this place was so far more than she'd ever witnessed in her few years as a paranormal investigator. Little did she know then things were only going to get worse.

****

Lonny stood at his post near the entrance. He didn't want to be any more in Veronica's way than absolutely necessary, so he kept his routine trips around the museum to a minimum. He stared into darkness, watching as the dim flashing lights from the exhibit monitors occasionally flickered shadows across the hall. And then he saw it: a misty figure swooping into the room like animated white smoke. It stopped a few yards down the corridor and remained still, except for the way her wispy, white tendrils swirled around it like steam caught in a slow breeze. Lonny couldn't make out whether or not it was male or female, but what he could tell was that it was lean, tall, and wearing what could only be described as… feathers? Yes, on its head was a crown or headdress of feathers. And there it hovered, motionless save for the rippling of its opaque outline. Lonny couldn't look away and was nearly knocked off his feet when the form appeared mere inches before his face with eyes as red as fire. He stepped back and sucked in his breath. The form pushed itself through him and Lonny felt as though he were being drown in ice water. He staggered and dropped to his knees as the misty figure swirled around him looking him dead in the face with a piercing snarl and those dire red eyes.

Veronica's equipment started going off erratically; lights flashed from dull to brilliant repeatedly and the static from the vocal reader started sputtering random words like WAR and SOULS. Veronica was frightened, not because of the activity but because of her inexperience. She decided the best course of action right now was to do an EVP session and see if she could catch any real responses or maybe even have a conversation. There was a small couch directly across from an exhibit featuring Indigenous peoples of the area, including Native

Americans who settled Michigan, and she figured this would likely be the best area. She sat, legs crossed, and took out her recorder.

"Hello. My name is Veronica. Is there anyone here who would like to talk? Please feel free to speak right into the little speakers here," She pointed to the top of the EVP box, her voice sounding strong and sure of itself, even if she was more nervous than anything.

The lights danced atop the recorder, "This LAND..."

It was loud and clear. Veronica could immediately tell whatever was speaking to her had just said This Land. Veronica cleared her throat, "I'm very sorry, but yes, this museum sits atop your land."

As the last word was spoken it felt as if all the air was sucked out of Veronica's lungs. She choked and collapsed onto her side. After a moment of blinding fear, she was able to inhale, and she choked a second time. "H-h-h-hey! That wasn't necessary!"

The glass case across from her began to vibrate. The artifacts: tools, weapons, clothing, it all began to smack against the enclosure. Veronica yelped as she sat up. Within the glassed-in box the statue of a settler from the 1700's turned its head and leapt forward smashing into the transparent partition rattling the entire thing. Veronica scrambled off the couch and backed away from the nightmare she witnessed in front of her. But it was too late. The glass shattered and antiques flew at her from across the hall. The statue lurched forward and fell to the ground. Veronica screamed.

****

Lonny heard Veronica's scream, and apparently so did the apparition because as soon as he turned his head toward the cry, it disappeared into nothing. Lonny took off at a sprint toward where Veronica had set up her equipment. She was there, lying on the ground against the wall across from the exhibit that showcased original settlers of the area. She stared at the glass case with her mouth wide open. Lonny skidded to a stop right next to her and offered a hand to help her up.

"D-d-d-do you s-s-see it?" She asked, stammering her words.

Lonny saw nothing. In fact, it looked as though nothing had happened at all over on this side of the museum, "What did you see, sweetheart?"

"The display… it was smashed to bits and all the contents…"

The exhibit was exactly how it should have been and the items within were as motionless as they'd been for as long as they'd been there. Veronica rubbed her eyes and slowed her breathing. Lonny took stock of the situation, and it became pretty clear that both of them had been on the business end of some very angry poltergeists. "So, should we talk about it?"

Veronica nodded her head and remembered her EVP recorder, "Yes, let's. But I also want to go over this. It was running the entire time. Unfortunately, I didn't have a camera over here, so I know that didn't catch anything. I heard voices, too."

"I did not. But boy that ghost was not happy. And it definitely looked like a Native American, too. I'm pretty sure I saw feathers, but I guess I'm not positive. I'm not really positive of much of anything at this point."

Veronica pressed the PLAY button on the EVP recorder. She and Lonny listened intently for anything that might sound like voices or words. It took less than ten seconds.

"OUR! LAND! REVENGE!"

They looked at each other on abject terror. The voice was crystal clear and seemed to echo throughout the hallways and corridors even though neither heard it live. "Wow," Veronica said, breaking the silence, "That was something. I have never, in any of my EVP sessions, heard a voice that pronounced!"

"Yeah, and did you hear how angry and mean it sounded?" Lonny asked, visibly shaken, "I'm really starting to have serios doubts about this gig tomorrow night. I mean if this thing is still hanging around by then... this just doesn't feel safe."

Veronica nodded, "I get it, Lonny, but Mr. Sandman is paying me a ton for this, and that diamond is going to set you guys up for the rest of your lives. I still have some work to do here, maybe I can get it to settle down even if it's just temporarily. I've done this -well, seen this done before. And I'm sure I can do it."

"What do you mean 'seen this', have you not actually removed a spirit before?" Lonny asked.

"I was present during several cleanses, as well as an exorcism. I know what I'm doing... based on that. But no, I've never actually done one myself. But don't worry, it's fairly straight forward. Go on, keep up your patrols, I'll handle it."

Lonny shrugged, still looking a bit confused, and went on about his night. But now he was far more on edge.

****

Jack Davis couldn't relax. He'd been out of a federal penitentiary for less than a week, and he was already working on scoring the biggest heist of his life. And, the more he thought about it, a stupid heist. First, he and his partner, Lonny were going to use Lonny's position as a night guard at the Eberhardt Museum to swipe one of the world's largest gems, the Iron Mountain Diamond, from its heavily fortified glass enclosure. Second, they needed to get it out of there undetected and without setting of any of the myriad alarms that were protecting it. And third -and somehow most important- the damn place was haunted by some malevolent spirit from the original Native Americans who occupied this land hundreds of years ago. So, yeah, Jack could not relax. He absently flipped through webpages on his laptop trying to find any excuse not to do the job. He's heard form Lonny only once since he'd taken the guard gig, and the way Lonny told it, the activity from something supernatural was pretty strong. Their employer, Mr. Sandman had brought in an investigator to check out the spirits, but Jack had no clue how that little venture was going. And worse yet, the theft was scheduled for tomorrow night. Jack took another swig from his beer glass and tried to think of all the practice he'd done the previous week to disengage the alarms and the laser array protecting the diamond. It was going to be a long night.

****

Veronica relocated her set-up. She wanted a more open space with a larger array of display cases. Now that she knew the ghost was simply playing tricks to scare her, she was no longer worried about ending up in a flurry of broken glass and animated antique objects. But she was wary just the same. She took a few precautions and made sure to have a way out to safety if something went sideways. Her spirit scanners and readers were strategically placed, and she was ready for another EVP session. This time she wanted to get a little pricklier with the entity and see if it would just leave on its own if it understood that it no longer had any control over the land on which the museum sat.

"Hello again! My name is Veronica! I am not here to hurt you or disrespect you in any way! But I do need you to know that this land no longer—"

"VENGEANCE!" The hollow baritone voice pulsated down her corridor like a thunderstorm. It shook Veronica to her core and vibrated her insides.

"You don't understand!" She shouted, using the surge of fear and adrenaline to urge her on, "No one here is going to hurt—"

"DEATH!" This Time the reverberations from the echoing voice dropped Veronica to her knees and knocked the air from her lungs.

As she slowly pushed herself up on her elbows, the air around her dropped fifteen degrees and she could suddenly see puffs of her own breath rapidly forming into clouds. She was freezing and her teeth began to chatter as she sat up and hugged her arms around herself. The atmosphere felt hollow, and the air tasted like old dirt and smelled of ancient decay. She blinked away tears and looked out into the distance. There was nothing. The expanse was empty and a cold shade of gray. "Hello?" She called out, watching as plumes of warm breath slowly dissipated into the frigid air.

"REVENGE!" Another booming exclamation filled the hall.

Veronica began to shiver so hard she could feel it in her bones. Her eyelids began to droop as the air began to feel thin and it took so much more to fill her lungs. Her heart beats were rapid, and she could see the beats through her shirt. Colors began to swirl just outside of her vision, and she knew instinctively that she was about to faint. Before her eyes, in a burst of angry red, a face exploded into her sight. Its nostrils were flared, its eyes burned raw fire, and the teeth dripped with hunger. It was the face of a Native nightmarishly amalgamated with that of a horse. Veronica could pick out features from both as she could slowly feel herself swoon out of consciousness.

"DEATH!" The terrifying mask bellowed into Veronica's face. She collapsed to the floor and saw nothing.

****

Lonny was heading to the bathroom. After four Diet Mountain Dews, his rental agreement with them was up. He pushed the door open and found the automatic sensor that flipped the lights on was not working. He waved his hand, jumped up and down- nothing. "Wonderful. Oh well, I gotta pee."

The lights flickered three times and the sound of broken circuits could be heard crackling through the restroom. Lon hesitated and stared into the emptiness around him. In front of his face was the vast mirror that took up all of the facing wall. He knew enough from horror movies he'd seen not to stare into that surface any more than he had to, nothing good ever came out of that. Hell, even if this place wasn't haunted, nothing good ever came out of staring into a mirror, Lonny comically thought to himself. As stress started to leak from his body, along with a urine stream, Lonny froze. He could feel someone directly behind him. As his body tensed, his urination stopped. He dared not move a muscle, even involuntarily. Hot breath tickled the back of his neck and goose flesh erupted across his skin. Then a sigh, deep and low filled the silence. Lonny couldn't help it: he peed even more. As he finished, he felt his body being yanked off its feet and thrown from the urinal. Lon crashed, back-first into the adjoining sing. The pain was excruciating, and it made him cry out. He couldn't stand, his legs refused to lift him. Sitting on the floor, Lon looked up directly into the face of an Indian Chief. Its face was a rotted mess of dried, dead flesh and worm-eaten tissue. Flaps of skin hung off in grotesque ribbons. Its remaining teeth grinned humorlessly in its gaping mouth and oozed with insects and skittering spiders. Those feathers Lonny had witnessed some hours ago were sitting atop this ghoul's fetid scalp, yet they, too were ruined. Broken, burned, caked with detritus and rot. Lonny couldn't move, his back was screaming agony. There was nowhere to run. He tried to scream but nothing except a weak squeak left his lips.

"DEATH!" The demonic Native American in front of him belched. A flurry of decay and the corroded smell of aged earth flew from the Chief's mouth.

With all the strength he could gather, Lonny pushed himself to his feet, turned toward the door, and fled. He made it two steps, and he was violently thrown to the floor. This time he heard and felt something snap. It was his shoulder and he cried out into the darkness. Struggling to sit, Lonny felt his other shoulder snap as his body was pressed to the tile floor. Sparks shot across his vision and the agony shot bolts of pain throughout his body. As he lay there moaning, the lights flickered once more and bloomed into life. The being he'd seen moments before was gone. And just as suddenly, the pain in his arms subsided to a mere whimper. Lonny sat up, looked around, and screamed.

****

Veronica fluttered her eyes. She had no idea how long she'd been out, but she certainly knew that she had a headache. Everything else seemed fine, her equipment was right where she left it, too. She glanced at her cell screen, it read 2:27. She was only out a few minutes. The activity in this museum was incredibly potent, very strong, and definitely evil. She had to find a way to get it to give up its ground. Fortunately, it was only using powerful scare tactics thus far and nothing doing any permanent damage. But she knew that could change at any time. Beneath her feet the ground began to rumble. It felt like an earthquake, but those were incredibly rare in Michigan. It steadily grew in intensity just as Lonny rounded the corner at a limping run.

"Holy hell! What is that?" Lonny shouted over the grinding din.

Veronica didn't have a chance to answer. The ground started to crumble away as mounds pushed their way to the surface, shattering tile and knocking displays from their fixtures. Exhibits cracked and shattered, spilling their contents in a cacophonous roar everywhere. Lonny and Veronica did all they could do just to avoid falling taxidermized animals, massive plant-life displays, tools, weapons, mannequins in full regalia, and thousands of pounds of breaking glass. As the ground continued its upward swell, more crumbling echoed above the clamoring of breaking antiques as massive headstones pierced their way through the surface. Five, ten, twenty tombstones crashed through the floor sending bits of concrete and tile flying in clouds of dust and earth. Lonny and Veronica scattered down the corridor not wanting to wait around for whatever awaited them. But their escape was cut short as a parade of Native warriors closed in on them. Spears waved in the air, tomahawks shook, battle cries were heard echoing down the hallway. They were trapped.

"This isn't real! It can't be! We didn't just see an entire graveyard open into the museum!" Lonny yelled as he cowered behind a support beam, "What the hell is going on here?"

"I don't know, but this is well outside my expertise!" Veronica yelled back.

The warriors surrounded them, thrusting their weapons at them to within inches of their heads. Lonny reached behind him and found a fake potted plant. He had a theory, he just hoped it was true. With a grunt, he tossed it at the nearest Native. It clamored to the ground, passing right through it. "Veronica! They're not real! They can't hurt—"

Veronica watched in horror as a tomahawk whisked through the air and cleanly severed Lon's head from his neck. Her final screams could be heard over the resonating war cries and Veronica was scalped and murdered.

****

Jack awoke with a start. His eyes wouldn't focus, and as he rubbed them, he sat up. He was freezing. His back hurt. He could hear voices coming from somewhere. He cleared his head, stood up, and as he curled his fingers around the bars of his prison cell, he fought to erase the remnants of another nightmare. Four years in and four to go.

The End

www.ingramcontent.com/pod-product-compliance
Lightning Source LLC
Chambersburg PA
CBHW060223030726
47499CB00004B/1173